Aru Shah

AND THE
NECTAR OF IMMORTALITY

Also by Roshani Chokshi

The Star-Touched Queen
A Crown of Wishes
The Gilded Wolves
The Silvered Serpents
The Bronzed Beasts

The Pandava Series

Aru Shah and the End of Time
Aru Shah and the Song of Death
Aru Shah and the Tree of Wishes
Aru Shah and the City of Gold

Aru Shah

AND THE
NECTAR OF IMMORTALITY

A PANDAVA NOVEL

BOOK FIVE

ROSHANI CHOKSHI

RICK RIORDAN PRESENTS

Disnep • HYPERION   LOS ANGELES   NEW YORK

First Hardcover Edition, April 2022
First Paperback Edition, April 2023
1 3 5 7 9 10 8 6 4 2
FAC-029261-23048

Printed in the United States of America

This book is set in Atheneum Pro, FCaslon Twelve ITC Std,
Teethreedee Std. Front, Clairvaux LT Std/Monotype; Adorn Roman,
Goudy Trajan Pro, Jenson Recut/Fontspring

Designed by Tyler Nevins
Ornament illustration by Keith Robinson

Library of Congress Cataloging-in-Publication
Control Number for Hardcover Edition: 2021043707
ISBN 978-1-368-07438-4

Follow @ReadRiordan
Visit www.DisneyBooks.com

For you, dear reader. May this book make you feel seen and loved, powerful, and infinite, because you are most certainly all those things. Barring that, may this book prove to be an excellent spider-squasher.

CONTENTS

Dear Reader,

I have a confession. What you are holding in your hands (or your ears/talons, etc., etc.) is none other than a feral, hungry... story.

"What nonsense!" you say. "Obviously it's *just* a story!"

Harrumph.

Tomorrow, I'd make sure your book is in the same place where you left it yesterday—stories are living things, after all. They're quite sensitive. There's no such thing as "just" a story, which brings me to my next point.

Like so many of the stories I have written in the past, I consider this one a living thing and believe it is important for you to know that this story's roots come from a living, active religion: Hinduism. One of the most beautiful aspects about Hindu mythology is that it is deeply intertwined with the sacred. As a practicing Hindu, I wanted to let my imagination take flight but also do my best to make sure that it doesn't stamp its feet on hallowed grounds. For that reason, the majority of the deities you will meet in these pages harken back to the Vedic Age, starting in roughly 1500 BCE. Many scholars consider Vedism a precursor to what we might now call classical Hinduism. That means you won't find deities like Durga-Maa, Vishnu, or Shiva as characters in this series.

This story is not intended to serve as an introduction to Hinduism or Hindu mythology, which is beautifully nuanced and varies from region to region. Instead, I hope you see this story for what it is: a narrow, vivid window peering out into an even brighter ocean of tales and traditions. As storytellers, we respond to what we love, and one of the things I loved most growing up was listening to my Ba tell me stories about gods, heroes, and demons. To me, this series is one long love letter.

I hope it sparks your curiosity, tickles your imagination, and, if I am so fortunate, sneaks into a corner of your heart and stays there.

With love,
Roshani

ONE

Not All Who Wander Are Lost

Kara's first reaction when she entered the labyrinth that hid the nectar of immortality was, well, disappointment. She'd imagined it would look like something out of the fairy tales she had read over and over until the book spines split down the middle. She thought it would be beautiful, with ginormous green mazes carved out of jungle plants where sleek panthers with glowing eyes would stalk and snarl at them from the sidelines.

But it wasn't. It was a cave. And it was dark.

The only light came from what she gripped tightly in her right hand: Sunny, her trident, forged from a drop of pure sunshine. Nothing could penetrate the darkness except Sunny, and as the daughter of Surya, the sun god, only Kara could lead the way through the labyrinth. No enemies would be able to follow, much less attack. She'd seen to that a few days ago.

Heat spasmed through her chest. She didn't know what to name this feeling.... Even the thought of feeling guilty made her feel...guilty.

You did the right thing, her father had told her over and over.

But then why did that moment feel so poisonous? Why couldn't she stop thinking about Aru's face? Or the way Brynne had almost bellowed in pain? Or how Mini, the gentlest of the Pandavas, had curled around herself like she'd been kicked?

"Are you ready, daughter?"

Kara looked up at her dad. He stood tall and noble, his blue and brown eyes beaming down at her.

"I'm proud of you," he said in his deep, rumbling voice. "You have been faced with difficult choices, and each time you have done the right thing."

The words glowed in Kara's heart. She was reminded all over again that Suyodhana was her dad in every way that counted. He had rescued her from a bad place. He had taken care of her when her own mother, Krithika Shah, had abandoned her.

Even so, Kara sometimes imagined a soft voice speaking to her in her dreams. . . .

He's lying to you.

The voice belonged to a young girl. If Kara really concentrated, she could almost see the girl's face. Dark brown skin, braids framing her cheeks, a pair of electric-blue eyes. She looked like Sheela, one of the Pandava twins.

You're not real, she once told Dream Sheela.

Sheela had regarded her mildly. *Or maybe you just don't want me to be real?*

Kara figured that her mind was simply reaching for an elaborate way to protect itself from the truth that she'd finally met her mom and now knew for sure that Krithika had given her up. *And who could blame her?* thought Kara with a pang.

Krithika had moved on with her life. She had another daughter: Aru. Aru was funny and clever. Aru had the soul of

Arjuna, the shining hero of all the stories. Kara had the soul of a mistake. *She* was a mistake, and it was only because of the Sleeper's mercy that she still existed.

"Remember what lies ahead," said her father now, placing a warm hand on her shoulder. "We will remake the world. We will all be together...as a family. Like I promised."

Family.

That was all Kara wanted. She'd meant what she said to Aru the moment she broke the *astra* necklace. She loved her mom and sister. She was doing this so they could be together, so they wouldn't fight one another anymore.

This was the only way.

He's lying to you...whispered that voice in the back of her head.

Kara shoved it aside and stood up straighter. "I'm ready," she said.

She raised her trident, and a stream of sunlight snaked through the darkness. This was the true path inside...the *only* path inside.

Behind her, her father's troops held their breath. His army was a strange mix of individuals. Some of them were pale and misshapen *rakshasas*, burned and scarred from fights with the *devas* long ago. Others were pristine *yakshas*, whose families had lost their homes due to human encroachment. With each passing hour, more beings joined her father's cause—celestial and woodland nymphs mistreated by human kings who had won the gods' favor, ghosts who had once haunted the edges of cremation grounds, members of the bear and monkey races who had fought in the devas' wars and won no glory.

Her father had promised them all that this time the nectar of immortality would not be stolen from them. This time, *they* would have the power. Whenever Suyodhana spoke, his followers listened. Hope shone in their eyes.

But sometimes Kara wondered what he really felt. When he thought no one was looking, Kara had seen him touch a pendant that he wore around his neck. He never took it off, and every time his fingers touched the stone, a look of pain crossed his face.

"Well, daughter?" prompted Suyodhana, snapping her back to the moment. "Lead the way. Be the hero to guide us into the new age."

Kara fought the urge to correct him. *Heroine*. That was what Aru, Brynne, and Mini always said.

But heroism was nothing like what she had understood from all her books. There was no shining armor to protect her from emotions she didn't want to feel. There was no magical horse leading her into a battle between clearly divided good and evil. Even the monsters weren't so monstrous.

So what does that make you? whispered a doubt deep inside her heart.

Kara ignored the voice and stepped into the dark.

TWO

I Hate It Here

Aru Shah's life was, to put it simply, an absolute mess. Her previous pigeon mentor, Boo, was currently a flammable chick of some kind. Her crush, Aiden, had kissed her and yet was now acting like she was invisible. Her friend Kara had turned out to not only be her real-life half sister but also the daughter of the sun god. And, as if that weren't enough for the past twenty-four hours, Kara had betrayed them, joined forces with the Sleeper to locate the nectar of immortality, and incinerated the Pandavas' celestial weapons.

On Aru's birthday.

But even though Kara and the Sleeper had vanished, at least Aru now knew where she could find them.

It was almost evening in Atlanta, and the February wind made her ears burn as she stared up at the stone gate marking the entrance to Lullwater Park. According to Krithika Shah, *this* was the current hiding spot of the labyrinth holding the nectar of immortality, but just for the next ten days. The only way to navigate the labyrinth was by the light of the sun, and now that the Sleeper had Kara's demigod solar powers on his side, the

Pandavas' chances of reaching the nectar of immortality first were looking, well, low.

Maybe it wouldn't be so bad if they could simply get through the magical barrier surrounding the park. For the second time since they'd arrived, Aru held out her hand. She could feel a pulse of energy near the gate. It was like a curtain drawn tight. She couldn't push past it.

"I told you, Aru," said Krithika softly, laying her hand on her daughter's shoulder. "You won't be admitted without your godly weapons. It's to be expected that the devas would come up with a way to keep humans out."

"But we're not humans!" said Brynne. "We're demigods!"

At that moment, a young white family walked past. The mom grinned at the Pandavas and thrust her fist into the air. "That's the spirit of the future! We're *all* demigods!" And then she laughed and kept walking.

"You okay, Brynne?" asked Mini. "Your forehead vein is sticking out a lot...."

"No, I'm not okay!" said Brynne. "We have *nothing*. We can't fight without our weapons!"

"Technically, we could..." said Mini, weakly holding up her fists. "It'd be a short fight, though. Because we'd die almost immediately—"

"Only someone with a godly weapon can control the Nairrata army," said Brynne. "We don't have them anymore! And we can't get into the labyrinth, either!" Her voice broke, and she looked away from them right before she mumbled, "We can't protect anyone."

"That's not true, Bee," said Aru. "We still have *this*."

Aru shoved her right hand into her pocket. Her fingers

instinctively searched for her lightning bolt, Vajra, which normally would either be coiled into a glowing ball of static electricity or wrapped around her wrist as a sparking bracelet. Aru felt a sharp ache. Without Vajra, the world was a little less bright.

Aru withdrew her hand. She had meant to pull out the IO(F)U coin from Agni, the god of fire. But she must have reached into the wrong pocket, because instead she drew out half an expired and possibly fossilized Twix bar. While her left hand fished around in her other pocket for the enchanted coin, Aru shrugged and took a bite.

"Aru! NO!" shouted Mini, smacking Aru's back so hard that Aru spat out the candy bar.

"That was perfectly good chocolate!" said Aru.

"What is wrong with you?" demanded Mini. "You *cannot* eat that! Expired candy can carry microbes! Some even have strains of salmonella! And if you eat it, you could *die*."

"We're already going to die!" said Brynne, crossing her arms. "Especially if Aru thinks a moldy candy bar is a way to avoid doom!"

"What I meant to take out was this," said Aru, holding up the glowing coin.

Brynne still didn't look convinced. "Yeah, but it doesn't seem to work, does it?"

Aru sighed. Nothing was going her way. She couldn't even eat some chocolate without the risk of death.

When they'd previously tried to contact Agni with the coin, Mini, Brynne, and Aru had taken turns holding it tight and making a wish. They'd even called out Agni's name and held it to the sky, but nothing seemed to make a difference.

"So how exactly are we going to find the god of fire, Shah?"

demanded Brynne. "If we set foot in the Otherworld and start asking questions, the devas are going to figure out we don't have our weapons anymore. Everyone will panic. What if they know already? What if Rudy goes back to the Naga realm and doesn't keep his mouth shut?"

"I think Rudy and Aiden are still at home fighting over who gets to hold BB," piped up Mini.

BB was what they had decided to name Baby Boo, who had hatched at the museum this morning and had already left multiple singe marks on the floor. Mini hadn't wanted to take him outside, worried that he would catch a cold—even though Aru had pointed out that he was literally a firebird—so they'd left him behind with the boys.

Brynne groaned. "There's no way to hide what's happened to us. Hanuman and Urvashi are bound to check in any minute now."

Aru flipped the coin between her fingers, weighing a new idea in her head. "Mom? Can you talk to Sheela and Nikita's parents? The twins may be able to help us."

"Of course," said Krithika. "But the girls are still too young to have inherited a godly weapon, so they won't be able to open the boundary either."

"But they still have their Pandava powers," said Mini.

Brynne looked like she was chewing on the inside of her cheek. Like Mini and Aru, she had lost her control of wind, her element. But she was part asura, which meant she could still shape-shift. The only problem was that she couldn't turn into anything big anymore.

Brynne shook her head. "So what? It's not like we can make the twins fight an entire battle on their own."

"I know," said Aru. "But we need a prophecy. Something that will let us get around in the Otherworld and look for Agni without anyone bothering us for the next few days."

Brynne kicked at a bottle cap on the sidewalk. "Right. We'll just pop over to a convenience store and pick a prophecy off the shelf."

Aru ignored her soul sister's tone. She knew Brynne was hurting—they *all* were—but Brynne was taking it even harder than Aru expected. A small part of Aru felt responsible for this whole mess.

On the drive over to Lullwater Park, she kept replaying all the things she could have done differently. She should have worded her answer better when the god of treasures, Kubera, had asked her to decide who could wield the Nairrata army. She should have stopped the Sleeper the first time she'd had the chance. She should have confronted her mom about the truth ages ago.

But it was too late for all that.

Aru squared her shoulders and frowned at the darkening sky overhead before she faced her mom and her sisters. "I never said it had to be a *real* prophecy."

THREE

I'm Sorry, but Your Call Cannot Be Completed as Dialed

One hour later, Aru found herself seated on a barstool at a kitchen counter that seemed to offer everything *but* food. There was a rotating shelf containing various multivitamins, a deadly-looking blender, jars of green powder, a whiteboard listing the multiple health benefits of fruits and vegetables, and a massive stack of books with titles like *Parenting a Prodigy* and *Unlock the Secrets to Ivy League School Admission*.

Across from her, Brynne slammed the fridge closed with such force that the magnets on the door fell off and papers on the counter were blown on the floor.

"Careful!" said Mini, bending to pick up a bright red card with golden script on it. "Nothing can look out of place or my parents will be suspicious when they get back home."

Mini's parents and Brynne's uncles, Gunky and Funky, had gone on a Valentine's Day cruise and wouldn't be back for another four days. Even Mini's brother had been dragged along, though Mini had refused to go because it was so close to Aru's birthday. When Mini's family heard about the Sleeper's attack, they'd almost turned around, but Mini had convinced them otherwise. Besides, it was safer for the Pandavas' families to be as far away as possible.

Brynne slouched on the stool beside Aru. "Mini, how come your parents have *no* ice cream but, like, ten different kinds of *plant-based muffins?*"

"They're health conscious," said Mini defensively.

"They're deranged," muttered Brynne under her breath.

Aru bit back a laugh. She liked Dr. and Mrs. Kapoor-Mercado-Lopez, but they were a little ... intense. Much like their daughter. Once, the Potatoes had been tricked into joining a horror-movie night at Mini's place. It was definitely horrific. But that was mostly because the movie was a documentary on diseases and viruses that could be contracted by kissing and other "activities of an age-appropriate nature."

Mini had henceforth been banned from hosting movie night.

"I don't know why Ammamma bolted so fast when we arrived," said Brynne. "I thought he'd want to see the twins once they get here. Maybe he got tired of babysitting? BB *is* a handful, and Rudy isn't around to help." The naga prince had been summoned home by his family but was waiting to help the Potatoes at a moment's notice.

Aru looked down at her lap, where BB was snuggled in a slowly charring sweater inside an oval baking pan. This was the closest they could get to a nest without setting something on fire. BB snoozed happily, puffs of smoke curling from his burning blue crest.

So smol! So deadly! thought Aru, resisting the urge to pat him.

"Maybe ..." said Mini. "Aiden just seems *off* lately. What do you think, Aru?"

There was a knowing sharpness to Mini's voice. Aru faltered. In the midst of everything that had happened, she hadn't had a second to tell her sisters about *the kiss*. But she didn't know what to say now. Aiden was acting really weird. He'd barely said a word to her. What if it had been a total accident? What if he'd tripped and she hadn't noticed and it just kind of...happened?

Aru was spared from answering by the sudden *squawk* of the cuckoo clock on the wall. As it chimed loudly, the wall cracked down the middle, revealing an enchanted entryway. Only the Pandavas had direct access to one another in emergencies. (Although Brynne had a very different definition of *emergency*. Once, Aru woke up to Brynne rifling through the museum apartment's kitchen for some sugar.) Through the portal, Aru could see the interior of a warm living room. Family photos lined the back wall. Although she couldn't see who was speaking, she knew it was her mom talking to Mr. and Mrs. Jagan.

"—promise they'll be safe and go to sleep on time."

Krithika poked her head through the portal. "Hear that, girls? One hour is all you get. The Jagans were just about to go to sleep."

"One hour," Aru repeated.

Her mom nodded. "I'll stay with the Jagans until you're done."

Aru's mom disappeared. A moment later, the twins stepped into Mini's kitchen. Sheela was wearing a pair of pink pajamas and fuzzy slippers, her hair under a pink bonnet. Nikita was also wearing a nightcap and pajamas, but her outfit was a lustrous gold.

"BIRDIE!" said Sheela, clapping her hands excitedly and rushing toward Aru. BB poked his head out of the burning sweater and blinked at Sheela.

Nikita glared and crossed her arms. "You couldn't just wait a couple of hours to dream-visit us?" But perhaps she saw something on their faces, because her frown instantly vanished. "Uh-oh... That serious?"

"Kinda?" said Aru. "I mean, the fate of the entire universe is on the line, so I'd rank that... mildly important?"

Over the next twenty minutes Aru explained the whole situation about the Agni coin not working, the impassable barrier of Lullwater Park, and the handful of days they had left to set things right. By the time she'd finished, two things had happened. One, Nikita—who'd been listening in silence and crocheting what looked like a dozen enchanted vines—had almost finished making a nest for BB. And two, Brynne had given in and eaten all the plant-based muffins.

Sheela bit her bottom lip. "I really don't like to lie, but I think I can fake a prophecy. Something to buy you time..."

"Something dramatic enough that no one will want to be anywhere near us," added Brynne. "Can you do that?"

Sheela nodded.

Brynne let out a sigh of relief. "Great. Now if only this stupid coin could actually end up doing something for us."

On the counter beside the fancy red card, the Agni coin glowed.

Sheela tilted her head, examining the coin with a dreamy look in her eyes. "Have you tried setting it on fire?"

"You sound like Aru," said Mini.

Sheela beamed.

Nikita looked up from her knitting. "Sheela has a point. I mean, he *is* the god of fire."

"How do you set metal on fire?" Aru asked.

Brynne looked around the kitchen. "We could try the stove?"

"It's broken," said Mini.

"Got any matches?"

"My parents hid them after the last time Aru visited."

"I'm both offended and flattered," said Aru.

At that moment, BB poked his head out of the baking pan, tilted it to the side, and chirped. His wavering blue crest of flames seemed a little taller, as if piqued by curiosity.

"What do you say, BB?" asked Aru, holding out the coin.

"Waaait!" said Nikita loudly. She closed her eyes and her fingers glowed as she made a complicated gesture with her wrists. A moment later, a pair of sunflower-yellow gloves tumbled to the counter.

"Wear these."

Dutifully, Aru slipped on the gloves. The fabric felt like cold silk but more durable.

"Flame-resistant, timelessly elegant, and also an homage to the 2008 Dior collection," said Nikita imperiously before smiling at BB. She set the crocheted nest of vines beside him. BB pecked it suspiciously.

"I used the same plant fabric for his crib," she said. "Honestly, Aru, you can't put a baby in a baking pan. It's ugly."

BB squawked in agreement.

"Wear the gloves, and that way you won't get burned when you hold him," said Nikita. "Brynne, yours will be blue. Mini, purple. Hmm...what about Aiden...?"

As Nikita tinkered with a new set of gloves, Aru reached for BB with one protected hand. In the past, touching BB had been like grabbing the handle of a hot pan, but now all she felt was the warm, fluffy weight of the firebird.

With her other gloved hand, Aru reached for the Agni coin and held it up next to BB's beak. "Okay, maybe you could just give me a tiny hiccup?" she asked him.

BB belched a flame the size of a dinner plate. Aru shrieked, reeling back and nearly dropping the chick as the Agni coin lit up. Sheela laughed. Mini screamed. Brynne started flapping her hands, which only made the coin burn brighter.

Nikita watched them for about ten seconds before rolling her eyes. Then she stretched out her fingers, flicked her wrist, and a moment later threw a tiny conjured blanket over the coin, immediately dousing it. "Voilà," she said.

Brynne lowered her hands, looking disappointed. Behind her, Mini had tugged her T-shirt over her nose and mouth. Sheela, still giggling, pulled off the blanket. If anything, the Agni coin gleamed a little more. But that was it.

Aru turned away, a hot flush of embarrassment creeping up her face. Coming up with a fake prophecy and looking for Agni had been *her* ideas, but what if they didn't work? Then what would happen?

Gently, she lowered BB into his new cradle. The firebird had already fallen asleep, and although Aru was happy to have Boo back in *some* form, she still felt lost. The old Boo might've been able to help them figure a way out of their predicament.

Aru stared at the counter. Luckily, the flames hadn't scorched the stone, but the bright red card now looked charred around the edges. *Oops*, thought Aru, as she tried to wipe it clean. It was, she noticed, an invitation dated for tomorrow.

You are cordially invited to the wedding of Ravi & Trena
~Portal entrances will be locked at the commencement of the ceremony,
so please arrive in a timely fashion.
At this time, the bride and groom are not accepting
any enchanted gifts. Thank you~

Brynne groaned. "Well, that was a total bust—"

Just then, an odd sound filled the kitchen. A very loud and incessant hum.

"It's coming from the coin!" said Mini.

The Pandavas stared at the golden disk. It began to vibrate on the stone countertop. A friendly automated voice said:

"HELLO. WE ARE SORRY, BUT YOUR REQUEST CANNOT BE COMPLETED AT THIS TIME. PLEASE CHECK YOUR CONNECTION TO A SACRED FLAME AND TRY AGAIN. THANK YOU."

The coin went still.

"Sacred flame?" demanded Brynne. "What does *that* mean?" She was frowning, but there was a new light in her eyes, and it looked a lot like hope.

"That makes sense!" said Mini. "Agni is always present at sacred functions that involve a fire! Like pujas done at home, or funerals, or—"

"Weddings," said Aru, holding up the invitation. "This one is *tomorrow*. We could go to it and talk to Agni."

Aru hadn't been to many weddings—most invitations kindly requested that Aru *not* attend—but she remembered that in Hindu ceremonies the bride and groom walked around a sacred fire while a priest chanted and invoked several gods...including Agni.

"Let's say we manage that," said Brynne. "What do we do

next? Stroll up to the middle of their ceremony and toss the coin into the fire? Won't someone, I don't know, NOTICE?"

"Not if we're careful," said Aru.

"You mean sneaky."

"Same thing," said Aru. "And if Sheela says the fake prophecy in the morning, no one will expect to see us anyway!"

"You'll each need a whole new wardrobe," said Nikita, raising an eyebrow.

"Excuse me," said Mini loudly. "But we can't go to the wedding! We're not on the guest list!"

Aru grinned.

Mini took one look at her face and her shoulders sank. "I'm not going to like this, am I?"

FOUR

And on That Note... BEGONE

With an hour to go before the wedding ceremony started, Aru held still as her mother fastened the final hook on the back of her blouse. Nikita had only been too happy to make them brand-new outfits overnight, and Aru, who loved Indian clothes but always ended up in the *itchiest* of garments, had found herself pleasantly delighted when hers was delivered in the morning. It was a rich, golden *lehenga*. The full-bodied skirt was covered with small mirrors in intricate shapes, and the cap-sleeved blouse boasted miniature lightning bolts in saffron thread.

It was gorgeous.

It was ridiculously useful.

And it was comfortable.

All the Pandava outfits (including the one belonging to Aiden, who preferred to call himself "Pandava adjacent") were flame-retardant and decorated with small enchanted mirrors that refracted light and turned the wearer invisible. Nikita had even charmed the threads to disguise the Pandavas' voices as well.

"You're beautiful, Aru," said her mom, smiling at her in the floor-length mirror's reflection.

Aru didn't really believe her, but she smiled anyway. All last evening, they hadn't spoken about the journey that lay ahead of Aru, or how this might be the last time the two of them would be together. Instead, Aru's mom had ordered takeout, put on *National Treasure*, and laughed when Aru recited every single line. It would've been a great day, if only Aru could've been sure there'd be more days to come.

"I wish I could go with you," said Krithika now.

Aru hugged her tight, once again feeling how thin her mom had become over the past few months while searching for the location of the labyrinth. "You just got back, Mom. I need you to stay here. I don't want anything to happen to you."

Krithika sighed and rubbed Aru's back. "I'll keep watch. I'll be waiting for you, Aru, and if by some chance you see Kara... Well, maybe one day there will be time to explain."

When Aru thought of Kara's crumpled expression and the pain on Krithika's face, all she felt was a deep sorrow. The Sleeper had twisted the truth. He'd made it seem like Krithika hadn't wanted Kara, and now what should've been a whole family was broken.

"What will you do?" Krithika asked.

Aru stayed silent. In a way, the plan was simple: Get their weapons back. Stop the Sleeper from stealing the nectar of immortality. And then the Pandavas were to do what they had been trained for from the very start:

End the war.

Which meant the Sleeper had to be stopped. The facts that

he was her dad, that he had loved her, that her own half sister was on his side, and that others who fought on his behalf were deserving of pity...they changed nothing.

"Try my best not to disappoint the universe?" offered Aru.

"Oh, *beti*," said Krithika. "It's like they say in the Gita, 'It is better to live your own destiny imperfectly than to live an imitation of somebody else's life with perfection.' You understand?"

Aru blinked. *No?* Sometimes she thought her brain involuntarily glazed over whenever her mom went down one of her philosophical roads. Krithika Shah loved quoting from the holy scripture of the Gita, but Aru only understood maybe a *quarter* of what she meant.

"Good advice?" she tried.

Her mom laughed. "What I mean is...be true to yourself."

Aru set her jaw. Since when had that worked out for her? Aru's instincts always seemed to be wrong. Her mom was just saying things to make her feel better. They both knew that her options were either to give up or fight back once and for all, and there was only one choice to make.

At that moment, the doorbell went off. Krithika released her. She swiped at her eyes, and Aru could've sworn she'd seen tears there.

When Aru went downstairs to open the door, her stomach flipped. Aiden was standing on her doorstep. His camera, Shadowfax, and his dark backpack were slung over his shoulders. He was wearing a black kurta with the sleeves rolled up around his forearms. His dark hair fell over his eyes, and the sun was doing that annoying thing where it seemed to illuminate only him. Aru hesitated, unsure of what to say.

But it was Aiden who spoke first. "Did you tell anyone?"

Aru felt like she'd been thrown into cold water. "About what?"

"About the..." He trailed off, glancing at the floor.

"The kiss?" She crossed her arms. "No."

Was it her imagination or did his shoulders fall just a little bit?

"Oh," he said. "Good."

Good?! thought Aru. She felt like someone had taken a cheese grater to her soul. *Good.* That meant he didn't want anyone to know... because it had been a mistake.

Why had she ever thought otherwise?

"I don't think we should've done that," he said, staring at the floor. "I'm sorry."

Aru gave herself roughly three seconds to be sad. Then she shoved the feeling far away from her.

"Are you... Are you okay?" asked Aiden. "Can we still be friends?"

Aru had never missed her lightning bolt more. Vajra would have happily electrocuted him on the spot.

"Am I *okay?*" said Aru, taking a menacing step toward him.

Aiden nervously stumbled back. "Aru...? It's not you, it's—"

"Finish that sentence and even without a lightning bolt I will *fry* you," said Aru.

Aiden shut his mouth.

"No, Aiden, I'm not *okay*. My birthday was crap. My half sister hates me, and my weapon is gone." Aru drew herself up. "I've literally got an entire world to save in nine days! I don't have time for this!"

"Uh—" said Aiden, his eyes widening.

Aru flipped her hair over her shoulder. "Sure, Aiden, we can be 'friends,' mostly because I don't need this nonsense on top of everything else. But when this is over, don't *ever* talk to me again. That should be easy enough for you."

And with that, Aru turned on her heel and stomped away. She caught sight of Aiden's reflection in the mirror. He looked stunned. And handsome...

But mostly stunned.

Ha, thought Aru, even though she felt a terrible digging sensation behind her ribs.

It was only when she'd reached the exhibit and saw Brynne's thunderous frown and Mini's shocked face that she realized she'd accidentally broadcast all that through the Pandava mind link.

Brynne spoke telepathically: *He might be my best friend, but I will beat the—*

I wish you'd told us! Mini cut in before Brynne could finish. *If you start crying, please drink water. Dehydration is serious!*

Brynne: *Really, Mini?*

Mini: *I'm looking out for her! Aru, what can we do?*

It doesn't make sense, said Brynne. *There has to be a reason why he'd backtrack like that. Let me talk to him—*

No way, said Aru. *Please, just let it go.*

Neither Brynne nor Mini looked convinced, but at that moment Aru's mom cleared her throat and raised her hand to get their attention.

"Oh, hi, Aiden," said Krithika. "I thought your mother was coming?"

"She's on her way," said Aiden. He lifted his camera, avoiding all eye contact with the girls. "I, um, I got the footage of Sheela's fake prophecy to show you."

He glanced at Aru, Brynne, and Mini. When none of them spoke, he pulled the images out of his screen, where they hovered in midair. Aiden must have filmed it secretly, because the angle was all off, and Aru could barely see the lower halves of Sheela's and Nikita's bodies. Judging from the glittering floor, they were in Urvashi's dance studio.

"—a vision?" said Urvashi off-camera. Her voice was pinched with concern.

Sheela began to shake. Aru heard Nikita whisper, "Don't overdo it."

Sheela's voice rang clear as a bell. *"You cannot see, you cannot know, where the Pandavas will go. . . . If you seek them, you shall find . . . destruction of another kind. . . ."*

"Aiden!" shouted Urvashi sharply. "Why are you filming this? Get help!"

"Sorry, *masi,*" Aiden muttered.

The camera's viewpoint careened toward the ground before going dark.

"And they bought it?" asked Brynne.

Aiden nodded. "Hanuman and Urvashi left after that. They're following some leads about the rest of the Sleeper's army."

"What leads?" asked Aru coldly.

Aiden didn't meet her eyes. "There's no way to access the labyrinth without a celestial weapon. But once you're inside, how do you let people *in*? Hanuman and Urvashi are trying to find out what his plans are."

Aru considered this, her stomach turning. All they'd been thinking of was how to get *into* the labyrinth. She hadn't even begun to consider how they were going to fit a whole army inside.

"Sorry I'm late!" called a musical voice down the hallway.

Malini Acharya entered the room and all the air seemed to leave it. Malini was tall and slim, with rich brown skin and beautiful eyes that looked like amber jewels beneath moonlight. Her supernatural grace was the only clue that she had once been a celebrated apsara before she had left her celestial city to marry a mortal man.

Malini smiled at Krithika and Brynne, nodded at Mini, and, as usual, ignored Aru completely. For some reason, Aiden's mom didn't seem to like Aru very much. Malini went to Aiden, resting her palm against his cheek.

"It's time," said Krithika, gesturing to Greg the stone elephant.

The statue's jaw unhinged, dropping to the floor.

"You have our blessings," said Krithika.

"And this," added Malini. "Should you need it."

She hummed a quick tune, and the music was what Aru imagined a shooting star would sound like. It filled Aru's senses, lifted her hair off her neck, and shimmered through her bones. When she blinked, Malini was holding a coin-size piece of light, which she handed to Aiden.

"Here. A pure note of music. It will let you call upon my family," said Malini. "But it is to be used *only* in emergencies."

Aiden took the note of music, a curious combination of fury and wonder on his face as he tucked it away.

"I believe in you. All of you," said Krithika. "Please come back safely."

Aru took a deep breath. Mini, wearing a purple lehenga covered in silver stars, stepped through the portal first. Next was Brynne, in a midnight blue *salwar kameez* with gold stripes. Aiden followed, and then it was Aru's turn.

"Don't forget to feed BB while we're gone," said Aru to her

mom. "And not too many Oreos—he'll get indigestion. And then the museum will be on fire."

Krithika laughed. "Noted."

With one last look at her mother and the place where she had lived for almost ten years, Aru stepped into the portal.

FIVE

That Time We Crashed a Wedding

A ru had imagined that crashing a wedding would involve a high-speed car chase, but what it really came down to was blending in with the guests and getting to the sacred fire before anyone saw them. After that, all they had to do was throw the Agni coin into the flames and get out. Easy enough.

The wedding venue looked pretty swanky. The outside of the fancy hotel was covered in twisting ivy and roses. Enchanted bronze lions yawned sleepily when they saw the Pandavas. Behind them, people jogged and walked their dogs without a second glance. To humans, the enchanted hotel looked like a pile of unfinished construction.

Calligraphy formed out of floating candles spelled out:

FOR THE RAVI AND TRENA PARTY, PLEASE ENTER!

"Where is everyone?" asked Mini softly as the four of them crept inside.

It was very quiet. *Too quiet,* thought Aru. The inside of the hotel opened into a marvelous atrium where enchanted snow sifted down from silvery clouds.

"They had those specially commissioned for the winter-wonderland theme," said Mini. "Superexpensive magic. My cousin threw a fit when the first artist tried to use cold Styrofoam pellets instead of real snow."

"Weddings are so overrated," said Brynne, dusting snow off her shoulder. "So, where's the food?"

"Guys?" said Aiden.

All three sisters snapped at him. *"WHAT?"*

Aiden flinched, then pointed to a pair of wide-open doors on the right. A faint shimmer on the threshold told Aru that the place had an enchanted sound barrier, which explained why they hadn't been able to hear anyone inside. Guests were already seated on either side of a long aisle decorated with snowy branches and floating candles. At the end of the aisle stood the *mandap*—the wedding tent—which had been adorned with hundreds of snow-dusted roses. From here, Aru could detect the faint whiff of the sacred fire. The bride and groom sat behind the flames while the priest threw in offerings.

"The wedding already *started*?" said Mini, starting to hyper-ventilate. "We were supposed to be here before all this! I must've gotten the time wrong! What are we going to do?"

Aru reached into her pocket—*All skirts,* she thought, *should come with pockets*—and touched the Agni coin. It was hot against her skin.

"Simple," said Aru. "We're going to walk down the aisle."

As long as we don't make a sound, Nikita said, our outfits SHOULD keep us camouflaged, said Aru through their Pandava mind link as they tiptoed down the long aisle in pairs. Fortunately, the eyes of the five hundred guests were all on the couple up front.

Super comforting, said Brynne.

She had insisted on bringing up the rear with Mini in case something tore out of the ground and attacked them, because "weddings never go according to plan." And since Aru had to be in front to throw the Agni coin in the fire, that left her walking down the aisle with . . . Aiden.

By now, they were about fifteen feet away from the sacred fire.

Slowly . . . No sudden movements, people, said Brynne.

What are we going to do when we get there? asked Mini. *What if we ruin the wedding?*

The entire world versus . . . a wedding, Mini, said Brynne.

Tell that to my mom's family.

The altar was coming up—less than ten feet away. The bride and groom looked radiant. They kept sneaking smiles and glances at each other. They didn't seem to notice what was going on around them, which was probably for the best, considering how the guests kept gossiping during the ceremony.

"Did she murder her hairdresser's family? That's the *only* way to explain that hairstyle. . . ."

"What a waste of money. . . . I hate capitalism."

"I heard from her cousin's sister's ex-boyfriend—"

Aru almost tripped trying to hear that last one, but Aiden caught her and gave her one of his Meaningful Looks™. There were a few small steps left before the sacred fire, barely two feet away. Aru half expected that the fire would be huge, but it was in an aluminum container the size of a large shoe box. As the priest chanted, he threw coins and petals into the flames.

If all went according to plan, nobody but the Pandavas would notice that something extra had been thrown in.

Okay, here goes nothing. . . .

Aru crossed her fingers on one hand, hoping that the magic of the coin would only affect them and no one else would see anything. She raised the coin high with her other hand, preparing to—

Throw UNDER, not over, Shah! scolded Brynne.

Whoops, thought Aru, adjusting her windup.

In one smooth arc, the Agni coin toppled into the smoke.

Aru braced herself. She thought the fire would explode or the ground beneath them would quake, but instead, there was nothing but the quiet crackle of the flames.

Aru was turning to look at her sisters when a short, light-skinned man in an unfortunate denim kurta stood up from his seat in the second row and said, "DON'T GO THROUGH WITH THIS, TRENA! He'll never make you happy!"

A loud gasp ran through the crowd. Even the priest stopped chanting. Aru bounced on her heels, rubbed her hands together, and said, "Well, *this* just got messy!"

Oops.

One moment the guests were staring in horror—and delight—at the guy who had just spoken up. The next, every eye was trained on Aru. The bride and groom stared at her over the flames.

"Who are *you?*" demanded the groom.

"Family?" piped up Mini.

"Congrats!" said Aru.

Aiden smacked his forehead.

The groom stood up. "What do you think—"

But he was interrupted by a loud gurgle coming from the fire. In the blink of an eye, the flames shot up fifteen feet. Then they parted down the middle like curtains drawing open.

"The decorations!" wailed one of the aunties.

"I told you we should've eloped," muttered the bride.

From within the flames, a woman's voice called out, *SACRED FLAME CONNECTION CONFIRMED. YOUR CALL IS BEING TRANSFERRED. PLEASE HOLD.*

"What is going on?" shouted the groom.

One column of fire spiraled toward the Pandavas, elongating into a flaming tunnel.

"Hold on tight!" yelled Aiden as he grabbed Aru's hand.

Aru flung out her other arm, and relief surged in her chest when Brynne and Mini drew close. A blast of hot air blew back Aru's hair as the flames pulled them all into the portal. She tried to blink, but the gusts of wind and flames forced her eyes shut.

The last thing Aru heard was one of the guests calling out, "Are you still serving lunch after this?"

SIX

A Warm Welcome. Honestly, a Little *Too* Warm.

Aru felt like she'd landed on hot asphalt. Her arms tingled as heat crawled through her skin. She blinked, trying to get ahold of her surroundings, but something blocked her sight. Something with coarse hair and . . . hooves? Aru shot upright, scuttling backward, only to find herself face-to-face with . . . a goat.

The goat didn't look like other goats. For one thing, it was wearing a shirt that read MULTIVERSE'S G.O.A.T. On top of that, its fur was the color of cinnamon and its horns were stubby orange flames. It regarded her with its rectangular pupils and then bleated indifferently, as if to say *Your presence is vastly underwhelming.* With a snort, the goat wandered out of her sight.

Only now could Aru finally get a look at where they were. Brynne and Mini were already standing on her left. Brynne had a scimitar out, and Mini was blotting her face with a moist towelette.

"This place is so hot!" said Mini. "I've run out of water, too. We could get heatstroke!"

Aiden, who was standing to Aru's right, held out a full water bottle.

Mini instantly brightened. "Thanks, Wifey!" she said, reaching for it before casting a guilty glance at Aru.

Aru knew, logically, that it was only a bottle of water. And yet some grumpy corner of her brain muttered, *Betrayal*...

"Need a hand?" asked Aiden.

Belatedly, Aru realized she was still sitting on the ground. She ignored him and hauled herself up on her own.

The Pandavas were standing in an empty chamber that reminded Aru of a fancy hotel lobby. The walls were slabs of shiny obsidian with rivulets of lava sliding down from the top and disappearing into the strangest floor she had ever seen. From one angle the floor looked like pieces of polished ruby and topaz interlocked in a dazzling array. But when she tilted her head, she could see images wavering in the jeweled tiles. In one, she saw a family's temple room, and even part of their kitchen. In another, she saw a woman in a white sari sobbing by the banks of a river. In a third, the same bride and groom from mere moments ago walked in slow circles with warm smiles on their faces.

"What *is* this place?" asked Brynne.

Aru looked up from the floor. Sweat broke out across her forehead, and her fancy lehenga felt too heavy. A ceiling of steam and smoke soared hundreds of feet above them, tapering like the funnel of a teakettle. It made her think of—

"Oh my gods, we're in a volcano..." said Mini. "An *actual* volcano..."

The goat, which had been ambling around them and occasionally snuffling the floor, bleated loudly. It stamped the floor with its hoof, and the ground began to tremble. All at once, a tall figure rose out of the jeweled tiles. Aru recognized the god of fire immediately. Agni's skin was burnished red, and his hair looked like shorn flames. He wore a scarlet kurta edged in fire, and around his neck was a bright chain. On it, a pendant the size of a robin's egg shone so fiercely that Aru had trouble looking at it directly.

Agni shook his head, then pinched the bridge of his nose. "It was *just* getting to the good part!" He inspected the floor, squinting at the tiles before groaning and craning his neck. "Argh! That guy just got kicked out by security! I wish I could've seen his face."

His goat trotted over, and Agni absentmindedly patted its head before looking at the Pandavas. "Can't you see I'm in the middle of, basically, *everything*?" he demanded, gesturing downward.

"You were . . . in the floor?" asked Mini.

"In a manner of speaking, yes," said Agni, closing his eyes. When he spoke, Aru felt as if his words sparked with heat. "I am . . . everywhere. I am the sacred flame. I am in homes and temples. I attend weddings and funerals. I purify all. I energize all."

Agni opened his eyes and stared at them. "So, who are you and what do you want?"

Brynne and Mini looked at Aru expectantly.

Your coin, your move, Brynne said telepathically.

"We thought it was a good time for a family reunion!" said Aru, smiling so hard she thought her face would break. "Remember me? Daughter of Indra? And Mini, daughter of the Dharma Raja . . ."

Mini waved.

"And Brynne, daughter of Vayu."

Brynne nodded.

"And then there's . . . Aiden."

"Another demigod?" asked Agni.

"No? More like a reincarnated former collective . . . wife?"

"Hi," said Aiden flatly.

"Oh, it's *you!*" said Agni to Aru, clapping his hands. "Almost didn't recognize you with the new hair. . . ."

Aru touched her hair. Minus the length, it was exactly the same.

"And height."

She *had* grown. . . . Two inches.

"Were you always wingless?" asked Agni.

"Sadly," said Aru.

"Hmm," said Agni. "There's something different about you lot—I can't quite put my finger on it. How long has it been? A millennium?"

"Uh, two years?" said Mini.

"Ish?" added Aru.

Agni blinked a couple of times, then started laughing. "Ah, time. The best cosmic joke in the universe."

"Yeah, so . . . Speaking of time," said Aru. "We have, um, *nine*—"

"Eight," muttered Aiden, glancing at his watch.

Aru's heart sank. Traveling to the god of fire's realm had robbed them of time. "*Eight* days left to get to the nectar of immortality before the Sleeper finds it and basically declares war on existence. And right now, he and our sister—well, technically *my* half sister, but we don't have to go into that today—are advancing through the labyrinth that's hiding the nectar, and we can't fight him without our celestial weapons."

"Ooh," said Agni. "Sounds dire! Do you think there will be a flame nearby so I can watch?"

Aru frowned. That was not the response she'd expected. "Maybe?"

"Awesome!"

"No, *not* awesome!" said Aru. "Look, a while ago you told us you have an arsenal of weapons that we'd need, and when the time came, we should call you. So . . . we have!"

Agni sucked in his breath. It was the kind of sound you make when you're about to tell someone bad news. Panic surged through Aru, but she pushed it down.

"So . . . what do you want us to do?" she asked, looking around the molten room. "Do you have an obstacle course? Are we going to do some training-montage stuff? You know, 'wax on, wax off'—you say cryptic, inspiring things and we sit around and despair until the cryptic things make sense and then—*boom!*—our weapons come back and everything is awesome?"

Agni looked confused. "'Wax on, wax off'?"

Aiden snorted back a laugh.

Through their Pandava mind link, Mini sighed. *This is not the right time to quote* The Karate Kid.

"Ignore that part," said Aru to Agni. "Point is, can you help us?"

Agni touched his glowing necklace and shook his head. "*Now* I know what's different," he said, before waving a hand in their direction. "Your weapons—they're gone."

Beside Aru, Brynne winced. Her fingers fluttered to her neck, where Gogo, her wind mace, had often rested in the form of a choker.

"Your weapons were proof of godly favor. Without that, you cannot wield my weapons, either," said Agni carefully.

Aru nearly swayed on the spot. Her plan had failed, and now they had no way to fight the Sleeper. She squeezed her eyes shut, her thoughts yanking her back to that awful moment when Kara had betrayed them.

I'm doing this because I love you guys.

Aru still didn't understand how it could've happened. How could Kara say she loved them and then leave them open to attack? And why, instead of trying to protect Aru, was the Sleeper choosing destruction?

If the Pandavas were on the "right side," why hadn't their weapons been restored? What was the point of any of this?

Brynne's voice pulled Aru out of her thoughts. "How do we win back godly favor?" she asked Agni.

"By way of a test, I imagine," said Agni, stroking his chin.

Brynne's face lit up. "We're ready! Let's do it. What's it gonna be? Obstacle challenge? Ten-course meal? I can do it all."

"It is, perhaps, more difficult than that," said Lord Agni. "I'll show you."

From Agni's back four additional arms sprouted and rose gracefully into the air. He reached forward and touched each of their foreheads with a different index finger. Aru was glad he didn't go for their noses. The day was bad enough without adding a cosmic *boop!* to it.

Aru felt a sudden pinch of heat on her skin, and her vision clouded over. When her eyes cleared, she was no longer in a volcano but standing on a palatial terrace in an ancient kingdom. She turned, looking for her sisters, but she was alone. Maybe they were all seeing this vision from Agni individually.

Helloooo, she called through the Pandava mind link. There was no answer.

The terrace looked out over a lush green valley. Not ten feet away, a tall, dark-skinned, and solemn-eyed king sat on a throne of gold, speaking to a group of advisers gathered around him. To his left was a large weighing scale with huge sacks of coins piled beneath it, guarded by two soldiers strapped with knives and swords. A sacred fire lay before the king, and as he threw an offering of rice into the flames, a soft caw sounded.

"Help!"

A pigeon swooped out of the sky, alighting on the throne's armrest. "You must help me, King Shibi!" said the bird.

"What ails you, creature of my kingdom?"

Aru made a mental note to use that line one day.

"I am being pursued by a hawk who wishes to eat me!"

The king nodded. "I will protect you."

Aru wondered if the king was going to offer the pigeon a job in his kingdom, but in the next moment, a huge red hawk dived toward the bird.

"Your Highness, give up that bird!" said the hawk. "It is mine to eat!"

"I cannot," said King Shibi. "It is under my protection."

"Am I not under your protection, too, great king? Am I not one of the creatures that lives in your land? Is my family to starve for lack of fresh meat?"

King Shibi bowed his head. "If you must have fresh meat, then take my own."

He gestured to a soldier to place the pigeon on one weighing pan of the great scale. Then he . . . well, Aru couldn't bring herself to watch, but from the cries of "Ah! My leg!" she gathered that the king was cutting pieces from his own thigh and putting them on the other pan to equal the bird's weight.

And yet, when Aru peeked at the scale, the pigeon's side was still lower.

She stared at the king's advisers. Some of them were crying in sympathy for the king's plight, but no one was *stopping* him. Not a single person was like, *Hmm, that's a weirdly heavy pigeon,* or *Wow, what are we feeding these birds?* Nothing!

Finally, there was a great clanging sound as King Shibi jumped onto the scale, shouting, "Take me! Spare the pigeon!"

A vivid glow enveloped the king, the scale, the birds, and the terrace. Aru blinked a couple of times as heat overwhelmed her senses. Two divine voices called out, their words shaking the floor and practically rattling her bones.

"OH, KING SHIBI, WE HAVE WITNESSED YOUR GOODNESS AND YOU HAVE PASSED OUR TEST. BE WELL, AND FIND YOURSELF RESTORED."

When Aru blinked, she was once more in Lord Agni's volcano lair. His extra arms had vanished, and he was regarding the Pandavas excitedly.

"Oof," said Mini, swaying a bit. "I feel woozy."

"Well!" said Agni. "I think that was clear enough!"

"Uh, no?" said Aru. "King Shibi couldn't ask his *royal chef* to make a chicken sandwich for the hawk? He had to jump straight to offering his own leg?" Aru briefly thought of Boo ruffling his feathers and quickly added, "Not that I wanted anything to happen to the pigeon."

"What was the point of that?" asked Brynne. "What's the test? Some kind of . . . food challenge?"

"No," said Aiden quietly, and all eyes turned to him. "The

test is about what we do when we think no one's watching, isn't it?"

Agni smiled. "You wish to enter the labyrinth containing the nectar of immortality, yes?"

The Pandavas nodded.

"Then do so," he said. "And perhaps the manner in which you do will win the favor of the gods."

"*Perhaps? Might?* These aren't exactly words of comfort," said Aru. "How will we know for sure?"

"Well, for starters, you'll possibly remain alive."

"*Possibly?*" repeated Brynne.

"But we can only navigate the labyrinth with the light of the sun," said Mini. "How are we going to do that? The Sleeper already has the advantage because Kara is the daughter of the sun god."

"You said you would help us," pressed Aru. "If you can't give us weapons, there has to be *something*."

At this, the goat—which had been persistently trailing after Aiden and trying to nibble Shadowfax's leather strap—bleated excitedly. Aru didn't speak goat, but if she did, she'd bet it was saying something like *Ooh! Show them the thing!*

"There is," said Agni. "Though it is known to do more harm than good...." The god of fire unclasped the bright necklace around his neck and held it out to the girls. "Only one thing can guide you through the labyrinth. This is one part of the Syamantaka Gem, but you might know it by its other name—the Sun Jewel."

SEVEN

The Sun Jewel

"This is perfect!" said Brynne, grabbing the necklace. "We'll use it to get into the labyrinth and—"

"That piece alone will do nothing," said Agni. "Only when it is whole can its light guide you."

"Why isn't it whole?" asked Mini.

Agni sighed. "The jewel has not always brought happiness. It caused strife amongst those who were so dazzled by its brightness that they could recognize no other light. To safeguard humanity from temptation, the jewel was chiseled into three pieces. One piece was given to me. Another went to Vasuki, great king of all the nagas. And the final piece is with Jambavan, king of the bears."

The longer Aru stared at the Syamantaka Gem, the more she kept hearing the Lord of the Rings soundtrack echoing in her head. *One ring to rule them all…*

"What?" said Agni.

"What?" said Aru.

"You just said 'And in the darkness bind them'?" said Agni, frowning.

"SO, ANYWAY..." said Brynne loudly. "All we have to do is reunite the three pieces and the jewel will work, right? And that way we'll be able to get into the labyrinth *and* win back the gods' favor?"

"That's assuming we can *find* the pieces," said Aiden.

Agni flicked his wrist. A small flame hovered above his palm. "Take this. It'll act as your ticket. Merely say where you wish to be."

Aiden braced himself as Agni poured the flame into his hands, but it didn't seem to hurt. Aiden's shoulders loosened. The flame crystallized into a ruby and he slipped the fire-red stone into the pocket of his hoodie. After that he gingerly swung his backpack to the front, unzipped it slowly, and peered inside. Aru rolled her eyes. Aiden was acting like his backpack was a treasure chest.

You're not that great, thought Aru.

"Where does King Vasuki live?" asked Brynne.

"Where does he *not* live?" returned Agni. "He is the lord of all the naga folk. He is as much in their blood as he is in their land."

Well, that's helpful, thought Aru.

Aiden looked like he'd bitten down on a lemon peel. "Pretty sure I know who can help us find him."

Mini's eyes dimmed. "Rudy?"

Aru thought she would've been excited, but Mini looked as if she'd forgotten her hand sanitizer.

"Well, he *is* a naga prince. I think King Vasuki might be one of his great-grandfathers..." said Aiden. "Plus, Rudy said he'd be standing by to help us whenever we need it."

"Then what are we waiting for?" asked Brynne, clapping.

ROSHANI CHOKSHI

"We've got a third of the jewel, eight days to go, and a clear directive. Let's do this."

Um, aren't we forgetting something? said Mini through their mind link.

"Oops," said Brynne.

The Pandavas knelt and pressed their foreheads to the ground before Agni, then put their hands together in prayer and *pranama*.

"Go with my blessings, Pandavas," said the god of fire. "But before you do, let me offer one last piece of wisdom. There is more than one kind of darkness, and none is darker than doubt, for the light required to illuminate it belongs not to a jewel or a flame, but your very soul."

Aru felt his words lasering in on the fears she had buried deep in her mind. Ever since Kara had destroyed their weapons, Aru's biggest worry had been what would happen if they didn't get them back. All the people they loved would be doomed... All the progress they had made would have been for nothing.

Lurking beneath that was a quieter dread of what would happen if they *did* win their weapons back. Then they would have no choice but to fight. Not against faceless, twisted enemies, but people they knew—people they'd cared for, in a way. Aru still felt haunted by Kara's heartbroken expression when she'd destroyed the Pandavas' weapons. And, no matter how much she wished she didn't see it, Aru remembered how the Sleeper had looked at her and her mom—not with hate, but with *love*.

I promised that, if I had to, I would break the world in half to make our family whole and happy, he'd said. *I intend to keep that promise.*

"And what will you do when you have your weapons?" asked Agni.

Aru opened her mouth, but Brynne answered first.

"What we're supposed to do," she said firmly. "We'll make sure the Sleeper doesn't get hold of the nectar of immortality."

"And then?"

Brynne's face contorted into a mask of fury. She punched her fist into her palm, her smile almost vicious. "And then we'll crush him and his army once and for all."

Aru flinched. She was glad she was standing behind Brynne and Mini so that her sisters couldn't see her face. What would they think of all the chaos inside her? She knew Brynne was right, but whenever she tried to picture herself standing on the battlefield, she felt paralyzed.

Could I do it? wondered Aru. She had two paths before her— destroy or be destroyed—and she couldn't stomach the thought of taking either one.

All the weapons in the world cannot help you if you do not know what you'll do with them, said Agni. *What will you do, Aru Shah?*

Aru looked up sharply. The god of fire's lips had not moved at all. He had spoken directly into her thoughts.

"Come on, Shah!" said Brynne from behind her now.

Aru looked over her shoulder. Aiden was holding out the flame-shaped ruby, Brynne and Mini on either side of him. Aru realized that she was standing alone and the god of fire was nowhere to be seen. Even the goat was gone.

Take it one step at a time, Shah, she told herself.

There was no point in panicking about what she would do in a fight until she was sure she could *get* to the fight. And right now, their only chance of catching up lay in the Sun Jewel.

Aru joined her sisters. For a moment, Mini's eyes met hers over the glow of the flame, and concern flashed over her features. She looked as if she wanted to say something, but it was too late.

"Take us to Prince Rudra's house in Naga-Loka," said Aiden. "But not inside! Definitely *outside* . . . please."

Heat burst around them. Aru squeezed her eyes shut as flames danced overhead and a powerful gust of wind shoved her through space. It hardly lasted a few seconds, but to Aru, it was like those agonizing minutes when you get into a hot car and have to wait for the air-conditioning to save you. When she could finally open her eyes, Aru saw the palatial underwater gardens of Rudy's estate. Above, a shimmering bubble arced through the water, letting them both breathe and swim at the same time.

"This way," said Aiden, gesturing to the huge front door covered in twisting coral and bright anemone.

Aru glanced at Mini. She looked crestfallen. Brynne didn't seem to notice—she was running over potential military strategies with Aiden, who was barely listening.

"What's up?" asked Aru, slowing down so that she and Mini were walking a little behind the others.

"Hmm?" said Mini, looking up at her. "Oh. It's . . . Well, it's not nothing." She gave a little laugh. "Have you ever thought about who we'd be if we didn't have our powers?"

"Slightly less awesome?" tried Aru, but it came out hollow.

"Some people don't need powers to be great," said Mini, as if to herself. "But I don't think I'm one of them. Without Dee Dee, I'm just . . . me."

"But you *are* great, Mini," insisted Aru.

Mini stopped walking and faced Aru, staring her dead in the eye. "Would you put up with me and my anxious spewing about fatal statistics and deadly bacteria if I wasn't *also* the daughter of the god of death? Would we even be friends if the Pandava-thing inside us hadn't woken up?"

Aru was stunned. She couldn't picture existence without Mini, but then her thoughts turned to how different her life would've been if she'd never discovered who she really was. She might still be walking past the Hall of the Gods every afternoon, never knowing what—or *who*—was waiting inside the lamp.

"See?" said Mini, taking a step back. "I knew it."

"No, I was thinking about something else," said Aru hurriedly. "Listen, if we weren't immediately friends, then that would've been a big mistake. *Huge.*"

Mini almost smiled.

"I would've been struck by your awesomeness eventually," Aru went on.

Mini didn't seem convinced. Her brow furrowed. "Sorry. It wasn't fair of me to ask you that. I know we're all struggling with this.... Maybe I need some space for a bit." Without looking at Aru, Mini picked up her pace.

Now they were outside the doors of Rudy's palace.

"Do we ... knock?" asked Brynne. "Does this thing even have a doorknob?"

Abruptly, the coral-covered doors swung open. The light from inside the palace silhouetted a person who practically jumped at them.

"WHAT'S UP, POTATOES?" said Rudy. His gaze went straight to Mini, and Aru suspected that he purposely made his voice lower as he said, "'Sup, Mini."

"Hi," said Mini shyly.

"Rudy ... what are you wearing?" asked Aiden.

ROSHANI CHOKSHI

Instead of his usual explosively colorful outfit, Rudy was wearing head-to-toe black and had slicked his hair to fall in a curtain in front of one of his eyes.

"Like it?" he asked.

"No," said Aiden, followed by, "Is that a fake earring?"

Rudy dropped his voice to a whisper. "It's part of my *disguise*."

"What disguise?" asked Brynne.

From somewhere behind Rudy, they heard a woman's voice call out, "*Beta?* Who's at the door?"

"NO ONE!" shouted Rudy. "JUST A DELIVERY OF MY ART SUPPLIES!"

He pointed down one of the outdoor walkways and whispered, "Meet me down there! I'll let you guys in through the back and fill you in on what's going on." He sniffed at the air. "And maybe I'll get you some towels so you can shower, too. You guys—except Mini—smell like two-week-old potatoes, if I'm being honest. You know, the kind Brynne sometimes forgets about in that closet where she spends all her time."

Brynne raised an eyebrow. "The pantry?"

"Yeah!"

"Nice to see you, too, Rudy."

EIGHT

Suffering for My Art, as Per Usual

As Rudy led them through his palace, Aru kept getting distracted by the artwork lining the walls. Some of the paintings she recognized from her textbooks. Others were posters from concerts long ago—1964, THE GANDHARVAS AND THE BEATLES, PERFORMING ONE NIGHT ONLY ON THE ASTRAL PLANE, SPONSORED BY LUCY IN THE SKY WITH DIAMONDS. Another poster showed a trio of beautiful women wearing golden gowns with elbow-length gloves. Aru paused. The women's skin was tinted *green*. The headline of the enchanted poster floated off its surface:

THE PRETTY POISONS ARE COMING TO LANKA! AND THEIR HITS ARE POSITIVELY *DEADLY*!

Those women were *vishakanyas* . . . poison maidens.

They were subtle and deadly, trained in all manner of arts and fed from a young age a special diet of poisons so that anyone who touched them would fall sick and die, her mother had once told her. *In the ancient times, they were sent to kingdoms as secret assassins, disguised as courtesans or artists.*

Aru had loved the story. How cool would it have been to say *Touch me and die, mortal!* Once, she'd even tried to turn herself into a vishakanya by chewing and spitting out a poison-ivy leaf.

That was... a mistake.

Hurry up, Aru! called Brynne's voice through the mind link.

Aru ran to catch up to the others. At the end of the gallery hallway lay the entrance to Rudy's chambers, marked by a pair of great silver doors. He waved his hand before the doors and they swung open. A jellyfish sentinel detached from one of the walls, floating down before the door and bearing a sign that read DO NOT DISTURB, ARTIST AT WORK.

Rudy's "room" was the size of a small but cozy house. Inside, hundreds of rocks lined the shelves on the walls, along with thousands of music records. Rudy's parents, despite being royalty, ran a jewelry business. Rudy, who was color-blind, didn't have the same talents in gemology as his parents and brothers. But while he couldn't spot the difference between some colors, he could see something else entirely—strains of magic. With that perspective, Rudy could make beautiful music that could throw off opponents and create force fields of noise.

Aru refused to tell him, but it was a pretty cool gift.

Rudy plucked one of his rocks, an egg-size piece of rose quartz, and stuck it under the door. The rock started emitting sighs and groaning things in Rudy's voice like *Why must I suffer to create?* and *No, Mother, I cannot eat! I need to be alone with the crushing splendor of my dark thoughts! FOR MY ART!*

Aiden frowned. "Rudy, what is that?"

"It's part of my disguise!" said Rudy. "I figured you guys would come find me when you, naturally, needed me to rescue you—"

"Rescue?" asked Brynne.

Rudy continued. "And news has trickled down to the underwater kingdoms that the Pandavas must be left entirely alone before the big battle, which didn't sound right, so I made up this whole disguise just in case. This way my parents won't go looking for me when I run off with you Potatoes."

"What exactly is your disguise?" asked Aiden.

Aru glanced between the two boys. With his dark hoodie and hair pushed in front of his eyes, Rudy kind of looked like—

"*You*. Duh," said Rudy. "The whole tortured artist, et cetera, et cetera. It's really convincing. My mom keeps having the courtiers leave huge feasts outside my door. It's great! I came up with the idea after I noticed how your mom is all 'Oh, beta, don't let me disturb you when you're daydreaming' and all that."

Aru howled with laughter while Aiden turned bright red. "WHAT?"

"So!" said Rudy, completely ignoring Aiden's meltdown. "What do you need?"

"I don't *sound* like that!"

"Yes, you do."

Just then, Rudy's wounded voice warbled from the quartz. *Oh no! Not another emotional spiral of despair! Oh, art, you CRUEL and beautiful thing!*

"I have *never* said that in my entire life!" said Aiden.

Brynne lifted her fingers to her lips and whistled so loudly that Aru winced. "Enough!" she said. "Rudy, we do need your help."

"As expected," said Rudy smugly.

"We need to get to Vasuki," said Brynne. She held up the Sun Jewel and filled him in on what Agni had told them.

When Brynne was finished, Rudy's eyes looked huge. "You want me to *rob* G-Thousand?"

"What's G-Thousand?" asked Aru.

"Nobody said *rob!*" said Mini, alarmed. "*Borrow,* that's all!"

"Possibly rob…" muttered Brynne.

"G-Thousand is what my brothers and I call Lord Vasuki," said Rudy. "Technically, he's like our great-great-great-times-a-thousand-grandfather, and that's kinda complicated to keep saying, so we nicknamed him."

"Maybe you can explain the situation to him?" suggested Mini.

"I've never talked to him," said Rudy. "I've met him—well, *part* of him—but everyone has."

Mini frowned. "How can you meet *part* of someone?"

"I mean, *look* at him," said Rudy, pointing up.

The ceiling of Rudy's suite was like a miniature Sistine Chapel. Only in here the frescoes were enchanted to create images of how the gods won back their power. After the gods lost their immortality due to a curse, they convinced the asuras to put aside their differences and churn the Ocean of Milk to find the nectar that would restore it. According to the story Aru's mom told, King Vasuki agreed to be used as a rope, and he was wrapped around the great Mount Mandara to froth the sea.

Aru didn't have much experience with mountains. She'd been to Stone Mountain in Georgia, which was pretty big, but even with that in her head she had trouble picturing how big a serpent had to be to wrap around it not just once, but *ten* times.

"Why is this on your bedroom ceiling?" asked Aiden. "I thought you'd make a constellation of your face so you can look up at it when you go to bed."

Rudy's jaw dropped. "Wait...That's such a good idea."

"I was joking."

But Rudy was tilting his head, examining the ceiling like he'd never truly seen it before. "My parents had this installed after I started failing all the jewelry-identification tests—it was a reminder of my illustrious heritage and all that. It was supposed to inspire me, and it did, but you're right, Aiden. *I* should be inspiring me. That's brilliant!" Rudy clapped his cousin on the back. "Thanks for believing in me."

Aiden opened his mouth, then closed it. "You're...welcome."

"Hug?" asked Rudy.

"No."

"Okay!" said Rudy, turning back to the Pandavas. "So you see why I've never really *met* him? I think once I saw a part of his tail when our parents took us camping. My brothers and I poked it, and then the scales started rippling and we got freaked out and swam away. I don't think anyone has seen G-Thousand's head in...centuries? He's so ancient and so huge that he's basically part of the infrastructure of the whole kingdom."

"How are we going to find the piece of the Sun Jewel if we can't talk to him?" asked Brynne. "Does he have a storage room or something? Maybe we can look through that?"

Rudy shuddered. For the first time, his bravado slipped away.

"What's wrong?" asked Mini.

"I know where we have to go," said Rudy. He walked over to one of his shelves. There, Aru saw a miniature model of a kingdom she'd never seen. It was made entirely of jewels and interlocking caves; the jagged mouths of caverns wove between shining towers and spires. He tapped the top of one miniature cave. *"Here."*

"And what is 'here' exactly?" asked Brynne.

"Patala," said Rudy. He whispered it like it was someplace sacred. Or haunted. "It's mostly ruins these days, but it used to be an old kingdom and now it's 'something, something, historical landmark, something.' I think one of my cousins is interning at the archive desk there. G-Thousand's treasures are supposed to be in one of the caves."

"But if we know exactly where to go, isn't that...good?" said Mini.

Rudy winced.

"What's the problem?" asked Aiden.

"Um, the *guards*?" said Rudy, wide-eyed. "I've never been down there, so I don't know *who* or *what* guards those treasures, but my dad says that it's protected by the greatest fear of the weakest men."

"What does *that* mean?" asked Aru.

Rudy shrugged. "I dunno. On our school trips, we just took a picture by the balcony vantage point. No one goes into the ruins anymore. Too dangerous." He squared his shoulders. "But I can get us there. We'll have to leave tonight, though."

Brynne threw up her hands. "Tonight? Why can't we go *now*? We've already lost so much time!"

"We have to wait until my parents go to sleep before we can use the fancy elevator," said Rudy apologetically. "In the meantime, I'm gonna grab us some food and stuff. Get comfy!" He flailed a hand at the different hallways shooting off from his own private lobby/room/thing. "There's a war arena down there. I didn't know what to do with it, so it's mostly my recording studio. Showers and pools thataway."

With that, Rudy opened his door and slipped out.

"This'll give us time to eat, freshen up, take a quick nap," said Aiden calmly. "I've got some chocolate. Want some, Brynne?"

"I've got no appetite," she said.

Aru and Mini exchanged shocked looks. Brynne Rao *never* turned down a snack.

You okay? asked Mini through the mind link.

Brynne sent a mental grunt down the line.

Gonna take that as a solid "maybe," said Aru, but Brynne didn't seem amused.

"C'mon, Aiden," Brynne said. "Let's run through some drills. I gotta stay sharp. I want to try out some new shape-shifting forms, and I can't get..." *Weak,* she finished telepathically.

Aru wondered if Brynne had meant to think that aloud, because without another word she turned on her heel and stalked off in the direction of the arena. Aiden looked over his shoulder at Aru. For a moment, it seemed like he was trying to catch her eye, but Aru didn't look back. Every time she did, she missed Vajra's electrocuting properties too much.

"I'm worried about her," said Mini when she and Aru were alone. "I'm worried about *all* of us. And that test Agni mentioned... What if I screw it up?"

"That's impossible, Mini," said Aru. "You're the most neurotic and good-est demigod I know."

"That's not a real word, Aru."

"See?" Aru grinned. "Nothing gets past you!"

Mini laughed. "I wish I was like you sometimes."

At this, Aru's grin faltered. She didn't know how to tell Brynne and Mini that, for all her plans, she still felt lost. What if, when the time came, she did exactly the wrong thing? Aru changed the subject.

"Well, for what it's worth, I think Rudy likes you just the way you are."

Mini's shoulders slumped. "Pretty sure what he liked most was all the power I had. Key word: *had*."

"Don't think like that," said Aru. "It's like what Boo said... We're more than the things we fight with, right?"

Mini held her gaze. "And is that how you feel?"

Aru paused. Mini had her there.

"Thought so," said Mini.

That night, Aru didn't think she'd ever fall asleep, but one moment she was staring at the wall, and the next...

"ARU!"

She was standing now. Sheela threw her arms around her waist. Nikita waved beside her twin. The girls were dressed in matching blue pajamas and hair bonnets. The outfits lacked Nikita's usual flair, which meant she must have designed them in a hurry.

Alarm bells went off in Aru's head. They were on a cold beach. Above was a gray sky, below was gray sand, and the water was the indistinct color of smoke. Sharks made of clockwork dived in and out of the waves. There was no sound but a constant ticking, like time running out....

"Where are Brynne and Mini?" asked Aru.

Nikita pressed her lips into a grim line. "Couldn't reach them. They're lost in their own dreams."

"But we could get to you, at least," said Sheela, still clinging to Aru.

"What can we do to help?" asked Nikita. "What happened when you went to Lord Agni?"

Aru quickly told them about the Sun Jewel, and how it had been cut into three pieces—one for Lord Agni, the second for Lord Vasuki, and the third for Jambavan, king of the bears.

"Jambavan's name keeps ringing a bell," said Aru. "But we don't know where to find him. Maybe you can do some digging for us in the Otherworld?"

"On it," said Nikita.

"I don't like this," said Sheela, stepping away.

"Like what?" asked Aru.

Sheela glanced nervously at her twin, who nodded her approval to continue.

"I tried to look into the future, Aru, and it...It was the first time I ever saw something like that."

Aru tried to keep the panic off her face. She wasn't sure she succeeded. "Something like what?"

Sheela looked up at her, and her blue eyes seemed to ice over. "Nothing," she said in her prophecy voice. "I saw *nothing*."

Aru frowned. "What do you mean you saw 'nothing'?"

But if Sheela was planning on answering, the moment was disrupted. The gray sea split in two. The sky churned overhead, and Aru felt her feet sinking into the ground. She tried to catch her balance, her arms shooting out to steady her—

"Whoa, Aru!" yelled Brynne. "You almost took my eye out!"

Aru blinked. Brynne and Mini were already dressed. Two moon jellyfish floated behind them like living lanterns.

"It's time," said Mini.

NINE

New Lifetime Achievement for Minimal Drool

Once Rudy's enchanted Sad Boi Rocks™ rocks were in place to throw his parents off their trail, Rudy led them through the passages of his palace until they arrived at a chamber with a dozen elevators floating a foot off the ground. The moment the Potatoes stepped inside the room, a pedestal swiveled out of the ground and a sparkling keypad appeared.

All the elevators looked more or less the same, except one. It was an ancient palanquin, the kind Aru imagined had once carried kings and queens. The palanquin was an elaborately carved and painted wooden box with open sides and two long beams underneath that four or more men would have hoisted onto their shoulders to carry the person within. The elevator was big enough for six people, but it didn't look like it wanted company. Frost spiderwebbed across its exterior, and though Aru was more than twenty feet away, she could feel an odd chill emanating from the interior.

"Don't worry," said Rudy, following her gaze. "No one goes in *that* one."

"Where does it lead to?" asked Aiden.

Rudy shrugged. "My mom says it goes to the end of the world."

"What?"

"Yeah," said Rudy. "I mean, technically, there's more than one end-of-the-world location. And I guess it also depends on the universe? Don't ask. Just thinking about it gives me a headache. But that particular end-of-the-world location is really cold and dark."

"Remind me again why we couldn't try to use a portal?" asked Aru, staring around the eerie elevator bank.

"Too risky," said Rudy. He placed his palm on the pedestal's keypad. "Patala isn't like other places. There's always maintenance going on down there. It's super unstable, too, because all the other worlds got piled on top of it. If you get stuck...you might not get found."

Welp, thought Aru, glancing at Mini. She was rocking on her heels, a clear sign of the beginnings of an MOMDPA, also known as a Mini Obscure-Medical-Doom Panic Attack. Probably something about oxygen deprivation. And death.

"It'll be fine, Mini," said Brynne, clapping her on the back. Brynne glared at Aru, signaling that she should say something reassuring to Mini, too, but Aru was still thinking about her dream with Sheela, the way her blue eyes had turned empty and unfocused.

Nothing. I saw nothing.

What was waiting for them in Patala? Rudy had said that Lord Vasuki's treasures were guarded by fierce creatures...*the greatest fear of the weakest men.* She didn't know what that meant.

"This way," said Rudy, ushering them inside one of the massive elevators.

This one wasn't as polished or modern as the others. Its glass was frosted and etched with designs of undulating snakes. In the corners winked huge, uncut chunks of rubies and emeralds. Instead of chairs, ancient silken pillows were arranged in the center.

"It'll take a while to get there," said Rudy, plopping onto the ground. "Might as well sit."

Aru leaned against one of the pillows. Dust puffed into the air. Mini coughed. "Why is it so musty? Don't your parents ever visit Patala?"

"Not if they can help it," said Rudy. "Patala is beautiful, but it's . . . not pleasant. You'll see."

The moment the doors closed, the elevator silently plummeted through the marble floor. Aru's ears popped as the landscape shifted. At first, the scenery seemed normal enough for the underwater realm. Every now and then she caught the occasional glow of a giant orange squid floating through the dark sea. After that came layers upon layers of striped rock embedded with pieces of lost ships. But then the setting became unfocused and oddly bright, like a molten rainbow was sliding down the elevator glass.

At some point she must have fallen asleep, because the next thing she felt was someone shaking her shoulder.

"We're here, Shah."

Aru woke to see Aiden's face barely a foot away from hers. Their eyes met. For a moment, it looked like he wanted to say something to her, but a second later he snatched his hand away from her shoulder as if it had burned him.

On the bright side, your drool was minimal this time! said Mini through their mind link. *I didn't even need to get out the wet wipes!*

Aru sighed. *Clearly, I'm winning at life.*

The elevator doors opened into a long, dimly lit cavernous passageway. A rocky ceiling soared hundreds of feet above them and the smell of wet stone and roots filled the air. At the end of the passageway, a bright light lit up the caverns. The moment they set foot on the ground, a trail of glowing rainbow quartz bloomed down the corridor and a voice echoed around them.

"Welcome to Patala, once the resplendent home of the ancient naga aristocracy and now one of the most celebrated historical ruins in the Otherworld," said the voice. "Witness the majesty of its architecture from the safety of our pavilion! See the world-famous cavern rumored to hold the treasures of Lord Vasuki himself! The deadly stage of the beautiful vishakanyas! Visit our exhibit to see a collection of ancient artifacts excavated through various digs. On behalf of the Society for Historic Preservation, thank you for supporting this landmark!"

Aru turned to Rudy, who had his hands jammed into his pockets. He looked skittish. "This way," he said.

Rudy had said that Patala was *not pleasant*, but so far, it didn't seem any different from the parts of the Otherworld she'd already visited. There was a tautness in the air, a pulse that Aru recognized as magic coursing through the rock. The closer they got to the "rainbow" end of the tunnel, the more Aru imagined she could hear something in the stone, like the softest of whispers. Aru shivered, and the sounds disappeared. Maybe she'd imagined them.

To her right, Aru saw glowing red words: AUTHORIZED PERSONNEL AND ARCHIVISTS ONLY. But beneath the sign there was nothing but solid rock.

Abruptly, the passageway stopped at a tall railing that hugged the edge of a pavilion jutting into midair. Aru's jaw dropped. She'd assumed that the light at the end of the cavern was created by powerful lanterns or maybe tons of candles, but no. The glow came from the ruins themselves.

All around the Potatoes stretched a city made of jewel-studded caves layered one atop another in a complex so vast that it seemed to extend into the multicolored clouds far above. Droplets splashed the railing, and Aru looked up to see a waterfall of molten silver thundering into the ground below. An enchanted moonstone the size of a dining table hovered in the air and parted the falling silver curtains, allowing Aru and the others to glimpse the ancient city of Patala.

It had looked beautiful in Rudy's scaled-down model, but in person, it was breathtaking. There were towers of raw emerald. Elaborate onyx carvings of tigers and cobras crouched over jagged cave mouths. Gardens sported blooms of intricately carved crystals spilling over pure diamond terraces. The walkways were constructed of gleaming golden bricks. All the caves opened over an ancient agora. In the distance, Aru could see the crumbling structure of a stage with ripped silk curtains as well as empty reflecting pools and the remains of what might have once been a bustling market.

The longer she stared, the more she heard an undercurrent of whispering. It was audible even over the thunderous roar of the waterfall. Aru took another step toward the railing, the hairs on her arm prickling as she tried to separate the thousands of voices. Rudy waved his hand to get her attention and held a finger to his lips. Then he pointed ahead.

Now Aru's immediate surroundings drew into focus. Not ten feet from them was a big slab of onyx rock with the words INFORMATION DESK carved into its front. A teenage naga was slumped in the chair behind it, snoring. Aru knew he was a naga by the scale pattern on his cheeks. He wore glasses and an official naval-looking uniform with a pin that read:

PARTH M.
MEMBER OF ROYAL FAMILY AND INTERN
HOW CAN I HELP?

Beyond the information desk was an archway marked EXHIBIT HALL. Beside it, Aru saw familiar cutouts and information plaques like the kind her mother had erected around the Museum of Ancient Indian Art and Culture.

AUTHENTIC CROWN OF KALIYA
3227 BCE
COMPOSED OF MOONSTONE AND ONYX
GIFTED BY THE ROYAL TREASURY OF THE KERR FAMILY
6TH CENTURY

"Niiiice and easy," murmured Rudy. He swung his backpack, drawing out a glowing blue rock. "No one make a sound, okay? I've got to steal his key to get past the personnel door, and then we can get to G-Thousand's treasure cave—"

Rudy tripped. The blue rock *clanged* on the floor, and Rudy slammed into the information desk. For three whole seconds, everybody held their breaths.

But Rudy's cousin kept snoring.

Rudy looked at them, then looked at his cousin and pumped his fist in the air. "WOO-HOO! Oops."

The teenage boy snort-startled awake. "*Rudy?* What are you doing down here?"

"Think quick!" said Rudy, tossing the rock at his cousin.

The boy caught it in his hands, still frowning, and the rock began to hum. Immediately, the boy slumped back in his chair and continued snoring. Rudy rummaged around in the desk, pulling out a paper-thin square of emerald rock that looked a lot like a key card.

"This way," said Rudy, gesturing them to one of the boulders behind the desk.

Rudy waved his key card. The boulder parted like the doors of an elevator, revealing a huge spiraling staircase in the darkness, which seemed to connect the various levels of the kingdom. But that wasn't all that appeared. A warning in bright red letters sprawled across the stairs.

DO NOT ENTER
CAVERNS CURRENTLY UNDERGOING MAINTENANCE
HIGH RISK OF DISMEMBERMENT OR
AWAKENING ANCIENT CURSES

"Ancient curses?" said Mini, practically squeaking.

"Eh, that's nothing," said Rudy, waving his hand. "I don't know anyone who went down here and got cursed."

"Or you never heard from them again?" said Mini darkly.

"Oh!" said Rudy cheerfully. "I never thought about it that way! Okay, let's go!"

Mini looked faintly nauseous.

The staircase had hundreds of steps and almost as many landings veering off into the rings of caves surrounding the public square. Sheets of cloth hung over many of the cave entrances. There was no wind, yet the cloths stirred. A moaning sound crept through the rock, and goose bumps prickled up Aru's spine. She listened harder, but the sound was gone.

"They say G-Thousand's treasure cave is that way," said Rudy, pointing to an opening on their right.

It was one of the few caverns not covered by a sheet. Gold particles shimmered in the air around it, and Aru saw jewels gleaming within.

"It's not," said Aiden.

He was holding up the Sun Jewel, and although Patala was bright, the jewel seemed like a caught star. Aiden must have taken it out of his backpack, which was, for some reason, slung against the front of his body. He had one arm around it, almost cradling it against him.

"What do you mean it's not?" asked Rudy. "Everyone knows where it is!"

The Sun Jewel pulsed as Aiden swung it in front of him. He lowered and lifted it, moving it from side to side before holding it right above his head. The necklace shone brightly, as if affirming the movement.

"Then they've been lying," said Aiden, pointing at the staircase right above them.

There, Aru saw the mouth of a cave that was far different

from the dazzling cavern far below them. This one was draped in a black cloth that did not ripple like the sheets covering the other caves.

As if it did not wish to be found.

Aiden led them up the staircase. With each step, those odd sounds kept finding Aru. She imagined she could hear bits and pieces of someone speaking.

Such soft hands she had . . .

He never removed me when he cooked and, oh, how I ate . . .

I was promised to her true love . . .

Aru paused on the staircase, shaking her head. "Am I going insane?"

"I think we're past that," said Brynne.

Aru was not amused. "I'm serious! Do you guys hear that?"

Brynne, who was a couple of steps ahead of her, blinked. "Hear what?"

"The stones," said Rudy, standing below her with Mini beside him. "You hear them, too?"

Aru nodded.

Rudy looked out over the ruins of the city. "The stones talk here," he said. "They tell you about who they met . . . who they saw . . . who loved who. I guess you could call them ghosts, in a way."

Welp. Definitely creepy. But on the plus side, thought Aru, if that was all that waited for them in Vasuki's cave, then at least they wouldn't need their weapons.

Aiden stepped onto the landing. In his hand, the Sun Jewel flashed with light before dimming. It seemed like a sign: *You have reached your destination.* Aiden returned the jewel to his backpack as they approached the cave. Aru calmed herself. She was fully prepared to yank open the sheet and run inside.

However, she was *not* prepared for a slender hand parting the cloth from the other side.

"We've been expecting you," said a silken voice.

The sheet opened to reveal a beautiful woman. Jeweled lights in the cave ceiling dappled her dark skin, so that it looked as if she'd been draped in rainbows. She smiled at them. "You must be here for the maintenance work. I am Aleesa. Come in, come in."

What Weak Men Fear Most

On the other side of the door, Aru stepped into a jewelry display half the length of a football field. She blinked, her eyes adjusting to the peculiar glow of the treasure room. A domed ceiling stretched a hundred feet above her, the glossy rock striped with bands of ruby and gold. Huge pieces of quartz and topaz, jasper and amethyst were embedded in the stone walls. Spanning the space were two glass-encased rows of exquisite jewels sitting on silk pillows. It was like a massive jewelry store—in every way except for one.

It was loud.

On their way to the cave, Aru had only been able to hear bits and pieces of frail voices. But here it was like someone was whispering in her ear, and though the voices were soft, the words were insistent.

I watched his face on the battlefield when he realized he would die. I felt his last heartbeat, and if I could have wept tears, I would have. . . .

I lived on her favorite garment, swept the floors of her great palace. No one speaks her name now, but I knew she was loved. . . .

Without me, he never would have remembered her. And yet they lost me. Why did they misplace me?

One phrase repeated every few seconds, echoing from the different gems strewn about the cave: *Did you hear me?*

"Yes, my darlings," said Aleesa, speaking to the cave. "Yes, I hear, I listen."

The whispering quieted.

"You're rather early," she said to Rudy.

He stared at her, his jaw a little slack until Mini helpfully elbowed him in the ribs.

"Um, early maintenance . . . rounds?" he said.

"But so many of you?" asked Aleesa. "Normally it's just one."

"Uh . . ." said Rudy, turning to stare at them.

"We're interns," said Aru quickly.

"And I'm acting as an archival photographer," added Aiden, lifting his camera to his face.

He considered *her* sneaky, but Aru knew what Aiden was doing as he snapped photos. Shadowfax had a high-magnification lens, which meant that with every picture he took, he was looking for a sign of the Sun Jewel somewhere amongst the treasures.

"Had we known there would be more than one inspector this time, we might have prepared different safety precautions for you," said Aleesa, tilting her head to one side. She gestured at the propped-open cave door. "Rest assured that this will provide sufficient ventilation and you need not worry."

Aru nodded, but she didn't understand what Aleesa meant. She stared around the cave, wondering if she'd missed something.

Worry about what? said Mini through their mind link. *Suffocating from a lack of oxygen? Because hypoxia is really serious.*

Maybe they just meant it can get too crowded in here, said Aru.

She couldn't imagine what else Aleesa could be talking about. Rudy had said that Lord Vasuki's jewels were protected by the fiercest of creatures, but all Aru saw was a woman with a kind face. Aleesa moved to one of the jewelry cases, stroking the glass and softly crooning to it. Inside, Aru spotted a golden arm cuff— it was polished and yet bore many scratches. Some of its jewels had been gouged out, and the remaining stones were cracked.

"I know, battles are a terrible thing to remember," said Aleesa to the arm cuff, before sighing and turning back to them. "Well, shall we begin? I imagine you'll want to check the numbers and test the strength of the foundations, as usual. Every year, our location becomes a little more tenuous. . . . It is sad to see a once-glorious city such as this sinking into ignominy."

"Absolutely," said Rudy with a straight face. "Inn-om-i-nee is bad."

"Do you even know what that is?" muttered Aiden.

"Clearly it is some kind of weird mud," shot back Rudy.

Aleesa continued walking down the rows of jewelry cases, her hands trailing the glass tops, singing softly as if she were in a nursery.

I don't see the Sun Jewel anywhere! said Brynne through the mind link.

Does anyone else feel kinda . . . woozy? asked Mini. *Did we even check the air-pollutant levels of Patala? What if there are weird microbes in the air? What if they attack our lungs? What if we—*

"Since we're, uh, interning and all that," said Aru to Aleesa, interrupting Mini's usual doomsday train of thought, "maybe you could give us some background on what you do? And, uh, the pieces that require the . . . most guarding?"

Aleesa stopped short, spinning around with an affronted look. "*All* the pieces require the same amount of love and care! We are the custodians of the tales the world has forgotten, collected by Lord Vasuki himself! We are the record keepers, guarding the place where the sun's rays do not reach."

"Speaking of sun…" tried Aru.

But Aleesa was not finished. "Why, see here…Look how precious they are." She gestured to the glass case a few feet away. Aleesa waved her hand, and the glass vanished so she could reach in and gently draw out a string of black pearls.

"*Shhh*, my beauties," said Aleesa. "These once adorned Princess Bhanumati, wife of Duryodhana, the great enemy of the Pandavas. People know him for his misdeeds, but he did not judge when others would. He had faith."

Aleesa held up the pearls, and their voices—like the chiming of delicate bells—filled the air as they spoke in unison:

We were there when the princess and Duryodhana's dearest friend, Lord Karna, were playing a game of dice. When her husband entered, Bhanumati stood, and Karna, who didn't see Duryodhana and thought the princess was abandoning a game she was losing, reached teasingly for her silk shawl. It was an impulsive, dangerous act for a man who was not wed to her. Our string was broken, and we spilled to the ground like rain hitting the earth. As we tumbled, we felt her shame and horror—for women have been harmed for less. . . . Yet Duryodhana merely laughed. He said, "Shall I pick up the pearls? Would you like me to re-string them, too?" We remember. We remember that she was loved. We remember her before she poured ash in her hair and mourned the deaths of all whom she cared for. We remember the time before the world forgot her name. . . .

Goose bumps prickled down Aru's arm. When she looked at her skin, she saw a patch of red above her wrist. She scratched at it, but the itching only grew worse.

"You see?" said Aleesa, gently placing the pearls back onto their silk pillow. "Or this one…"

Through her Pandava mind link, Aru heard Brynne triumphantly yell *FOUND IT!*

Aru looked out of the corner of her eye. Aleesa's back was to Brynne and Aiden, who were pointing at a bright speck that wasn't encased in glass but tucked into a fold of rocky ceiling a hundred feet away.

"This is one of my favorite pieces," said Aleesa, drawing out a small ring. The stone looked like a drop of rain.

Aru nodded, trying to hide her distraction. In the background, Brynne drew a dagger from her sleeve.

If I transform and jump off the glass case, I think I can pry it out with my dagger, said Brynne. *Just keep her distracted!*

Aru turned her attention back to the guardian. Beside Aru, Mini slumped to one side.

"I…I'm not feeling so great," said Mini.

Good distraction! said Brynne through the mind link.

I mean it, replied Mini.

"What should I do?" asked Rudy, grabbing Mini's hand and then abruptly letting go of it.

Mini didn't even notice. Her face looked bloodless.

"Have you no mask?" asked Aleesa, frowning. "I assumed you would've put one on by now considering how far we are from the door."

Mini started rubbing her temples. *I don't think I can talk, Aru. You have to distract her.*

"The ring!" said Aru loudly even as alarm bells went off in her head as she watched Mini sway on the spot. "What were you saying about it?"

The sooner Brynne and Aiden could retrieve the piece of the Sun Jewel, the sooner they could get out of this creepy place and help Mini.

Aleesa held the ring close to her body. "It once belonged to Queen Gandhari.... Go ahead and speak, my darling. You see, I am not the only one listening."

A voice clear and low—and achingly mournful—rose from the clear stone.

She held me tight, for she could foresee the destruction of all one hundred of her sons at the hands of the Pandavas and their allies. We turned the color of her tears that no one noticed. We remember her strength that others forgot....

Behind Aleesa, blue light flashed as Brynne transformed into a hawk, her dagger pinched firmly in her beak. Aleesa didn't notice. Her eyes were fixed on the ring.

"Well!" said Aru loudly. "This was very illuminating and not at all disturbing!"

She took a step back, one hand steadying Mini. Rudy was on her other side, looking more concerned about Mini by the second.

"That was all?" asked Aleesa, frowning. "What about the foundations? Are our jewels safe for the next year?"

Here we go! shouted Brynne.

"Yup!" said Rudy. "Supersafe!"

"So glad that whole *deadly creature protecting the stash* thing turned out to be fake," said Aru, laughing.

A terrible crashing sound tore through the cavern. Dozens of voices cried out jaggedly:

Mothers! Help us!

Breaking!

Who will hear—

Aleesa spun around and shrieked. The cave shook, and several women rushed out from niches in the walls. The light behind them was a pure, vivid white, and in its glow, Aru saw something she hadn't noticed before about Aleesa and the other guardians of Vasuki's treasures. Their skin was tinged *green*, like emeralds, or...

Like poison.

"Brynne!" yelled Aiden, brandishing a scimitar.

Near the roof of the cave, Brynne was on a ledge, her blue wings beating uselessly against the rock. She cawed, and Aru knew she was trying to transform, but she was stuck as a hawk. The shard of the Sun Jewel still glowed brightly in the wall behind her. Brynne stopped flapping. Her blue glow faded as her bird form went limp. She plummeted to a ledge not far off the ground, wings feebly stirring.

BRYNNE! Aru screamed through the mind link. She couldn't catch her breath. Panic choked her, and the air around them turned thick with something foul and claggy.

"Let us go!" Aru tried to yell, but her voice came out as a whisper.

"We do not answer to the demands of thieves," said one of the women advancing toward them.

The exit was a hundred feet away, but the moment Aru looked at it, the door slammed shut. The two rows of jewelry stands, once cast in a soft glow, now held the menacing gleam of two sharp blades.

"Mini?" asked Rudy, terrified.

Aru flung out her arms, but she couldn't catch Mini as she crumpled to the floor.

Poison, said Mini weakly through the mind link. *There's poison in the air....*

As the women stalked toward them, their features seemed to

change in the eerie lighting of the cave. Their hair waved around them. They grew taller, the silken hems of their gowns rising and twisting into what looked like vast tentacles. They were no less beautiful, but their beauty now belonged to something dangerous. Something deadly.

"You dared to *steal* from Lord Vasuki?" demanded one of the women.

"You dared to *injure* our beloved charges?" sneered a second.

"It will be the last thing you ever do..." said Aleesa.

From the tips of her long fingers a silver vapor emerged. It rose up like a cloud, drifting toward Aru, Rudy, and Mini. Aru tried to wave it away, but the moment she touched it, pain lanced through her thoughts. It was as if the vapor were made of razor blades. Her skin started to blister. The women moved closer.

When Aleesa smiled, Aru saw the sharp points of her teeth. Ice shot down Aru's veins as she finally realized who, exactly, the guardians were. Rudy's story hadn't been fake at all. The guardians of Vasuki's treasures were none other than the vishakanyas of legend....

The deadly poison maidens.

ELEVEN

The Tale of the Vishakanyas

Aru tried to pull air into her lungs.

The corners of her vision turned fuzzy. She tried to look past the vishakanyas, but it was as if the whole cave were choking on black smoke. Aru squinted at the floor where Brynne had been lying unconscious. But she couldn't see any sign of her. Or Aiden. Her heart sank. The vishakanyas had surrounded her, Rudy, and Mini in a careful circle of poison. Already, Aru could barely keep her thoughts straight. If she tried to make a run for it, she'd die.

Brynne! Aru called through the Pandava mind link.

There was nothing but static in response.

Aru swayed. She fumbled for something, *anything* she could use to fight back, but her grip slid on the jewelry cases. Beside her, Rudy shouted at the vishakanyas. He was the only one who didn't seem affected by the poison. Instead, the scales along his cheekbones were glowing. Dimly, Aru realized he must have transformed into his half-snake form in the last few seconds, because now he towered above Aru and Mini. The coils of his naga tail wound protectively around Mini, who was still and unresponsive.

"I'm a prince!" said Rudy desperately. "Like, *a real prince!* You can't do this! I'll…I'll tell my dad?" Rudy shrank down on his coils. "Are you going to kill us?"

"You, princeling, are exempt from our justice, but your friends have violated sacred lands," said Aleesa. "And now they shall pay the price."

"Get away from them!"

Aiden cut through the black fog of poison, his scimitars blazing. His face was half hidden by his hoodie, which he had pulled up to cover his nose and mouth. Then he slammed down a blade.

One of the poison maidens shrieked, but Aiden's weapon hadn't touched her. Instead, he'd crashed it into the jewelry case, shattering the glass. From inside, a necklace of pearls began to speak in a quivering, frightened voice.

O Mothers, who will listen to me now?

Aiden whirled back to face the poison maidens. For a moment, his eyes went to Aru's. Something fierce and determined flashed in the depths of his gaze before he jerked his sword at the vishakanyas. "Hurt them and I'll—"

But he never got to finish the sentence.

The roof of the cave trembled. Aiden frowned, glancing up.

"Look out!" yelled Aru hoarsely.

Aleesa blurred forward. In one movement, she swatted the scimitar out of his hand. Next, she grabbed Aiden by the throat and dragged him up and across the cave walls. He kicked out wildly, but his feet found no purchase.

"You shall never touch our charges *again*," hissed Aleesa.

Time seemed to slow around Aru. Rudy thrashed his tail as if trying to help his cousin, only for three vishakanyas to step through the black cloud around them.

One of them pointed a red-taloned finger at Mini. "Another move, and I'll aim all my venom at her heart."

Rudy's tail went slack. "Please, you can't...."

"Oh, but we *can*, little princeling," said another poison maiden.

"And, oh, we *will*," said a third, smiling.

A patch in the poison cloud cleared enough for Aru to catch sight of Brynne. She was still in the form of a blue hawk, sprawled on the high ledge right in front of the gleaming Sun Jewel. They'd been so close, thought Aru with a pang. But now the poison was starting to twist her thoughts. For a moment, she imagined the roof of the cave undulating like the glossy scales of a snake.

There was nothing she could do.

If she'd still had Vajra, Aru could have shocked the poison maidens. Brynne could have used Gogo to clear the air of all its fumes. With Dee Dee, Mini could have kept them invisible as they stole the Sun Jewel and escaped.

What did Aru have now?

Her tongue felt heavy. When she opened her mouth to speak, it was like dragging each word through a wall of lead.

"We're sorry," said Aru.

"It is too late for an apology," said Aleesa. She had not released her hold on Aiden. Aru felt a sharp jolt of panic as she watched his kicking slow and weaken.

"We *need* the Sun Jewel," said Aru. "There's a war coming, like the great one from before—"

"A war?" whispered the vishakanyas closest to Aru.

The black cloud of poison drew back, allowing Aru to suck in some clean air. Aleesa growled, dropping Aiden. He fell to the ground, choking.

"And what do *wars* matter to us?" asked Aleesa. "We were made to be weapons! A weapon does not care whose hand holds it! A weapon merely seeks to aim true! We do not care about the battles of mortals and gods."

The cloud of poison rose up once more. Aru felt her thoughts flicker dimly at the back of her skull, and yet one word stuck out in the painful haze: *Care.*

"But you *do* care," said Aru. "You care about those jewels.... You treat them like they're your kids."

Aleesa cocked her head.

"You care about them because . . . because you listen to them, and they . . . they help you remember what everyone else forgot," said Aru. "This war isn't about gods and humans."

"Then what is it about?" asked another vishakanya.

Aru swallowed hard. "It's about immortality...."

But as she said the words, she realized the answer was more nuanced than that. The Sleeper wanted to rewrite his fate, to escape "the tyranny of destiny." The people he had lured to his side wanted the same thing, like Lady M, who'd wanted her true story to be told, and Takshaka, who'd sought revenge for the senseless murder of his family at the hands of the original Pandavas.

"It's about being able to live the life you choose . . . and who gets to be remembered, and how," continued Aru. She coughed and inhaled with a gasp. "If we can't reunite the pieces of the Sun Jewel, the Sleeper will destroy this world and everything in it will be lost. Forever."

This seemed to have an effect on Aleesa. She stilled, giving a last burst of hope to Aru.

"You guard them, you...you listen to them," Aru said, gesturing to all the precious gems. "But what about *you*?"

"What do you mean, thief?" asked Aleesa.

"What about *your* story?" asked Aru. "If you...If you let us go—if you let us borrow the Sun Jewel—then we'll...we'll be like *your* guardians. Just like what you do for the jewels. And if we win the battle, I'll...I'll make sure everyone listens."

The cloud of poison drew back, and Aru drew in a huge gulp of air. Above her, the top of the cave rippled. The six other vishakanya women stumbled backward, whispering among themselves.

"Impossible!"

"Do we trust them?"

"Never spoken—"

"Silence!" said Aleesa, holding up her hand. "What a clever proposal, thief. And yet what you do not realize is that it is impossible for you to trick us. Our poisons always draw out the truth."

"It *is* the truth," said Rudy.

He was bobbing slowly, the long coil of his tail carefully propping up an unconscious Mini. Not ten feet away, Aiden was bound by ropes of enchanted smoke, his backpack clutched in his arms. He caught Aru's eye and mouthed, *You got this, Shah*.

Aru felt a small burst of warmth in her bones. She turned to face the poison maidens. "I'm not lying. I'll hear your story. Honest."

"Ask what you wish, then," said Aleesa with a casual flick of her wrist. "You cannot hide what you truly think of us, thief. We shall know by the end if you intend to keep your promise."

Aru wasn't sure where to start. "I need to take notes or—"

"I've got it," said Rudy, swinging around his backpack. "Special recording quartz coming right up."

A moment later, he set the chunk of rock on the ground before them. The vishakanyas faced Rudy, Aru, and Mini, forming a V-like shape to keep them in one place. Aru could feel the intensity of their stares like a sunburn.

"So . . . uh, how did you get into the business of . . . being poisonous?" tried Aru.

"You assume we had a choice," said one of the maidens with a sharp laugh.

"You didn't?" asked Aru, frowning.

"Many of us were simply poor and sold by our own families for food," said the third poison maiden. "Or we were destined to become young, childless widows, and no one believed our families would want to keep us, so they gave us to the harems."

"We were fed delicacies laced with poison," said another. "We were taught to sing and dance, to converse like the best courtesans. We were made beautiful."

The poison maidens stamped their feet against the cave floor, and Aru saw images flicker across the rock as if it were a screen. In one flashback, young girls wept in dark chambers. In another, a girl whose skin was tinged green reached eagerly to play with a kitten that had wandered into the courtyard. One moment the kitten purred and rubbed against the girl's wrist. The next moment, the kitten stopped moving.

The images vanished.

"We were made to be weapons," said Aleesa softly. "We were made to be loathed, not loved. We were made to carry out murder, not carry any children."

Aru thought back to how the poison maidens had tended to

the jewels, how they had touched them with a motherly gentleness. They were, Aru realized, the only things the poison maidens could touch without killing.

"When the wars ended, we were nothing more than deadly entertainment, like cobras released from a basket," said another maiden. "There are those who can live that kind of life, but we could no longer bear it. Lord Vasuki gave us sanctuary in his treasury halls." She gestured to the cave. "He gave us something to love and to tend. A place where we would never have to do harm again."

Aru looked around the cavern, which held jewels but nothing else. "What about, um, food?"

"We eat nothing," said Aleesa. "Our captors fed us a poison that gave us long life but not immortality. Without constant feeding, it leaves our systems little by little." She bowed her head. "One day we will know the death we inflicted on others. Some deaths we regretted. Others... we relished."

The poison maidens didn't need to cast more images on the floor for Aru to picture what they had done. She could imagine how enemy kings and princes might have seen one of them as merely another beautiful girl. Perhaps some of their victims had tried to court them, writing poems or singing songs.

Perhaps some had tried to take what they wanted.

That thought turned Aru's stomach even more than the poisonous fumes hanging in the air.

"So, thief, do you intend to remember our tale, as you promised?" demanded Aleesa, her chin at a defiant angle. "We know you think of us as monsters now."

Aru did not hesitate. "I don't think you're monsters."

Aleesa's eyes widened. "What?"

Aru thought of all the individuals she had met over the last few years. Her father, who had wanted to be her dad and ended up her nemesis. Lady M and her lost beauty, the identical wives of the sun god, and even the Palace of Illusions, living in a place between life and death. All of them would have been called monstrous at one point or another.

"Even a monster isn't the monster of their own story," said Aru. "If you let us go, we'll remember yours."

The vishakanyas looked at one another. One by one, they each took a step back.

"You mean it," said Aleesa, shocked.

"No one has asked to hear our tale before," said another, turning her head.

"What say you, Lord Vasuki?" asked Aleesa, looking up.

Uh, thought Aru, *pretty sure that's a slab of rock.*

But then a loud screech tore through the cave. The poison maidens lifted their arms and the last vestiges of the noxious fumes reversed, streaming through the air and disappearing into their skin. The ledge holding Brynne suddenly broke off.

"Brynne!" screamed Aru.

The ropes surrounding Aiden vanished. He lunged forward to catch Brynne before she hit the ground. Her wings stirred.

What's happening? asked Brynne through the Pandava mind link.

You're okay, Bee! You're okay, said Aru, grinning.

Gently, Aiden laid Brynne on the floor. In a flash of blue light, Brynne transformed back into her normal self. She was crouching, her body bent and one hand clenched tight. Light streamed through the gaps between her fingers as she opened them slowly.

The second piece of the Syamantaka Gem sat in her hand.

TWELVE

Whaddaya Know! Another Family Reunion!

Jagged beams of light hit the ground as the ceiling opened. In the distance, Aru could hear a rumble, like an avalanche building momentum. She looked up...and *up*...as the ceiling transformed. It had never been a ceiling at all, but the great hood of Lord Vasuki.

"I have heard quite enough," said a low, ancient voice.

As he reared up, the cave city of Patala glittered behind him. Vasuki's huge cobra hood was the length of at least six semi-trucks put together. He was the color of twilight and so old that thick stalks of quartz and precious jewels had formed between his scales—scales Aru had mistaken for cave rocks.

Vasuki hissed and a warm wind gusted through the rows of treasure. The vishakanyas bowed low, and Aru quickly followed suit. Rudy crumpled down on his coils. Aiden bent down and Brynne, still disoriented, wobbled something like a curtsey. Only Mini didn't move. She was breathing, but the poison had knocked her out cold.

"So, it has begun again, has it?" asked Vasuki. *"The nectar of immortality is fought over once more.... All things repeat...but not as they seem...."*

Aru couldn't see his mouth. She could barely stand looking at his eyes, which seemed huge as planets and were a fiery red.

"My adopted daughters do not wake me for trifles, and I see now that you have taken a piece of my treasure."

"I...W-we..." stuttered Aru, gazing up at the serpent lord.

The remaining cavern walls trembled, and Aru realized the great snake was laughing.

"You think I shall give you my piece of the jewel because you imagine yourselves to be, what...heroes?"

And heroines, grumbled Aru to herself.

"There is nothing that surprises me," said Vasuki. *"Drop the jewel, take your lives, and go. That is my mercy."*

"I might surprise you? I'm pretty sure I'm not like your other descendants."

It took Aru a moment to realize that Rudy had spoken. The naga prince was shaking a little as he rose on his coils and stared up at his ancestor.

The great snake sniffed the air, and his eyes narrowed. *"You are one of mine?"*

"Yes," said Rudy.

"Then what do you mean you are different? You are, I imagine, like all of mine...a gatherer of jewels, a lover of all that glitters and glows. Majestic, yes, but not different from me."

"Actually, I don't really...like...jewels," said Rudy carefully. The gems in their cases hissed. "I mean, they're great and all, but I can't see their colors the way other people do. I appreciate them for something else." Rudy reached into his bag, pulling out the chunks of rock. "I...I make music with them."

"Music?" asked Vasuki, tilting his head a little.

As he did so, bits of rock and debris clattered around them.

"Yeah," said Rudy. He shoved some of his rocks forward. "Like this."

Rudy's music flowed through the cave, and it felt like that first time he'd saved them, when he'd shown up with speakers and annoyed the naga king Takshaka so much the Pandavas were able to escape the treasury. Only this time the music was of Rudy's own making, and it was unlike anything that had ever played on a radio. It sounded like thunderstorms prowling across a mountainside and it felt like running your finger along the edge of a knife—dangerous and sharp.

Vasuki's great eyes closed. His head swung a little. Aru crouched, ready for the snake king to lunge...but he didn't.

Instead, he...bopped to the music?

Did not expect that one, said Brynne.

"A musician in the family," said Vasuki warmly, opening his eyes. The music stopped. *"That is...surprising."*

"Surprising enough that you'll give us your piece of the Sun Jewel?" tried Rudy.

Aru sighed, thinking he had pushed things too far.

Vasuki paused, and then, ever so slowly, bowed his great head in a nod.

"I am amused by the possibility that you will do something different with it. Let us see whether you succeed in surprising me again...."

"Thank you," said Brynne, clutching the jewel to her chest.

Vasuki gave a great rumbling laugh. He moved closer, his forked tongue darting toward Rudy.

"Hmm," said the great snake thoughtfully. His eyes turned a hypnotic shade of green. *"I like you, child."*

"Yay?"

"So I shall give you this final warning. You have awoken me. And when I move, so too does the world...."

Lord Vasuki lowered himself farther to inspect his treasure. Around him, Patala began to crumble. Chunks of the cave wall broke off and fell, crashing into one another. All the poison maidens except Aleesa retreated into the wall, and the Potatoes ducked for cover.

Aleesa flung out her hand, and the door at the end of the hall swung open. "Go!" she told them. She tossed a small lantern in their direction. Aiden caught it one-handed. "And take this! It shall contain the pieces of the Sun Jewel and guide you."

"C'mon!" yelled Rudy. "I've got Mini!" He gathered her up while he was still in his naga form. His hood flared above her like a shield.

Aiden and Brynne ran ahead. Aru knew she had to leave quickly, too. She could feel the ground trembling and hear more rocks falling. But she couldn't look away from Aleesa. For all Aru knew, no one would ever see the poison maidens again.

Aleesa smiled. She tugged one of her bangles off her wrist and threw it to Aru. When Aru caught it, she winced. It felt like she'd touched a too-hot pan.

"Go and remember us, daughter of the gods."

"I will," said Aru. "I promise." She turned and ran, shoving the bangle deep in her pocket.

"Aru!" yelled Brynne from the doorway. "The whole city is falling apart! We've got to go *now!*"

Aru sprinted. She had just stepped across the threshold when the rocky floor beneath her gave way. A hundred feet below, a great cloud of dust and rock spewed from what had once been the city's agora.

The jewels embedded in the caves screamed *EMERGENCY! EVACUATE! EMERGENCY! EVACUATE!*

Aru teetered backward, her arms pinwheeling as she scrambled for secure footing. Someone caught hold of her wrist.

"I've got you, Shah," said Aiden fiercely.

It was the last thing she heard before something thudded against her head and the whole world went dark.

THIRTEEN

Finally! Paradise! And by That, I Mean Home Depot.

When Aru opened her eyes, she found herself in the
only place in the world that made her feel like she
could breathe a bit easier, a place where broken
things could be fixed, where all the answers lay
in plain sight, where the aisles held the rare perfume of possibility tinged ever so slightly with the sweetness of mulch and wood
chips. . . .

"Aru, you really need to get over your Home Depot obses-
sion," said Nikita, staring down with her hands firmly planted
on her hips. "Can't you dream about someplace else?"

"Nope," said Aru.

Of course, in the dream, Home Depot didn't really look
the same. First, Aru was sitting in an armchair that seemed to
be made of cotton candy for no apparent reason. For another,
the aisle banner over her head said FLOORING, but instead of the
shelves being filled with things like wood laminate or vinyl plank,
she was staring at a rotating row of moon jellyfish and miniature
thunderclouds. At the end of the aisle, which somehow seemed

as if it were hundreds of feet away and yet close enough to touch, stood a huge podium where an endless supply of doors rotated. Staring at it made Aru's heart race faster.

"We took a wrong turn and ended up in your subconscious," said Nikita, pointing at the doors. "You've got *a lot* of stuff rattling around in there."

"Everyone does!" said Sheela, materializing beside her twin and beaming at Aru. "Although yours is a little ... different."

Aru peeked at the podium of rotating doors. Each, unfortunately, was labeled.

A pink one read WHO AM I IF NOT A DEMIGOD?

A black one read "LUKE, I AM YOUR FATHER" AND OTHER PARENT-RELATED HORRORS.

A white one read DO I QUOTE MOVIES BECAUSE I DON'T TRUST MY OWN THOUGHTS?

A door in a garish shade of red was labeled THE THING THAT HAPPENED WITH AIDEN/FEELINGS ARE INCONVENIENT.

"What's *that* one?" asked Nikita, raising an eyebrow.

"OKAY, THAT'S IT! OUT!" said Aru, clapping once. The dream Home Depot vanished and was replaced with a fuzzy rendering of the lobby of the Museum of Ancient Indian Art and Culture. "Why can't you be like normal little sisters and raid my closet or something? Why do you have to poke around in my brain?"

"I like your brain," said Sheela. "It's funny."

"And I would rather wear an actual sack of potatoes than the clothes in your closet," said Nikita flatly.

Aru glared at her.

"I'll get the others!" said Sheela brightly, before vanishing once more.

Nikita tapped her foot on the dream floor. Today she was wearing a long red velvet sorcerer-esque robe with gold trim on the cuffs and a matching sleeping turban. She flicked her wrist and thorny green vines twisted up her arm, sprouting bloodred flowers.

"I got worried," said Nikita, not looking at Aru. "I hate that. It messes with my designs."

"I love you, too," said Aru.

Nikita grunted, but a slight smile touched her lips. "Things aren't looking so good in the Otherworld, Aru. People are nervous."

"I know."

The thorny vines climbed down Nikita's hand and tumbled onto the dream floor. Their vivid green had been replaced with a ghostly pallor. Aru knew her sister well enough to understand that sometimes her creations spoke what she couldn't bear to say out loud.

"Everything will be okay," said Aru, but her tone didn't sound very convincing.

"You can't promise that," said Nikita. "And what about Sheela's dreams?" Nikita stared into her eyes. "Aru, what about the battle? What happens if we *lose?*"

Aru was saved from answering by a loud *pop!* In a flash, Brynne, Mini, and Sheela appeared.

"Aru!" said Mini, hugging her.

"Glad to see you're okay," said Aru.

"Apparently I'm still unconscious," said Mini, wrinkling her nose. "Acute inhalation injury is serious. Any more exposure to the poison and we could have, well, you know."

"Rudy brought us back to his place, and we're recovering

now," said Brynne. "It was really close.... We almost didn't make it out in time."

Panic spiked in Aru's chest, and she remembered Aiden's hand reaching for hers. "Is everyone okay? What about the Sun Jewel?"

"It's inside that lantern the poison maiden gave us," said Brynne grimly. "But we still have to get the last piece."

"How much time do you have left?" asked Nikita.

"Five days now according to Aiden's watch," said Brynne.

To Aru, that sounded like a lot, but she knew it wasn't. Time in the Otherworld was slippery at best. But at least they had the second piece of the Sun Jewel. That had to count for something....

"I hate this, Shah," said Brynne, staring at her hands as if they were strange things she'd never seen before. "I...I can't do anything. Without Gogo, I'm just...weak. And useless."

"Brynne, that's not true," said Mini, putting her arm around her. "You were great back there!"

"How do you know? You were unconscious the whole time!" said Brynne, shaking off her touch.

Mini looked stung.

"Brynne, we're all struggling," said Aru.

"*I'm* not," muttered Nikita.

"Okay, well, *most* of us are," said Aru, shooting a frown at the twin.

"What if this whole thing *fails* on us?" asked Brynne. "Sheela told us about her vision, the one where she literally saw *nothing*? You kept that from us, Shah. That's messed up."

"I'm sure Aru had a reason," said Mini carefully. "You *did* have a reason...didn't you, Aru?"

"I didn't like that vision," said Sheela.

Nikita crossed her arms. "Me neither."

Aru felt the weight of her sisters' expectant gazes like a great wave threatening to break over her. She hadn't told them because she wasn't sure what it meant and she didn't want to scare them. The truth was, she was *still* unsure. And yet, something about their encounter with Vasuki needled at her thoughts....

I am amused by the possibility that you will do something different with it. Let us see whether you succeed in surprising me....

Something different. Something other than the choice of destroy or be destroyed?

Aru was reminded of the vishakanyas—how there was so much more to them than what was on the surface. War was just as complicated. People fought for many different reasons. Up until now, Aru hadn't considered the fact that there might be a third option. Maybe she had to get to the battlefield before she could see the whole situation properly.

"Well, Shah?" asked Brynne. "Why didn't you tell us the truth?"

Aru took a deep breath. "Because I didn't understand what it meant...until now."

Nikita peered at her sharply.

"Look, the fact that no one can see what's coming next isn't necessarily bad," said Aru. "It means the future can still be changed. *We* can still change it."

Sheela tilted her head as if she were daydreaming about that idea.

"We may not understand it yet, but we're also not done," said Aru. "We have to focus on what we can do right now, which is getting the third part of the Sun Jewel. Lord Agni said himself that if we can prove we can get to the labyrinth on our own, there's a good chance our weapons will come back."

"A *chance*..." said Brynne darkly.

"It's better than nothing," said Aru.

Brynne looked at her for a long moment and then sighed. "Fine. I guess you're right."

"What was that?" asked Aru, cupping her ear. "I couldn't hear you over the sound of your ego shattering...."

Brynne shoved her. Aru grinned.

Mini turned to the twins. "So, the third part of the jewel is with Jambavan," she said. "What'd you guys find out? Who is he? Where does he live?"

Nikita snapped her fingers. The air shimmered as an image took shape of a huge bear with black fur and a spot of white on his chest. A constellation encircled the head of Jambavan, the bear king.

Aru remembered him as part of the Council of Guardians. He'd been there when she and Mini were put on trial for supposedly stealing Kamadeva's bow and arrow. Aru wasn't sure she'd ever heard the bear king speak. And she'd never seen him anywhere else in the Otherworld.

"He's *really* reclusive," said Nikita. "That crown is excellent, though. I wonder where he got it from...."

Brynne studied the image of King Jambavan. "Gunky and Funky used to tell me stories about him. They called him the Hero-Maker. Supposedly, defeating him in combat is the mark of a great warrior, or something like that."

"You love combat!" said Sheela before pausing thoughtfully. "And cake. That one dream with the tiramisu locked in mortal combat with a stack of macaroons was..."

"Both disturbing and delicious?" suggested Aru.

"Yeah!" said Sheela.

But Brynne didn't smile.

"Maybe we don't have to fight him at all," said Mini soothingly. "If he's part of the Council, can't Hanuman and Urvashi get the Sun Jewel piece from him?"

Nikita shook her head. "Hanuman and Urvashi have been out of touch throughout their whole mission."

"Do we at least know where his house is?" asked Aru.

"Everyone knows where he lives," said Nikita. She dragged her hand through the air, and the image displayed a cold, craggy chunk of land surrounded by snowcapped trees. Aru could almost feel the freezing wind of that place reaching out to touch her.

"Whoa," said Mini. "Where *is* that?"

"Literally the end of the world," said Nikita.

"King Jambavan does *not* want to be disturbed," said Sheela.

"Do we know if he's, um, dangerous or anything?" asked Mini, nervous.

"This place looks just like Ahch-To!" said Aru excitedly.

"Bless you?" said Sheela.

"Oh, not again," said Brynne.

"Ahch-To, from *The Last Jedi*!" repeated Aru. "You know, the place where Luke Skywalker is hiding out when Rey goes to find him? The place with the porgs! What if King Jambavan is just like Luke? Kinda gruff and reclusive, plagued with secret guilt ... just waiting for heroes like us to come along and save the world."

Brynne rolled her eyes. "You watch too many movies, Shah."

Aru ignored her and reached up to touch her hair, which she normally kept in a loose braid. "Maybe I could—"

"I'm telling you this now, out of love. You cannot pull off

Rey's hairstyle," said Nikita. "One, you don't have the forehead for it. And two, you *will* look like a hedgehog that got into a fight with a lawnmower."

Aru scowled and tossed her braid over her shoulder.

"Rudy said he can get you guys to the outskirts of Jambavan's home," said Nikita.

"How?" asked Mini.

"Something about an elevator bank?" said Nikita.

Aru shuddered. She was in no rush to go back to that eerie place in Rudy's kingdom.

"We asked him when we stopped by in his dream," said Sheela.

"I needed his address so I could send over a cold-weather wardrobe," added Nikita.

"I like Rudy's dreams," said Sheela, clapping her hands. "They're so loud and fun!"

"And full of mirrors so he can look at himself," grumbled Nikita.

"Aiden's dreams are a lot sadder..." said Sheela. "We tried to talk to him, but he got mad when he saw us. He was in the museum. Actually, you were there, too, Aru...."

"What?" asked Aru.

Nikita shushed her twin. "Astral projecting is serious stuff. We're not supposed to share what we see."

"But you just shared the thing about Rudy and the mirrors!" said Aru.

"That was different," said Nikita primly.

For some reason, Brynne now looked very guilty. That was weird. Aru made a note to ask her about it later.

"Time to go," said Nikita, glancing up. A thunderstorm was coming. Lightning flashed across the sky.

Sheela shivered, her blue eyes flashing icily the way they always did when she caught a vision. *"I see such sorrow and such cold. I see what greatness weakness holds."*

FOURTEEN

I Was Told There Would Be Porgs Everything Is a Lie

"Rise and shine, your hero has arrived!" announced Rudy. Aru blinked and found herself staring into the eyes of Rudy's favorite mortal celebrity: Dwayne Johnson, aka the Rock. Dozens of posters of him lined the walls of Rudy's private living room. Everywhere Aru looked, she was met with either a fierce or a smiling image of the celebrity fixing the room with an eyebrow so arched that, according to Rudy, it deserved to be a national monument.

"He's *the best*," Rudy had once explained during one of the Potatoes' epic movie nights. "I mean, the guy used to be a *rock*. And then someone with special powers came along and was so impressed with how *cool* he looked *as* a rock that he turned him into a *human* rock!"

Everyone had stared at Rudy. Eventually, Aiden had said, "Dude, that is not why he's called that." But Rudy had refused to listen.

Aru sat up on the couch. Mini, Brynne, and Aiden were gone. Rudy tossed her a parcel. Only now did she notice that he was dressed in a tie-dyed faux-fur getup. With velour. It was so transcendently awful that it looked almost...cool?

"Nikita sent over a cold-weather wardrobe a couple of hours ago," said Rudy. He did a little spin. "Mine is *obviously* befitting of my new status as savior of worlds, et cetera, et cetera, you're welcome. Now I'm kinda mad my family isn't home and I can't tell them about it, but these are the sacrifices that a real hero— like myself—makes."

Rudy beamed, and Aru cracked a smile. "Thanks, Rudy. You did save us."

"I know," said Rudy, lifting his chin. "Everybody else came to before you did, so get dressed! We're leaving in ten."

According to Rudy, his parents and brothers had gone to secure their vaults while he'd been left behind after playing his Sad Boi Rocks™. News coming out of the Otherworld was only getting worse. There were reports of escalating violence and stories of people throwing their support behind the Sleeper and his vision of a world remade....

Sheela's prophecy might have kept people from looking for the Pandavas, but it didn't stop the rumors. Some were beginning to whisper that the Pandavas had recognized the war as a lost cause and had abandoned the effort altogether. Aru tried not to think about all that as she walked the lonely, stately halls of Rudy's palace.

She felt curiously weightless without her ball of lightning warming her pocket or Boo's talons lightly digging into her shoulder. She thought of BB snoozing in his nest of vines. The firebird might have had Boo's soul, but he seemed very different. At peace, and perhaps a little wilder. A little freer.

Would she ever feel that way? Or would she always feel like she'd folded away her fears and tried to make them as small as possible so she could keep going?

Aru stepped over the threshold to the elevator bank and stopped short. No one else was here...except Aiden. Unlike Rudy in his riotously colorful outfit, Aiden wore a dark green ski jacket and matching pants. The moment he saw her, he shoved aside his backpack, a guilty look on his face. But that look—the downcast eyes, his chin tilted to his chest, hands shoved into his pockets—hit Aru like a kick. It was way too close to pity. And more than anything, Aru did not want to be pitied.

She straightened her shoulders and—without even a *hint* of wobbliness—proudly strode into the chamber and plopped onto the ground, where she leaned against one of the glass elevators. She looked calmly at Aiden, who was, once more, staring at the floor as if it were a long-lost friend. If he couldn't stand to look at her or talk to her, that was *his* problem, because Aru Shah did not give a—

"You were great back there," said Aiden suddenly.

"Say what now?"

"With the poison maidens," he said. "The way you realized what they wanted most—it was brilliant."

Aru stared at him. Was this a trick?

"Thanks," she said.

Aiden took a deep breath. "Listen, I know that—"

"THE TIME OF THE POTATOES HAS COME!" hollered Rudy, as he hopped across the threshold.

Mini and Brynne walked behind him, wearing matching somber expressions.

Where were you guys? asked Aru through the mind link.

Rudy had a change of heart about his outfit ten different times and said he required our opinions, said Brynne. *Of course he finally chose the first one he put on.*

Mini merely nodded.

You feeling okay, Mini?

I'm tachycardic, perspiring, and think I have angina, said Mini through the mind link.

I don't think that's a surprise to most girls....

It's a heart attack, Aru.

Oh.

Brynne snorted, which was almost a laugh, and therefore a victory to Aru.

"When you guys get your powers back and win the battle and all that, we can totally use these elevators to go on cool trips," said Rudy.

"And all that?" echoed Aiden weakly.

"Where's the first place you'd go?" asked Rudy.

"The beach," said Brynne.

"Mountain cabin," said Aiden.

"Beach, all the way," said Aru.

"I want to see the plague pits of London and the bone-filled catacombs beneath Paris," said Mini thoughtfully.

Aiden, Brynne, and Aru stared in horror at Mini.

Rudy clapped and pointed at her. "I can take you!" he said. "It'll be great! You can tell me all about diseases!"

Normally this would've brightened Mini's mood exponentially. But this time she only shrugged. Rudy didn't seem to notice. He gestured excitedly at the palanquin at the far end of the chamber, the one that was covered in frost and cloaked in shadows.

"Aiden, help me out," said Rudy as he went over to fuss with the wooden beams of the conveyance. "I've got to get it into the right position."

The Pandava sisters hung back, and Aru knew she wasn't alone in feeling miserable.

Kinda thought you'd be excited that Rudy clearly worships at the altar of Yamini Kapoor-Mercado-Lopez, said Aru to Mini through their mind link.

Me too, said Brynne.

He doesn't know what he's saying, said Mini. *He thinks my powers are going to come back and I'll be the cool daughter of the god of death again.*

You still are, said Aru. *That hasn't changed?*

It's not the same, said Mini.

Aru could tell her sister didn't want to talk, but she recalled the moment when Mini lost consciousness in Lord Vasuki's treasury and the way Rudy had shifted his shape and coiled protectively around her. She wasn't so sure Mini was right.

The palanquin had a wooden roof, open sides with a pitiful-looking railing, and three rows of cushioned benches. Everything felt rather cramped, and the wood held the smell of rot. Rudy sat on the front bench, tapping the ceiling. Aru could see fragile levers next to him and a small knobbed stick that might be some kind of steering device.

"Go forth!" commanded Rudy.

The palanquin didn't move.

"Are you sure that's what you're supposed to do?" asked Aiden, leaning forward. He was sitting next to Brynne on the middle bench, while Aru and Mini were in the back.

"No backseat palanquin drivers!" huffed Rudy, tapping once more at the wood. "Honestly, it's just supposed to move—"

FWOOMP.

The Potatoes screamed as the palanquin dropped straight through the marble floor. Aru's stomach swooped. She grabbed tightly to the flimsy wooden railing, which was all that stood between her body and an immense amount of *nothing*.

"EVERYTHING IS FINE!" Rudy shouted over the noisy wind.

Aru felt the palanquin tilt hard. Mini's elbow slammed into her ribs. Aru slid to the left, her hands grappling for some kind of purchase. She would've opened her eyes, but every time she tried, cold wind lashed at her face.

"I thought there'd be some kinda windshield!" said Rudy.

"What do you mean *thought?*" shouted Aiden over the wind. "What are you using to drive this thing, Rudy?"

"INSTINCT!"

Aru flew backward, her spine thudding against the rear wall of the palanquin as the structure began to climb through the air. Her neck felt tight, like when a roller coaster inches toward the top of a free fall. She opened her eyes a crack, and then quickly wished she hadn't. The palanquin looked like it was aiming straight for the side of a mountain.

"RUDY!" shouted Aiden.

"INSTIIIIINCT!" roared Rudy, toggling maniacally with the driving levers.

Aru turned her head as the mountain loomed closer. Suddenly, the vehicle made a sharp right. Mini screamed, her body sliding sideways and nearly tipping out of the palanquin. Aru flung out her hand, but Mini's fingers were too slippery. Just when it looked like she was going to fall, Mini thudded against something.

"Ow!" she said, scuttling upright as the palanquin straightened out.

Mini pressed her palm against the air, her fingers splaying as she met the solid surface of a windshield that hadn't been there moments ago. The roar of the wind died away, replaced with a faint *whooshing*.

"See?" said Rudy. "Windshields! Instinct! Told you it'd be fine!"

Brynne looked like she was going to vomit. Rudy didn't look so great himself. Naga scales had bloomed all the way down his neck, as if he was transforming into his full snake form out of pure panic.

"Rudy," growled Aiden.

"Look around you!" said Rudy, with a slightly guilty smile. "I mean, the views are great, right? Perfect for picture-taking..."

Aru looked to her right, trying to fight the wooziness that came with the realization that very little was protecting you from a thousand-foot plummet to certain death. When she peered through the windshield, she saw the sharp peaks of mountains cutting through a snowy mist. It was terrifying. Yet Aru had to admit it was beautiful.

They flew through the mountains and blankets of mist. At one point, Aru thought she saw the solemn eye of an elephant regarding them through the fog. But when she blinked, it disappeared.

"PREPARE FOR LANDING!" hollered Rudy.

There was no time to get ready. One moment, the palanquin calmly sailed through the air. The next moment...it dropped.

Aru screamed as the top of the palanquin popped off and her cushioned seat slipped out from under her, transforming into a parachute that erupted as the bench catapulted her into the air. For a few weightless seconds, cold blasted across her face, stealing the world from sight. When she could finally open her eyes, the mist cleared and the ground rose to meet her—

Thud.

"Ow!" said Aru.

The parachute collapsed around her, the ropes magically untethering from her gold winter coat. She stood up, wincing at the pressure of something jagged in her pocket. Aru fished it out and groaned. Welp. There went her phone. This was the seventh one she'd broken in a year.

"My mom is going to kill me," said Aru.

"That's amazing," said Brynne.

"Wow, rude?" said Aru, only to realize that Brynne was pointing at something else.

They were a hundred feet away from the end of the world. It was lovely and exhilarating, like holding your breath underwater and opening your eyes, knowing you wouldn't be able to see this forever. Snowflakes swirled around them and made a line of trees on their right dissolve into a silvery mist. The Potatoes stood on snowy slabs of gray rock interrupted by occasional tufts of blue grass. A hundred feet away, the slabs ended at a cliff, and near the edge, carved into a huge rock face, was what looked like a cave. But its entrance was blocked by boulders. The cave was flanked on one side by a ginormous gray pillar that disappeared into the snow clouds overhead.

"I bet whoever lives there is extremely welcoming," said Brynne dryly.

Not two yards away lay a twelve-foot-wide circle of small, sharp-looking stones that glittered in the snow. It was surrounded by patches of dangerously slick ice. Was this some kind of barrier King Jambavan had set up?

"What do we do?" asked Mini. "Just...step over these like they're nothing?"

"Should we announce ourselves?" asked Aru. "Like, 'We are heroes seeking the shiny thing'?"

"We should work on that wording," said Aiden.

Aru ignored him.

"Or— Wait. Rudy, what are you doing?" asked Mini, looking deeply alarmed.

Despite the freezing temperatures, the naga had shucked off his winter jacket and hat and was doing jumping jacks in the snow.

"I—heard—he—wrestles—everyone—who—comes—in—so—I'm—warming—up," he said.

Brynne shook her head. "Let's just get this over with." Aru held her breath as Brynne stretched her neck from side to side and then stepped into the circle of white stones. "KING JAMBAVAN! We respectfully ask that you let us enter so we may speak to you!"

"About the shiny," whispered Aru.

"ABOUT THE SHINY—I mean, THE LEGENDARY SYAMANTAKA GEM!" said Brynne.

Nothing happened. The wind howled. The stones creaked.

"Maybe there's a front door we're not seeing?" asked Mini.

They turned away from the cave, scanning the line of trees as if there might be a sign hidden in plain sight. Aru was studying the circle of stones when she saw something else—a shadow sprawling over the snow-packed earth. She barely had a moment to wonder at it before a hot, wet wind ruffled her hair. She whirled around.

"Uh, guys?" she said. "I . . . I think he knows we're here."

Jambavan panted behind them from atop a flat boulder. He looked nothing like the being Aru remembered from the Council meetings. For one thing, he was *huge*. Aru had never seen a bear as big as three mature elephants.

Jambavan lumbered off the rock, his sharp claws sinking into the snow. He was covered in shaggy black fur broken only by a white moon on his chest. His muzzle was long and narrow, the fur around it matted and wet with . . . blood? Aru gulped. Jambavan swung his head at them. He looked feral. His shiny black eyes registered nothing. When he snorted, steam puffed into the air.

"O Lord Jambavan—" started Aru with a squeak.

"BEGONE!" he roared. "NO VISITORS! EVER!"

"It's not like we're here out of choice!" shot back Brynne.

Jambavan roared. The ground quaked.

"Run!" said Mini.

The Potatoes had turned on their heels and started running when the white rocks began to tremble. One moment, they were hardly more than triangles on the ground. The next, they had shot up tall as towers, sharp as teeth, and thin as needles. The gaps between the poles were barely more than a foot.

Aru skidded to a stop just inches away from the barrier. Behind her, Jambavan charged. Snow kicked up around his claws. His head was lowered, gums pulled back to reveal blood-stained teeth.

"Squeeze through!" said Mini, turning sideways and trying to work her leg through an opening in the stones.

Brynne grabbed hold of one white bar only to wince. "It stings just to touch it!"

Jambavan was closing in. Fifty feet…now twenty.

Aiden jumped in front of Aru, brandishing his scimitars.

Rudy was digging through his satchel of enchanted musical rocks. "Where did it go?!" he said, panicking. "I thought I packed the enemy-interference quartz, but THIS IS THE SOUNDTRACK TO *BEAUTY AND THE BEAST*!"

"Why do you even have that?" Aiden asked.

Jambavan reared up a foot away from them. Aiden swung out his scimitars and Jambavan knocked one aside with a lazy brush of his paw, sending it spinning fifty feet away. Then the bear king growled, slamming back down onto all fours.

"We were sent here by Lord Agni," said Mini in her best calming voice. "I'm sure we can talk this over?"

Jambavan rose again on his back two legs. He stood at least seventy feet tall. When he stared down at them, his eyes were totally black.

"No."

The monster opened his mouth, and all the blood drained from Aru's face. Her back was pressed against one of the white rods. She could feel its stinging sensation like a soft pinch through her winter clothes.

This is it, she thought. *Eaten by a* literal *bear. What is life?*

The bear king loomed over them, claws outstretched, jaws rippling in a snarl….

Then a loud *creak* made him stop. Aru, who had closed her eyes for the final moments, cracked one lid open. Jambavan looked like he'd been caught in the world's weirdest game of freeze tag.

"Uh, what?" asked Rudy, staring up at the immobile bear king.

Jambavan still didn't move. Aiden, who still had one scimitar outstretched, lowered it slowly. He stepped forward cautiously and poked the bear king in the side.

Nothing.

"I KNEW THAT THING WAS BROKEN!" called a voice in the distance. "Stupid robot."

Aru craned her neck around Jambavan to see... Jambavan. He looked almost identical to the frozen, murderous bear king looming above them. *Almost.* For one, this Jambavan's belly happily protruded, and where the automaton stood tall, the real bear looked stooped and tired. He wore a red knit scarf around his neck, thick beige socks, and a pair of sandals. The biggest difference, however, was in his eyes, which shone with warmth and alertness.

"Ah, human children!" he said, clapping his paws in delight. "You must be cold! I don't know why my fireplace didn't alert me to guests—perhaps I slept through the alarm. Sometimes that happens." He shrugged, then tilted his head. "Why, you remind me of my own cubs when they were your size...."

Aru, whose heart was still racing, tried very hard not to think about bear cubs that were five feet tall.

"Come in, come in, get out of the cold!" said the real Jambavan, yawning and squinting at the desolate, frigid land outside his cave. "I was rather in the mood for hot chocolate. Anyone else interested?"

FIFTEEN

The Bear King

Jambavan's cave palace was surprisingly cozy. The floor was polished rock, accented with woven rugs. From the main hallway, the cave opened into a spacious chamber. At its center was a huge, unlit floating fireplace, its rock funnel disappearing into the ceiling. Soft emerald-colored moss studded with small purple and pink wildflowers covered the right wall of the chamber, while the left had a panel of glass overlooking the vast, desolate tundra. Aru frowned. In the distance, she saw something that looked like massive gray tree trunks. She'd never seen trees like that.

"Must remember to dust those photos," said Jambavan, aiming a critical eye toward the large frames that dominated the back wall.

"Are you from the Council, hmm?" he asked, tottering around in an old bathrobe. "Some kind of interns for the census, perhaps? I do hate traveling to the Otherworld. Hanuman and Urvashi deeply disliked that I only sent my facsimile, but what of it?"

He waved an indifferent paw, not bothering to wait for the Potatoes to answer. "Have you ever added salt to hot chocolate?" asked Jambavan as he strode ahead of them. "It's my secret ingredient for the most exceptional cup of cocoa, if I do say so myself."

Aru glanced nervously at Brynne. Normally when any sort of recipe-related talk came up, Brynne would bellow about the superiority of her ingredients. But she hadn't had an appetite lately. She hadn't even bothered making any snacks before they left. Instead, the Potatoes were relying on some kelp-and-algae protein bars that Rudy's older brother ate "strictly for the gains."

They tasted like salty old socks.

When Brynne didn't respond at all, Aru and Mini exchanged worried looks.

"Make yourselves at home by the fire!" said Jambavan, extending a paw toward the massive couches. A single cushion looked like it could comfortably seat a family of five. Jambavan glared at the craggy ceiling overhead, which had a chandelier of bleached antlers. "Music! Lights! You know the drill!"

Instantly, a fire coughed and sputtered in the fireplace. The scarlet flames cast huge shadows on the mossy wall, and the smell of burning wood and the gentle crackling of sap eased the tension between Aru's shoulders. Soft music filled the air, broken only by the occasional sound of Aiden's camera shutter. Aru looked around the room, but there was no sign of the Syamantaka Gem. And there weren't any obvious halls, doors, or archways leading to other rooms in Jambavan's cave palace.

The bear ambled toward a table set against the back wall. Aru watched as his furry arm went *straight through* the rock. There was a slight clattering sound, as if he was rummaging around on a shelf they couldn't see. When he withdrew his paw, it held a golden tray with six steaming mugs of cocoa and a platter of cookies.

Part of Aru rejoiced. CHOCOLATE!

The other part despaired. Where was Jambavan keeping the Sun Jewel? What if Agni was wrong and the bear king didn't have it? Then what would they do?

"Ooh, what is this couch made of?" asked Rudy, rubbing the soft, ruby-colored leather. "I like it!"

Aru studied the pattern. It had odd grooves in it that looked somewhat familiar.

"Oh, the usual," said Jambavan happily as he made his way over to them. "The skin of an enemy, I can't remember which.... Was it a naga, or some kind of winged thing? I've lost track of my victories."

Rudy immediately stopped petting the couch.

Jambavan handed them each a mug, then plopped into a comfy armchair and let out a huge yawn. "Well, we might as well get started, since you came all this way!" he said. "I'm due for my nap any time now."

"Get started?" asked Mini, confused.

The great bear smiled in a warm, pitying sort of way. "I understand. It can be overwhelming to be in the presence of a legend, but if you came all this way for an interview, I don't wish to disappoint such enterprising youngsters!"

Aiden lowered his camera, looking from Brynne and Mini to Aru.

"You think we're journalists?" asked Aru.

"Journalists!" echoed Jambavan, chuckling to himself. "That's a mighty grand word. Who would trust the voices of *children*? You're census takers, right?"

Aru felt a little prickly. Jambavan reminded her of one of those uncles who was good-hearted and genuinely well-meaning but nevertheless couldn't imagine anyone being remotely as important as himself.

"I thought only heroes come all the way out here," said Aru. "That's why you're called the Hero-Maker, isn't it?"

"Oh sure, sure. Many have come to my home thinking that if they can throw me off-balance in a wrestling match, they'll earn everlasting fame and renown," said Jambavan, clearly bored. "But, I mean, look at you lot. You don't strike me as particularly heroic."

Aru's face grew warm. Beside her, Brynne lifted her eyes from the ground and frowned at the bear king.

"I'm used to warriors striding into my cave!" thundered Jambavan. He slapped his thigh for emphasis. "Why, take a look at my wall of fame here!" He smiled indulgently at Aiden. "You can take a picture of it for your school project, if you want. But do be careful with that camera, child. It looks a little beyond your skill set."

Aiden opened his mouth to respond and Brynne gave a small shake of her head. *Not worth it.*

"What does that wall tell you about me?" asked Jambavan, sipping his cocoa.

Aru studied the framed items. There were trophies and ribbons, awards that declared Jambavan the "best wrestler of all time," and tons of photos taken with men who looked like they could crush a block of cement just by sneezing. Each photo was signed by the loser, with some variation of *It was awesome to be vanquished by you.* And there were about a dozen pictures of Jambavan pointing excitedly at a snowcapped mountain.

Aru crossed her arms. "You're superstrong and you like... hiking?"

Mini choked on her cocoa.

"Hiking?" repeated Jambavan, looking at the pictures. "Oh, those are just some family pictures that snuck in. That's my brother, Himavant. He doesn't smile very often."

Aiden squinted at the picture. "I don't see anyone?"

"How can you miss him? He's right there! He's huge!"

"Your brother is... a mountain?" asked Mini.

"Don't be fooled by the icy exterior. He's a real laugh riot," said Jambavan. He leaned back in his chair, examining his claws. "And yes, you're right! I am wildly strong. Why, I was strong enough to wrestle Lord Krishna for *twenty-eight days* before he revealed his divine nature and I yielded! *Twenty-eight*, mind you! With the Lord of the Universe!"

"Why would you wrestle with Lord Krishna?" asked Aru.

Jambavan tutted. "Come all this way without doing your research? You should know better than that, child."

Aru swallowed back a retort by taking a sip of her hot chocolate. Meh. Brynne's was way better.

"It's my claim to fame, obviously," said Jambavan. "Lord Krishna came here seeking the Syamantaka Gem. He had suggested that a nobleman named Satyajit relinquish it to their king so its wealth could be shared with the people of Dwarka. But Satyajit refused out of greed and selfishness." The bear shook his great head. "Mankind is stubborn. You can lead them to a pool of righteousness and they will still prefer their poisoned wells. After a while, all that is lovely and bright tarnishes beneath their gaze...."

As he said this, Jambavan stared into the fire. For all his

might, he looked old and tired. Silver streaked his broad chest and long muzzle. Scars that Aru hadn't noticed until now roped his haunches with thick, pale stripes.

"The jewel had been a gift, you see," continued the bear. "From the sun god, Lord Surya, to Satyajit. Whosoever possessed the gem was promised riches and freedom from sickness, and when Satyajit wore it, people mistook him for the sun god himself."

Aru could see the story unfurling in the flames. A middle-aged nobleman donning a necklace of illustrious light. The way his smile turned from shy ... to smug.

"Satyajit lent the jewel to his brother, Prasena, who wore it as if it were nothing more than an ornament."

The images churned, and Aru saw a different man hunting in the forest. He was surrounded by such a light that even the animals were momentarily transfixed by its brightness. Suddenly, a lean, furred body leaped out of the brush....

"He was killed, of course, as foolish men should be," huffed Jambavan. "The lion made off with the jewel, and that was how I came to obtain it."

The flames flashed, revealing a tussle between the massive Jambavan and the muscular lion. Aru looked away when Jambavan's claws took hold of the feline's jaws.

"By that time, Satyajit had accused Lord Krishna of having killed Prasena to get the Syamantaka Gem. To clear his name, Lord Krishna sought me out. I care naught for the jewels of men, and I had given it to one of my children to play with," said Jambavan airily.

Sure enough, the flames showed a small bear cub knocking around the huge jewel. Behind him, a figure that could only be

Lord Krishna appeared. He was wearing a small crown with a peacock feather tucked into the ornate metalwork.

"I am the strongest living entity," said Jambavan. "If anyone wished to take anything from me, they had to prove themselves worthy of my belongings."

The images shifted, revealing a clearing before the cave. Lord Krishna had removed his peacock crown. Jambavan wore a dhoti around his hips and legs. With a furious roar, he charged at the god, who smiled mischievously in return. A crowd gathered to watch them. The opponents' heels dug great trenches into the ground while the sun and moon spiraled above them.

"After twenty-eight days I conceded and gave him the jewel," said Jambavan. "As a sign of goodwill, I even offered him my own daughter, Jambavati, as a wife!"

In the flames, Aru watched as a tall lady bear draped in silk and wearing a crown of flowers took Lord Krishna's hand in her paw. He looked at her lovingly, and slowly she was engulfed in light. When the light receded, a beautiful woman stood before him. Her hair was the same color as the bear's fur, and when she smiled, her teeth were a little more pointed than a regular human's. Lord Krishna beamed at her all the same and hung a garland of flowers around her neck.

"When Lord Krishna passed from the material world, a piece of the Syamantaka Gem was returned to me," said Jambavan. "Many have come looking for it, but none deserve it. Humans are simply not fit for such a treasure, and yet they all believe otherwise. Why, every warrior who has stepped foot in my cave hoped that by defeating me they would wrest it from my possession!"

"*Would* you give the jewel to someone who beat you in combat?" asked Brynne.

Jambavan only laughed. "It is impossible. No one but Lord Krishna was strong enough to make me forfeit my treasure. Which is just as well. The world is at its end...I can feel it." He paused, stretching a paw toward the fire. "No one, not even myself, is strong enough to stop change."

"Maybe that's not true," said Aru.

Jambavan arched the tuft of white fur above his eyes. "Pardon?"

"We're not interns," said Aiden, rising from the couch. Rudy joined him, looking only too happy to leap off the skins-of-my-enemies cushion.

"We are the reincarnations of the Pandavas," said Mini, raising her chin. "We're demigods."

"Things in the Otherworld are *bad*, King Jambavan," said Aru. "Right now, the Sleeper and—" Her voice caught. She couldn't bring herself to say Kara's name, and the words *my sister* had almost snuck up on her. "And his, um, *accomplice* are making their way through the labyrinth to find the nectar of immortality and end Time. We can't stop them without that last piece of the Sun Jewel."

"If you give it to us, we can change all this," said Brynne. "We can prevent the end of the world."

Jambavan stared up at them, his rheumy eyes aglow. Slowly, he set down his hot chocolate and stood. Before, the king of the bears had walked with a stoop, but now he stretched to his full height. He towered over the fireplace, rising to almost twenty feet.

"Oh, children, you are operating under a misconception," said Jambavan in his low, gravelly voice. "You see, I'm quite ready for the world to end."

"What?" asked Aru, nearly dropping her mug of hot chocolate.

Jambavan smiled, and the sight raised the hairs on the back of her neck. Slowly, the bear king steepled his claws.

"But we're ... we're the Pandavas," repeated Mini, confused. "We can change—"

Jambavan started chuckling. It was a soft, pitying sound, and he made a great show of trying to spare their feelings by turning his head.

"Children," he said, wiping at his eyes. "If that were true, it would prove my point even more! I've *seen* the past reincarnations of the Pandavas. The one who was a judge, the other who was an Olympic athlete ... and if *you* are what the universe has to offer as we draw to the end of an age, well, surely you can agree that all the powers in the world have no faith in you."

Aru's mouth turned dry and her shoulders caved as Jambavan's words found their mark. What if he was right? What if this was all some terrible cosmic joke? Her heart beat even faster and her palms began to sweat.

"Where are your celestial weapons?" asked Jambavan, studying them.

"There was a fight, a-and—" Mini stammered.

"And you lost them," finished Jambavan, *tsk*ing. "Well, there you have it! The fact that your weapons haven't been restored to you speaks of your inadequacy. And I mean that, of course, in the kindest way possible. Why, you must have known from the start you were not intended to be the agents of change. You're far too young! And, forgive me, but I've never heard of a girl—"

"That's enough," said Brynne loudly.

Aru turned, stunned, to see Brynne propel herself off the couch, eyes blazing.

"You don't know what you're talking about," said Brynne.

"You haven't left this cave in forever. And you don't know what we're capable of."

Yeah, take that! Aru wanted to shout, but Jambavan was looming over them, the hot chocolate had gone cold, and this, perhaps, was not the best time to speak up.

"It is good to dream, child," said Jambavan, with a dismissive wave of his paw.

"I'll prove it," said Brynne. "Let's fight it out. You and me."

Mini's eyebrows shot up her forehead. Even Aru had to bite back a wince. Was that really the best idea? Brynne was superstrong, but strong enough to defeat Jambavan? The odds didn't look good.

Jambavan laughed. "Though I have grown tired of the world, I have not lost my appetite for victory. If you wish to taste loss, who am I to stop you?" The fire picked out a proud gleam in his eye. "The rules are simple. Either you manage to knock me off my feet or you agree to forfeit all efforts to take the Sun Jewel from me."

SIXTEEN

Brynne Rao Didn't Come Here to Play

Brynne Tvarika Lakshmi Balamuralikrishna Rao had always been strong. Like, so strong that even her shadow bristled with muscles and other shadows would wither away in its presence. Probably. But ever since she'd lost her wind mace, Gogo, it seemed like all that strength had vanished along with her celestial weapon.

Brynne knew that sometimes being strong demanded the courage to be weak, but weakness wasn't a choice right now—it was something that had been forced on her the moment Kara used the astra weapon to destroy their celestial gifts. Without Gogo, Brynne was so...less than. When she shape-shifted, she could no longer transform into gargantuan creatures. When she reached into the air, she could no longer weave cyclones out of nothing. It was as if the world was telling her that there was really nothing special about her.

But at this moment...Brynne was pretty sure she'd been wrong.

Beside her, Aiden touched her arm. "You don't have to do

this. We can find another way to get the Sun Jewel. We can go to the Council—"

"Look at your watch. We're already down to four days, Ammamma," said Brynne. "If we leave now, we'll have to find our way to the Otherworld, explain that we lost our weapons, and then what? We'll lose time and confidence. This is the only way."

The Potatoes were standing in an arena hidden deep inside Jambavan's cave palace. It was a large domed space in the brown rock. In deep niches in the walls, lit candles twisted the shadows. The floor was swept earth, broken only by a circle drawn in white chalk.

On the other side of the room, Jambavan shrugged off his heavy robe. Underneath he wore a pair of loose white pants. He did not stretch. He did not warm up. He merely watched Brynne, waiting for her to be ready.

"Bee?" said Aru. "I know what he said was, well, awful, but—"

"It wasn't awful," said Brynne. "It was *wrong*."

Mini, who had her arms wrapped around herself, looked up.

"It's like what Boo told us," said Brynne. "We're so much more than what we fight with."

It was one of the last things Boo had ever said to them. Brynne had been thinking about it ever since Aru had made them all quote something from Lord of the Rings and pledge to get their weapons back.

More than anything, Brynne wished she could ask Boo what he meant, ask him to prove it to her.... But right now, Boo was a baby firebird far more interested in cookies than warfare. Brynne didn't blame him.

"Do you know what you're doing?" asked Mini, nervous. "He could really hurt you, Bee."

Brynne looked between her sisters' faces. She knew what they'd been thinking these past few days...that she'd been too lost in her own world to notice what the two of them were going through. But they were mistaken. She saw how haunted Aru looked when she thought no one was watching. She saw how Mini's confidence had plummeted. And then Jambavan had made his big speech.

Speaks of your inadequacy...

You were not intended to be the agents of change....

I've never heard of a girl...

The moment Brynne had seen Mini's eyes shine with tears and Aru's lower lip tremble, something in her had snapped.

"I know what I'm doing," she said. "At least...I do now."

Brynne took one step into the arena, smudging the chalk on the ground, which was cold under her bare feet.

Behind her, Rudy whisper-hissed, "I have a *try-not-to-die* playlist....Do you think Brynne would like it if I put that on? *Ow!* Don't pinch my scales, Aiden. That's rude—"

"I'm ready, Jambavan!" roared Brynne.

No sooner had the words come out of her mouth than the floor shook. Clods of dirt and pebbles bounced around her. The candles flickered in their rock sconces. Brynne barely had a second to catch her breath before Jambavan's huge frame came into focus. For an old bear, he moved with uncanny grace. He shredded the air with his claws, then pressed down on Brynne's shoulders. Brynne dug her heels into the ground, wincing as sharp rocks tore into her skin.

"GIVE UP, LITTLE ONE!" roared the bear king.

Brynne grunted, trembling with the effort to stay upright. She gripped his shaggy arms and tried to push them away. She lifted her chin, meeting Jambavan's gaze head-on. In the half-light, his rheumy eyes looked wild.

"You first," she said.

Jambavan laughed. "Child, I am not even trying."

He pushed down harder. Brynne tried to resist, but it was like poking a skyscraper with your pinkie and expecting it to topple.

Brynne, this doesn't look good, said Aru through the Pandava mind link. *We can figure something else out, I promise! But it's not safe!*

Bee, c'mon, this is scaring me, said Mini pleadingly. *You're not strong enough!*

Brynne gritted her teeth as she smiled.

That's the point, said Brynne.

Wait, what—?

Brynne blocked her sisters' voices. With a duck and a twist, she slipped out of Jambavan's hold, and then she scrambled out of his reach.

The bear king spun around, snarling. Steam plumed from his nostrils. "Don't congratulate yourself for that maneuver," he said. "I am not used to fighting opponents so small."

Brynne let his words roll off her. She jumped back, putting even more space between herself and the bear king before she roared and ran at him. Jambavan caught her, his claws sinking through the thick enchanted coat Nikita had made, and forced her back onto the earth floor. Brynne felt something pop in one of her knees as she resisted the bear king's attempt to make her crumple. He loomed over her, blotting out the light.

"Yield," he snarled. "You are neither strong enough nor big enough to topple me, child."

Brynne dug in her heels once again. The effort made her pulse hum in her ears. When she blinked, spots danced across her vision. Her spine felt like it was being compressed, and still she held firm....

She held firm because she'd realized something when Jambavan had talked down to them. He didn't know who they were or what they'd done—he'd taken one *look* at them and assumed they were weak. The moment Brynne had heard that, she'd understood something.

Yes, she was smaller.

Yes, she wasn't as powerful.

But there was strength in that perspective. When someone chose to see you only as small and weak, it made them careless. Careless enough not to notice when a small and weak thing crept past all their expectations and laid a trap they didn't expect.

Jambavan rose on his back paws and pressed harder on Brynne's arms. The room grew dark and cloying. This close, she caught the animal stink from the king's bared teeth. She waited until her knees buckled, until she could see Jambavan wobbling in his effort to push her down. And then, Brynne closed her eyes... and transformed.

In the past, she would have made herself huge. She would have morphed into an elephant or bear or gorilla. This time she changed into a small blue chickadee.

Instantly she felt the relief of being out from under Jambavan's claws and the sudden weightlessness that came with flight. The bear's eyes widened. He'd leaned too far over to get her to yield, and it had cost him his balance.

Brynne beat her wings furiously. She flew backward just as Jambavan toppled to the ground. A huge cloud of dust and dirt puffed into the air. The rocks in the cave trembled. There would've been a shocked silence after Jambavan fell if Rudy hadn't put on his playlist. In the background, Brynne heard Aretha Franklin belting out:

R-E-S-P-E-C-T
FIND OUT WHAT IT MEANS TO ME

Followed by Rudy saying, "Fine, fine! I'm turning it off! You guys have no sense of atmosphere...."

Brynne closed her eyes and took on her human shape once more. She rolled her shoulders and stretched her neck from side to side as she walked over to Jambavan. The bear king rolled onto his back, a stunned expression on his face. From the sidelines, her sisters had recovered from their momentary shock and were screaming and whooping.

"How did you do that?" asked Jambavan. "You are not—"

"I know," said Brynne, cutting him off. "But I don't have to be stronger or bigger to beat you. I am *so* much more than the things I fight with."

At that moment, Brynne felt a soft wind stirring through the cave. The candles flickered out, then roared back to life. A cold sweetness enveloped her senses, and for the first time in days, Brynne's stomach gave a loud growl. She licked her lips hungrily.

"And by the way, your hot chocolate isn't that great," she said, planting her hands on her hips. "For a truly *exceptional* hot chocolate, add a pinch of cayenne!"

The wind picked up, swirling the pebbles and ruffling Mini's hair.

"Use a splash of double cream for richness! Grate nutmeg into it and add two sticks of cinnamon to the pot!"

Something blue glinted in the air, and dimly, Brynne realized her feet had lifted off the ground and her hair had lifted off her shoulders. But she couldn't stop mid-recipe!

"And then coat the rims of the mugs with Nutella before pouring in your cocoa concoction!" said Brynne, throwing up her arms. "THAT IS HOW YOU MAKE THE BEST HOT CHOCOLATE!"

The moment she put her hands in the air, Brynne felt something fly into them. The blue wind wrapped around her like a soothing breeze. It swirled inside her rib cage as if a humming cyclone had rooted itself to her bones.

Brynne's feet slammed onto the ground. She blinked a couple of times as the dust settled. And then she looked at what was in her hands, her mouth falling open.

Laid across her palms, gleaming turquoise and aglow with the power of Vayu, god of the wind, was Brynne's celestial wind mace.

SEVENTEEN

I Am Officially Intrigued

Aru couldn't stop staring.

"It's *back*," she said. "Your weapon came back...."

It was, perhaps, the fifteenth time she'd said that in the past ten minutes. Mini had been stunned into silence. Gogo had transformed from a wind mace to its usual glowing blue choker at Brynne's throat. Aru couldn't help putting her hand in her pocket and feeling a twinge of sorrow when her fingers didn't find her lightning bolt.

That wasn't the only change. Jambavan was almost unrecognizable. At first, Aru had panicked, wondering if they'd have to make a run for it with an ego-bruised bear king on their heels. But instead, he'd been *ecstatic*.

"AT LAST, A WORTHY OPPONENT!" he'd roared, shaking the stalactites hanging from the cave. "I AM OFFICIALLY INTRIGUED!"

The fact that Brynne had proceeded to transform into a large blue bear had only delighted him more.

"Perhaps we are related!" he said, patting his stomach. "That would explain why you could defeat me. Are you of my blood?"

"Uh," said Brynne. "Maybe?"

Jambavan had let out a big, rumbling laugh. "And now my descendant will have a hand in the remaking of the world! How excellent. Come. There is something I must give you."

Jambavan led them out of the arena and through the honey-combed passages of his home until they stood before another wall lined with photos.

"What do you see? Look closely, children."

The Potatoes stepped up to the wall. Aru tilted her head, scanning the images of Jambavan with his various opponents, but it was hard to make out everyone's expressions. Every photo was covered in a thick layer of dust.

"I am little more than a relic," said Jambavan in his sonorous voice. "My descendants have long passed, and I am all that remains of the old world and its time of heroes. I am blessed—or burdened, perhaps—with longevity. I was meant to witness history, and now I am reminded to look at the world anew." He took a deep breath. "You have earned my piece of the Syamantaka Gem."

Jambavan reached into the wall, and when he withdrew his paw, the final piece of the Syamantaka Gem sat in his palm. From his backpack, Aiden pulled out the lantern holding the other two pieces of the Sun Jewel. Brynne took the gem from the bear king, and when she reunited the last piece with the others, the glow that burst through the caves might have been the rising of a second sun. In that light, the bear king smiled and laughed.

Jambavan refused to let them go without a meal, and considering that the Potatoes had been subsisting on algae protein bars, they didn't fight him. Down the hallway next to the photo gallery, the cave opened into a beautiful vaulted room. A low silver table stretched almost fifty feet, and at least a hundred soft silken cushions lay all around it.

"This is no ordinary table," Jambavan said proudly. "A single meal at it will restore your strength and make you feel as though you've had seven nights' sleep. Above all, one must never shirk one's rest! Even the most powerful of beings do not neglect what they owe to Nidra, goddess of sleep."

As a gesture of thanks, Brynne had offered to make a feast worthy of the bear king, and he had only too happily agreed.

In an alcove next to the silver dining table was Jambavan's sort-of kitchen. As a bear, he ate raw food, so the shelves were laden with jars of nuts and dried fruits and baskets of dark, gleaming berries. One side of the wall was nothing but beehives, beneath which streams of honey lazily collected in a golden basin. Fat bees drowsily swooped in and out, disappearing into the hidey-holes of the cave.

"You were so partial to the skin-of-my-enemies couch, just wait until you see the wonders of the other relaxation chambers!" said Jambavan, gesturing at Aiden and a faintly nauseated-looking Rudy to follow him on a house tour.

Now that the three of them were alone, Aru plopped onto the floor and Mini sagged against one of the counters.

"How did you earn back Gogo?" Mini asked Brynne. "What happened? Was there a sign? A voice? Walk us through *every single detail*."

Brynne started preparing a fruit cobbler. She sifted flour, nutmeg, and cinnamon together. Then she sliced a couple of spiky plums to add to the rainbow-colored berries.

"Honestly, I don't know," she said. "I was just thinking, I guess, about strength and weakness?"

Aru stared at her. "What?"

"I know how it sounds, Shah, but it's the truth."

"Lord Agni said that the gods test in mysterious ways," said Mini slowly. A look of horror crept onto her face. "Do you think Aru and I have already been tested and...*failed*?"

"Of course...not?" said Aru, but she had the same worry herself.

"I don't think the test works like that," said Brynne thoughtfully. "It's more about figuring things out. For yourself."

"And you figured out that...?" prompted Aru.

"I figured out that I'm...strong."

"That's nothing new!" said Aru.

"I don't know how else to explain it," said Brynne. "But it's a good sign, right? I mean, if I can get my weapon back, so can you guys!"

Hopefully that was true. Aru felt genuinely happy for her sister, but envy gnawed at her, too. What if Aru ended up being the only one who didn't get her weapon back? But there was no point wandering down that brain road. Worrying wouldn't make a difference.

"Gods, I miss my lightning bolt," said Aru.

"I miss Dee Dee, too," said Mini, flexing her hands. "What will you do when you get Vajra back, Aru?"

"Electrocute Aiden," said Aru flatly.

Mini snorted. "Poor Wifey."

Brynne went oddly silent.

"Okay, what aren't you saying?" demanded Aru. "You're being shady."

Brynne's face turned red. She turned to reach for a bowl of honey.

"It's, um, not what you think," she mumbled.

"What isn't?" asked Aru.

"What he said to you in the museum lobby," said Brynne, the words coming out in a rush. "There's just more that he's not saying. Or can't make himself say."

Aru's pulse kicked up a bit. "Okay, so tell me."

"Can't," said Brynne.

Mini looked between Brynne and Aru, her eyes wide.

"Why not?" asked Aru.

"Because he's my best friend!"

"And I'm *literally* your soul sister!" shot back Aru.

Brynne groaned, her shoulders sagging. "Yes, I know. That's why this is literally killing me."

Aru crossed her arms. "You look like the picture of health to me."

"I knew him first," mumbled Brynne.

"What is this, the worst game of dibs ever?" said Aru. "I am your sister!"

Right then, Jambavan's booming laughter filled the room. Aru peered through the archway to see Aiden and Rudy following him. Aiden was looking pleased as he scrolled through the photos on Shadowfax.

Rudy, however, still seemed nauseous as he collapsed into the nearest cushion. "So...many...couches..." he said.

"Just give him some time, Shah," said Brynne under her breath as she put the cobbler in the oven. "And trust me, okay? It's really not what you think, but it's not my place to say it."

"I hate you."

"Love you, too," said Brynne, walking past her with a tray full of delicacies.

Aru hadn't realized how hungry she was until she sat down to the feast. There were huge platters of cut mangoes and jackfruit, bowls of passion fruit mixed with cream, delicate knots of edible flowers, hanks of cheese, and steaming mounds of paratha slathered with ghee. Jambavan snapped his fingers and silver pitchers full of honeyed water appeared on the table and emptied their contents into sparkling glasses that rose out of the silver table.

"The table grows its own plateware and cutlery," said Jambavan proudly. "Can't say I use much of it, but it is lovely to look at."

Light rippled down the surface of the silver table, as if it were delighted with the compliment. It then proceeded—for no reason Aru could guess—to produce a soup tureen, several flowerpots, a pair of grilling tongs, and a pinkie-size sorbet spoon.

With each bite of food, Aru felt her strength returning to her. When she looked across the table, Mini's face was glowing, Aiden's hair was shining, Brynne was positively beaming, and even Rudy now looked well-rested and happy.

Eventually, the food was nearly finished and the old bear king was no longer smiling. He turned his head toward the dark archway leading out of the banquet hall.

"There is much ahead for you," he said.

"Just the labyrinth," said Brynne, shoveling another piece of cheese into her mouth.

Jambavan made a low grumbling sound. "It will be well protected. Places like that do not have just a single entry point—they have multiple layers of access. Those who guard the doors could either be allies, enemies, or like I was—eager to see the world end. Desperate for everything to start over."

"We're ready," said Brynne.

Hooray, thought Aru dully.

"But how are we going to get there?" asked Rudy. "The elevator's totally demolished."

Aru grimaced, thinking of the shattered palanquin.

"That I can easily help with," said Jambavan. He tapped the table. A drop of liquid silver rose from the surface and spread out into a long oval mirror. When Jambavan touched the mirror, Aru saw the view from outside his palace. It was exactly what they had seen when they first arrived—the bare branches of thin trees hugging a crescent of the world that seemed to drop straight into oblivion. In some places, fog curled on the horizon, turning the star-flecked sky beyond it dark and hazy. The only thing Aru could detect amid that fog and starry space were those odd gray tree trunks, the tops of which disappeared into a thick blanket of clouds.

"We…fall off the edge of the world and hope for the best?" asked Aiden.

"Of course not!" said Jambavan. "You take the stairs straight to the doors!"

"Stairs?" repeated Mini.

"Doors?" echoed Aru.

Jambavan pinched the mirror with his thumb and index finger, as if he were zooming in on a screen. There, through the trees and almost invisible thanks to the silver mist, appeared the beginning of a white staircase.

"Take those stairs up to the platform right beside the elephants' knees, and the Sun Jewel will lead you to the door, which shall take you to the labyrinth," said Jambavan.

Aru stared at him. "Elephants?"

"Why of course, child!" said Jambavan. "What else did you think those were?"

He pointed to the huge gray pillars, then looked back at Potatoes. When Jambavan saw their expressions, he slowly zoomed out...and *out*...and *out*...past the silver mist on the crescent of land, past the white staircase winding through the dark space, past the cloud bank that had cut off the tops of the *surprise,-it's-actually-an-animal!* pillars until Aru found herself staring at outer space. Frosty planets and distant stars moved in a slow cosmic dance. Rivers of dust and light wound through the dark, linking it all together. In a way, it was too vast to comprehend, but one thing was certain....

All of it was balancing on the backs of four gigantic elephants, each of whom faced one of the four cardinal directions. Aru couldn't imagine what would happen if one of them sneezed. Or, heavens forbid, caught a sudden, uncontrollable case of the itchies.

"Right beside their knees is a platform with revolving doors that will take you anywhere you need to go," said Jambavan. "Just...be careful when you're near them. The doors can be, well..." He paused, thoughtfully scratching his muzzle.

"Kinda hard to open?" suggested Aru.

She knew firsthand how some doors went out of their way to mock you. After all, Aru had lost many minutes of her existence pushing on doors that were clearly marked PULL. She did not like to talk about this.

"No," said Jambavan, lowering his paw and not meeting their eyes. "The doors can get . . . hungry."

Rudy's eyes went wide. "Say what now?"

"The doors go everywhere, into any time," explained Jambavan. "They are sustained by the daydreams and nightmares of humanity. The doors rarely meet individuals in the flesh. Whatever thoughts you have will, I imagine, deeply intrigue them."

"Naturally," said Rudy, puffing out his chest.

Aiden sighed, pinching the bridge of his nose. "I can't believe we're related."

"So what do we do when we get there?" asked Mini.

Jambavan nodded to the lantern beside Brynne, which held the Sun Jewel's three fragments. Its brightness was now a pleasant glow, as if it were sleeping. "Now that the three pieces have been reunited, the gem will act as a compass and guide you to the correct door. But you must move quickly. Try to focus on only one thing, so as not to draw the doors' attention. When the correct one appears, open it, and go through."

That sounded easy enough, thought Aru, relaxing. All they had to do was follow the Sun Jewel. It was bright enough, so at least that wouldn't be a problem.

"One last thing," said Jambavan. "Whatever you do, don't touch the elephants' legs. They'll panic."

"Don't worry, we won't," said Brynne, patting the lantern.

Just then, wind began to howl through the arches of Jambavan's cave. The shrill, swooping sound raised goose bumps on Aru's arms.

It sounded like someone shrieking.

EIGHTEEN

No Thoughts Head Empty

The wind may have been howling, the clock may have been ticking down, and the Potatoes may have been growing more anxious about catching up with the Sleeper, but at least they had the Sun Jewel.

"How much do you think this thing is worth?" asked Brynne, weighing the lantern.

"I dunno," said Mini. "But you could probably feed a whole country with it."

"Or *buy* a country," said Brynne. "Or, like, several private islands."

"I vote for that last one," said Aru, pointing at her.

Mini sighed, sharing an aggrieved *why-are-they-like-this* look with Aiden. He only laughed, while Rudy mused about the cost of various objects in the human world that had caught his attention.

"I bet you could buy at least *five* thumbtacks with the Syamantaka Gem," he said as they prepared to leave Jambavan's kingdom. "Or a *whole* case of paper clips..."

Rudy was under the impression that thumbtacks were the

most advanced weapons humanity had to offer. Nobody had bothered to tell him otherwise. As for paper clips, he just liked putting them on the tips of his fingers and pretending they were claws.

"Are you ready?" asked Jambavan with a determined look on his face. "I'll accompany you to the staircase, but then I must turn back."

Earlier he had gone outside to clear a pathway to the stairs leading to the World Elephants. Snow still dusted his long muzzle and the thick black fur on his shoulders. The old bear king seemed rather sad to see them go. Since the battle with Brynne, there was more sparkle in his eyes and he stood a little straighter.

The Potatoes looked at one another, something unspoken passing between them. As of now, there were four days left until the entrance to the labyrinth closed for good. Four days in which Aru hoped to win back her celestial weapon the way Brynne had.

Even now, Gogo glowed on Brynne's neck. A steadiness had taken over her sister, and Aru felt even more weird and off-balance. She tried to shrug it off, but the feeling clung.

"We're ready," said Aru.

Jambavan nodded toward the door. A stray winter wind had followed him inside, and even though Nikita's jacket kept her warm, Aru felt a chill creeping past her coat.

The moment they set foot outside Jambavan's palace, Aru kept her eyes focused on the lantern. Since Brynne was the only one who had her celestial weapon back, the Potatoes had decided that she should be at the front of the line with Jambavan. Behind her was Aiden with his two scimitars sticking halfway out of his sleeves. Rudy followed him, holding an enchanted rock to create a sound barrier and keep them from getting distracted. Next came Mini, then Aru.

Aru tried to think of nothing but the light on the snow as they trekked through the sparse trees and damp ground for what felt like eons. Finally, they came to a stop.

"Take a final look, children," said Jambavan.

Aru lifted her head. They were standing at the base of a huge staircase carved out of white stone. The steps were at least twenty feet wide and they wound up so high into the sky that they disappeared into a layer of clouds. Beneath the glowing staircase was nothing but space . . . and the single leg of a massive elephant whose gray hide was crisscrossed with old scars. The rest of its body was too large to comprehend from where they stood.

"Go now," said Jambavan. "Be careful of what will greet you on the other side, for as I said, there are many amongst us who simply wish for the world to begin anew."

Brynne nodded, then took the first step. Aiden, Rudy, and Mini followed, each of them bowing their heads and pressing their hands together as they walked past Jambavan. When it was Aru's turn, Jambavan held out his paw.

"This is for you, daughter of Indra," said Jambavan. In the middle of his palm was the tip of a sharp black claw, roughly the size of a pencil. Aru took it gently. It was lighter than she thought it would be, as if it were hollow.

"What's it for?" she asked hopefully. Maybe it was a cool weapon she could use and then not feel quite so useless.

"To remember me by," said Jambavan.

"Why me?" asked Aru, trying to mask her disappointment.

The bear king glanced at her sisters and friends slowly making their way up the stairs. "Because I think you see more than you let on," he said in his rumbling voice. "Perhaps this token will help you when the time comes for you to make your decision."

"Decision about what?" asked Aru as she turned to place the claw gently inside her backpack.

When Jambavan didn't respond, she looked up . . . but the old bear king was gone.

No one spoke as they walked up the stairs. No one complained about how their feet ached and their back hurt, how it seemed like they'd been climbing for ages. Aru knew the rules.

Stay focused.

Don't catch the attention of the doors.

Eventually, Aru could sense the clouds parting around them. The surface of the steps became smooth, flattening out into a platform that had the feeling of a wide space. Like a school gymnasium. On the white stone, she could see the stark shadows of dozens of doors spinning around them. It looked like the Potatoes were standing in the middle of roving teeth.

The lantern seems to be shining brighter at one of the doors, said Brynne through the mind link. *Let's take this slowly. Four steps ahead on my count. Three . . . two . . .*

On *one*, Aru took a step forward. Mini followed Rudy, and Aiden moved in sync with Brynne. Aru exhaled, her shoulders relaxing by a fraction. They were doing it. . . . They were almost there. . . .

On the third step, Aru closed her eyes. It was only supposed to be for a second. The light from the Sun Jewel was giving her a headache.

But the moment Aru closed her eyes, she did something she never meant to do . . .

She hoped.

And with that hope, she saw the entrance to the labyrinth at Lullwater Park, where her mom had taken them. Aru imagined her mom smiling with pride, while Vajra's glow rivaled that of the Sun Jewel itself. . . .

WHAT'S HAPPENING? came Brynne's panicked thought.

Aru's eyes flew open. The shadows of the doors had moved closer, like a circular trap drawing shut. Now they were near enough that Aru caught the shape of something instantly familiar. It was the smooth mahogany entrance to Krithika Shah's office. In one corner of the wood was the tiny cat Aru had drawn with a black Sharpie when she was eight years old. Aru quickly turned her head.

Too late. She had looked at the door . . . and the door had noticed.

It's spinning away! said Brynne through the mind link. *Now it's on our left! Everyone take six steps! Do NOT look. . . .*

Focus, Aru told herself as her breaths began to come a little more quickly. She tried to keep her head empty, but it was as if the doors knew they'd found an opening in her. With each step, Aru caught sight of a different entrance drawing closer. Here was the swinging glass door that led to her principal's office. There—

I'm being followed, said Mini through the mind link. *I can* smell *it. Are we almost there?*

Don't think about it, Mini! said Brynne.

It's just like my—

Alarm bells went off in Aru's head. *NO, MINI, DON'T THINK IT!*

Basement, said Mini.

Once Mini said *basement,* it was as if she had summoned it into being. Aru felt the shadow of the opening falling over her. She tried not to look at it, but it caught her eye anyway. The door was wooden and painted a cheery shade of pink. A tarnished metal latch dangled at eye level like a lolling tongue. It creaked open.

One day last summer, the power had gone out in the Kapoor-Mercado-Lopez house, and all the food in the basement fridge had gone bad. No one had discovered it until weeks later. Aru still remembered the stench of rotten meat, the sight of puckered fruits thick with maggots. The stone floor of the platform vanished beneath her feet to be replaced by the rough red carpet that Mini's parents had brought back from a trip.

"NO!" yelled Aiden.

Aru looked up to see that Mini's expression was glazed over, her eyes blank and staring. At least fifteen doors crowded around them. Aru recognized the sunlit door of her favorite library, swinging open so she could lose herself in its warmth. Then the menacing door of her eighth-grade geometry teacher's room. Next, a door strung with lights, which Aru recognized as the entrance to an Italian restaurant her mom had taken her to—

"Look at me, Shah," said Aiden, grabbing her hand.

Aru jerked her gaze away from the doors and stared into his eyes. She sensed the doors circling her, getting closer and closer. Aru could feel the rough brush of wood and the whine of distant music, as if a door was desperate to suck her in.

But Aiden's gaze steadied her and for the first time, she could see what was happening around them.

Up ahead, Rudy held up one of his enchanted gemstones.

The doors recoiled from the sound it loudly emitted—a wood-chipper? A lawnmower? Next to him, Mini swayed on the spot. Her basement door noiselessly slid forward until it was barely three feet away from her. Aru was on the verge of grabbing Mini's hand to pull her away from it when Brynne shouted.

"FOUND IT!" she yelled. "The lantern says this is it!"

Sure enough, the door in front of Brynne was a rectangle of molten gold. Beside it, a glass door that looked like violet-tinged smoke angled for their attention. And next to that one stood a door covered in sheet music.

"I just have to get it open!" yelled Brynne. Then her eyes widened. "MINI, NO!"

Brynne raised a hand. Her wind mace flew into her grip, its head aimed at the basement door that had swung open at Mini's touch.

I want to go home, thought Mini. *I want everything to be okay. I want my friends to be safe. I want us all to wake up from this awful dream....*

Brynne aimed her wind mace, and a jet of air hit the solid wood. Aru thought it would slam shut instantly, but it only quivered a little on its hinges. It was as if Mini's thoughts were keeping it open. Mini edged toward it.

Brynne growled. This time she chucked her whole wind mace at the door. The force of the impact snapped it shut with an angry screech of its hinges.

Mini stumbled backward. She shook herself, looking around wildly. "What just happened?"

"Nothing," Aru said. "Well, almost something, but it's okay—"

Before Aru could finish her sentence, the platform tilted to one side to avoid a sudden storm cloud brewing in the void. Brynne—who had her hand outstretched to catch her boomeranging wind mace—slipped. She missed Gogo by mere inches.

Aru watched the arc of the wind mace as time slowed around them.

"Uh-oh," said Rudy.

Aiden leaped into the air to catch the rogue mace. His fingers skimmed the metal—only to lose it. With a *thud*, the mace hit the crusty gray hide of a World Elephant. A moment later, it bounded back to Brynne, who caught it one-handed. Beneath their feet, the platform righted itself.

All five Potatoes froze. Even the doors around them went still. Aru looked at her sisters. "Maybe the elephant didn't notice?"

Far, far above them, a trumpeting sound echoed through the air. It was an angry sound, and it sent a tremor through the floor, cracking the stone.

"Okay, we gotta move fast," said Brynne, holding out the lantern.

But if the World Elephant they'd hit was mad, that was nothing compared to the doors. Now they all clanged together, spinning in a whirlwind about the platform. Aru couldn't keep track of which door was the entrance to the labyrinth. The light of the Sun Jewel bounced around like a deranged flashlight, skittering over the different surfaces.

"Where do we go?" asked Aru, squinting as she tried to see through the blur.

"This way!" said Brynne, taking a step forward before doubling back. "No, I mean, *this* way!"

Aru reached out, one hand locked tight with Brynne's, the other grabbing hold of Mini, who reached for Rudy, who clasped Aiden's shoulder.

"Here!" said Brynne.

The light threw open a door. Aru couldn't see the surface. Everything was utter darkness, as if a jaw had unhinged around them.

"This way!" said Brynne, as they tumbled into the void. "I think?"

NINETEEN

A Brief Interlude from Madness

"This is weird," said a familiar voice.

Aru opened her eyes. She felt weightless, like she was in a dream, but her surroundings didn't look anything like a dream. She, Mini, and Brynne were standing on a white disk. All around, prismatic lights flashed past, as if the Potatoes were barreling through a tunnel.

Floating in front of them were Sheela and Nikita, but they weren't totally there. For one thing, the twins had only emerged halfway through the tunnel wall, and for another, they were *translucent*. When Aru reached out to touch them, her fingers went through empty air. Aru jerked back her hand.

"What's going on?" asked Brynne, turning around. "Where are we?"

Sheela licked her finger, then held it up like a sailor trying to feel the direction of the wind. "Tastes like daydreams," she announced.

Nikita sniffed the air, frowning. "You're definitely moving, but you're not unconscious. This isn't a normal dream. My guess is that one of the places you're passing through is the realm of sleep. Or maybe an astral plane?"

"How are we able to talk to you guys?" asked Aru.

"Well, *we* always have access to the astral plane," said Nikita haughtily.

"I thought we were going to the labyrinth entrance," said Brynne, looking around the tunnel of prismatic light. "This doesn't feel right."

Sheela licked the air, shutting her eyes tightly. "No. This tunnel is *kinda* near the labyrinth, but...backward? I don't know how to explain it."

Mini whimpered. She was staring at her hands, huge tears welling in her eyes. "We opened the wrong door, didn't we? It's all my fault. I'm so sorry. I didn't mean to get distracted."

"It's okay, Mini," said Aru. "Those doors were *creepy*. I almost got sucked into one—"

"Almost," echoed Mini. "But you didn't. *I* did. What if I do it again? It's like my instincts are all turning against me."

Aru shot a pointed look at Brynne.

"That's not true, Mini," said Brynne, but her tone was unconvincing.

"Tell us something good," said Aru pleadingly to the twins. "We got all three pieces of the jewel together, at least!"

Sheela and Nikita exchanged awkward glances, and Aru's heart plummeted.

"What is it?" asked Aru.

"There's been news," said Nikita, her eyes darting around the light-filled tunnel as if something was going to jump out at them.

"The Sleeper has almost gotten through the labyrinth," said

Sheela. "Soon, he'll start burrowing pathways out to where his soldiers can meet them."

"How is that possible?" asked Aru. "I thought you can only enter with a celestial weapon?"

"True, but you don't need one to *exit* it," said Nikita. "That's how he'll get his army inside."

"Well, then, what are we doing here? Why don't we just stalk his soldiers and enter the labyrinth that way?" asked Brynne.

Nikita shook her head. "If you do that, it will only lead you straight to his camp. Hanuman and Urvashi are already searching for those entrances and trying to block them off. Besides . . ."

"It won't do us much good unless we have something to fight him with," said Aru glumly.

"The good news is that the Sun Jewel lantern won't just get you through the labyrinth, it'll also break all the barriers at once!" said Sheela. "So once you get inside, we'll be able to meet you! To fight with you!"

Aru's ears were ringing. A tightness wrapped around her chest. What if that never happened?

Nikita looked her in the eyes, and it didn't matter that she was nearly translucent—Aru felt the intensity of her stare like a slap. "He's telling people he's already won, Aru."

"And do they believe him?"

"If you guys don't come back soon," said Sheela, her fading eyes acquiring that frosty look of prophecy, "they will."

"How do we get out of this place?" asked Brynne. She tried to take a step off the platform, but some kind of invisible barrier threw her backward.

Nikita raised her head as if she'd caught sight of something in the distance. But to Aru it just looked like a never-ending tunnel of multicolored lights.

"Any minute now," Nikita said. She closed her eyes, made a fist, and then opened her fingers. Five vivid—and solid—petals lay in her hand. "Place these on your clothes. They'll act like camouflage stickers and keep you hidden."

"How did you—" started Aru.

"Do it!" said Nikita.

Aru grabbed them.

"Now what?" asked Mini.

"Now, I guess, it's up to you," said Sheela. "I can't see clearly anymore. You have to move fast, or else—"

TWENTY

The End of the World!
But, Like, Fun!

"O uch," said Aru, stumbling forward while massaging her temple.

"Hey!" shouted someone far behind her. "No cutting! We were in line first!"

Line? thought Aru.

She blinked, trying to get a sense of her surroundings. She tapped her foot and felt sand beneath her. Something huge, winged, and fanged moved across her sight and she jumped back to see a ginormous bright-green headdress swaying a couple of feet away from her. The person wearing it swung around. They had the narrow, flat head of a lizard, pink skin, and a pair of bulbous eyes that did a quick head-to-foot scan of Aru, followed by a dismissive flick of their forked tongue.

FIRST OF ALL, RUDE . . . thought Aru.

"Ugh, my head," said Mini, beside her.

All the Potatoes, except Aiden, swayed and blinked, clutching their heads as if they'd just survived the World's Worst Migraine. For some reason, Aiden looked completely normal. By the time Aru's vision had fully returned, he'd already grabbed the Sun

Jewel lantern and stuffed it into his *oh-so-precious-no-one-can-touch-it* backpack. He was still staring into the bag, looking deeply concerned.

"Here," said Aru groggily, holding out the camouflage petals from Nikita. "Stick them to your clothes."

With an equally groggy grunt, each of them took a petal and stuck it to the front of their shirt.

As her head slowly cleared, Aru realized that they had stumbled out of a low mirrored wall and into a line that stretched *at least* a mile in either direction. People were appearing right and left, stepping out of the same wall with a bright *pop!*, which meant that the mirror was some kind of gateway.

But to where? Judging by the half day/half night sky above them, they were somewhere in the Otherworld. But it wasn't terrain Aru had ever visited before. It was a black-sand desert formed of ever-shifting, glittering dunes that reminded Aru of a great creature's ridges rippling.

Aiden raised Shadowfax to his eye and snapped a couple of pictures. "I don't see anything nearby. No buildings, no signs—"

"HEY! Why are you kids holding up the line?" demanded someone a few steps away. It was a very tiny pale-skinned woman with flames for hair wearing what looked like chain mail made out of Q-tips. "Keep it moving! You're not the only ones hoping for a last chance at stardom!"

Stardom?

Brynne, still dizzy and frowning, pushed Aru forward with a vague grunt. Aru glanced at the front of the line. It was moving *very* fast. Before, it had seemed like they were smushed against strangers. But now the lizard-faced creature with the headdress was a hundred feet away.

The Potatoes jogged to catch up, rounding the bend in the wall until a structure came into view. Aru blinked. On the other side of the wall loomed a glass pavilion. Animals made of smoke—leaping fish, soaring eagles, and prancing horses—circled its cupola, and from within came a dull thrum of music. But the glass was frosted, so there was no way to see inside.

"Definitely enchanted," said Rudy, holding up a hand. "It's like some kind of . . . music venue, I think."

"A *music venue?*" repeated Aru. "In the middle of nowhere? Why would they even have that?"

"Where's the labyrinth?" asked Mini, biting her lip. "I really messed up, didn't I?"

Aru wanted to say a comforting word to her sister, but someone started yelling at them from the back.

"KEEP MOVING OR I WILL ROAST YOU!"

Aru spun around, a retort ready to fly off her tongue, only to see that the being talking to her was, in fact, a living column of flame. Who happened to be ten feet tall. Aru changed her mind.

"Yeah, okay, let's go," said Aru, hustling forward.

The line moved so fast there was no time for the Potatoes to chat. Every now and then they would hear an ear-piercing screech or a deep, bellowing sob from the front of the line, but things quieted down as they got closer. The mirrored wall faded away. A new part of the structure became visible: a big red door that floated a foot off the ground.

Beside it stood a very bored-looking yaksha. He was short and skinny, with mint-green skin and mossy patches above his pointed ears. He wore a white T-shirt with holes in it, a pair of distressed leather pants, and an elaborate brocade *sherwani* atop it all. A pair of glowing sunglasses was perched on his bulbous nose above an unsmiling mouth. On the other side of the green yaksha was the curtained entrance to the massive tent. From where Aru stood it was still hard to see much inside, but through a crack she could just make out a field. Dark shapes moved on the other side of the glass wall.

"Yeah, listen, you're, like, the *seventh* person to tell us that you're *really* good at the ukulele," the green yaksha was saying. He was speaking to a small band of *vanaras* at the front of the line. They were wearing palm fronds and banana leaves and carrying a variety of musical instruments.

Their leader, who was clutching a bagpipe to his chest, started to weep. "But we've been practicing for *years!*" he said. "We just want *one* chance to perform on the Final Stage!"

The yaksha yawned. "No."

"Please! Think of my family!" said the leader, thrusting a photo at the yaksha's face. *"What will I tell my son?"*

"Sir, this is a cat."

"WELL, IT'S THE CLOSEST I HAVE TO OFF-SPRING...."

"Next," said the yaksha in a bored voice.

"We can do a great rendition of Dolly Parton's 'Jolene.' Just give us one more chance—"

The red door lurched forward. It swung open and the band disappeared into it with a yelp. All that was left of them was a single photograph drifting onto the sand. In it, a very fat orange cat in a Santa hat was sitting on a chair. It did not look happy.

Now the lizard-faced creature with the green headdress swanned forward, allowing Aru to get a better look past the entrance. Inside was a wide mowed field of grass at least twice the size of a football stadium. Bleachers lined the sides of the pavilion, and in the center was a rectangular stage made of glimmering crystal. Floating directly above it was another door, this one purple and faded around the edges. Curls of smoke seeped from it and combined to form fantastical winged horses and narwhals that twisted in the air.

Brynne peered over Aru's shoulder, scowling. "I recognize that door from the World Elephant platform," she said. "But it's not the one the Sun Jewel picked."

"I think it was *right next to* the labyrinth door," whispered Mini. Her gaze darted to the yaksha, who was less than ten feet away from them and locked in some kind of argument with the reptile-faced person. "So we can't be too far away from where we're supposed to be, right? It's like Sheela said—"

"Near the labyrinth and backward?" said Aru, repeating what their sister had mentioned in the astral plane.

"What if we can't find the door to the labyrinth in time?" asked Mini, her pitch going up a notch. "Should we just take *that* one? How? What are we going to—"

"NEXT!" bellowed the mint-green yaksha.

The lizard-faced creature had vanished. Beside the yaksha, the red exit door swelled, then flattened. As if it had burped after devouring something.

A single pink feather twirled in the air.

Aru gulped. That did not bode well.

"Hi," she said, taking a step toward the yaksha.

She darted a look at her sisters and then at the floating purple door above the stage. How exactly was she supposed to ask for directions to the labyrinth?

"Well?" asked the yaksha, tapping his foot. "What's your talent? And don't tell me ukulele. I've had, like, a hundred of those.

And if you start off by saying you were 'great in marching band,' I've got news for you, kid—you weren't."

Aru frowned. First of all, she wasn't even *in* marching band! There'd been an incident with a trombone and, well, Aru had been "encouraged" to try a different extracurricular activity. She was still bitter about it.

"Um, do we need to have a talent to go inside?" piped up Mini. "It's just that we were hoping to enter the, um, labyrinth—"

The yaksha lowered his sunglasses. His eyes were the color of rocks at the bottom of a river, and the look he gave them was just as cool and indifferent.

"And *you* are?" The yaksha sneered at Mini.

Behind Aru, Rudy seemed to puff up in indignation, but Aiden elbowed him sharply.

"The only ones who get *access*"—the yaksha emphasized the word by waggling his fingers and glaring at them—"to the Final Stage are the artists who are deemed worthy of performing *upon* it. And just to have the *honor* of auditioning, one must be wildly talented! And even then, the door may not open. It requires the presence of true genius! True je ne sais quoi—"

The Sun Jewel will open the door for us! thought Mini through their mind link.

I could easily blast us up to it with Gogo in hand, said Brynne.

Aru grinned, hope sparking in her ribs. They could *do* this! They just had to get through the talent-whatever.

"We'll do it," said Aru loudly.

The yaksha snorted. "My dear, *thousands* have tried to get past the first round and failed. Do you think you're the only one eager to perform on the stage of the apocalypse? When the great Lord of Destruction dances and obliterates existence, we intend to join him in that dance! And we're not going to have some two-bit performers ruining the end of the world!"

Aru blinked. "Wait—everyone here wants to watch the world...get destroyed?"

When King Jambavan said that there were others like him, Aru had pictured hermits in a cave making peace with the end times. Not people showing up in chicken costumes and singing opera in the background.

"Some dance with the hope that as we are folded back into the universe, we might find the happiness we missed out on in this existence," said the yaksha, a wistful look in his eye. "Others dance because there is no hope left. The Sleeper's army is unstoppable. Even the Pandavas have abandoned us."

"That's—" started Brynne, but Aru silenced her with a quick glare and tapped the camouflage petal on her clothes.

"Okay, so your solution is to, what, throw an *Apocalypse X-Factor* contest?" asked Aru.

The yaksha ignored her. "You've wasted enough of my time. Do you have a talent or not?"

Uh-oh...She hadn't thought this far ahead. "It's, um, a secret," said Aru.

The red door inched closer. It looked alarmingly glossy...as if it were slicked with blood. The yaksha smirked.

"But if you give us a chance, it's *really* going to blow you away," said Aru, trying to angle her steps backward. "It's just so overwhelming that we honestly can't share—"

The yaksha gestured at the red door of rejection to move a little closer. Mini winced.

Brynne tapped into their mind link. *What if we just made a run for it? I could use Gogo to blast us through—*

"And don't even *think* about running in," said the yaksha, bored. "That arena is protected by living hurricanes. You would be shredded to ribbons before you even got a chance, so unless you know some higher-ups, I'd say it's time to go—"

"We know people!" said Aru. "Right?" She looked at her friends and nodded, encouraging them to follow along.

"Oh yeah?" said the yaksha. "Who?"

Rudy's mouth opened, no doubt to drop his trademark *I'm a prince* line, when someone else spoke instead. Someone Aru hadn't expected.

Aiden stepped forward, his face a little pale, his camera hanging dejectedly from his hands. He set his shoulders, stretched his neck, and said, "The apsara Malini."

The yaksha squeaked. "Malini?"

Aiden merely shrugged. "Yeah, you know, formerly one of the biggest celebrities in the cosmos? With a voice that once summoned a tsunami?"

The yaksha's sunglasses dropped off his nose. "No one has seen her in ages! You can't possibly know her!"

Aiden held out his camera, the display reeling backward to show a picture of his mom. It must have been the last picture he took at home before this quest. His mother's expression was both hopeful and worried. The sun was streaming through their kitchen windows, capturing her Otherworldly loveliness. Aiden changed the display so it revealed something more casual—a selfie with his mom.

"Oh my god…" said the yaksha. "It's really *her*. You really *do* know her!"

A stray wind ruffled Aiden's hair. The outline of his body took on a glow.

"This is kinda overkill," muttered Rudy.

Uh-oh, here comes the Wifey smolder, said Mini.

"I'm her son," said Aiden. "I'm the only one who inherited her gifts before she renounced the Otherworld completely. I mean, c'mon, look at me."

Don't look, said Brynne through the mind link.

Aru squeezed her lids shut. The apsara powers Aiden had inherited from his mother were a fearsome weapon. When he *really* wanted to—and he rarely did—Aiden could make it seem like all the light had been sucked out of the world and into his eyes. His voice would take on a starry, velveteen quality, and mortals taken by surprise would end up doing something stupid in response. Like waltzing without music. Or singing. (Not that Aru had *ever* done anything remotely embarrassing when Aiden showed off his apsara powers....)

"You believe me," said Aiden.

When he spoke, a warm breeze swirled around them. The air took on the sweet smell of lilacs. Aru's cheeks warmed.

"You know who I am," said Aiden. "You'll let us in without any more questions."

"I see," said the yaksha in an entranced voice.

"Good."

Aru opened her eyes when Aiden's voice lost its sparkling quality and became normal again. The red door seemed a little farther away now.

"The son of Malini is always welcome," said the yaksha pleasantly. A moment later, a hard look reentered his eyes as he considered the rest of the Potatoes. "But what about *them*?"

Aiden glanced at them all, and Aru could see a small battle being waged in his face. Then he sighed.

Next to her, Rudy sucked in a breath, whispering, "Oh my god. It's happening, isn't it?"

"What is?" asked Mini.

Aiden closed his eyes as he turned back to the yaksha. He raised his hand, gesturing at the Potatoes. "This…"

Oh no, thought Aru.

"This is my band."

Rudy barely restrained a squeak.

The yaksha watched all this rather indifferently. He shrugged. "Very well. I'll give *you* this chance, son of Malini, but the judges will want some real proof that your band deserves a spot on the Final Stage, or you're out. Understand?"

The big red door moved back sulkily.

Part of Aru was delighted. They'd gotten in!

The other part was not so thrilled. Aru wouldn't exactly call herself musically gifted.…She could play what she called "the nose guitar"—humming a tune while holding down one nostril and pretending to strum the other side of her nose—but it was not very popular at parties. In fact, Brynne had said on more than one occasion that it would be a very useful torture technique for prisoner interrogations.

The yaksha swirled his hand in the air and a pink clipboard appeared. His sunglasses—which had magically levitated back onto his face—transformed into a pair of reading glasses.

"And what's the name of your band so I can add it to the roster?"

Aiden frowned. "Uh—"

"IT'S RUDY ROCKS!" shouted Rudy. "WE'RE KNOWN AS RUDY ROCKS. THERE IS NO OTHER NAME."

Rudy was so excited that Brynne had to grip his shoulders to hold him in one place. Even Mini, who hadn't smiled once since the incident with the World Elephants, cracked a grin.

Aiden sighed again and turned back to the yaksha. "What he said.... Our band is Rudy Rocks."

TWENTY-ONE

Rudy Rocks, Rudy Rocks, Rudy Rocks

The moment the Potatoes were admitted into the pavilion—with a brisk "Someone will be with you shortly. NEXT!"—its interior changed. From the outside, it had looked beautiful and tranquil, with its glass stage and the floating portal door.

Inside, however, it was *chaos*.

Aru could now see dozens of tents behind a giant semicircle of bleachers. Performers disappeared in and out of the flaps. Various acts were warming up on the field: jugglers, winged dancers, a trio of treelike creatures sprouting roses as they sang, and a band of fire performers who were literally walking flames. Wooden platforms with numbered flags floated in the air to the left of the main crystal stage.

"Those are definitely the audition stages," said Rudy, glaring at the other contestants. "We gotta crush the competition."

Just then, a boulder rolled up to them. It paused twenty feet away from Rudy. Craggy hollows opened in the middle of its surface, making what looked like a glowering face.

"*Most* of the competition," amended Rudy.

The boulder slowly rolled away.

"Forget the competition," said Brynne, pointing at the glass stage about a hundred feet away. "*That's* our goal."

Hovering above it, like a spotlight angling down, loomed the violet portal. Aru felt a lump in her throat when she looked at it. If they were lucky, it would be the last boundary between them and the labyrinth.

Aru stared at her empty hands. They were so close to the entrance, and yet Aru was no closer to getting her powers back.

"Those things do *not* look friendly," said Rudy.

Aru snapped back to attention. The yaksha had said that the stage was well protected, but it hadn't looked like it when they were standing in line. Now that they were past the threshold, she could see huge jaguars stalking around the stage. Were these the "living hurricanes"? Their eyes were nothing more than points of light, and their long teeth were as bright as polished knives.

"I could take them," said Brynne, her wind-mace choker glowing.

"But the rest of us can't," said Mini sullenly. "And that's not to mention who or whatever else around here might attack us if we try to make a run for the portal. Which means we've got to get through the audition round and onto that stage."

"Rudy Rocks, Rudy Rocks, Rudy Rocks," chanted Rudy happily until he caught Mini's glare. "Rudy Rocks . . . but for the common good?"

Mini did not look amused.

"Except we don't have any musical talent," said Aru.

"*Yet*," said Aiden, but he muttered it mostly to himself, his fingers tapping nervously against the strap of his backpack.

Brynne looked highly affronted. "I play the harp."

True, thought Aru. *But not well!*

She did not express that thought telepathically, but Brynne scowled at her anyway.

"I tried violin once," said Mini, frowning. "It gave me a nosebleed."

Aru was on the verge of asking how in the world that was even possible when she heard a commotion behind them. Three important-looking yakshas stalked past them, followed by an entourage of a dozen assorted Otherworld creatures.

"YOU'LL GET YOUR TURN! MAKE WAY!" shouted one of the entourage members. "JUDGES COMING THROUGH!"

Judges? Uh-oh, thought Aru.

The yakshas' padded-shoulder suits were identical except for the colors: one was bright gold, another a glowing silver, the third a dazzling array of glitter. All three judges wore sunglasses with elaborate frames that covered most of their dark-skinned faces. Some of the performers on the field tried to draw closer to them, but the entourage batted them away.

The judge in the silver suit shouted, "HOW IS LADY MOONLIGHT SUPPOSED TO JUDGE WITHOUT HER LUCKY TOE RING? HAS ANYONE SEEN IT?"

Half the entourage scattered across the field, dropping onto their bellies to inspect the grass.

The yaksha judge in the gold suit yelled, "THE LORD OF THE AFTERNOON DEMANDS THAT HIS ROOM BE SET AT SIXTY-SEVEN DEGREES *PRECISELY*, WITH A BOWL OF ONLY YELLOW STARBURSTS WAITING FOR HIM POST-JUDGMENT."

Aru made a face. *Only yellow Starbursts?* Gross. Truly the worst flavor in existence.

"THE ARTIST FORMERLY KNOWN AS STARLIGHT DEMANDS TO KNOW WHY THEY CAN'T REMEMBER THE THING THEY WERE JUST THINKING OF!" hollered the glittery yaksha. "DID SOMEONE STEAL THEIR LAST THOUGHT?"

"You must be Rudy Rocks," said a new voice.

Aru nearly jumped out of her skin when someone popped out of the ground. She was a petite milk-skinned yakshini with dark, liquid eyes framed by long lashes. She had a pert nose and an unsmiling mouth, and her black hair was cut in a severe bob around her chin. A pair of raven wings folded neatly on top of the sleeves of her red velvet suit and transformed into an embroidered feather pattern. An ID card on a lanyard around her neck read:

NATALIE D.
PROGRAM COORDINATOR, FINAL STAGE

"Yup, that's us!" said Rudy proudly as he shouldered his way to the front of the group.

Natalie didn't smile. Despite being shorter than all of them, she managed to look down her nose at the Potatoes. "The judges are *very* interested in your performance," she said before pivoting on her heel. "Follow me to your tent, please."

Natalie led them across the field. Soon they arrived at an unmarked tent on the eastern side. It was far larger on the inside than it was on the outside, and it reminded Aru of Brynne's penthouse living room. Except it had very few furnishings. There was only a bathroom stall, a tall mirror, a closet, a couple of chairs, and a coffee table.

"Meals will arrive three times a day," said Natalie, dropping a bunch of folders onto the coffee table. "If you have any dietary restrictions, please note that we do not care."

She reached into her jacket pocket and pulled out a pen. "By signing this agreement, you acknowledge that you are willing to submit to the rules and the decision of the yaksha judges for the opportunity to perform on the Final Stage, the only talent show in the multiverse dedicated to marking the apocalypse with the performance of a lifetime to, well, *end* all lifetimes," said Natalie calmly. "You hereby accept all risks inherent to performing in a doom-laden arena and release us from all liability in the event that you are—including but not limited to—maimed, transfigured, or reduced to ash."

Aru, Brynne, and Mini wore matching looks of horror.

"Uh, maybe we can discuss—" Aiden started to say before Rudy grabbed the pen.

"YES," he said.

"Never mind, then," said Aiden.

Natalie pulled back her sleeve to examine her watch. "Your audition will be in approximately twelve hours."

"*Twelve?!*" said Brynne. "But we're running out of time!"

Natalie pinned them with an icy look that even Nikita would've admired. "We all are, contestant."

The moment they were alone, Aiden plopped onto the couch and dropped his backpack between his feet. He tugged at his hair, his eyes wide and frantic. "We are so—"

"FORTUNATE!" said Rudy, hauling out all his crystals and setting them delicately on the table. "Okay, so I know you guys were just joking about not having any musical talent. What can you *really* do?"

"Well, I can play—"

"Aru, do *not* say nose guitar," said Brynne.

Aru harrumphed.

The look of joy on Rudy's face faded. "You really can't play anything?"

Brynne opened her mouth.

"Bee, do not say harp," said Mini.

Brynne closed her mouth. The three sisters glared at one another.

"If you don't have talent, they're going to throw us off the audition platform and we'll never get to the Final Stage!" said Rudy.

"Don't you think we know that?" demanded Aru. "Maybe we can do something else, like . . . interpretive dance?"

"No," said Rudy, Mini, and Brynne at the same time.

"Well, there goes my first, last, and only idea," said Aru. "It's not like we can magically summon up some talent."

"Actually, we can," said Aiden.

They turned to face him. He was quiet. Something glowed in his hands. Aru recognized it from earlier—a single note of music torn from the air by Malini herself.

It will let you call upon my family.

Aru remembered how a look of disgust had stolen across Aiden's face when his mom had said that.

The note glowed in Aiden's hand, releasing a perfume of song. It made Aru feel drowsy and delighted, like she'd spent the whole afternoon in the pool and was unwrapping a Popsicle to eat in the shade before she returned to the water.

"This will take us to my mother's family," said Aiden darkly. "The celestial musicians and dancers are known to give out blessings from time to time.... We can ask them for help. Twelve hours should be plenty of—"

Rudy let out a whoop. "First we started a band, and now we get to meet apsaras! I love quests. I'm gonna go fix my hair. The rest of you Potatoes should, too. Except Mini." He turned and beamed at her. "You don't need fixing."

Mini turned her head away from him.

Ouch, thought Aru. But Rudy hadn't seemed to notice.

Brynne put her hand on Aiden's shoulder. "It's going to be okay," she said. "They're your family."

Aiden snorted. "Not by choice."

"She wouldn't have given that gift to you if she didn't think they'd help," said Brynne softly.

She, as in Malini. Once she made the decision to marry a mortal man, Malini had to give up her place in the celestial court, and her exile from the Otherworld was permanent.

"Urvashi is your aunt, and she's nice enough," said Mini.

"She's actually my mom's cousin—it's different," said Aiden gruffly. "Not like the person my mom wants me to see."

"A terrible aunt?" asked Aru.

"Worse," said Aiden. He took a deep breath. "My grandmother."

Aiden closed his eyes. He curled his fingers around the musical note and the inside of the tent changed. Light slashed out between his knuckles, turning into bright ribbons that began to weave a staircase in midair. The stairs ended just before the tent's ceiling and dissolved into a golden pool. Far above, Aru could hear the distant sound of music.

Aiden stood up. For a few seconds, he just stared at the first step. Then he started to climb. Without looking back at them, he spoke in a toneless voice. "Let's go."

TWENTY-TWO

I'd Like to Speak to a Human Now

In Aru's imagination, the divine halls where the celestial dancers and musicians lived was like a constant party in the clouds. All the stories made it out to be a place bursting with joy and beauty and raucous songs, an endless heavenly revel. It was not supposed to be boring, she thought as she emerged from the sunny portal into a room that was utterly pristine, empty...and silent.

The apsara halls looked and felt a lot like a fancy spa.

The moment they stepped off the staircase, the Potatoes found themselves in a great hall. In the distance were slender reflecting pools and a gently gurgling fountain set into marble. Beyond that was a closed pair of ornate silver doors. The floor was solid marble. The walls were frosted sheets of glass on which hung dozens of plaques and framed headlines and ads:

> MENAKA'S SPA EARNS FIVE~STAR
> RATING ACROSS THE MULTIVERSE

> "A NEW AGE FOR A NEW APSARA,"
> PROCLAIMS SPA DIRECTOR MENAKA.
> "TIMES HAVE CHANGED, AND SO HAVE WE."

WELLNESS AND WONDER ABOUNDS IN FORMER PLEASURE HALL OF THE GODS! MAKE YOUR RESERVATION *TODAY*!

Aiden looked around the hall, frowning.

"Are we in the right place?" asked Rudy, deflating. "What about all the dancing? The—"

"Gorgeous apsaras?" suggested Mini.

"Yeah!" said Rudy and Brynne at the same time.

"I mean, no?" said Rudy when Mini raised her eyebrows.

Just then, a figure rose from the floor. She was just over four feet tall and made of clouds. A thick veil of mist formed her long dress. Her eyes were nothing more than depressions in the fog, but they still managed to feel warm and friendly. When she spoke, her voice was gentle and soothing, but it reminded Aru of one of those automated recordings.

"Welcome," she said. "I'm a cloud attendant. How may I assist you?"

"We're here to speak with Menaka," said Aiden.

"Do you have an appointment?"

"Well, no, but—"

"I would be happy to assist you in making a reservation," said the cloud attendant. "The next available appointment is in"—she paused, and her voice turned robotic—"three years. Would you like to book a massage, a facial, a sound bath, a private meditation, or—"

"No," said Aiden calmly. "We need to see Menaka today—"

"We also offer private music lessons with Tumburu, celebrated gandharva of the ages, and private dance instruction!

Converse with your ancestral heritage through art! Discounts are available—"

"Stop!" said Brynne loudly.

The attendant blinked. "Welcome," she said. "How may I assist you?"

Aru felt her eye twitch. Brynne looked like she was about to explode.

"We need to speak to Menaka," said Aiden again.

"Do you have an appointment?"

"That's it!" said Brynne, brandishing her wind mace. "I will render you *mist*—"

"Make it stop!" moaned Rudy.

"Do you have an appointment?" repeated the cloud attendant. "If not, I would be happy to assist you in making a reservation."

"I WANT TO SPEAK TO A CUSTOMER SERVICE REPRESENTATIVE!" yelled Mini.

A faint glow appeared in the hollows of the attendant's eyes. Aiden grabbed her hands and pressed the musical note into it. "Show this to Menaka immediately."

"Please wait by the Fountain of Compliments and someone will be with you shortly," said the cloud attendant.

"Fine," said Aiden.

A moment later, the attendant disappeared into the floor.

"How'd you know what to say, Mini?" asked Aru.

"Yeah, nice work!" said Rudy.

"Experience," said Mini. "I'm used to calling companies to get answers. I don't trust the safety advisories on products."

"Ah, that makes a lot of sense now," said Brynne.

Aru bit back a laugh as they followed Aiden down the hallway to the fountain.

"So...how's this going to work?" Aru asked him. "Are we going to be like, *Hey, give us a blessing,* or do we have to make a blessing reservation with Menaka?"

Even though she was still mad at Aiden, Aru just wanted him to crack a smile. But he was lost in his thoughts.

Don't take it personally, said Brynne through the mind link. *When his parents split up and his mom was having a rough time, he kept trying to get ahold of her apsara family members. But no matter what he did, they wouldn't answer.*

Yikes, thought Aru.

That's so cruel, said Mini. *Poor Wifey....*

Aiden walked past the pretty reflecting pools holding white and pink lotus blossoms and went straight to the Fountain of Compliments. Aru didn't think it looked very impressive. It was about ten feet high and carved out of marble. A stream of water gently arced from its plain spout and splashed into a circular basin.

Aiden had only just sat down on the edge of the fountain when the water began to froth.

"Hello!" said the fountain.

"Gods, not again," said Aiden, dropping his face into his hands.

"My, you are *gorgeous!*" said the fountain. "It's so wise of you to come to our spa to take care of your mental and emotional needs. Treat yo'self, am I right?"

Aiden looked at the fountain warily.

Rudy stepped up and peered into the water.

"Gosh, I *love* that outfit on you!" said the fountain.

"Really?" said Rudy, plucking at his shirt. "I was kinda on the fence about it...."

"Oh no, you definitely pull it off."

Aiden pushed himself off the fountain's edge and went to stand by the wall.

Aru didn't know why he was so annoyed. After all the yelling and shouting and other awfulness they'd experienced on this quest, who couldn't use a compliment to perk up their spirits?

Brynne approached the fountain next.

"You're so strong!" said the fountain. "I admire that. I bet people look up to you all the time."

Brynne grinned and stood a little straighter.

Mini joined her.

"I love those glasses on you—so chic."

Mini touched her frames self-consciously, a small smile on her face.

OKAY, MY TURN, thought Aru as she strolled up to the fountain's edge. She waited expectantly, but the fountain only gurgled a bit.

"Oh, wow," it finally said. "You're really *brave* ... to wear those clothes!"

Okay, that was technically a compliment.

"That's it?" she said.

"Clearly you don't care what other people think about you! I wish I had that confidence!"

Aru frowned. "And what's that supposed to mean?"

"You haven't peaked yet!" said the fountain. "So there's still time!"

"Time for *what?*" asked Aru.

The water seemed to be churning a lot faster, as if getting more nervous.

"Aren't you supposed to be the Fountain of Compliments?" demanded Aru.

"I'm trying!" said the fountain.

"Wow," said Aru.

"Aru, did you break the fountain?" asked Brynne, roaring with laughter.

In the distance, Aiden was laughing, too. This was *not* the way she'd imagined making him smile.

"Maybe there were just too many people!" said Mini, moving in front of Aru.

"Has anyone ever told you your smile is somewhat above average?" returned the fountain.

"Thanks," said Mini flatly.

"Okay, that's it," said Aru. "I hope people throw dirty pennies in you!"

The fountain splashed Aru, and she spluttered as the water hit her face.

At that moment, the silvery doors swung open. The cloud attendant had returned. Beyond her, the pattern of glass walls and reflective pools continued.

"Lady Menaka will admit three people only," said the attendant.

"I'll stay here," said Mini. "I might mess something up again, like when I touched the door."

Mini, that wasn't your fault, said Aru.

Anyone would've made the same mistake, said Brynne.

But you guys *didn't*, said Mini. *I'm staying behind. Please don't ask me again.*

Mini drew up a wall in her mind. When Aru tried to say something else to her, she got an instant headache. Ouch.

"Me too!" said Rudy, beaming at Mini. "I'll stay!"

From the cloud bank, a low marble table appeared. It held platters of cut-up mangoes and guavas and slices of banana dipped in chocolate. There were pitchers of sparkling fruit juice, too. A pair of plushy robes and slippers peeled off the cloud bank, along with two reclining chairs.

"Oooh...hello, spa day," said Rudy, rubbing his hands together.

"Kindly follow me," said the attendant to Aru, Brynne, and Aiden.

As they followed her down the cloudy pathway, Brynne kept trying to catch Aiden's eye, but his gaze was fixed ahead.

Do you know anything about Aiden's grandmother? Aru asked Brynne through the mind link.

Superpowerful, super-old apsara, said Brynne. *And really strict. But that's about it.*

Old and powerful and mean. Great, thought Aru. None of these family reunions ever seemed to go well. And yet the name Menaka tickled something in the back of Aru's head. She felt as if she'd heard it before, but she couldn't remember when.

Before long, the cloud attendant stopped in front of a pair of golden doors. They were engraved with scenes, and when Aru looked closer, she saw that the pictures actually *moved*. Beautiful apsaras danced before a host of gods. In another image, an apsara flew down to earth toward a sage who was deep in meditation. In the stories Aru's mom had told her, every time a man renounced the world and began to perform a lot of religious rites, he gained power. Sometimes too *much* power. In that case, the gods would send a heavenly nymph to distract the sage.

When Aru was younger, that part had always confused her. "What do you mean 'distract'?" Aru had once asked her mom. "Did she start blasting music? Throw water in the guy's face?"

At that, Krithika Shah grew deeply uncomfortable. Like she'd stepped on an anthill and still had to continue with polite conversation. "Not exactly…"

The cloud attendant knocked lightly on the golden doors. They swung outward, revealing a dimly lit room.

"The Lady Menaka will see you now."

TWENTY-THREE

The Lady Menaka

As they stepped inside to meet Aiden's grandmother, Aru felt a lump in her throat. She'd never met her own grandparents. Krithika Shah's family had cut them off before Aru was born, and by the time they were willing to reconcile, Aru was six years old. She remembered getting all dressed up and waiting for her mom at the bottom of the staircase. They were supposed to go on a four-hour drive to meet them.

While she waited, Aru had imagined what her grandparents would be like—all crinkly smiles and pockets full of candy, and milk and cookies at night with a bedtime story, the way it looked in movies. It was almost two hours later before Aru learned she wasn't going to meet them after all. Her grandfather had suffered a stroke and her grandmother didn't want any visitors that day. When Krithika got the news, she'd been so upset that she forgot about Aru waiting for her downstairs. Krithika had felt awful about it and had apologized a thousand times. Aru had forgiven her, of course, but she'd never forgotten that awful plunge from hope to disappointment.

Hope *hurt*.

Aru felt each one of her hopes as if it were a fresh bruise. She hoped she could earn back her lightning bolt. She hoped she would make the right choices. She hoped there would be a light at the end of the darkness.

Maybe it would start with Menaka, she thought. Maybe Aiden's grandmother would be like the crinkle-eyed, smiley ones in all the stories. . . . Maybe it would be okay.

"Why have you come here?" snarled a voice in the dimness.

Aru, who had been lost in thought and staring at her own feet, looked up suddenly. At first, she couldn't see the speaker. The room was vast enough to hold a dozen elephants, and its walls seemed to expand and contract, as if it were breathing.

Unlike the rest of the apsara wellness center, this place had an ancient look and feel to it. The floor was dark wood, scratched and dimpled by furniture and footpaths. The back wall, more than a hundred feet away, was shrouded with fog. In the gloom Aru could make out what she thought were large chairs with sheets thrown over them. The wall on the right moved closer, until it was a dozen feet from Aru, and on it she saw a faded tapestry where twelve apsaras performed an intricate dance to the accompaniment of the celestial musicians, including one at the forefront who had the head of a horse.

"I said, *why have you come here?*"

There was a *whoosh* above their heads. Aru looked up just in time to see a woman descend from the ceiling. Her outfit was simple enough—a white linen shift with matching pants and a flowing *dupatta* that hung from her elbows—but on the apsara, it looked worthy of royalty.

The word *beautiful* wasn't adequate to describe Menaka. Her shiny black hair cascaded to her ankles. She had a long, regal nose and full red lips, proud cheekbones, and dark brown skin. The color of her eyes, Aru noticed, was identical to Aiden's—like the surface of the ocean beneath moonlight. Although Menaka had to be *way* older than his mom, not a single wrinkle marred her skin.

"*That's* your *grandmother?*" asked Brynne, her jaw dropping a bit.

"Not by choice," said Aiden.

Menaka huffed. She flicked her wrist and a throne from the back of the room shot forward, catching her as she sank into it.

"That you dislike me comes as no surprise," said Menaka, looking not at Aiden but somewhere beyond him. "Which begs the question, why are you here? Why did you use the note of music? It was intended for your mother alone."

Her voice was deep, as if weighed down by something. It didn't match her youthful appearance. But it was lovely nevertheless.

Aiden stiffened, and his fingers nervously tapped his camera strap. "Maybe she thought you wouldn't answer," said Aiden coldly. "You never did before."

"She knows why I did not," said Menaka. "When I heard the note, I thought..." She shook her head. "Never mind. It was clever of her to give you that."

"You asked why I came," said Aiden, stepping forward. "My friends and I are in need of your blessing."

"For what? Beauty? Fame?" asked Menaka, tilting her head. "As the child of Malini, you already have the potential for both. Not even your human father's mediocrity can change that. Or are you to be the exception among apsara descendants?"

Aiden's grip on his camera strap turned white-knuckled. His mouth pinched to a thin line as if he was holding himself back.

Jeez. Grandma is really going in for the kill, said Aru through the mind link.

Makes sense, said Brynne. *Aiden said she was the worst.*

"What we need is a blessing of musical talent," said Aiden.

"Why?" asked Menaka quietly. "From what I gather, you already possess quite the voice. Just like her."

Aiden's eyebrows shot up his forehead. "How would you know that?"

Menaka's face turned cold and expressionless. "Answer me. Do not tell me you have come here on some whim—"

"Not *whim*," said Brynne, stepping up and putting her hand on Aiden's shoulder. *"War."*

Still Menaka kept her eyes averted. "There is always a war."

"Not like this one," said Aiden.

"This time, the fate of the gods hangs in the balance," said Brynne. "If the Sleeper gets the nectar of immortality, he will take all its power for himself." She slapped her palm with Gogo, emphasizing every word. "He'll destroy the world. We're fighting on the side of the gods. You *have* to help us."

Aiden winced, and Aru immediately realized that was a bad choice of words.

"Have to?" repeated Menaka in a poisonous voice. Her hair slowly billowed around her shoulders as she gradually rose off her throne, still in a seated position. "I do not *have* to do anything. We apsaras no longer do the gods' bidding. We fought for our own choices, and no one can take them from us."

Brynne scowled. "But we—"

"I am not addressing you, mortal child," said Menaka, turning her chin. "You are no one to me."

Brynne looked infuriated. *"I am a—"*

Don't! warned Aru. *We're supposed be undercover!*

But it didn't matter.

"Trust me, I already know, and I do not care," said Menaka, waving her hand. "A reincarnated Pandava, yes? Those flimsy camouflage petals won't work on me. Judging by the look of you, it appears Bhima's temper was inseparable from his soul. Congratulations."

Brynne glared directly at Aru, wanting her to share in the outrage, but Aru's thoughts were being pulled in another direction. Menaka's name had stirred something in her memories. Aru kept thinking about those golden doors and their engravings of apsaras performing for the gods and occasionally descending to earth to "distract" mortal sages.

Brynne looked as if she was going to say something else when Aiden put out his hand and stepped in front of her.

You know this is not our fight, said Aru.

Brynne responded with a mental growl.

"Just give us the blessing and we'll go," said Aiden. "We'll never have to see each other again."

Menaka didn't look at him when she spoke. Instead, her gaze was fixed on the wall tapestry, which had once more moved farther away. "I could do that with ease, but it is not going to happen."

"Why not?" demanded Aiden. "It's the *least* you can do. You haven't given me or my mom anything else."

"Your mother did not tell you how it works, did she?"

"How what works?" asked Aiden.

Menaka laughed. "In order for an apsara to grant you a

blessing, you must approach with at least a drop of love and understanding in your heart. You must harbor no ill will, or the blessing will go awry. Look at you. You cannot manage that."

"Look at *me?* You haven't looked at me *once*," said Aiden heatedly. "Is it because I'm only half apsara? Is that it?"

Slowly, Menaka turned her eyes in his direction. Aru saw that they shone with tears. "Is that what you have thought this whole time?"

"What other reason could there be?" demanded Aiden. "You wouldn't see my mom even when she needed you."

"It was not possible," said Menaka, growing agitated. "Malini understood what she was doing when she left our realm to marry the mortal and give up her celestial essence. It was her choice."

"Choice?" said Aiden. For the first time, his skin started to glow. "That wasn't a choice! That was an *ultimatum!*"

His feet rose off the ground and his glow turned brighter, sharper. Aru winced and turned her head to avoid looking at Aiden directly. In front of them, Menaka levitated even higher off her throne. Her apsara glow bathed the room in light. The tapestry on the wall rippled and changed. In the new image, Aru saw an apsara who looked like Menaka fleeing from a sage who had flung out his hand. Menaka was carrying a baby in her arms.

"Uh...Aiden?" said Brynne, tugging on his pant leg.

But Aiden wasn't listening. "You told Mom she couldn't come back. *Why?* Because you can't stand the sight of me? You abandoned her when she needed you—"

"Do not speak to me of abandonment, child!" said Menaka, outraged. "You know nothing of what you speak."

"HELLO?" said Brynne, waving her hand in front of Aru's eyes. "What are you staring at? We've got to stop this!"

Aru looked up at Menaka, a story from long ago clicking in her head. "You're Shakuntula's mother, aren't you?"

The light in the room dimmed and then flared as Menaka swung around to face Aru. "What did you say?"

"Shakuntula," repeated Aru. "I . . . I remember that story. My mom used to tell it to me when I was a kid."

Menaka slowly drifted down. Aru risked a glance at Aiden, who was still hovering above them, his skin faintly aglow and his eyes furious.

"Shakuntula?" asked Aiden. "My mother never mentioned—"

"She was long before your mother's time," said Menaka, her face stricken with grief. "I did not want history to repeat itself, and yet it did."

"What do you mean?" asked Aiden. "What happened to her?"

Menaka's feet landed softly on the floor. She looked toward the tapestry, her eyes distant. "She fell in love, which, for the descendant of an apsara, is never a simple thing. We are plagued with curses. With prophecy . . ."

Out of the corner of her eye, Aru felt Aiden's gaze swivel to her before he looked away.

"And with pain," continued Menaka. "Her lover was cursed to forget her, and many years passed before they were finally reunited. I tried . . . I tried to bring her to the heavens to live with me forever, but the gods would not allow it. Her choice made her mortal. It didn't matter who I was or what I did . . . I could not protect my daughter from death."

The room changed with Menaka's words. The images on the tapestry slipped down the wall and spread across the ornate tile.

"You do not know what it was like for us back then," said Menaka, staring at the floor. "When the gods demanded that we disrupt a sage's penances to prevent them from gaining too much power, who paid the price? *Apsaras.* Some of us were turned to stone for thousands of years. Others lost their hearts—"

Aru watched the scene unfurl on the ground. Menaka, too, had visited a sage, not intending to fall in love with him. After their child was born the sage realized that she had been sent to deceive him, and he banished her from his sight.

"Others have lost children," said Menaka softly. "In the olden days, some of us married human kings. We spent years together in happiness. But no matter how wise and kind they were, they always died. And eventually, no matter how brilliant, pious, and beautiful our offspring were, they died too, and we were always left behind."

Aiden fell gracefully to the ground, his glow disappearing. For the first time, Menaka lifted her eyes and looked directly into his face. Her expression was raw and almost hungry, as if she would never be able to look at him enough, and that hurt.

"When Malini chose to leave, she became mortal. She chose death," said Menaka. "I could not endure that slow grief again."

Brynne's eyes went wide, her glance flicking between Aiden and his grandmother.

"You ask if it is because you are only half immortal that I cannot bear to look at you," said Menaka, turning her face away again. "But that is not it. It is because *I* am fully *immortal* that I cannot bear it."

Aru watched as Aiden's mood changed. The hard set of his mouth softened. His hand went to Shadowfax, then stopped. Aru couldn't guess his thoughts in that moment—it was like a storm was raging in his head.

"Now that you know all this, can you really bring yourself to ask me for a blessing?" challenged Menaka. She shook her head, a haughty slant returning to her mouth, her spine straighter. The images vanished from the floor and the tapestry resumed its faded appearance. "Or will you curse my name and leave this place?"

Aiden nodded at Brynne, who took a step back. Watching out of the corner of her eye, Menaka braced herself as Aiden walked forward. Slowly he knelt to the ground and pressed his hands together in respectful greeting.

"Menaka...Nani..." said Aiden, his voice catching. "We seek your blessing."

Menaka turned toward him, her lips parted in awe. She touched her heart, as if it were feeling each word Aiden had uttered. When she gazed at him, there was something like hope in her face.

"Then I shall give it."

This was one of those moments when Aru couldn't decide if she wanted to shout at people or demand popcorn and watch the drama unfold. She kept looking back and forth between Menaka and Aiden, who, in Aru's opinion, were now locked in the Most Painful Small Talk of the Century.

"So, your mother. Is she...well?" asked Menaka cautiously.

Aiden nodded. "Yes."

"Good."

"Good," said Aiden. "She started taking up baking."

At the same time, Menaka asked, "Has she any new hobbies?"

"Baking? That's...good," added Menaka.

"Yeah," said Aiden.

WHY WON'T THEY JUST HUG SO WE CAN MOVE ON WITH OUR LIVES? demanded Aru through the mind link.

Grandmother and grandson were now locked in an *I'm-not-staring-I'm-staring-at-you* contest.

OKAY, I'M JUST GOING TO SAY IT—

No, Aru! scolded Brynne. *Leave them alone!*

I can't take this.

"So, Aiden, how much time do we have?" asked Aru.

He frowned, glancing at his watch before his face went a little pale. "We've got two hours until our audition for the Final Stage."

"TWO?" repeated Aru. "That's not enough time to learn some kinda magical instrument thing!"

"Trust me, that's plenty," said Menaka, snapping her fingers.

On the wall thirty feet to her right, a golden archway appeared. Aru caught the flicker of screens in the distance, and the muffled sound of music.

"There's only one person who can help you," Menaka said. "Come."

"We also brought our friends Mini and Rudy…" said Brynne, gesturing to the front door.

Menaka closed her eyes, and when she opened them, she smiled. "They've been summoned. They'll meet up with us. Now come. Tumburu, lord of the gandharvas, is waiting."

The hallway was very short and very dark. The walls seemed to function like two-way mirrors, allowing the Potatoes a glimpse of the inner workings of the apsara wellness spa. Here and there, Aru saw Otherworld denizens in the middle of yoga classes or struggling through cardio choreography sessions led by apsaras who floated through the studio and adjusted people's posture. Aiden walked ahead, a few paces behind Menaka, who kept sneaking glances at him, though he didn't seem to notice.

In a matter of moments, the hallway opened into a large

recording studio. To the right, enclosed by a panel of mirrors, stood a platform with microphones and floating headphones. In the middle of the room was a circular mixing board with a thousand lit-up switches and buttons and a huge wingback chair facing away from them. Two walls were covered with instruments. There was a guitar-like sitar and an elongated drum called a tabla, along with a *venu* and a *bansari*, two kinds of wooden flutes. Aru recognized them from her mom's exhibits on Hindustani and Carnatic musical traditions.

The last wall held multiple television screens, all of them showing the same video feed. A blue-skinned yaksha in a sparkling suit spoke into the camera: "We're coming to you *live* from the audition field of THE FINAL STAGE, the multiverse's *only* talent show for what may very well turn out to be the *last* and *final* age!" The yaksha let slip a frantic laugh. "Which is fine! Everything is…*fine*. So, um, let's meet the newest contestants, shall we?"

"WHAT DRIVEL," groaned a voice from the chair.

"Tumburu, I have some people I'd like to introduce you to," said Menaka.

Aru braced herself as the chair slowly swiveled around. She knew that a gandharva was a celestial musician, but she'd never heard the name Tumburu before they arrived here. Was he going to be awful and condescending? What if he refused to help them?

Do you know anything about this guy? asked Aru through the mind link.

Nope, said Brynne. *But he's a gandharva, so he's probably going to be super tall, super handsome, and—*

TWENTY-FOUR

A Horse

Tumburu was a horse. Well, at least he had the head of a horse, which was not what Aru had expected. Short, glossy sea-green hair covered his face and neck. His mane, which was sea-foam green with white ends, had been artfully coiffed to one side. From the neck down, he was a well-dressed man. A white silk scarf hung around his throat, and beneath it he was wearing a navy Nehru jacket with golden cuffs, black pants, and a pair of satin loafers with the words THESE COST A LOT embroidered along their tops.

Tumburu must have been just as surprised as Aru, because when he saw them he skittered backward in his chair, hand clutching his scarf.

"OH, DEAR LORDS!" he exclaimed.

A moment later, there was a loud *pop!* as Mini and Rudy appeared beside Aru. Mini was wearing the same clothes as before and she still looked a little sad, but she flashed a smile when she saw Aru and Brynne. *That didn't take too long,* Mini said through the mind link. *How'd it go?*

Aru was about to respond when Rudy groaned. He was

draped in a cloud robe and wearing a face mask. "I was *right* in the middle of a meditation session." Two cucumber slices peeled off his eyelids and hit the floor. "HORSE!" he yelled, jumping back.

"EW!" said Tumburu, cringing before he looked at Menaka. "My dear, what in the world is this? Why are you accosting me with"—he wiggled his fingers at them—"*lower life-forms?*"

"Calm down. We're just teenagers," said Aiden flatly.

"I stand by my choice of words."

Touché, thought Aru.

"Tumburu," said Menaka, pointing to Aiden. "*This* is my grandson. And these young ladies . . . are the Pandavas."

"Don't mind me," muttered Rudy. "I'm just a prince among peasants."

"They need a blessing of celestial musical talent," said Menaka, talking over Rudy. "And I have sanctioned it."

"A musical blessing?" repeated Tumburu. "Whatever for?"

Behind Tumburu, the now-muted televisions showed auditions for the Final Stage. A group of naginis in matching outfits and glittery eye makeup hissed and flared their cobra hoods at the indifferent judges before disappearing in a cloud of smoke. Tumburu followed Aru's line of sight. He turned his head, looking at the monitors and then back at the Potatoes.

"You're joking."

Brynne's lip curled. "Yeah, we're trying to prevent the end-of-the-world war. Hilarious."

"But what does *that* abomination of entertainment have to do with war?" asked Tumburu, watching the screens.

Just then, the cameras panned out from the auditions, revealing the crystalline Final Stage and the violet portal hanging above it. The portal that was all that stood between the Pandavas and any hope for a future. Aru's heart sank. Maybe the Sleeper and Kara had already gotten hold of the nectar of immortality. Maybe this whole thing was a waste of time.

Understanding flickered in Tumburu's eyes. "You wish to enter the labyrinth and make it a last battlefield," he said in quiet awe. "But surely you can just go there directly? Aren't there buzzing, deadly whatnoticals you might avail yourselves of?"

"You mean our godly weapons?" asked Brynne, touching her choker.

Gogo gave off a faint and, Aru thought, offended glow.

"Sure," said Tumburu. "We of the heavens rarely bother to concern ourselves with human affairs. Though I have to admit that *this*"—he paused to look at the screens, which were now showing a pair of jugglers being forced off the audition platform with flamethrowers—"is concerning on many levels. First and foremost, do they really believe that, if the world is ending, a person wants to watch professional *clowns* before he shuffles off this mortal coil?"

Menaka coughed loudly.

"And secondly," said Tumburu, removing his glasses to clean them with his scarf, "I'm simply not ready to bid farewell to existence. There's far too much music still to experience. Too many rhythms begging to exist! Too much inspiration that I must guide into the universe!"

As he said this, he raised his arms dramatically in the air. Then he brandished his eyeglasses at them. "So, what's the meaning of this?" asked Tumburu. "Why can't you simply... flee to the labyrinth? As I understand it, the maze will certainly allow entrance to those with a godly mark of approval."

Beside Aru, Mini looked crestfallen. Aru knew her sister

was thinking about how they should've already been inside it by now ... but it wasn't only her fault. Aru felt the burden of guilt, too. All the wrong choices she'd made reflected back at her like a poisonous mirror. There were a thousand things she should've done differently.

"Our weapons were destroyed," said Brynne before touching her wind mace. "Well, most of them."

Tumburu gasped. "And so you find yourself cursed and forlorn? Cast out of all that was familiar?"

Aru's ears turned hot. "This isn't some kind of joke, okay?"

"Oh, my dear, I am *not* joking!" said Tumburu. "Trust me, I've *been* there. It was awful."

He swept a hand in front of the televisions behind him, whickering sadly. Behind him, a creature took shape on the screens. It was huge—the size of ten oaks stacked atop one another. Its flesh was the color of expired yogurt, and yellow fangs curled out from underneath its flared nostrils. A mane of neon-orange hair fell down its back and arms, and it wore a loincloth of jaguar pelt.

"I mean, *look at me*," said Tumburu. "Look at what I was *forced* to wear!"

"Wait a minute.... That's you?" asked Rudy.

"Well, *was*," said Tumburu. "Lord Kubera cursed me to become a demon—it's a long story, but he and I eventually made up eons ago. Rather unfortunately, I was cursed to be impervious to weapons. Then I ran into the god king Rama and his brother, Laxmana, and I had to do the whole *Roar!-I-kill-you-now* thing, even though I really did *not* want to."

Mini raised her hand. "But if you couldn't be killed by any weapons, how did you ... uh ..."

"Get liberated from my mortal existence as that Hell Muppet?" asked Tumburu.

Aru knew better than to say YUP.

"Well, it wasn't pretty," said Tumburu, scratching the end of his muzzle. "I think they had to bury me alive?"

Rudy looked horrified.

"I don't remember much of that existence, to be fair," said Tumburu. He waved his hands, and the television screens returned to live coverage of the Final Stage auditions. "What I *do* remember, however, is the curious beauty of the mortal lands. The poetry of thunderstorms. The song of the wind in the trees. The loveliest ragas one could imagine ... Why, it was those recollections of my mortal existence that I used to inspire other musicians who won my favor. So I suppose even the worst moments in one's existence have some purpose."

Tumburu's words wound through Aru. She wanted so badly to believe that there was a reason they'd lost their weapons and were down to the final days to fix things, but she wasn't sure what it could be. Brynne had already managed to prove herself, but what about Aru and Mini? And even if Aru succeeded, what would she *do* with her lightning bolt?

In the back of her head, Lord Agni's warning words echoed softly. *All the weapons in the world cannot help you if you do not know what you'll do with them. What will you do, Aru Shah?*

"So ..." said Aiden, shoving his hands in his pockets. "Does that mean you'll help us win this competition?"

Menaka, who was floating above them, looked down at him. Aiden couldn't see it, but pride glowed on the apsara's face. Tumburu leaned forward in his chair. He steepled his hands for a moment and then snapped his fingers. The instruments lifted off the wall one by one and circled the Potatoes. The strings of the sitar began to vibrate. The flutes whistled. The drums began a steady *thump, thump, thump.* It was all very beautiful and majestic, but also creepy, and Aru had a brief vision of what it might be like to be stalked by a harmonica in the dark....

"Oh, yes," said Tumburu. "I can see it now.... The melody is all coming together. You will be my grand project. You will be the greatest band the world has ever seen—"

Rudy clapped eagerly.

"I will select an instrument for each of you, and forevermore you will be considered a *master* player of it," said Tumburu.

Aru's eyes went wide.

"We are about to *break* the world with all the talent I shall bestow upon you!" said Tumburu, rising from his chair.

"You mean *save* the world," said Aiden.

Tumburu scowled. "Yes, that, too."

TWENTY-FIVE

ME? Shocked at This Latest Instance of Disrespect? NEIGH!

Brynne was the first to be matched with a talent.

Tumburu had her stand in the middle of the small circular stage right across from his mixing board. The original four instruments had been joined by others—an electric guitar, a tambourine, a xylophone, and a keyboard—all floating in the air.

"Do you possess any musical skill?" asked Tumburu, flexing his fingers.

"I play the harp," said Brynne proudly. "I'm pretty good at it."

Aru was glad she wasn't the only one holding back a wince. Mini studied the ground. Even Aiden suddenly looked very preoccupied with the wall.

"She does?" said Rudy. "I've never heard—"

Aiden shushed him.

From there, Tumburu's line of questioning proceeded at rapid-fire pace.

"Favorite color?"

"Blue."

"Fire or water?"

"Fire," said Brynne.

"Clean bathrooms or vacuum the house?"

"Vacuum," said Brynne. "But what does this have to do with—"

"Final question!" said Tumburu, pressing his hands together. "Is cereal a soup?"

This time Aru did wince.

Brynne looked outraged. Wind began to gather around her ankles, ruffling the hem of her shirt and the ends of her hair. "Are you serious? What kind of gastronomic blasphemy—"

"For you, the backbone of the group, your instrument is..." said Tumburu, clapping, "THE TABLA!"

A dozen feet above them, the two-sided hand drum perked up at the sound of its name. It somersaulted in the air toward Brynne. She threw up her arms to block it, but the drum seemed to take that as an invitation and thudded against her palms. A pink light gloved Brynne's hands, from the tips of her fingers to her wrists, before vanishing.

Brynne frowned. She rotated her wrists. The tabla hovered before her, quivering.

Tentatively, Brynne's fingers tapped the drum skin—slowly at first, then faster. Her wrist flexed as the rhythm sped up. Aru found herself nodding along to the beat. Even the instruments above them began to sway happily.

"Whoa!" said Brynne, staring at her hands in awe.

The straps on the sides of the drums stretched as if they were grinning.

"Now someone will actually compliment your musical abilities!" said Tumburu.

"I said I could play the harp," said Brynne.

Tumburu blinked, then repeated, "Now someone will actually compliment your musical abilities!"

Brynne opened her mouth to protest, but Tumburu was already waving his hand to usher her off the stage. "You there! Glasses! Let's go!"

Mini startled. With a slight *hmpf* she pushed her glasses up the bridge of her nose and walked to the circular stage.

"Oh yes, I see it now," said Tumburu, circling her. "You're the enigma of the band. You're the mystery! The girl with secrets behind her eyes!"

"Um—"

"It's settled," said Tumburu, pointing into the air.

An electric keyboard hovering just above Menaka zipped out a quick scale and snaked toward Mini. The moment her fingers brushed the keys, a bluish light surrounded her hands before sinking into her skin. Mini gasped. She closed her eyes and lifted her hands off the piano before slamming them down. Her digits flew over the ivory, and a wild, beautiful tune filled the air. Aru's jaw dropped. Mini's mom had made her take piano lessons, but until now, the only thing Aru had heard Mini play was "Chopsticks."

"How long do these blessings last?" asked Aru enviously.

Brynne shrugged and looked at Aiden, but it wasn't he who answered.

"A blessing given from the apsaras lasts forever," said Menaka.

The whole time Tumburu was working his magic, the apsara hadn't said much. She floated just shy of *close* to Aiden. While Aiden was watching Tumburu and the instruments, Aru noticed that his grandmother looked like she wanted to start talking at any moment. In the end, though, Menaka stayed silent. Maybe she thought that would be the wiser thing to do.

The idea saddened Aru. She thought of all the times she'd wished that she and her mom had said things out loud. Maybe if they had, things would be different now. As a former (and rather excellent) liar herself, Aru knew that, sometimes, speaking the truth felt like wrenching a thorn out of your side. But doing the opposite meant pretending it wasn't there. And that made every single step ache.

It was no way to live.

"Good, good," said Tumburu, ushering Mini off the stage. He stretched his neck from one side to the other, tossing his mane behind him, and then pointed at Rudy. "I suppose you're the next one in need of some musical talent?"

Rudy looked highly affronted. "I don't *need* musical talent. I already have plenty."

"I've heard that one before," said Tumburu, rolling his eyes.

Aiden's eyebrows rose a little. "Well, actually..."

Rudy lowered his backpack and took out his various rocks—a chunk of quartz, a raw ruby, amethyst pebbles, and three sapphires. He closed his eyes, and the jewels levitated. "Here's *my* music."

One by one, they lit up at his touch. Rudy's music—his *true* music—had always been different. It was less of a tune and more of a truth. It captured a beautiful feeling rather than a frenzied beat. The amethysts released a sound like rain hitting a window, and Aru thought of all the sleepy, happily boring times in the car when she'd watched raindrops race down the glass. Next came the sapphires, unleashing a sound like ocean waves crashing against the shore. Then the ruby, with the crackling of flames. Last, the quartz, which overlaid the other sounds with a Bollywood song Aru couldn't remember the name of—a slow build, a lash of heat, the majesty of the sea, and the familiarity of an old melody. It was the sort of music that made Aru want to cry for no reason. Rudy let the rocks play for about fifteen seconds before cutting them off with a snap of his fingers.

"And that's just a sample," he said haughtily.

"That was amazing," said Aiden.

Tumburu stared at Rudy. "YOU ARE MY STAR! You are the GENIUS behind the group!"

Rudy puffed up a little. "I know."

Tumburu started pacing in a circle. "You know, we could make this act really *big*. We could sell out stadiums across the multiverse. Maybe I can talk to Ixtab—and yes, I am referring to *the* queen of Xib'alb'a—about a concert next time we meet up for happy hour...."

"Tumburu..." said Menaka quietly.

The gandharva sighed. "Once more, my dreams have to take a backseat."

"To the apocalypse," added Aiden.

Tumburu ignored this and turned his attention back to the group. "Well, who's next, then?" He looked at Aiden. "There's nothing to be improved upon with you, and you've got the look of a lead singer."

The tops of Aiden's cheeks turned red. "Okay."

"Which leaves...you," said Tumburu, rounding on Aru.

She perked up, rising on her tiptoes a bit. Everything was absolutely awful, but *what if she could play the electric guitar?* That would be amazing. She would be the stuff of legends! Maybe she should get highlights in her hair....

"Come forward, please," said Tumburu.

Aru walked to the stage.

"How would you describe yourself?" asked Tumburu.

Aru considered this. And then, in a very measured voice, she said, "Kind."

Brynne snorted. "You mean sneaky."

"Uh, imaginative," said Mini, a touch defensively. "*Very* imaginative."

No one asked you to elaborate! Aru said through the mind link, but her sisters only laughed.

"Kinda weird," said Rudy.

Aiden glanced at her. The corner of his mouth tipped up. "Chaotic."

"Ignore them!" said Aru, trying to catch Tumburu's eye, but the celestial musician wasn't listening.

"Feral," he said, stroking the end of his muzzle. "That odd, quirky factor—"

"Electric guitar!" said Aru. *"Please!"*

"Something almost comical to look at—"

"Wait, no," said Aru.

But it was too late. An object sailed out of the ring of instruments. It was rather large and shaped like a crescent moon. With the light behind it, Aru couldn't tell what it was at first. *Another drum?* she hoped. She could live with that. Aru reached out and caught it one-handed. That same pink light gloved both of her hands. It felt like someone had outlined her muscles in glitter. Movement jerked through her body and she found herself raising her arms, one hand striking the instrument. It made a loud jangle that was joyous and annoying at the same time.

It was—Aru realized with dawning horror—a *tambourine.*

"You're joking," said Aru.

Across the room, Brynne and Mini had fallen against each other laughing. Rudy winced and Aiden shook his head sadly.

But there was no time to linger on the fact that, for the rest of her mortal existence, Aru Shah would forever be known as someone who played the tambourine. Menaka cleared her throat. "Your audition draws near," she said.

Aiden checked his watch. "One hour left."

Tumburu sniffed. "Go make me proud. Remember, if they ask who your manager is, it's Tumburu, lord of the gandharvas, et cetera, et cetera."

"There is one more thing you must do," Menaka said to Aiden. "You cannot simply show up on a stage without a plan. You must unify the audience, Aiden. Sing a truth to sell an illusion. The sincerity of your message will see you through."

"Sing a truth?" he repeated hesitantly.

Menaka nodded. "Something you have told no one. Perhaps something that frightens you to your core. In such honesty there is powerful magic."

"Okay," said Aiden, a determined look crossing his face. "I will."

"Go, go, go!" said Tumburu, pointing to the screens.

The television camera was focused on the latest contestants who had disappointed the judges. This time, it was a group of break-dancing cave yakshas. They seemed angry, but Aru couldn't really tell for sure because of their sunglasses.

Tumburu pinched the air in front of him, and a small gateway opened up about ten feet away from where the Potatoes stood.

"This will take you back from whence you came," said Menaka, turning to leave.

"Wait," said Aiden.

He lifted Shadowfax and frowned as he adjusted some settings before reaching into its enchanted screen. A moment later, he pulled out a photograph. Aru caught a glimpse of it as he handed it to Menaka. It was an image of Aiden and his mom.

"If you...If you want it," he said awkwardly.

Menaka touched the photo reverently, tears shining in her eyes. "I haven't looked upon her face in almost..."

"Sixteen years?" guessed Aiden.

Menaka nodded.

"Well," said Aiden. "You know where we are if you want to find us. But if you don't"—he paused, taking a deep breath—"I won't hold it against you. Anymore."

Menaka bowed her head. "Thank you."

Brynne gently put her hand on Aiden's shoulder. "Ready?"

"Yeah," he said.

Rudy walked to the portal first.

"Should you ever want an internship, find me," Tumburu said to him.

Rudy grinned and disappeared. Next went Brynne with her tabla under her arm, muttering, "I *can* play the harp." Mini followed with her electric keyboard, and then Aiden.

Aru, still distracted by her newfound talent for tambourine, was about to join them when Menaka drifted forward and touched her shoulder.

"A moment of your time, daughter of the gods," she said.

Aru looked up at her, confused.

Menaka's dark eyes met hers. Her mouth was pinched with anxiety. "You knew who I was," she said. "That is a rare thing for me."

Aru wasn't sure what to say, so she stayed quiet as Menaka seemed to work up the courage to speak.

"I cannot predict what will happen, whether the world might be remade, and what place I might have in the future. I do not know, after this war is done, whether anyone will remember who I was," said Menaka quietly. She held out a fist. When she opened it, Aru saw a single golden earring gleaming in the center of her palm. "So will you take this as a memento? It is the jewelry I was born with when I emerged into the world."

Aru nodded, taking the earring and carefully stashing it in her backpack. When she did so, her tambourine made an obnoxious jangling sound.

"And will you watch over my grandson?" asked Menaka, grabbing Aru's hands.

"What?" said Aru. "Why me? I mean, he—"

"I do not know whether I will ever find the strength to see my daughter again, for each time I have loved, it has almost destroyed me," said Menaka.

"Uh—"

Aru heard Aiden's voice calling her. "Shah! Where are you? It's showtime!"

"I gotta go," said Aru, pulling away and jogging toward the portal. "I'm sorry."

When Aru reached the opening, she looked over her shoulder. Tumburu stood in the shadows, his hands in his pockets, his horse head swiveled toward the television screens. Menaka stood alone and apart, an ethereal glow rising off her body.

Aru remembered the visions she'd seen across the floor—Menaka clutching a child to her chest, torn between the earth and the sky. In the human lands, the sage she loved forsook her because she'd been sent to weaken him. In the heavenly realms, she was not permitted to raise a half-mortal child. She'd been trapped, over and over again. But no one ever talked about that part of her story. They only spoke of her dazzling beauty, as if that's all she ever was—someone to be looked at but not listened to.

"I'll do it," blurted out Aru.

Menaka's face brightened. "I thank you, daughter of the gods."

TWENTY-SIX

Tambourines Are Underrated

Aru had thought the portal guiding her back was bright and flashy, but it was *nothing* compared to what awaited her when she hopped down the last step into the Final Stage performers' tent and looked around.

"Half an hour to go," said Aiden.

But Aru could barely hear him. Just outside the tent, camera flashes spangled the white canvas. Aru saw someone's shoulder bump into the fabric only for the tent to spring them backward. Reporters tried to speak to them through the open flap, each one yelling louder than the last.

"Hi! I'm here from NBC, the Night Bazaar Channel. We heard that one of you is a *direct* descendant of the apsara Malini? Can you comment on this— I SAID, BACK OFF, ARNOLD, OR YOU'LL GET THE HORNS—"

"My interview! I was here first!" shouted someone else.

"But who are the *other* performers? Are they also apsara descendants? How many of you are there? WHY WON'T YOU TELL US ANYTHING? THE SUSPENSE IS KILLING— Oh no, not you, Spence. You're doing great camera work, believe me!"

POP!

The Potatoes looked up. A square brown paper package sailed through the tent flap.

"Urgent delivery for a Mr. Aiden Acharya!" the package announced before it dropped itself with a loud *thump* onto the ground. The Potatoes moved closer. A note was taped to the top, written in the large, loopy, and slightly uneven letters that Aru instantly recognized as Nikita's handwriting:

S. saw that you might need this.
The helmets should block Aiden's hypnotic apsara stuff
so no one does anything embarrassing…again >:)
—N & S
P.S.: The tambourine? hahaha

"Amazing," said Aru, crossing her arms. "Little sisters can troll you at any distance."

Brynne reached for the package. As she tore off the paper, the materials within cast a bright glow around the room. Aru blinked a couple of times, peered through the packaging, and grinned.

"Helloooo, shiny," said Aru.

Fifteen minutes later, the Potatoes were unrecognizable. Nikita had made each of them a whole new outfit—stylish padded-shoulder blazers with shiny pants and a colorful bejeweled helmet to match. Aiden was in head-to-toe emerald green, Rudy in fierce scarlet, Brynne in soft turquoise, Mini in a smoky violet, and Aru in bright gold. Aru examined herself in the mirror. The helmet was lightweight and comfortable over her coiled braid. When Aru lifted the visor, she saw a pair of intense dark eyes staring back at her. She looked sharp. And she felt…powerful.

Maybe there was some truth in what Nikita had once told her: *Dress like victory and the war is halfway won.*

"I am NEVER taking this off," declared Rudy.

"All right, you guys," said Aiden, pacing the center of the room. His green helmet was tucked under his arm. "Instruments?"

"Check," said Mini, patting her floating keyboard.

"Sound system?" asked Aiden.

"Got it," said Rudy, waving around a gemstone.

Aiden turned to Brynne. "Sun Jewel?"

Brynne nodded, patting the front pocket of her blazer where the lantern was stowed in one of Nikita's magical pockets.

Aiden took a deep breath. "Okay, so, as far as I can tell, our audition platform is about ten feet from the actual Final Stage. If we play well enough—"

"You mean when we *kill* it in front of the judges," said Rudy.

"Sure," said Aiden before continuing. "We might be able to go straight from the audition platform to the Final Stage, and from there we can access the next portal."

"According to Jambavan, the door should open the moment it recognizes the Sun Jewel," said Brynne. "I just need to get close enough to the portal, and then—*boom!*—we're on the other side."

"But even then we won't be *in* the labyrinth," said Mini, speaking faster. "There's one more entrance to get through. And now there's only two days left before the labyrinth closes up for good and the Sleeper and Kara get the nectar of immortality and—"

"And we'll deal with it one step at a time," said Brynne gently.

Mini didn't look reassured.

"The biggest thing is the song, Ammamma," said Brynne, lifting her eyebrows at Aiden. "We've got the fancy instruments, but you're the one who's supposed to keep this illusion going with a truth."

"I know," said Aiden.

"If the illusion breaks, everyone will see what we're doing, and they'll probably kick us out."

"I know," repeated Aiden.

"Or throw us into some celestial void."

"Bee," said Aiden firmly, "*I know.*"

"But do you know what you're going to sing about?" asked Brynne.

Aiden's gaze was fixed on the floor. "Yeah. Yeah, I do."

Aru, Rudy, Mini, and Brynne exchanged glances.

Aru cleared her throat. "So … are you gonna tell us?"

Aiden looked startled that she'd addressed him. He glanced at her, frowned, and then jammed his helmet over his head. "No."

Aru rolled her eyes. So they were back to *that* version of Aiden. Great.

"Artists are extremely temperamental," said Rudy sagely. "Trust me, I am one."

Aiden checked his watch, straightened his shoulders, and then patted his backpack as if it was good luck. "It's time."

One by one the Potatoes walked out of the tent and headed to the platform. Through the narrow strip of her helmet visor, Aru couldn't get more than a glimpse of the throng. She felt jostled as she walked behind Brynne and Mini. Rudy was at the rear, and Aiden was nearly invisible up front.

Beside them, a pair of towering yaksha bouncers in black shirts parted the crowd. "Talent coming through!" one of them shouted. "Make some room!"

Despite the shouting, Aru was able to pick up some of the onlookers' comments, including *"Is that one carrying a* tambourine?"

Aru swiveled her head, wanting to shake the instrument at the rude speaker, but she was quickly pushed ahead. The walk to the audition platform took almost ten minutes. By the time they stepped onto it, Aru's nerves had spiked.

Aru looked out and saw an audience of hundreds. Cameras flashed. Harsh spotlights in the ceiling of the great pavilion pivoted in her direction. To her right the crystalline Final Stage loomed fifteen feet above them, and above that, more than fifty feet in the air, hovered the door that would bring them one step closer to the labyrinth with barely a day to spare. Aru really wished they'd had time for at least a dress rehearsal.

This was bad, thought Aru. Her hands turned clammy. What if Tumburu's blessings randomly failed? What if the plan didn't work and they got booed off the stage? This was a thousand times worse than being called on in class when you were on the verge of falling asleep and had *no idea* what was going on....

Aiden took his place in front as the lead singer. A microphone magically appeared before him. The three judges sat ten feet away, their expressions inscrutable behind sunglasses. Aru remembered hearing their names earlier—Lady Moonlight, the Lord of the Afternoon, and, if she had this right, the Artist Formerly Known as Starlight.

Lady Moonlight leaned forward. "We are ready to be grossly underwhelmed. Begin at your leisure."

Aiden looked over his shoulder, lifting his visor. "Ready? Brynne, you start. Rudy, introduce some effects. Then it's your turn, Mini."

"What about me?" asked Aru. "The tambourine deserves its moment to shine!"

"Try to punctuate the words, I guess," said Aiden. "On three. One, two—"

"RUDY ROCKS!" hollered Rudy. "LET'S DO THIS!"

"Three," said Aiden solemnly.

He lowered the visor over his eyes.

What about me and my tambourine?! asked Aru through the mind link.

I don't know! said Brynne, rotating her wrists and stretching her fingers.

Just follow the beat once he starts singing? suggested Mini.

Brynne struck the tabla. The beat juddered through the stadium, and the crowd fell silent. The rhythm built, becoming faster and faster as Brynne's fingers hit the drum.

The Artist Formerly Known as Starlight uncrossed their legs and sat up a little straighter.

Moments later, Rudy threw down three amethysts and a sapphire. The sound crescendoed over the stadium, conjuring an illusion of waves crashing down. The audience gasped.

Lady Moonlight lowered her sunglasses, staring up at the pavilion's ceiling and then at the stage.

Next, Mini bent her head. As she brought her fingers to the keyboard, a tune soared around them, at once bright and friendly and strangely sorrowful, too.

Aru lifted her tambourine. Now? Should she just go for it? But she paused when Aiden began to sing.

His words poured like honey over the crowd.

Aru lowered her hand, but the movement jangled the

tambourine. The instrument seemed to know, on instinct, how to punctuate the rhythm. Aru found herself wrapped up in the words, sung so vividly that she imagined they were meant for her.

> *"They said I have to be honest,*
> *So here's something you don't know . . .*
> *You scare me, but I try not to let it show. . . ."*

That was all it took.

As one, the judges shot out of their seats and began clapping wildly.

"CHAMPIONS!" shouted the Lord of the Afternoon.

Lady Moonlight flung her sunglasses on the ground and started to weep.

Behind the judges, the crowd surged forward, their hands waving in the air. But Rudy Rocks wasn't finished.

Mini leaned over the keyboard, lost in her rhapsody, while Brynne thunderously beat the drums. Rudy spun a tornado of jewels above them, drawing out the strands of the music and overlaying them with his own magic: the weightless wonder and terror of falling from a great height, the breathlessness that comes after laughing too hard, the way October sunlight feels on your face. It was mesmerizing.

But then something odd happened beside them. The huge crystalline stage began to glow. A set of stairs emerged from its side and lowered to meet the Potatoes' audition platform.

"The Final Stage has acknowledged its champion!" shouted one of the judges before collapsing on their side.

Aiden sauntered up the dozen steps, singing all the while to the huge cheers of the crowd. Brynne, Rudy, and Mini followed.

Aru was the last to head up. She felt overwhelmed by Aiden's lyrics. They made her heart hurt, but she didn't know why.

"They said she'll be the death of me,
And honestly, I agree...."

Once she had climbed a few stairs, Aru could see the crowd stretched out before her as Rudy's jewels rippled light over their faces. The ceiling of the pavilion was awash with color. Even the animals made of smoke had curled up in one spot, their tails whipping lazily to the beat.

Here goes nothing, said Brynne through the mind link.

Out of the corner of her helmet visor, Aru watched as Brynne slowly removed one hand from her drums. With her left hand, she kept the beat going. With her right, she touched her choker and Gogo slowly tugged the Sun Jewel lantern from the pocket of her blazer.

Aiden turned his head. His voice grew louder. Rudy threw a handful of quartz pebbles up in the air. They absorbed all the sunlight in the pavilion, and the crowd screamed. Multicolored beams began to spin around in the darkness like light from a feral disco ball.

Aru watched, still thumping the tambourine against her hand, as Brynne levitated the lantern higher and higher. The smoky purple edges of the door brightened in response. Its hinges glowed.

Aiden gasped for air, and the disco lights spun faster. Aru watched as one of the judges turned toward Brynne, a furrow appearing between their eyebrows.

"Keep going, Wifey!" shouted Mini. Hunched over the

electronic keyboard, she looked a lot like a mad scientist. Colors bounced off her jacket.

Aiden began to sing again in earnest.

"I think you're chaos walking and we probably won't get through today,
      But, for what it's worth, I wouldn't have it any other way...."

Aru stilled. Why did those words make her heart race? Aiden was singing to the crowd, not her....

But then she remembered the joke he'd made in Tumburu's recording studio. *Chaotic,* he'd called her, with the corner of his mouth tipped up.

There was a faint ringing sound in her skull. But what about the whole *Let's be friends—*

IT'S OPENING! yelled Brynne through the mind link.

Aru looked up just as the purple door swung open. Whatever lay on the other side was impossible to see. All she could make out was a dim purple glow against a star-flecked background. A thick beam of indigo light shot down from the portal and onto the stage. The moment it touched the crystal floor, billowing silver clouds gusted across the pavilion. It was as if an odd drowsiness had poured into the space. When Aru looked out into the crowd, she saw people dropping to the ground like they'd fallen asleep on the spot.

Fortunately, the clouds had no effect on the Potatoes.

"I'll send you up one by one!" said Brynne. "Mini, come on!"

Mini sprinted toward the purplish blue light. When she reached Brynne, her feet lifted off the ground. Brynne whirled her wind mace and with one gust sent Mini straight through the opening.

For one terrifying moment, Aru wondered if something had

happened to her, but then she heard Mini shout back through the mind link, *I'm okay!*

"Rudy, you're next!" said Brynne.

Rudy took off at a run, jumping into the beam at the same moment Brynne sent a wind to push him through the door.

"Keep singing, Wifey!" shouted Brynne.

Aiden was edging closer and closer to the ray of light.

"Aru, c'mon!" said Brynne.

Aiden's words had rooted her to the spot. He turned to face her and she realized he'd lifted his visor. Time froze for Aru. She knew that in a matter of minutes she would tell herself this had never happened, he hadn't meant it, he hadn't really been singing *to* her.

But in that one shining moment, she didn't listen to that voice in her head. Instead, she listened to him.

> *"I'm sorry that I lied,*
> *But I've got too much pride. . . ."*

"Aru, *now!*" shouted Brynne.

Aru shook herself. She banged the tambourine one last time, and then ran up the last few stairs to the stage and toward the midnight-blue light. The moment the beam hit her skin, she felt Brynne's breeze gather around her ankles. The wind grew stronger, propelling her up and through the portal. Far below, she saw Aiden's head still turned toward her. Their eyes met across the stage and the lights and the music, and she imagined his words were meant for her.

> *"Maybe, when we reach the end,*
> *We can finally start again. . . ."*

TWENTY-SEVEN

Hoodwinked

"Sir, they've been spotted."

Kara looked up. She blinked. Her limbs ached with exhaustion, and her eyelids felt leaden. "Who?" she asked weakly.

"Do not concern yourself with these matters," said Suyodhana. "Take your rest, daughter. We are so close to the end."

He smiled, then rose from her side and left to go speak with the tortoise-faced lieutenant. Kara propped herself up on one elbow. She'd been lying in the makeshift tent her father had constructed roughly a dozen feet from the crater holding the nectar of immortality.

This was Kara's appointed rest time, and for the past hour her father had been reading the plays of Kalidasa to her. Kara had almost been soothed to sleep by the sound of his voice conjuring the tales to life. Sleep was hard to come by these days. Every time she closed her eyes, she was back at Aru's birthday party and the world was splintering around her.

Now that she was fully awake, a familiar panic seized her. Kara had lost track of the number of days they had spent beneath the ground. She knew it had to be less than ten, because otherwise the labyrinth would have vanished around them, but it felt like years.

Through a flap in the shadow-tent, Kara could see the nectar of immortality in its great *kalash*. The pot holding the *amrita* was smaller than she'd imagined, roughly the size of a kitchen oven. Even from this distance, she could see the still, mirrorlike surface of the gold drink. And yet, for all its closeness, it was proving nearly impossible to access.

They had spent days winding their way through the dark, and the whole time Kara had felt her confidence flagging. Their provisions were shrinking faster than they'd imagined, and she could feel the eyes of the soldiers on her back, hear their whispers in the dark.

He said she would be the answer to our problems. . . .

Nothing but a child with a weapon she cannot use!

Who's to say she is capable of leading us?

The glares and grumbles had stopped—for a while, at least—when Kara's seam of sunshine led them to the lip of a vast crater that glowed like a fallen star. The army had cheered, and Kara had basked in their smiles.

But the feeling of victory didn't last.

A shimmering sphere protected the nectar of immortality. It was impenetrable to blades and acids, and Kara's magical trident had only managed to make a teeny hole in it . . . and *that* was after an hour of concentrating all her strength. Even so, a hole was a hole, and it was a start to opening it completely.

For the past two days, Kara had done nothing but stand at the lip of the crater and focus all her energy into destroying that protective sphere. The whole time, her father had been warm and attentive. He made sure she had regular breaks for water and rest. He read stories to her before her naps.

Even so, Kara could detect his impatience. She could read worry in the tightness of his smile and the lines around his eyes. He wouldn't say it, but he didn't have to. The soldiers whispered, and even when they thought they were out of earshot, she heard them. *We are running out of time.*

News of the outside world came to them in bits and pieces. With Kara's celestial weapon to guide them, a route to the labyrinth's core had been established, allowing a select group of soldiers to start hacking out paths that would eventually let in their allies. Even deep underground, news and rumors reached them. Including, most recently...

Video footage.

Kara spied an enchanted bubble levitating just outside the tent's entrance. Within the bubble, silent images flickered back and forth. Kara slipped out of her bed of cool shadows and crept toward the tent flap where her father conversed in urgent tones with his lieutenant.

"Where was this taken?" her father asked.

"A desolate field outside the Otherworld," said the lieutenant, pausing to consult a sheaf of papers in his hands. "The Final Stage? Some sort of... apocalyptic entertainment. It's actually rather enjoyable—"

Her father snarled faintly, and the lieutenant cleared his throat. "Their faces are obscured by helmets, as you can see, but the likeness—height, size, number—to the Pandavas is indisputable. The singing boy is rumored to be the son of the apsara Malini, and he is often in their company."

"I remember him," said Suyodhana grouchily. "He has a soft spot for her."

Aiden, thought Kara. *They were talking about Aiden.* Her cheeks turned hot. On Aru's birthday, she'd worked up the courage to tell him that she liked him. What a mistake. She wished she'd never done that. When she recalled the pity in his eyes, or the realization minutes later that it was Aru he'd liked the whole time, she felt worse than a fool.

She'd been hoodwinked by hope.

Hoodwinked, Kara had discovered during her reading breaks, was a word that originated from the practice of falconry. When people used to train falcons to hunt prey, they'd calm the bird by putting a hood on its head. These days the word no longer meant to blindfold.

It meant to trick.

They tricked you, her father had said. *They made you think things that weren't true.*

At first, in her anger, she'd clung to those words. But lately when she fell asleep she found herself trapped in a nightmare where Aru's birthday party never ended. And each time Kara got stuck on the way Aru had pleaded with her, her eyes shining.

We *love you, Kara. You're one of us.*

Somewhere deep inside her, Kara felt that Aru's words had the ring of truth to them, and she didn't know what to make of that. Kara's father's assurances that he loved her and that he believed he was doing the right thing also rang true.... So where did that leave her?

Kara took another step toward the entrance of the tent, and there she saw the video her father and his lieutenant were fiercely examining. In it, the Potatoes were onstage. Kara's eyes widened. She didn't have to see their faces to know immediately that it was Aru, Brynne, Mini, and Aiden. They were all dressed up in fancy suits and wearing gleaming helmets. They looked like rock stars! Even Rudy was there, she realized with a stab of envy. When they started performing, the sound wove its magic around her, and Kara realized she was *grinning*.

Since when did Mini play the piano? Or Brynne know what to do with drums?

Kara almost laughed thinking back to how all of them tried to sneak out of Brynne's penthouse whenever she started "practicing the harp." *Torturing the harp* was probably the better word choice, as Kara had once said, making Aru snort with laughter. Only Hira would stick around, which Kara suspected was because she liked the player, not the playing.

In the video, a beam of purple light opened up from a source Kara couldn't see. One by one, the Potatoes flew up and vanished into the glow.

Kara thought back to her own adventures with them, and without meaning to, she chuckled.

Her father spun around, catching her at the threshold of the tent. With an abrupt wave of his wrist, the images vanished. Kara froze.

"You should be resting, my dear," said her father.

"What was that?" asked Kara.

"It's nothing," said Suyodhana in a strained voice.

"But—"

"You need your rest," her father insisted. "Perhaps you are having trouble sleeping, child. I can fix that."

"Wait, Dad. What happened to Aru—" Kara started to say,

but her father had already raised his hand. He snapped his fingers and a ribbon of black shadow snaked out from his palm, wrapping around her eyes.

Hoodwinking me, thought Kara drowsily.

It was the last thing that crossed her mind as her eyes closed and her bed of shadows rose to steal her away from the world.

Kara had braced herself for nightmares, but instead she found herself standing inside what looked like a large warehouse. There was a wall of frosted windows on one side, and Kara sensed movement—*memories*—shifting behind them like sea creatures trapped under a layer of ice.

"There you are," said a familiar voice.

Before her appeared Dream Sheela, wearing a pair of black pajamas patterned with tiny yellow ducks. "I kept trying to bring you here, but your dreams are kinda hard to get through."

Kara blinked and rubbed her eyes. "This is *such* a weird dream. I know you're not real. Well, I mean, I know you can't *really* be right here."

Dream Sheela shrugged. "I dunno. That's probably what you want to believe, but deep down, I think you know the truth."

Kara hung her head. "I don't know anything anymore."

Dream Sheela reached out her hand. "I've seen your dreams, Kara."

Kara shrank from her. "So? What about them?"

"It's scary to love people," said Dream Sheela. "Nikki says it's like walking off a cliff on purpose."

Kara almost laughed because it was so true. It took a lot to trust someone, and once you did, you gave them the chance to hurt you.

"Yeah. I guess you could say that."

"But you're wrong, you know," said Dream Sheela. "They *do* love you. Even Krithika. I saw it in her dreams. I stole them, one by one. The Sleeper's, too. I can show them to you if you'd like, and then you'll know the truth." She gestured behind her to the blurred-out windows, and Kara held her breath.

"None of this is real," said Kara.

"Then I guess it doesn't hurt to look," said Dream Sheela. "But I think...um, actually, I *know* there will come a moment when you have another chance. I can't see what you'll do with it. But at least this way, you can decide for yourself."

Kara stilled, glancing up at the windows. She saw the slender silhouette of a woman moving behind one of the windowpanes, and Kara felt a painful urge to see her face. She caught the scent of the neroli perfume that Aru's mom—*their* mom—wore on her neck and wrists. Kara remembered walking through Krithika Shah's bedroom before she'd known they were mother and daughter. Kara imagined Krithika now, sitting on the edge of her bed, checking the clock and waiting for her daughter Aru to come home. The image made her ache with envy. She so desperately wanted a mom who would worry about where she was and when she'd be back, a mom who would let her borrow her perfume and try on her shoes until, eventually, they fit.

"So...will you look?" asked Sheela.

Kara couldn't recall if she answered. All she knew was that one moment she was standing in the dark and the next she was holding the little girl's hand as together they walked into the light.

TWENTY-EIGHT

The Halls of Nidra

Aru blinked. Once more she was back in that curious void between realms. Only this time she seemed to be in a tunnel filled with purple smoke. The walls around her moved, but she stayed still. Looming ever closer was a door that looked as if it had been made of the darkness between stars. Aru patted her own head, bemused. Her helmet was gone, and so was—she realized with a surprised pang—her tambourine.

The longer Aru looked at the door, the more unease she felt creeping into her heart. Her eyelids were heavy. If she closed them, she imagined she'd sleep for years.

But she sensed it was not a good sleep that lay ahead. Frost grew over her skin. The hairs on the back of her neck prickled as if bad dreams were lurking just out of sight.

"So . . . that was kinda weird," said Mini.

Aru startled and her drowsiness burned away. Unlike Aru, Mini seemed perfectly content in the space between the portals. She looked graceful and at ease. Her toes were pointed as if she were mid-flight, and her chin-length hair flowed in the wind.

"What's weird?" asked Aru.

Mini opened one of her eyes. "Aiden's song?"

Aru's face burned. When she'd heard it, she'd thought that . . . well, that maybe it was for her. But that was ridiculous. . . . Wasn't it?

A loud snore interrupted her thoughts. Rudy was fast asleep with his knees curled to his chest and his hands tucked under his head.

"Oh good, you're back!" shouted a familiar voice.

To her right, Sheela and Nikita partly manifested in the void, their features translucent again. Nevertheless, Nikita had dressed for the occasion and was sporting a turban of stars and a robe embroidered with constellations. Sheela wore a comfortable-looking silver sweat suit. She grinned at Aru and Mini, waving vigorously.

"How'd you find us?" asked Aru.

"We've been taking turns sleeping in case you showed up in the astral plane," said Nikita, yawning. "It's very tiring. I couldn't stay awake for my last shift."

Aru crossed her arms. "I'm so sorry *napping* has been difficult for you while we run around trying to avoid death and all that."

"Apology accepted," said Nikita.

Aru rolled her eyes.

"Brynne and Aiden are on their way," said Sheela, looking beyond them. "You'll have to tell them."

"Tell them what?" asked Mini.

"Where you're going next, of course," said Sheela, pointing to the door.

It was closer now. Aru didn't like the look of it. There was something eerie and endless about what lay ahead.

"That's the entrance to the labyrinth, right?" said Mini.

"Wrong," said Sheila.

"WHAT?" asked Aru. "How many more strange doors do we have to—"

"It should look familiar, not strange," said Nikita. "You've been here before."

"I have?"

"Oh yes," said Nikita. "But you might not remember it. You're going to the Halls of Nidra."

Aru paused. She knew that name. Nidra was the goddess of sleep. She recalled Jambavan and his great silver table. *Above all, one must never shirk one's rest,* he'd said. *Even the most powerful of beings do not neglect what they owe to Nidra....*

Those words made her shiver now.

"Do we have time for this?" asked Mini. "The labyrinth will be closing soon, and we still don't have our weapons back. What if we're too late?"

Aru shared Mini's concern but wanted to get as much intel as possible from the twins while she could, so she jumped over her questions. "What's going on in the Otherworld?"

"Well...some people have gone into hiding," said Nikita. "And others are trying to join the Sleeper."

Aru's heart sank.

"But there's *lots* more who want to fight with *us,*" said Sheela.

Aru lifted her head. "Really?"

Nikita smiled. "Really."

"They want to know how to help," said Sheela. "We can see it in their dreams."

Aru thought of all the people they'd met over the years...the Maruts, those thunderous warriors who lived in the immortal city of Amaravati; the monkey-faced *vanaras* of the Kishkinda Kingdom who had fought in the first war against Lanka....

All had said they would fight. *Whenever you have need of me or my people, we will honor your call*, Queen Tara had promised.

The Pandavas weren't alone.

That realization knocked down walls Aru hadn't realized were around her. It was as if she'd stepped into a bigger, brighter room and she could see more clearly than she had before.

"Well, if they want to help, then let's send them a message," said Aru.

Mini caught her eye and smiled.

"Fine," said Nikita. "But I'm not making any more outfits. They just get blown up, incinerated, or thrown into *washing machines* instead of being treated like the priceless works of art they are."

Aru groaned. "It was *one* time, Nikita! I'm sorry I ruined the dress!"

"The instructions very clearly said DRY-CLEAN ONLY!" retorted Nikita. "What monster doesn't look at care instructions?"

Sheela tugged on her sister's sleeve. "Time to go, Nikki. They've reached the door. And there's someone else I need to talk to.... Someone I've been visiting."

Aru frowned. She was on the verge of asking Sheela who she was talking about when the door to the Halls of Nidra creaked open. Pale wisps of smoke uncoiled in the air like tentacles reaching out for them.

"Send word to our allies," said Aru. "Tell them where the battle is.... They won't be able to get in unless we can use the Sun Jewel to blast apart the barriers, but at least tell them ... Tell them we'd be honored if they fought...."

She almost said *with us*, but only Brynne had her celestial weapon back. Which meant that only Brynne could get through to the labyrinth right now. And anyway, without Vajra and Dee Dee, Aru and Mini would be useless in a battle against the Sleeper and his army. There were only two days left, and the gods hadn't seemed to test her at all. What if they thought they had a better chance of winning without her?

The thought left her nearly breathless.

"Aru?" asked Mini. "Is something wrong?"

When she looked at Mini, Aru felt a stab of shame. She knew how much Mini was hurting without her weapon, too, but at the same time, Aru was glad. She was glad she wasn't the only one who was powerless.

It didn't change the fact, though, that Aru didn't know what she would do if she regained her powers. And she didn't know how to tell her sisters that she was still torn about the war. But now wasn't the right moment to share these worries.

Will there ever be a right time? whispered a tired voice in her skull.

"Aru?" said Mini, snapping her fingers in front of her face.

"Sorry," said Aru, shaking herself. "Yeah, I'm fine."

She glanced at the twins. Nikita looked indifferent, but Sheela's head was tilted to the side, and Aru wondered if she could see straight through her.

"I wish you could come with us," Aru said to the twins.

"Me too," said Sheela. "But we have work to do. Dreams to visit."

"Be careful, okay?" Nikita told Aru and Mini. "Once you're inside, you'll have to move fast. Dreams don't last forever, and neither do the Halls. And in the Halls of Nidra not all the dreams are nice."

TWENTY-NINE

Well, This Isn't Awkward at All

A ru tumbled through the door and found herself in a realm she knew she'd never visited. And yet...

"Doesn't it feel like we've been here before?" asked Mini.

"Yeah," said Aru.

Nikita had said they'd all passed through the realm of sleep and the Halls of Nidra, and Aru wished she'd remembered it simply because it was a landscape of wonder, like a meadow from a fairy tale—full of dozing poppy flowers and pale, graceful trees. Daydreams roosted in the trees' branches, and when they took flight in the forms of finches and sparrows, peacocks and ravens, Aru *felt* the tiny moments of escape they carried in their beaks: floating in a pool, sudden superpowers, unexpected cake in the fridge.

"I like it here," said Mini.

Rudy grunted. Of the three of them, he was the only one still bleary-eyed and disgruntled from waking up. "Where's Aiden and Brynne?" he mumbled, rubbing his eyes and yawning.

"They should be here soon," said Mini, looking over her shoulder.

The door still glowed faintly behind them. It hovered above the ground, which was gray and pebbled like a rocky beach. A few feet ahead, the surface changed, blurring into night-darkened clouds that rose and fell like gentle waves. A few children—dreamers—swam through the clouds with their eyes closed. Others bobbed in the waves, their brows furrowed in sleep. A couple of them opened their eyes in Nidra's realm and giggled with delight before vanishing.

"Don't you think they've been gone a long time?" asked Rudy nervously.

At that moment, the door shuddered, contracting for a moment before swinging open. Brynne and Aiden tumbled onto the ground.

"My tabla!" moaned Brynne, staring into the void.

The door, indifferent, slammed shut behind her.

"I know," said Mini, glancing at her empty hands. "I lost the keyboard, too."

Aiden winced, looking like he'd been violently shaken out of a dream. He blinked a few times before his eyes went wide. *Where's my backpack?* Did I lose it—"

"Calm down, Ammamma," said Brynne. "It's on your back. Like it's supposed to be."

Brynne tugged one of the straps and Aiden relaxed. He gingerly adjusted the pack, unzipping it and reaching inside to fuss with something.

"What's in there, anyway?" asked Brynne, trying to peer into it.

Aiden wrapped his arm around it protectively. "It's a surprise."

"Ooh!" said Rudy.

"Not for you."

"Cruel."

With his backpack decidedly secure, Aiden lifted his gaze to scan the Halls of Nidra. A few moments later, he looked at Aru. She froze. Up until now, she'd told herself that those moments on the Final Stage were all in her imagination. But the way he stared at her now was different. He seemed . . . determined. Emboldened. The intensity of it made her palms clammy. And this time it was Aru who looked away first.

"I'm sad we lost the instruments," said Rudy, looking downcast. But then he brightened. "AT LEAST THE BAND IS REUNITED!"

"That was a one-time thing, Rudy," said Aiden firmly.

"That's what *you* think," muttered the naga. "Rudy Rocks will be immortalized as the greatest band of all time. . . ."

"I think I see a way out!" said Brynne, pointing.

Aru followed the direction of Brynne's outstretched arm. All around them, an undulating, star-flecked purple mist rolled through the Halls. From one moment to the next, it changed shape. Where it had first looked like an ocean, now it had narrowed, transforming into an elaborate corridor with night clouds for a floor.

"Wait," said Brynne, faltering. "Maybe I was wrong."

Out of the corners of her eyes, Aru saw dozens of silver doors appearing and disappearing on either side of the cloud floor, but looking at them was like trying to remember the details of a dream after waking up.

And then, far ahead, the thick mist cleared long enough to

reveal a door different from the others. It was larger and looked like poured gold.

"That's weird," said Brynne, frowning. "I . . . I can't get a sense of how close it is."

Aru knew what she meant. The labyrinth entrance had all the logic of a dream. On the one hand, Aru could sense the details— its impressive height and lustrous color. But when she blinked, her perspective changed so that it seemed small and bright and almost two hundred feet in the distance.

But even from this far away, Aru saw something appear next to the door. The star-flecked mist half hid it, but it looked like a large, oddly spiky shrub? It wiggled a bit, and something about it made Aru recoil. . . .

How come the longer they stayed in the Halls of Nidra, the more it seemed to *move*? The whole space rose and fell gently. At first, Aru had thought it was the waves formed by the night-darkened clouds on the floor. But now it was as if this realm of sleep was, well, asleep. A body breathing in the dark.

Beside Aru, Mini shivered. "Something's not right. It's like one of those dreams where the exit gets farther and farther away."

"Even if we have to walk for hours, we'll get there," said Brynne.

"We may not have hours," said Aru.

Brynne looked sharply at them. "What do you mean?"

Mini glanced at Aru. "Sheela and Nikita were able to visit us in the astral plane. They said that the Halls of Nidra don't stay in one place for long. We have to move fast."

"Well, then let's go!" said Brynne. "This could be *it*. The final test! Once we get through, we'll be in front of the labyrinth!" She smiled at Aru and Mini. "I bet the *moment* we go through that portal, you guys will both have your weapons back. It's going to be *good*."

There was an edge of forced cheer to her voice, and Aru wondered if Brynne felt it, too—that trace of frost in the air. Or the unsettling sensation that the Halls mimicked the shallow breathing of someone dreaming restlessly.

Or someone wide-awake and watching.

After guzzling some water and eating the last of Aiden's protein bars, Brynne took the lead. Far ahead and yet impossibly close, the door to the labyrinth's entrance taunted them.

"I wonder if we can take any of the daydreams with us," said Rudy, squinting at a swan made of music notes. A pale magpie flew past, with a note tucked in its beak that said EXTREMELY WITTY RESPONSES.

Aru frowned as Nikita's words floated back to her. *In the Halls of Nidra not all the dreams are nice.* Aru looked around warily, as if one of the daydreams might suddenly sprout teeth and dive at them....But everything seemed serene.

"Move out, Potatoes!" said Brynne, taking the first step.

Beneath her feet, the night-darkened clouds yielded, and Aru's stomach swooped a little as she sank up to her ankles in their softness. The clouds moved coolly against the fabric of her pants, and instantly a sense of calm stole through her body.

"Ahh!" said Rudy. "Watch where you put your feet! I almost stepped on someone's nose."

Mini sniffed the air. "I wonder what kind of microbes exist in the dream realm. Do those trees have pollen? Is this why I sometimes wake up with a stuffy nose? What if someone got a severe allergic reaction out here?"

As if on cue, Brynne, Rudy, Aiden, and Aru all said, *"They could die."*

Mini was not amused. Aru smiled a little as they walked across the clouds. She was still scanning the narrow hallway when Aiden fell into step beside her. He shoved his hands into the pockets of his dress pants. His emerald-green costume blazer from the Final Stage glimmered. When he looked at her, his expression was serious and intense, like he had been working up his courage for this moment.

"Hey," said Aiden. "Do you have a second?"

Alarm bells went off in Aru's head. She lifted an eyebrow. "For what? Clearly Brynne, Mini, and I are in the middle of apocalypse-thwarting. I don't want to risk getting distracted."

Just then Brynne and Mini started arguing about poached eggs.

"Undercooked eggs carry a risk of salmonella!" said Mini.

"*Poached* eggs are rich and luxurious, and I won't hear them slandered," said Brynne.

Aru groaned inwardly. Why weren't they ever talking about some kind of brilliant military strategy against nefarious enemies when she needed them to be?

"Yeah...I can see that," said Aiden.

Aru walked a little faster. If this was going to turn into another *Sorry about what I said before, but yeah, it's true, I think you're repulsive,* she did *not* need that energy. Nope, nope, nope.

"Shah, wait up," said Aiden, touching her elbow. "Please."

Aru paused. When the others passed, she turned to him sharply. "What?"

"I'm sorry."

"Yawn—"

"I was scared, Shah," said Aiden in a rush.

"Scared of what?" Her voice came out annoyingly fragile, and she wanted to shake herself.

"This . . . This *thing* . . . got into my head, and I chickened out after we, uh, you know, because I was just . . . terrified, I guess. And that terror made me say stuff I didn't mean."

Terror.

One moment, a flimsy hope lit a match in her soul. The next, it was as if the word *terror* had become a sentient being. Aru felt it like a shadow passing overhead.

Under any other circumstances, she'd be yelling, *TIME OUT! AIDEN ACHARYA IS HAVING A MOMENT OF HONESTY!*

But something was wrong.

The Halls juddered. Their soft breathing became a panting, slavering sound.

"Hold that thought," said Aru, hating that she had to say those words to him. "Everyone, stop. Do you feel that?"

A few feet ahead, Rudy, Brynne, and Mini slowed down. Aiden touched his wrists together and his scimitars flashed out. Aru held still, watching a tremble work its way through the cloud floor. Tall blades of grass replaced the pillowy softness. Some of the dreamers vanished. Others looked trapped in the thicket, their foreheads wrinkling.

"What is that?" asked Brynne.

Around them, the Halls of Nidra expanded once more, transforming into a grassy plain. But instead of being green and bright, it was dark and bleak, crammed with shadows. The trees and daydream birds vanished. In the distance, the labyrinth entrance had been reduced to a spark of light *miles* away. Ten feet to their right, a building materialized. It was one story and long, with dozens of stalls.

"I don't feel so good," said Rudy woozily.

"Why is it so cold and dark now?" said Brynne.

Aru shivered. Was she imagining things, or was the ground trembling harder now? Pebbles bounced up and down in the grass.

"Something's coming," said Aiden. He moved to the front with Brynne, who immediately brought out her wind mace.

"What's that sound?" asked Mini, edging closer to Aru.

A hundred feet away on their left, the dark mist began to harden into shapes—glossy flanks, serrated hair, flaring nostrils. *Nightmares.*

Night *mares.* Nothing at all like the nightmare hounds she'd met ages ago in the Dreaming Grove of Ratri. This was a different kind of creature entirely.

A dozen Otherworldly horses galloped out from the darkness of the dream world, towering nearly ten feet tall. Their black tails swished behind them, the ends dissipating into smoke. Blue flames burned in their eye sockets, and when they huffed in the air, Aru could smell fear burning off their bodies. It was acrid and salty, like a combination of metal and tears.

"Nice . . . horsies?" said Aru.

The night mares regarded them with their burning eyes. One of them took a step forward. Where its hoof met the ground, the blades of grass turned to ice.

"We're just trying to go that way," said Aru, pointing toward the door in the distance. "So, you know. We'll go do that."

I do not like this, said Brynne through the mind link. *Maybe I should blast them—*

No! said Mini. *They're probably frightened. . . .*

You mean frightening, right? said Aru.

Mini broke from the line, holding out her hand. "There's nothing to be afraid of... see? We just need to pass."

One of the mares snorted and stepped forward. Its muzzle was maybe less than a foot away from Mini's outstretched hand.

"See?" said Mini, smiling.

Aru stared at her sister, amazed. Mini would refuse to put her hands on a kitchen counter if she suspected it wasn't thoroughly disinfected, but give her a twisted living creature, and she'd cuddle it.

The blue infernos in the horse's eyes began to dim. It angled its head down, huffing steam, when movement flared behind it.

"Watch out!" yelled Brynne.

Skeletal wings whooshed out from the night mare's shoulder blades. Aru gasped. Brynne grabbed Mini's arm, hauling her backward.

"No, wait!" said Mini.

The horse reared, towering above them, its hooves punching the air. The other night mares screamed. Around them, the air churned with shadows and wings.

Brynne raised her wind mace, aiming it at the line of creatures. A jet stream of air shot out, hitting a night mare square in the chest. The horse brayed, and the sound raised the hairs on Aru's neck. It was an unearthly screech, and in the echoes of it Aru heard all her worst nightmares reflected at her....

The vision the Sleeper had showed her years ago, of her sisters turning away from her.

Her father's smug voice ringing in her ears. *You were never meant to be a hero.*

Kara's heartbroken face twisting into a superior grin. *I'm the daughter they wanted. Not you.*

The shock of these fears struck Aru like a punch to the gut. She staggered back, avoiding the night mare's landing hooves by mere inches.

"Aru!" shouted Brynne, aiming Gogo again.

A jet of blue light struck the night mare in the forelock and the horse cried out, vanishing.

But only for a moment.

Smoke rushed in to fill the absence and the horse rematerialized moments later. It swung its head toward Brynne, baring its blackened teeth.

"You're making it worse!" said Mini angrily.

The night mares' manes bristled, and their blue eyes sprouted more flames. They opened their mouths, and their jaws unhinged as their terrifying screams were unleashed.

"They're going to charge!" yelled Rudy. "We need to go, now!"

"I'll hold them off," said Brynne, gritting her teeth. She twirled the mace over her head and then sent out a blast of wind, creating a cyclone between the night mares and the Potatoes. The horses reared back, their hooves churning against the funnel.

"It won't last forever....C'mon!" said Brynne. "We can regroup in that building."

They raced across the field. The closer they got to the structure, the more its details came into focus. It was a stable! There were individual stalls for each night mare, and a nameplate hung from the top of each frame.

Aru thought the fancy horses from races like the Kentucky Derby had weird names, like Spectacular Bid, or California Chrome. But *those* were nothing compared to the names of the night mares—

THE THING THAT CHASES

CREEPY PARTY CLOWN

INEXPLICABLE NATURAL DISASTER

SLEPT LATE AND MISSED THE BIGGEST DAY OF YOUR LIFE

DON'T LOOK UNDER THE BED

BUGS IN YOUR HAIR

EVERYONE YOU LOVE MOCKS YOU BEHIND YOUR BACK

EVERYONE YOU LOVE IS DEAD

ENDLESS FALLING

TRAPPED

LOOSE TEETH

A GHOST IS RIGHT BEHIND YOU

"This one's empty!" said Aiden, running into the stall at the end. It was huge and cavernous, more like a living room than a stable. Aru wrinkled her nose. Inside, it smelled like wet hay and horse sweat.

The moment the door swung shut behind them, plunging them into darkness, Mini spun toward Brynne. "How *could* you?" she said.

"What?" said Brynne.

"I totally had that under control!" said Mini. "You should've waited!"

"For *what?*" said Brynne. "For them to eat us?"

"I don't think they were going to do that, but you didn't listen to me!"

Aru tried to step backward and melt into the shadows when Brynne turned to face her. "Well, what do *you* think?" demanded Brynne.

Mini raised her chin, an imperious look on her face. "Yeah, Aru, what *do* you think?"

Trapped! sounded an alarm in her head.

"Uh, well..." said Aru.

Honestly, she understood where both of them were coming from, but she was pretty sure that was not the answer her sisters wanted. She was spared from responding as her shoulder hit something solid. Something solid...and warm. Aru looked into the darkness, and the darkness looked back.

Slowly, a pair of blue inferno eyes flickered open right above her.

THIRTY

Hello Darkness, My Old Friend

The night mare whinnied loudly as Aru scuttled back.

Rudy squeaked. "I thought you said the stable was empty, Aiden!"

Aiden backed up, too. "I was wrong." His scimitar cuffs glinted in the blue glow of Brynne's wind mace.

"Okay, maybe if I'm up close when I blast it," said Brynne, "it'll stay away longer."

The horse screamed, and a wave of dizziness crashed over Aru as her fears rose again.

"WAIT!" said Mini, stepping in front of the horse. "Just *wait*."

"Mini, get away!" shouted Brynne. "That thing could hurt you!"

"The nightmares are both outside and inside us!" said Mini. "Blasting the horses isn't going to help us get to the portal! There has to be some other way. Just . . . Just *trust me* for one second, okay?"

Through the mind link, Mini uttered one word: *Please*.

Brynne frowned. After a few seconds, she lowered her wind mace. "What's your plan?"

Mini took a deep breath as she faced the night mare. It whinnied, its great wings beating the air and gusting fear around them. But Mini didn't flinch.

"I need more light," she said calmly. "Not the Sun Jewel—nighttime and sunshine don't really mix. Rudy? Help me out?"

Rudy, who was cowering behind Aiden, took a few steps forward. Slowly he opened his backpack and set two quartz stones on the dirt floor. He tossed a third one to Mini, who caught it smoothly.

A cool moonlit glow washed over the stable. A few feet away from Mini, the night mare huffed. In the silvery light, Aru saw that it was indeed a mare, not a stallion, and it had one front hoof raised.

"I'm Mini." She glanced up at the plaque inscribed with the horse's name. "And you're ... Loose Teeth?"

The horse whickered. She still looked more demon than animal, but now when she swung her head, there was something gentle in her movements. Something ... shy.

Mini took a step forward. "Why aren't you out with the others?"

Loose Teeth snorted. Smoke plumed from her nostrils. Aru thought she looked somewhat offended by the question. She reared back and then hit the floor—except for her right foreleg. She kept that hoof bent toward her belly.

"Oh ..." said Mini. "You're hurt, aren't you? Must be some kind of obstruction. ..."

She was using her best *trust-me-I'm-a-doctor* voice. And it seemed to be working. The night mare didn't startle when Mini moved closer, and when the Daughter of Death knelt and held out her hand, it took only a few moments for the horse to tentatively offer her hoof. Mini held up one of the stones for light and made a loud *hmm* sound.

The night mare's ears pricked and swiveled backward. Aru imagined her asking *Is it bad, Doctor?*

"You have a rock stuck in there," said Mini. "May I?"

The horse's ears pointed forward. Aru wasn't sure what that meant, but Mini must have found it reassuring enough to reach for her backpack. Whereas Brynne's backpack was full of candy and Aru's was full of candy wrappers, Mini's backpack was a portable hospital. She had gauze and a few EpiPens, two first-aid kits, suturing thread and a wickedly sharp needle, several tweezers, and enough sanitizer to dissolve a person. With quick, practiced motions, Mini disinfected her hands and then removed a pair of tweezers from its plastic packaging. "This won't hurt."

Lie! Aru wanted to say. *Whenever a doctor says that, they're lying!*

"Mini..." said Brynne, her voice coming out low and distressed. "You sure about this? If it gets mad, then what?"

Mini ignored her. The night mare looked down at her, curious, ears bent back. Mini poised the tweezers over her hoof, humming a little. "Okay, on the count of three, I'll pull it out," said Mini. "One..."

The muscles of the horse's flank rippled.

"Two..." said Mini. Quick as a flash, she pulled out the piece of gravel.

The horse whinnied in pain. As much as Aru hated night mares, she had to sympathize with this one. *I told you they lie!*

Brynne panicked and raised her wind mace, but Rudy laid a hand on her arm.

"She's got this," he said fiercely.

Brynne backed off. The night mare spread her wings, and Aru felt a fresh gust of fear.... Only this time, it wasn't *her* fear, but the animal's. Loose Teeth gave Aru a vision of what the mare's life was like. Though she was massive to Aru, she was tiny compared to her sisters, and she also walked with a limp. When she tried to nuzzle the other horses, she would often get a wing to the face.

In her mind's eye, Aru saw how the night mares grazed in the long, dark grass of the Halls of Nidra. When the clouds changed to grass, not every dreamer made it out. Some were trapped in the meadow.

The night mares would search for stragglers, and when they found them, fear would roll off the horses' dark bodies like smoke until the sleepers breathed it in. Within seconds, the victims' eyelids would scrunch tight and their mouths would flatten into a panicked line as they started to toss and turn. Bad dreams would make the sleepers glow in the dark, and the night mares would drink in that flush of despair until the blue infernos of their eyes blazed brighter. Eventually, the sleeper would wake up and disappear, and the horses would wander off, their meals concluded.

The night mares fed off fear.

It struck Aru as monstrous, but Mini didn't seem to think so.

"It's okay," she said, holding her hands palms-up to Loose Teeth to show that she meant no harm.

Loose Teeth trembled. Her withers quivered and she swung her great head toward Mini's chest as if angling for... a hug? Mini smiled. The horse moved closer and sighed. Her tail whipped lazily behind her.

"She's sweet," said Mini, stroking her nose.

"Mini, that is *literally* a monster," said Brynne. "You can't keep it!"

ROSHANI CHOKSHI

"I wasn't going to!" said Mini defensively.

Brynne and Aru exchanged a look that said, *She absolutely was.* But before they could confront their sister, the door slid open and a new voice entered the stall.

"How did you do that?"

Aru turned to see a woman standing at the entrance. She was light-skinned with shoulder-length black hair that fell in tight curls. Her features were small, pretty, and doll-like, and she wore a men's riding outfit.

"Who are you?" asked Aiden.

The woman ignored him and stepped inside. Loose Teeth recognized her and whinnied happily. The woman smiled, but the smile did not reach her eyes. Silently she looked around the stall, her gaze darting from Mini's supplies to Loose Teeth's foreleg firmly planted on the ground. Mini stepped back as the woman approached the horse and stroked his nose.

"Curious," said the woman, turning to look at Mini. The woman's voice was sweet and high-pitched. "Few can bear to be so close to these creatures."

Aru felt a flash of nerves. Was this Mini's test to win Dee Dee back? Did that mean Aru's was next...or had it already passed?

"Yeah, well, Mini's really brave," said Rudy, crossing his arms.

Mini glanced at him gratefully.

"Either that or she's all too familiar with fear," said the stranger, lifting an indifferent shoulder. "Are you often scared, child?"

Mini opened her mouth, then quickly shut it, hurt flashing across her eyes. The confident girl who had been standing tall and proud a moment ago had disappeared.

The stranger didn't seem to notice Mini's silence as she

238

scratched Loose Teeth's velvety muzzle. Loose Teeth snorted with pleasure.

"Night mares are terribly misunderstood creatures," she said. "People think they're evil, but they serve a beautiful purpose. They force you to behold yourself more clearly. They make you honest."

"Can they, uh, make a path for us to get out of here?" asked Aru.

Mini's weapon hadn't returned, so maybe that meant this wasn't the test. Aru's relief was short-lived and followed by a wave of guilt. Was she really that selfish?

Not selfish, said a kind part of herself. *Just scared. That's okay.*

"Oh, you'll leave soon enough," said the woman. "He's bound to wake up soon, and then the Halls of Nidra will vanish and re-form elsewhere."

Rudy raised his hand. "Um, who's going to wake up?"

Brynne shushed him.

"Yeah, about the whole vanishing thing…" said Aru, taking a step toward the woman. "We don't want to be thrown out of the dream—we need to get to the end of it. To the labyrinth entrance—"

"And *soon,*" cut in Brynne. "There's—"

"A battle brewing?" guessed the woman.

"How did you know that?" asked Aiden nervously.

"The Halls of Nidra are ripening, for the realm of dreams loves a good battle," said the woman, looking around. "It is only in dreams, after all, that one's dearest wishes and fiercest terrors may be realized."

"Right…" said Brynne. "Well, it was nice to meet you, stranger! We've got to get going now!"

The woman chuckled softly. "You'll never make it. The realm of dreaming will detect that you are not part of this world, and the door you seek will only grow farther and farther away."

"So that's it, then?" said Mini. "We can't get through?"

"Nonsense," said the stranger. "I will help you."

At that moment, Loose Teeth stepped forward. Her wings arced up, and her shadow fell over Mini, who smiled and reached up to tickle the mare's chin. The dark horse grunted, its blue eyes aglow.

It could have been the low light playing tricks on her, but Aru could have sworn that a look of annoyance flashed over the woman's face.

"Why?" asked Aru warily.

"I do not enjoy being in anyone's debt," said the woman, gesturing to Loose Teeth's foreleg. "You healed one of my charges. In return, I shall supply transportation to the end of the dream world."

Brynne, Mini, and Aru looked at one another, all silently asking the same question: *Can we trust her?* But could they afford not to? Nikita and Sheela's warning was clear: the Halls of Nidra would not last forever. And their chance of ever getting into the labyrinth would soon be lost.

"I have no reason to harm you," said the woman mildly. "I can tell by the celestial weapon your friend carries that you are doing the great work of the gods themselves. Why should I not offer assistance?"

Brynne's chest puffed out a bit, but Aru was still wary.

"Normally I would not concern myself with such matters, but, as I said, I owe you a debt."

"Okay, but who are you?" asked Mini.

The woman bowed her head. "I am the one who tends to the dreams. You may call me The Lady."

Aru raised an eyebrow. "Is that a first or last name?"

"Names are dangerous here," said The Lady. "They make the dream world...specific to you. Give it your name, and you've given a part of yourself that perhaps you may never be able to take back." A look of sorrow crossed The Lady's face. "Now, you will have to ride a dream to make it to the other side. Come. I shall introduce you to the herd."

THIRTY-ONE

They Must Use a Lot of Soap

Normally when one hears *You will have to ride a dream,* that sounds unequivocally *awesome.* Ride atop a dragon made of marshmallows? Excellent. Hurtle through space and time inside a cozy, hand-painted bathtub? Sign me up!

End up face-to-face with gigantic monster horses?

Hard pass.

The Lady had lined up the night-mare herd, and they snorted eagerly, the blades of grass under their hooves brittle with frost. Rudy whimpered. Brynne tried to stare down the demon horses while Aru positioned herself somewhat behind her sister.

Aiden seemed to have won over Inexplicable Natural Disaster by snapping her photo and showing her the result. The horse had whinnied appreciatively, even tossing her mane, which dripped like some sort of toxic sludge down her thick neck. Then she took a gentle step toward Aiden.

"She has chosen you as her rider," said The Lady, scanning the rest of the line.

Don't Look Under the Bed sniffed at Rudy, who ducked to one side...

Mistake.

DLUTB huffed. The sound raised goose bumps on Aru's skin. Rudy tried to move out of the horse's line of vision, but the creature only mirrored his movements.

"She thinks you're playing," observed Mini, who was standing a couple of feet away. Behind her, Loose Teeth snuffled Mini's hair. Compared to the rest of the herd, Loose Teeth did look rather small. Her wings were stunted, as if they hadn't grown properly, and she kept them tightly folded along her back.

"The girl is right," said The Lady, nodding at Rudy. "Don't Look Under the Bed has chosen you."

Rudy, horrified, inched sideways toward the steed.

"I'm not scared of you," said Brynne, pointing to the horse who hadn't broken eye contact with her. "You're mine."

The Lady arched an eyebrow. "That one is Bugs in Your Hair."

Brynne's hand instinctively went to her hair as the horse stepped toward her. The moment Brynne touched the mare's nose, the horse whinnied. Brynne whinnied back.

The Lady surveyed the herd. Most of them had broken off from the line, tails swishing as they nosed through the grass, looking for dreamers. Only one remained. It looked at Aru as if she were a piece of food dropped on the ground and it was deciding whether or not she was worth eating.

The Lady smiled. "Which leaves you with..."

Aru cringed. "Creepy Party Clown?"

The horse bared its teeth in what looked like a huge grin. Its muzzle had a ruddy hue. Like a red foam nose.

"Yay me?" said Aru.

As far as creepy party clowns went, at least this one wasn't trying to talk to her.

Aru sat in the saddle waiting for everyone else to get settled on their mares and found herself petting Creepy Party Clown's shoulder blade. The horse's bristled hair was surprisingly soft, and a shiver of delight ran through its muscles.

I still don't like clowns, thought Aru.

"With the night mares beneath you, the Halls of Nidra can no longer sense your presence," said The Lady. She had levitated a few feet into the air, turning on the spot to survey the area.

The landscape changed. A secret wind rippled across the meadow, as if the dream world were breathing a sigh of relief. The plain stretched for miles in all directions. On either side of them, a thick, dark forest jutted out from the ground and threw shadows over the Potatoes.

"Look!" said Brynne, pointing to something up ahead.

The final portal door, once constantly shifting between near and far away, was no longer moving. It was still some distance from them—at least a couple of hundred feet—but for the first time, it looked like they'd actually be able to reach it.

Aiden, sitting astride Inexplicable Natural Disaster, frowned. "What is *that*?"

Aru knew immediately what he was talking about. It was the odd shape in front of the portal door. Earlier, Aru had thought it looked like a piece of coral. But from here she could see that its protrusions were too long and thick.

Aiden lifted Shadowfax to his eye and adjusted the focus. "That can't be what I think it is...."

"What can't?" asked Brynne.

Aru knew what he would say, and she braced herself for it.

"It looks like a *hand*."

As one, the Potatoes gazed up at The Lady, who was still floating in the air, serene and unbothered.

"But it's not....Right?" said Mini. "Because that would be extremely disturbing."

"Of course it is a hand," said The Lady.

The Potatoes fell silent. Rudy looked nauseated. "What happened to the person it belonged to?"

"Oh, he is here," said The Lady, glancing in the direction of the door. "He is always here...and soon, he will wake up. Which is why we shall take a shortcut through the forest. No need to announce our presence. Once he wakes up, the Halls of Nidra will move elsewhere, and you, human children, will be thrown out."

"Who is *he*?" asked Brynne.

It looked like The Lady was going to answer, but then she glanced at the hand and thought better of it. "When we are out of earshot, I shall tell his tale."

She waved her hand, and some fifteen feet away, the dark trees parted to reveal a shadowed archway.

"This way," she said, floating toward the opening.

The Lady whistled, and the five horses turned and fell into step behind her. Brynne was at the head of the group, Rudy and Mini followed her, and Aru and Aiden were at the rear. As the horses jostled into line, Aiden caught her eye. Aru realized she'd never given him the chance to finish his apology. But she couldn't exactly turn around in her seat now and yell, *WHAT WERE YOU TALKING ABOUT?*

She could tell, though, that he hadn't forgotten. And as the night mares trotted into the forest, she felt his eyes on her even in the dark.

Branches parted and the cool shadows slid aside to make a path. The only light came from the night mares' burning-blue-inferno eyes. They snorted, stamping their feet against the undergrowth. It crunched like broken glass.

Where the horses stepped, puffs of smoke rose into the air, and Aru caught faint images in the tiny clouds—a man being greeted at the door by his children, an outdoor wedding, a rug beside a crackling fireplace. The pictures vanished within seconds.

"What is this place?" she asked.

Up ahead, The Lady looked over her shoulder. She was faintly illuminated, and her hair wavered in the air around her like a ghost's, making Aru wonder if she was one.

"This is the burial ground of dead dreams," said The Lady. "Dreams that were once held dear and then abandoned when the dreamer realized they would never come true."

Aru felt a pang of sorrow as they moved through the trees. Though the forest was thick with brambles, she could see the last portal between the branches. The hand, bathed in the door's golden glow, was more visible now, too. It towered over them like a roller coaster. Huge rings glinted on the sandy-colored fingers, and the nails were filed to a long, elegant taper. Aru couldn't begin to imagine the size of the person the hand belonged to.

"So . . . whose hand is that?" she asked, darting a glance at The Lady.

"I thought the answer would be obvious by now," said The Lady. "He made a poorly worded wish some eons ago...and a part of him will always pay the price."

Aru felt a name squirming in the back of her thoughts. A rakshasa prince...brother of Ravana, the demon king. Aru opened her mouth, but Mini spoke first.

"Kumbhakarna?"

The Lady turned and smiled. "You know the tale?"

"Sorta?" said Mini.

The Lady waved her hand. The forest around them vanished and was replaced by a rocky field. A large *yagna* fire burned at the center, the flames towering almost a dozen feet in the air. The demon king Ravana was seated before it, all ten pairs of his eyes shut tight in prayer. Behind him, looming taller than the flames, sat Kumbhakarna with his hands pressed together.

"They were very pious demons," said The Lady. "And after they performed great penances, even the gods could not ignore their goodness."

The air crackled with thunder and lightning. Aru startled, and the night mares pricked their ears, their heads swiveling as if unsure of this new landscape. Mini reached out and scratched Loose Teeth's ears. The horse's tail swished happily as she continued to walk.

Just reminding you that you cannot *keep a night mare as a pet,* said Aru through the mind link.

I would never! said Mini.

Brynne made a snorting sound of *Yeah, right* through the mind link.

Loose Teeth can't exist outside the realm of sleep anyway, said Mini. *I asked.*

Before Aru could point out that this was the *wrong* question, Kumbhakarna's voice boomed across the rocky field.

"I, Kumbhakarna, humbly ask for . . . for . . ." He paused.

At his massive height, Aru couldn't see his face clearly. It was blurred by shadows. But she saw that the rakshasa prince listed to one side, as if he had suddenly become tired.

"The demon brothers had already agreed that Kumbhakarna would take the throne of the gods themselves by demanding *Indraasana*, or the seat of Indra," said The Lady. "But instead he asked for—"

"I DEMAND *NIDRAASANA!*" boomed Kumbhakarna.

Below him, Ravana looked up sharply. Aru didn't think she'd ever be able to sympathize with a demon king, but she recognized his expression immediately. It said *Bro, that was* NOT *part of the plan. What are you doing?*

The Lady laughed softly. "And he was also supposed to ask for the annihilation of the gods, or *nirdevatvam*."

"AND I DEMAND . . . I DEMAND . . . *NIDRAVATVAM!*"

To Aru's ears, the words slurring from Kumbhakarna's mouth sounded almost identical.

Almost.

In the image, Ravana's face fell. He stood up and darted out of the way as his huge brother fell into the earth beside him and promptly began to . . . snore.

The vision faded, and once more the Pandavas were back in the forest with The Lady, who was laughing to herself.

"Ah, the fool," she said, delighted. "A goddess tied his tongue so that when he meant to ask for the seat of Indra, he asked for a *bed*, and when he asked for the annihilation of the gods, he asked instead for *sleep*."

Maybe Aru would've laughed, too, but the trees looked different now. When she turned in her seat, she could no longer see the path they'd taken. Impossibly, the forest was even thicker and darker, and no matter how hard she looked, she couldn't catch sight of either Kumbhakarna's outstretched hand or the final portal that had set it aglow.

"Where are we?" asked Aru.

"I told you," said The Lady, "we're taking a shortcut. And anyway, we've arrived. Time to dismount from your steeds."

The night mares stopped. Mini bent over her horse, frowning. Loose Teeth swiveled her head to look at her rider, and in the blue infernos of her eyes Aru detected something like *sorrow*.

Something feels off, said Aru through the mind link.

Loose Teeth looked forward again and whinnied, trotting sideways. She bucked slightly.

"Whoa, what's wrong?" asked Mini, rubbing Loose Teeth's neck, but the mare wouldn't calm down.

"I said *dismount*," said The Lady.

All the horses except Loose Teeth began to roar. Creepy Party Clown slowly turned her head toward Aru. The horse's lips pulled into another terrifying grin. Aru scrambled out of her saddle, nearly tumbling headfirst to the black forest floor below.

Rudy slipped sideways off his horse, hollering, "HOW DARE YOU!"

Mini dropped gracefully from her saddle, and while the other horses backed away, Loose Teeth stayed with her, nuzzling her shoulder, her tail flicking nervously like a cat's.

"What's going on?" demanded Brynne. "You said you'd show us a shortcut out of here!"

"And this is, in a way," said The Lady.

ROSHANI CHOKSHI

Aiden hopped down from Inexplicable Natural Disaster and walked straight over to Aru. He stood in front of her, and Aru could feel the heat coming off him as he raised his scimitars defensively. Brynne's hand moved to the choker at her throat. Aru's gaze whipped around the forest. She hated this feeling, that she was trapped and couldn't do anything to help her friends. She watched, horror climbing through her, as fallen leaves and pine needles on the forest floor swirled into the unmistakable shapes of five little beds.

The Lady, now hovering twenty feet off the ground, turned to face them. "You want a shortcut out of all this mess? Out of all this *pain*? Oh, don't try to tell me otherwise, children. My horses relayed your sweet fears as they quietly feasted upon them."

Aru glanced over her shoulder. Ten feet away, Creepy Party Clown met her gaze and licked his nose with a tongue the color of dried blood. She felt sick.

"The horses told me that you're just so . . . *tired*," said The Lady. "I'm doing you a favor, really. You'll see that it's better this way. Besides, the goddess Nidra would consider herself robbed if you didn't visit her realm of sleep. All your fancy enchantments and wake-me-up amulets mean *nothing* here. It is time to pay your debts in another manner."

The leaves and needles rose up, swirling around The Lady and choking off the forest around them. "It's time, sweet heroes . . . to *rest*."

THIRTY-
TWO

Worst Lullaby EVER.
Can I Get a Refund?

T he debris churning around The Lady exploded.
The horses scattered, whinnying loudly as they fled
the forest. The pine needles hurtled toward the Potatoes
like tiny darts.

"Ow!" said Mini when they hit her skin. "They're drawing
blood!"

"Get together!" shouted Aru.

The five of them huddled, standing back-to-back as if that
might offer some protection. Aru had just raised her hands to her
face, bracing herself for impact, when a shadow fell across her.

"Loose Teeth, what are you doing?" asked The Lady in a shrill voice.

Aru peeked between her fingers to see the needles hitting the
horse's wings, which were spread in front of them like a shield.
Loose Teeth neighed, her forelegs kicking at the air as the needles
settled once more onto the ground. Mini broke away from the
group and patted the horse's shoulder. The night mare grinned.

"No matter," said The Lady. She snapped her fingers and a
black root snaked out of the ground, heading straight for Mini.

"Move!" yelled Aru.

"Mini!" screamed Brynne, spinning to cast her mace.

But it wasn't Aru or Brynne who reached Mini first.

It was Rudy.

The naga prince darted out, transforming in a flash into his half-serpent form. His eyes glowed red, and his red-and-gold-banded tail slapped the root away as he snarled at The Lady. He looked surprisingly formidable. And it wasn't missed that he had tapped into his own power to protect Mini. Her eyes widened.

Rudy opened his mouth. Clearly he was going to say something epic and awesome, and maybe even romantic....

"What about Plushy Scales? I'll get nightmares without Plushy Scales—" Rudy slumped to one side. The bed of pine needles zoomed over to catch him. His tail curled up, and within seconds he was snoring.

Never mind, then, thought Aru.

"Plushy Scales?" asked Aiden, raising an eyebrow.

"Why are you doing this to us?" Mini asked The Lady. "You'd better not hurt him!" Her face blazed with fury. Beside her, Loose Teeth stamped the ground.

"There's a war on the other side of this realm, and we have to be there—" started Brynne.

The Lady laughed humorlessly. "I have heard it all. I know all about the wars that end all wars, and the truth is, nothing changes. People die. Lives are sacrificed. And who bothers to remember? No one."

The Lady gradually began to descend. Black debris swirled around her feet once more. Brynne raised her wind mace again and Aiden fumbled with his scimitars. The edge of one of his golden blades touched the ground, and it seared the grass with a *hiss*. A small pile of leaves briefly caught fire. Aiden watched it, his brow furrowing as if he'd just had an idea.

Aru's eyes flicked from the burned leaves to the grinning Lady. "But this time it might actually be different," Aru said quietly. "This time, we have the chance for true change. The chance for a life in which no one needs to be sacrificed ... or hurt. Or forgotten."

The last four beds inched closer, and Aru felt a terrible drowsiness wash over her. She swayed on the spot until she felt a warm hand close around her wrist, and she looked up to see Aiden staring at her. The starry flecks in his eyes held her steady.

"Don't you dare, Shah," he said. "Stay with me."

His words helped Aru shake off her drowsiness. Aiden let go of her hand, and Aru imagined she felt sparks chasing one another across her skin.

"Who *are* you?" Mini demanded of The Lady.

"I am Urmila."

She stared at them and Aru felt a stab of guilt when she looked at the woman's face. Urmila's eyes looked vengeful, but there was also the faintest trace of *hope* on her face. As if this might be the moment someone recognized her.

Urmila's shoulders sank. "But of course you wouldn't know."

"Then tell us," said Aru. "What do you want? Maybe we can help?"

Urmila waved her arm, and the scene around them changed. They were standing in the front hall of a beautiful palace, and there were three people before them—a man with sapphire-colored skin and a bow and arrow slung across his back, a dark-complexioned woman with a queenly bearing despite the plain cotton sari she wore, and another man with a bow and arrow, the color of his skin like sunlight hitting bronze.

Aru recognized them instantly. Rama, the god king; Sita, his wife; and Laxmana, his brother. She also knew what was about to happen based on the tales her mother had told her. Rama, Sita, and Laxmana were on the verge of their exile in the forest, and soon the demon king Ravana would steal Sita away and ignite a war.

A fourth person appeared in the scene, running into the hallway breathless and tear-streaked—Urmila. She wore a diadem of amethysts around her head, and she was dressed in rich purple silks.

"Sister, why have you come?" asked Sita. "Go. Return to the palace. Our fate is not for you to bear."

"But I wish to," begged Urmila, reaching for Laxmana's hands.

The look that passed between them was loving. Intimate. They were, Aru realized, husband and wife. It made sense that Laxmana had a wife, but Aru had never heard her name spoken.

"You cannot, my love," he said. "I have to protect my brother. You know that. To ensure his safety I will not close my eyes for a single moment—"

"But that is not for you to decide," said a voice, interrupting the scene.

Laxmana, Rama, and Sita looked up. A great pair of eyes opened just above them. *A goddess's eyes*, thought Aru. They were thickly lashed and lined with kohl, with irises the color of a thousand midnights.

"You must take your sleep, for it is owed to me. . . ."

"I cannot, goddess Nidra," said Laxmana, pressing his hands together in prayer.

"Then who will?"

"*I* will," said Urmila, raising her hand. "I...I will take my husband's rest."

The goddess's eyes roved to Urmila, who looked as though she was trying her best to stand tall beside Laxmana.

"Sleep...unending...for years. The world will change, and you will not. Dust will be your bed of dreams. Is this truly the sacrifice you wish to make?"

Urmila faltered. Laxmana stared at her, his shoulders thrown back, his expression unreadable.

Urmila nodded. "For my husband, I will sacrifice those years."

The moment the words left her mouth, Urmila swooned and fell to the ground. Laxmana knelt beside her, and the vision faded.

Aru looked up at Urmila, who was now dressed in a gown as in the story and silvered like a ghost. Nearly transparent.

"I lost years of my life," she said. "I heard the courtiers laughing at my 'sacrifice' while I dreamed my way through autumns and monsoons, trapped in the Halls of Nidra for the sake of my love. My life held but a sliver of importance to the great quests and greater wars of godly kings and princes.... Where were those who would sacrifice a night of rest for me? Where is the life I dreamed away? Perhaps a part of me has always been stuck here... in a dream that will not end."

"Maybe we can change that. It may take us a while, but if you let us go and we win the war, then we can come back for you—" tried Aru, but Urmila shook her head.

"No," she said. "I will wait for no one. Not anymore. And frankly, child, why should you carry such burdens? What do you owe the world after what it's done to you?"

Aru felt Urmila's eyes burning into hers, and shame curled around her thoughts. Shame because Aru *agreed* with her. What *did* she owe the world after all that had happened? Why *did* the Pandavas have to do this? Where was everyone else?

"Good-bye, children," said Urmila. "Sweet dreams." She hovered off the ground, angling forward.

"Get back here!" yelled Brynne. She spun out her wind mace, but the stream of air merely went through Urmila. The forest debris swirled around them, agitated by the sudden blast of Brynne's power. Aru uselessly swiped at the hem of Urmila's gown, as if she could tug her back to the ground, and her hand met something solid....

Urmila turned and glared at her before vanishing into the trees along with the rest of the night mares. A silver anklet now lay in the middle of Aru's palm like a token. It was so cold it burned her skin, and she nearly dropped it.

"ARU!" screamed Mini.

Aru glanced up as a wall of black detritus shot from the ground. The sound of the swirling leaves, twigs, and needles was like the buzz of a thousand flies. Aru looked over her shoulder. A few feet away, Rudy snored on, oblivious to the storm around him. Next to him, the four little beds of pine needles glowed softly ... *invitingly.*

"Aru, get back!" said Brynne. "What are you doing?"

The wall of debris and sleep moved closer. If she lifted her arm, it would be inches away. Sleep would be instantaneous. Urmila was right. Aru was so tired and so angry, and so tired of *being* angry that all she really wanted in this moment was a good long nap. If she touched the wall, she wouldn't even know that she'd let everyone down. She wouldn't know anything. And there was a dangerous escape in that blankness that made the muscles in her arm twitch.

Aru, come back. . . . You have to come back!

But the words were lost in the sound of the dead leaves, which no longer seemed so noisy. It made Aru think of one of Kara's favorite words: *susurrus.*

It sounds like what it means, Kara had once said. *It's . . . it's an honest word. No tricks to it, just sound and poetry. I think that's why I like it so much.*

No tricks to it . . . There was something comforting in that knowledge. *Susurrus* was the quiet *shush-shush* of rustling things—autumn leaves, blankets, thoughts on the edge of sleep. Aru had just closed her eyes when a voice sliced through the comforting buzzing. . . .

"Please, Shah?"

Aru opened her eyes. The swarm of black leaves and dirt was barely six inches from her face. She shuddered, jumping back and colliding with something warm and solid. She caught her breath and inhaled that familiar fragrance of spice and fresh laundry. *Aiden.*

His hand moved to her waist, drawing her against him. "I've got you, Shah," he said. When he spoke, his voice ruffled the wisps of hair that had escaped from her braid. "Don't go."

It was hardly more than a few seconds, but Aru felt each of them crash against her like waves.

"I can't get rid of it!" yelled Brynne.

Turquoise jets of air ripped into the wall of debris, creating holes in it, but seconds later the dead leaves merely fell back into place. The wall began to encircle them. Brynne roared, twirling her weapon overhead. A powerful cyclone blasted the wall apart. . . .

Only for it to re-form and close in tighter.

Aiden and Aru sprang away from each other. Once more, Aiden drew his scimitars. Loose Teeth neighed loudly and kicked the air. Mini stroked her neck, trying to calm her, but it made no difference.

"What do we do?" shrieked Mini.

One of Aiden's scimitars dropped to the ground, and yet again Aru heard that searing *hiss*. The leaves and twigs under Aiden's sword began to smoke.

"The heat!" said Aru, pointing at the blade. "We need more of it!"

Aiden followed the direction of her gaze and then looked up at her. "Uh-oh."

"What *uh-oh*?" said Aru. "You've got scimitars— Whoa, what are you doing?"

Aiden dropped to his knees and took off his backpack, laying it gently on the ground.

"Ammamma, what are you *doing*?" demanded Brynne. "We don't have time for this!"

Aiden ignored her. He unzipped his bag. Detritus whirled overhead, blotting out the night sky. Aru and Brynne inched closer together, the wall now less than a foot away from them.

"Okay, just"—Aiden's eyes flashed between Aru, Mini, and Brynne—"don't be mad."

Aiden reached into his backpack and brought out a pair of gloves. As he slid them on, realization struck Aru.

"Are you serious?" she demanded.

Aiden made soft cooing sounds as he lifted something bright and glowing from the depths of his pack.

"Oh no," said Mini.

THIRTY-THREE

Post-Nap Baby Boo

"WHAT?!" said Brynne.

A significantly larger—and apparently fresh from a nap—Baby Boo appeared in Aiden's hands. The firebird was now the size of a laptop. He blinked at them and chirped happily. Smoke spiraled off his ruby-red plumage. His flaming blue crest flickered happily. He looked up at Aiden, ruffling his feathers.

Mini just spluttered. "The...the hygiene! The air circulation! What about his food?" And then, at a loss for how to convey all her fury at once, she finally blurted out, "Baby Boo has a very strict sleep schedule!"

"The backpack is enchanted and extremely comfortable, and of course I know about BB's sleep schedule!" snapped Aiden. "Why do you think I kept checking my backpack?"

"Focus, Ammamma!" said Brynne. "Battle first, baby later!"

"Right," said Aiden, awkwardly bouncing BB.

The wall swirled closer. Aru was almost scared to breathe, convinced that if she sucked in any of the debris she'd fall asleep on the spot.

"Wifey…" said Mini warningly.

"On it," said Aiden.

His scimitars lay glowing on the ground. "BB always gets some indigestion after a nap, so this is our best chance."

Baby Boo made small sounds of distress, evidently annoyed at being jostled up and down. His little blue flame towered higher. Steam rose from his beak. The bird swiveled around, squawking angrily at Aiden.

"I know, I know," said Aiden, his eyes fixed on the forest floor. "Just get it out of your system."

BB screeched. The little scarlet feathers on his throat puffed out. He lifted his wings. In the distance, Rudy looked completely swallowed up by leaves and pine needles. Loose Teeth had stopped kicking at the wall. Instead, her blue-inferno eyes regarded the firebird curiously. She stepped forward, looking as if she might snuffle BB, when Aiden shouted, "Duck!"

Baby Boo hiccupped. A tiny spark shot out of his mouth and fell onto the ground.

Aru, crouched beside Brynne, glared up at Aiden. "Is that it?"

Baby Boo's wings rose again, his small beak opened, and—*FWOOMP!*

"Was that a sneeze?" asked Brynne.

It wasn't a kind of sneeze Aru had ever witnessed. Flames shot out of Baby Boo's beak. When the fire hit the dirt, a metallic screech ripped through the Halls of Nidra. Aru and Brynne huddled closer to the ground while Brynne cast a wind wall shielding Rudy in his bed of pine needles. Mini ducked behind Loose Teeth. The night mare swiveled her great head and closed her burning blue eyes. Through the gaps in her fingers, Aru watched as the stream of fire turned the forest floor molten. The wall of debris melted into glass and exploded, showering them with shards. Heat washed over Aru, and she sucked in a lungful of hot air.

Cheep!

Baby Boo hiccupped loudly. A chiming sound had replaced the gnat-like buzzing of the swirling leaves and sticks. When Aru removed her hands from her face, she saw that the forest floor looked like it was littered all over with diamonds. She stood up carefully. As the ring of smoke around them began to clear, Aru spotted a glow in the distance. A shadow quivered in front of it, only to be swallowed up once more by the smoke.

"Shhh, there, there," said Mini, soothing Loose Teeth, who was anxiously swishing her tail.

Rudy groaned and stirred. Light skittered across his tail, and within seconds he had morphed back into a fully human shape. He shook himself, then swung his legs off the bed and yawned, blinking at the scene around him. "I'm either way more powerful than I thought...or I missed something," he said.

"The latter," said Brynne, patting Baby Boo's head. The bird seemed very pleased with himself. The long feathers of his tail fanned out, scattering sparks along Brynne's sleeves. She screeched, batting out the fire while Aiden held back a laugh.

Rudy squinted. "Wait. So I *didn't* save everyone?"

"You were great, Rudy," said Mini.

At this, Rudy beamed. The tops of his cheeks turned red and his eyes widened. "Um, why is BB here?"

"That's what I said," said Mini.

"I made a promise to Boo that I would always take him with us," said Aiden stiffly. "Besides...he needs us."

"Why don't I ever get to hold him? He likes me best anyway!" said Rudy, outraged. "Give him to me!"

"No!" said Aiden.

While the boys argued, Brynne took out her wind mace and aimed it at the smoke still curling around them.

"Poga mayam aipo!" said Brynne.

A faint blue light snaked out from Gogo and dragged back the smoke as if it were a curtain. Many of the dark trees around them had snapped in two and now lay in smoldering chunks. Beyond the forest was the shadowy meadow of the dreaming world. Above was an endless twilight sky, and less than a hundred feet away stood a golden door. . . .

The final door.

Beside it, poking out from another dense thicket of shadows and trees, was the outstretched hand of Kumbhakarna. Aru stared at it. Had the fingers always been curled like that?

"Well, at least Urmila wasn't totally lying," said Brynne. "This was definitely a shortcut. And the portal isn't moving anymore, so that's good."

"Path's clear, too," said Aiden.

Baby Boo cheeped in agreement. Aru couldn't say why she felt a sudden prickling at the back of her neck, as if she were being watched. Loose Teeth snorted, and Mini frowned at the night mare.

Something wasn't right.

"Well, then let's go!" said Rudy. He strolled toward the edge of the woods. "Honestly, I don't know why we can't play some music while we walk. It's so boring otherwise— Ow!"

Rudy frowned. He tried to move forward, only to find himself blocked. He lifted his hand in the air and his fingers splayed out as if he'd hit a pane of glass.

"What the—"

Aru looked up to see a pair of eyes blinking open in the twilight sky. Nidra's eyes. Large and slightly lifted at their corners, thickly lashed with shadows for eyeliner and irises the color of midnight. Two thin clouds suggested eyebrows angled downward, giving Aru the impression that the goddess was frowning at them sympathetically.

"I am afraid that there are no exceptions to the rules. All who pass through my Halls must pay."

THIRTY-FOUR

You'll Be the Death of Me

Aru was sure that one of them had spoken. Maybe Rudy had yelled. Or Brynne had made a retort. Maybe she herself had gasped when she saw those great big eyes in the sky....

But all the sounds were swallowed up in a sudden roar.

The Halls of Nidra quivered. The remaining trees shook. The sound flattened the grasses in an instant, and a crack appeared in the sky.

Nidra's eyes rolled to the left, as if sensing something just out of sight. *"My realm is waking."*

Oh, thought Aru, her stomach sinking. It was not a roar at all....

It was a yawn.

Kumbhakarna's hand twitched, and the golden glow of the portal door flickered. Nikita's warning rose sharply in her thoughts—the realm of sleep was not built to last in one place forever.

"What do you want from us?" demanded Brynne.

"Bee..." said Mini warningly.

Mini was the first to press her hands together in pranama before touching the glittering ground. Aru and the others quickly followed suit. When Brynne straightened up, she looked a little ashamed. "Sorry," she mumbled.

"What can we give you, goddess?" asked Mini, one hand on Loose Teeth's flank.

"I've got lots of rocks!" said Rudy, thrusting his backpack at the sky.

The pair of eyes regarded them mildly.

"They're very shiny?" added Rudy.

It is your sleep I want. I need your dreams to build the borders of my world. You must give them to me if you wish to pass. Even demigods grant me what I am owed.

Aru thought back to Urmila, the way she'd fallen into a sleep and lost years that no one remembered.

"I can't do that," said Brynne.

I have already selected one among you. I want dreams rich with wonder, tinged with sadness, and flavored with hope that will sweeten my land like the rarest of nectars.

Don't let it be me, don't let it be me, don't let it be me, prayed Aru. But even as she did, she had a sinking sensation that it was.

And indeed, the pair of eyes focused on Aru. A pale violet light hovered in front of her. It was soft and inviting, and when Aru looked at it, she tasted dust on her tongue.

You, child. I can feel your exhaustion....

Oh, well. Maybe it was all for the best, thought Aru, swaying on her feet. Better her than someone else.

Let me take it from you....

"No," said a firm voice behind Aru. "Not her."

Aru turned. The light washed over Aiden. He stood tall, his eyes hard and glittering.

"Take me instead," he said.

"What?" said Aru. "*No way.* I can't let you do that."

"I always knew this was going to happen," said Aiden. "I'm not scared, Shah."

His eyes skipped over Aru's and met Brynne's. Aru saw that Brynne looked horrified...but not surprised. Her mouth was a grim line, as if she'd been steeling herself for this moment.

Did you also know this would happen? Aru asked her through their mind link.

Aru could feel Brynne's hesitation like a wall of debris slowly growing up between them. She lashed out, screaming through the barrier. *DID YOU KNOW?!*

Brynne and Mini winced at the same time. Aru didn't apologize.

It's the prophecy he heard, said Brynne. *Remember? I wanted to say something, but it wasn't my secret to tell. He made me promise not to.*

The prophecy. Aru cast back in her mind for words that were uttered what felt like eons ago.

The girl you love will be the death of you.

But that would mean...

Aru's mind stopped short of comprehension. She swung around to face Aiden. He looked achingly handsome. His emerald-green jacket stretched across his broadening shoulders. The violet light of the dreaming world tinted the tops of his cheekbones, the glimmer in his eyes, and the glossy curls of his hair. His apsara bloodline shone through as if he were partially made of starlight, and if he had looked at her face just then, Aiden would have seen all the things Aru refused to say.

But he wasn't looking at her. His gaze was fixed on Nidra's eyes in the sky.

"Do you understand what you are doing?" asked the goddess.

Aiden didn't hesitate. "Yes."

"You understand that my realm is its own form of death."

Death. The word shuddered through Aru. Aiden didn't flinch, but Aru watched—frozen in horror—as his jaw clenched. He nodded. "I know."

Nidra blinked and then closed her eyes in assent. *"You have always known, haven't you?"*

Aiden said nothing, but he looked straight at the goddess and didn't move away.

Aru felt as if something inside her was pulling taut to the point of breaking. She kept trying to speak, but the words stuck in her throat.

He was sacrificing himself for her.

"You understand that you will not be returned to the waking world if there is no world to wake up to."

"I understand."

"What does that mean?" asked Brynne, frantic. "He's going to die?"

Beside her, Mini and Rudy looked stricken. Even Loose Teeth pawed at the ground, dismayed. Baby Boo made a soft, inquisitive chirp, and looked up at Aiden. The blue flame crest on his head wilted.

"What is the point of returning him if there is no chance of a world worth returning to?" asked Nidra. *"Whether he dies or not depends on you, daughters*

of the gods, for it is your world to save, is it not? And if he does die, that in itself will be a blessing. To die in one's sleep is the hope of all mortals. You should be thanking me."

Thirty yards away, Kumbhakarna's fingers curled. His hand flipped over and his palm pressed into the dreaming world as if it were a mattress he was pushing himself out of.

"You are running out of time. Make your choice now or be thrown from my world."

The choice was an impossible one. Aru knew that she was the one who had to confront Kara and the Sleeper, but Aiden was...

Before Aru could protest, or Brynne could lunge forward, or Rudy could raise his hand, or Mini could plead for a different request, Aiden spoke.

"I accept."

The words thundered through the Halls of Nidra, and Aru knew in her bones that his offer had been accepted. The violet light slipped sideways, abandoning Aru and drifting toward Aiden. She wasn't sure how she knew, but that same instinct told her that the moment he touched the light, he would vanish.

Forever, whispered a dark voice in her thoughts.

"Aru."

She looked up, startled by the sound of her name.

"I can't let you do this!" she said.

"It wasn't your choice to make, though," said Aiden, smiling sadly. "It was mine. You'll find a way out of this, I know it. Watch BB for me, okay?"

Aiden set down his backpack and the firebird. BB nestled into the bag, cooing and chirping at Aiden.

Hot tears slid down Aru's cheeks. "What if I can't?"

"You will," said Aiden. "You always do."

The violet light turned brighter. It was suspended right next to Aiden now. He and Aru were less than a foot apart, but it might as well have been miles. The growing illumination threw the rest of the world into shadows, transforming Mini, Brynne, Rudy, and Nidra's great, wide eyes into nothing more than blips of darkness.

"I lied, Aru," said Aiden, reaching for her face. His fingers slipped into her hair, and he drew her closer. "I don't regret anything."

"Wait—" she tried to say, but the rest of her words were stopped by a kiss.

A first kiss...and now a last kiss? In some secret part of her heart, Aru held the hope that they would have a thousand more. She closed her eyes. It was only for a blink or two, but when she opened them a moment later, Aiden was gone.

Nidra's silken, starry voice echoed in the sky. *"No time for dreaming, Pandavas. Kumbhakarna is already rising."*

THIRTY-FIVE

The Daughter of Death Opens Her Eyes

Yamini Kapoor-Mercado-Lopez was used to being scared.

While other people were trailed by their shadows, Mini was convinced that it was fear that followed her, constantly dogging her steps and whispering *Are you sure? Is this right? Is this safe?*

Dimly, she heard Brynne's heartbroken cry and she watched in shock as Aru sank to her knees, her face pale. She saw Rudy's face crumple in grief. In the aftermath of Aiden's disappearance, he had picked up his cousin's backpack and now held the small firebird in the crook of his arm, supported by a fireproof blanket.

"But...But that wasn't supposed to happen," he said dully. He turned to Mini as if she knew all the answers. "Aiden's coming back, right? *Right?*"

I don't know, thought Mini, feeling hollow.

They should have been staring at Aru and Aiden in the aftermath of a kiss. They should have been breaking into awkward laughter. Brynne should have been rolling her eyes and saying something about how it was *about time* and how any more pining would've ruined her appetite for good. Mini should have been trying not to tell them about the number of bacteria that lived in the human mouth.

Everything felt wrong.

Loose Teeth snorted and pushed Mini's shoulder with her cold nose, her damp breath ruffling Mini's hair. She was looking to Mini for direction. Rudy was, too.

"My stomach hurts, and my heart is doing this rhythm thing that might be cool as a bass beat, but it doesn't feel so good," said Rudy. His breaths were coming fast and shallow. "What's happening to me?"

"You're having a panic attack," said Mini.

"How do I make it go away?" asked Rudy.

Before, Mini thought she knew the answer to that question. With her Death Danda in her hands and power flowing through her veins, fear couldn't touch her. But all that had changed in an instant. Aru's birthday party at the museum had turned into a battle, and the shadows Mini summoned began to pop and bubble. But much worse was the moment she realized Dee Dee was melting into the floor tiles and she was left scrabbling uselessly at the marble.

Without her weapon, her fear had returned with a vengeance. Maybe that was why it couldn't take her by surprise anymore. After all, it was the condition in which she always existed.

So, when Kumbhakarna sat upright in the distance, Mini didn't bat an eye. Neither did she shriek when the dream world around them shook and the stars trembled overhead. Mini was always braced for the worst. Thus, when the worst happened, time didn't speed up for her . . . it slowed down.

"I SMELL STRANGERS," said Kumbhakarna.

Even at a whisper, his voice covered miles.

Rudy whimpered.

"WHERE ARE YOU, LITTLE STRANGERS? ARE YOUR DREAMS SWEET? HAS YOUR HOPE SOURED? COME TO ME SO I MIGHT TASTE IT FOR MYSELF."

"We have to get out of here," said Mini, her hand on the night mare's warm flank.

Loose Teeth snorted. The Halls of Nidra grew darker, and the stars winked out one by one. The only remaining brightness came from the glowing portal door about a hundred feet away. But the terrain had changed—it was no longer covered in soft grass or rolling clouds but pitted all over with the glass shards from Baby Boo's fire blast.

Kumbhakarna stood. The only way Mini knew was because the Halls of Nidra tilted and the remaining stars were momentarily blocked out. Otherwise he was nothing more than a silhouette set against the dimness.

"I can barely see anything," said Rudy, turning around in the dark.

Mini pushed her glasses a little higher on the bridge of her nose. It didn't help her see any better, but it gave her hands something to do as her mind began to turn.

"I've got it," said Brynne flatly.

Aru still hadn't said a word. She was just staring at the spot where Aiden had disappeared. Mini wasn't even sure she'd noticed that it had grown darker around them.

"Got what?" asked Rudy.

"The Sun Jewel," said Brynne. "I bet—"

Loose Teeth whinnied loudly.

"Wait," said Mini, holding up her hand. "I don't think that's a good idea."

"We won't be able to see where we're going without some light!" said Brynne.

"And if we bring out a light like the Sun Jewel, then Kumbhakarna will be able to see us," said Mini.

As if he'd heard them, the giant's whisper stretched over the desolate dream plains once more.

"ARE YOU SCARED?" he asked. "GOOD. MEAT TASTES SWEETER WHEN THE PREY IS STARTLED, YOU KNOW. FEAR IS SUCH A SUBTLE FLAVOR."

He inhaled and then exhaled with a loud *ahh*. "ALREADY IT BUILDS AROUND YOU LIKE THE SWEETEST OF PERFUMES."

Fear. *That* was what was swallowing the dreamscape. Its darkness was slowly rolling over the portal, eating away its light.

"IS THAT A SPARK I SEE IN THE DISTANCE?" asked Kumbhakarna.

Adrenaline shot through Mini. "Rudy, hide BB! Now!"

"Sorry, buddy," said Rudy, lowering the firebird into Aiden's backpack.

Immediately the Potatoes were shrouded from sight.

Kumbhakarna laughed. "WELL, YOU CANNOT HIDE FROM ME FOREVER."

"How are we going to get out of here?" asked Brynne, her voice barely above a whisper.

Instinctively, both Brynne and Mini looked to Aru. She was the one who always had the ideas—Aru, whose imagination was so slippery that it could sneak its way through any problem. But she was still as a statue.

Brynne, the strongest of all of them, cowered a little.

The sight jolted something loose inside Mini.

She wasn't sure what made her act, but now she found herself reaching for Loose Teeth's bridle. She swung her leg over the saddle. The night mare's ears pricked and swiveled.

"Mini, what are you doing?" asked Brynne.

Mini reached for Loose Teeth's reins and looked out. She could see a trail of blue light winding through the dark toward the dimming portal.

"There's a path," she said.

"What are you talking about?" asked Brynne.

"The *path*," said Mini, pointing at the snaking blue line.

Brynne followed Mini's finger and shrugged. "I don't see anything."

"Me either," said Rudy.

Brynne looked up at her. "Why can only you see it?"

Mini paused. "I...I don't know."

It was like what had happened in the stable with Loose Teeth. For some reason, she wasn't scared. Mini flinched, remembering Urmila's indifference when Aru had said that Mini was brave.

Either that or she's all too familiar with fear.

Urmila had said it like it was a bad thing, but Mini's fear had alchemized into something precious—something that, apparently, was letting her see what no one else could.

Are you often scared, child?

"Yes," said Mini softly. "But that's not going to stop me."

"What?" asked Brynne.

Mini realized that she'd spoken out loud. "Nothing," she

said. "C'mon. I'll—" She took a deep breath and tried out words that felt spicy and strange on her tongue: "I'll lead us."

Aru held Brynne's hand, and Brynne held Rudy's, and Rudy clutched a strap on Loose Teeth's saddle. The mare had grumbled at first, her head swinging dangerously close to Rudy's, but she stopped short of biting when Mini, sitting astride the saddle, had shushed her.

"Quiet," she hissed. "He could be anywhere."

Mini searched the clouds as she followed the path of blue light in the darkness. The ground yielded like thick mud beneath her. Once or twice she slid in her seat, and yet with every step, Mini found herself sitting up a little straighter. They were moving forward. They were making their way.

I don't know how you're doing this, Mini, but KEEP DOING IT, said Brynne through the mind link.

Mini grinned. Up ahead, the portal was nearly hidden beneath a cloud of fear, but Mini could still see it clearly enough.

"WHERE ARE YOU, SWEET MORSELS?" asked Kumbhakarna.

His voice came from behind, and it was edged with irritation. So far, he hadn't been able to find them. Mini smiled and urged Loose Teeth forward. For the first time in days, she felt as if some of her panic had receded. And yet she was still empty-handed. Stripped of her celestial power. So why did she feel that way? There was a tingling sensation at the back of her skull, as if she were on the verge of understanding something.

I see the portal! said Brynne. *Twenty feet away! Keep going, Mini!*

Mini urged Loose Teeth forward.

Brynne ran ahead. The Sun Jewel lantern tucked inside her

jacket pocket emitted a faint glow, and the portal door loomed larger.

It's opening! said Brynne.

Up close, the door was the size of six cars stacked on top of one another. It was made of molten gold, like sunlit water rushing over a mirror. Mini saw herself in its reflection. In the past, Mini had always looked away from her reflection, uncomfortable with the sight of herself, as if more was supposed to meet her eye and just hadn't.

But this time she really *looked* at herself. She was sitting astride Loose Teeth. The glow of the portal picked out the glossy shine of her chin-length hair. It bounced off her glasses, and when Mini tilted her head to the side, she saw her wide brown eyes staring back at her. She thought she would look owlish and scared, but she didn't.

She looked *powerful*.

You did it, Mini! said Brynne, patting her leg and flashing a grin as she crossed the remaining five feet to the slowly opening doorway.

I don't know how, said Mini shyly.

For the first time since Aiden was taken, Aru looked up at her. She smiled, and even though her gaze looked hollow, Mini knew she was proud of her. *I know how,* said Aru through the mind link. *It's because you're the Daughter of Death.*

Yup, echoed Brynne.

A moment later, Aru and Brynne were guiding Rudy toward the door. The labyrinth was waiting on the other side. Around them, the Halls of Nidra had shrunk to the size of a dim living room, all of its trees and dreamers swallowed up by the darkness.

Almost there, said Brynne excitedly through the mind link. She held the Sun Jewel lantern up to the portal. Mini was about to smile when she felt it—a soft gust of air against her neck like someone's breath. She stilled, looking around. The last time they'd heard Kumbhakarna he'd been far away.... Had he noticed the glow? Had he made his way back to them?

Did you feel that? asked Mini through the mind link.

Feel what? said Brynne.

Mini turned in the saddle, her hands still on Loose Teeth's reins. In the darkness, a wet roving eye blinked open. It was the size of a couch. But that wasn't the worst part. The worst part was that it was less than ten feet away. The portal light bounced off Kumbhakarna's dull gray teeth, their ends jagged as if he'd broken them when crunching down on his still-screaming food.

He smiled. "FOUND YOU."

"Bee!" yelled Mini.

Brynne flung out her wind mace, but Kumbhakarna merely laughed in the dark. Mini tensed. A powerful jet of air blasted all around them as Gogo scoured the Halls of Nidra. Beneath them, fissures formed in the ground. The dreaming world began to crumble. Loose Teeth screamed as a gap snapped open inches from his front hooves.

"Just get through the door!" yelled Brynne.

Aru grunted as she hauled it open. "Go, Rudy!"

Rudy looked alarmed. He cast about, as if he might find some way to solve this.

"What about Mini?" he asked, looking up at her. "I'm not leaving without her!"

A flicker of warmth touched Mini's heart. Earlier she had thought that the naga prince would only care about her when she had power, but as it had turned out, that wasn't the case at all.

And so it was with much gratitude and affection that Mini said through the mind link, *Please push him through, Aru.*

Don't have to ask me twice, said Aru.

"I am a *prince!*" railed Rudy in the dark. "You can't— HEY!"

Aru grinned, took Aiden's backpack from Rudy, and shoved his chest. He toppled backward into the light, hollering, "I AM, LIKE, REALLY DISPLEASED!"

Another time, Mini might have laughed, but her attention felt scattered right now. The light of the portal door flickered, and once more Mini was taken aback by her own reflection. The cut of her hair, the depth in her eyes, the set of her chin.

She wasn't scared.

"Mini, ride through!" shouted Brynne. "Just go!"

Mini knew she should move, but she didn't. She kept thinking about Aru's words from earlier. *You are the Daughter of Death.*

"I am the Dharma Raja's daughter," she said to herself. "Even without Dee Dee."

It was such a quiet shift in her mind, but it was as if a secret part of her were blinking open and adjusting to new light.

Yamini Kapoor-Mercado-Lopez was the Daughter of Death.

Mini saw death everywhere she went, felt its presence in everything from a fight against a demon to a moldy candy bar. Death was a subtle shade over her life. Because of death, Mini savored each breath she took, knowing there were only so many she'd be given for one life. Because of death, Mini felt things more deeply, knowing that at any moment, all feeling could end.

All this time she had thought that Dee Dee had cured her of fear... that her celestial weapon had somehow overcome all her panic and made her powerful. But Mini wasn't powerful *in spite* of her fear. She was powerful *because* of it.

Fear made her anxious, yes, and panicky, yes, and sometimes oversensitive, yes, but it also made her feel deeply, see clearly, think carefully.

And it was that perspective that dragged her gaze upward at the barest flicker of pressure just above their heads.

"Mini, what are you waiting for?" yelled Aru. "Run!"

Mini was done running.

A jet of blue light caught the outline of a large hand swinging down over their heads. Brynne's back was turned, her wind mace aimed toward the portal. Aru was beside Loose Teeth, grabbing the reins to lead Mini out of danger.

Nobody saw the hand. . . .

Except Mini.

The world went silent. She thrust her own hand into the sky as if she might catch Kumbhakarna's fist. . . . But instead, something else happened.

A wrinkle of violet light shimmered just above her, hardly larger than the span of her arm. It blinked in and out, and then it *burst.*

A violet screen mushroomed over the Pandavas, the night mare, and the portal door. Kumbhakarna howled, grabbing his hand in pain after his fist crumpled against Mini's shield.

He snarled, "WHAT MANNER OF SORCERY IS THIS?"

Energy pulsed through Mini's veins, and it made her feel as if she were full of shadows and starlight. Her hair blew back as something solid *thudded* into her palm and caused her arm to sag. Mini blinked and looked at it. Her Death Danda shone like a scepter. Mini grinned and stared up at Kumbhakarna.

"It's my power," she said.

She raised her hand again and a violet light streamed from the shield, wrapping around Kumbhakarna and flinging him far away from them. In the afterglow, the violet light fell over her sisters' shocked and happy faces. Brynne looked slack-jawed. Aru's eyes sparkled.

More than anything, Mini wanted to savor this moment, but the ground beneath them cracked even more. Loose Teeth whinnied, rising up and nearly shaking Mini off her back. Mini jumped down and hugged the night mare's head.

"I'm really happy for you, Mini, but we've *got* to go!" shouted Brynne.

Loose Teeth nosed Mini sadly, huffing hot air over her face and fogging her glasses. The mare pawed the ground.

"Good-bye, sweet horsey," said Mini. "I'll see you in my dreams."

Then, with the Death Danda in one hand and power still racing through her veins, Mini turned her back on the dark.

THIRTY-SIX

Good News Bad News

Kara stumbled out of her recollections of the Sleeper and Krithika. She fell on the floor of the dream bubble Sheela had put her in. It looked like the sea beneath her fingers, but it felt like cold glass. Kara's lungs ached.

Sheela walked up to her and patted her head. "It's a lot," she said.

"What *was* that?" asked Kara.

"Memories. Genuine memories!" said Sheela. "It took me ages to piece it together from everyone's dreams, but I did it in the end."

Genuine.

Kara had always liked the etymology of that word. It came from *genu*, Latin for *knee*, from the ancient Roman custom of a father placing a newborn baby on his knee to acknowledge that the child was his. From *genu* came words like *genus*, like the categorization of a species, and in the sixteenth century it transformed into a word that meant natural and, most importantly, authentic.

Real.

Kara forced herself to stand. When she turned around, Sheela had remade the dream bubble, fashioning it into an underwater glass tunnel with vivid sea creatures swimming outside. The two of them sat down at a fancy white-clothed table set with a full tea service. Instead of a chair, Kara found herself bouncing on a large pink sea anemone.

"I saw something like this in a magazine," said Sheela, grinning. "Nikki said it would be a good place for a fashion show, but *I* think it's way better for tea parties."

"None of those memories were—" Kara stopped herself before she could say *real*.

Something told her that wasn't the case, and yet she didn't know how to make sense of them. In the scenes Sheela had led her through, Kara had seen Suyodhana as a young man. She saw the prophecy foisted upon him, the way he had struggled in his search for the Tree of Wishes, the final moments when Krithika locked him in the lamp where he would remain for eleven years.

"Why did you show me all that?" asked Kara.

Sheela fidgeted with the end of one of her braids before shrugging. "Because you needed to see it."

"What do you want me to do?" asked Kara angrily.

"What do *you* want to do?" responded Sheela.

What Kara wanted to do had never changed. She wanted to do what was right. It was the reason she had taken the astra necklace and destroyed the other Pandavas' weapons. But now, when she thought back to that moment, she felt nauseated.

Kara had a way with light. Whether it was because she was the daughter of the sun god or something else, she usually had good instincts when it came to telling what was true and what was false. But, unfortunately, that didn't make the world any easier to navigate.

True: Her father loved her.

True: Her father had lied to her.

True: Her mother had given her up.

True: Her mother had never given up on her.

Suyodhana did love her. Kara knew that in her bones. And she knew that he loved Aru, too. He even loved Krithika Shah. It was a truth he'd let fester inside himself like a poison he couldn't get rid of. But those things he had said about her mother ... and about Aru pushing Kara away ... and about Kara being unwanted ... all that was false.

"But he saved me," said Kara.

Part of her thought she was saying those words just to see how they felt on her tongue. They felt sticky. Slimed.

"From what?" asked Sheela, tilting her head.

"A bad childhood," said Kara automatically.

"Is that what you saw?"

Kara blinked. She'd seen her mother, Krithika Shah, touching a tree and watching Kara play in the large backyard of a low-slung house. A younger version of Kara squealed with delight as she picked up limes that had fallen from a tree. The little girl also gathered kumquats and jacaranda blossoms and piled them in the lap of a large woman whose face was out of focus.

"I was happy," said Kara softly. "Wasn't I?"

Her hands curled into fists in her lap. For some reason she couldn't get past that image. Once upon a time she'd had a lime tree in her backyard, and she'd picked purple flower blossoms knowing there was someone to give them to. A smiling adoptive mother.

Kara should have been able to remember how that lime had felt in her hand, whether it was cool from the shade or warmed by the sun, whether it was fragrant or rotting, whether it was later used for sugary limeade. But she couldn't remember, and that lack of knowledge, which had once felt like a sweet mercy, now turned sour.

"You're lying," she said to Sheela, ice in her voice. "It's not real. *You're* not real."

If the images Sheela had conjured were true, then...

Then her father was every bit the monster Aru had said he was. He had stolen her memories, but not to protect her. To manipulate her.

Kara blinked and felt the cold chain of the astra necklace as she'd yanked it off Aru. She saw Aru's heartbroken face, heard the way Brynne's voice broke and Mini called out, *Kara? Wait! No, no, no!*

What had she *done*?

"I don't know what real is," said Sheela, looking around them in the dream world.

A jellyfish pulsed gracefully alongside the tunnel. The sea anemone cushions beneath them shaded from pink to a vivid blue, and Sheela giggled.

"Like, none of this was here before, but I believed it and now it is," said Sheela. "So, I guess that makes it real."

"What are you saying?" asked Kara. "That the only thing that matters is what I believe?"

Sheela began to dissolve at the edges. Her voice seemed far away. "Uh-oh, gotta go. Nikki's going to be mad at me. She hates it when I'm gone too long."

"Wait!" said Kara, reaching for her, but Sheela was transparent now. It was this sudden fading that let her cry out loud, "I don't know what to believe!"

Sheela turned to look at her with sad eyes. "You either will or you won't, Kara."

When Kara opened her eyes, her father was sitting beside her. He beamed at her, and Kara remembered walking through the memories that may or may not have belonged to him. She saw him in a hospital room, rocking a small bundle that could only be an infant Aru in the crook of his arm. She saw him waiting in front of the home where Kara had played happily in a backyard with jacarandas and lime trees before he stole her away and wiped her memories.

"What is it, child?" he asked now. "I have good news."

"Nothing," said Kara, but she was lying to herself.

As her mind readjusted to her surroundings, she heard shouts of joy near the makeshift tent of shadows. She glanced over her father's shoulder at the entrance. His army had swarmed outside, a dull golden glow silhouetting their heads, horns, and the sharp tips of the weapons they thrust happily into the air.

Kara's stomach sank. She predicted her father's words before he said them.

"We did it," he said. "The sphere around the amrita is broken. Your last efforts proved to be more than enough. An hour ago, it split down the middle."

Kara took a deep breath. A curious sweetness, like nectar and honey, had entered the air, mingling with the stale sweat and rancid breath of her father's soldiers. Beyond them, Kara imagined the fragrance rolling over the field surrounding the crater where they had located the nectar of immortality. She pictured the endless, bruise-colored sky, and her sister, a world away, stripped of her weapon. Her heart broke.

"Daughter," said the Sleeper, folding her hand in his. If he felt the tremor in her fingers, he didn't show it. He smiled with all his teeth. His one blue eye and one brown eye seemed to belong to two different people. And maybe, thought Kara, they did.

Kara opened her mouth, but she couldn't make herself utter all her fears. *Did you kidnap me? Did you promise me a family knowing I already had one?*

She was a coward. The word came from the Latin word *cauda*, which meant *tail*. It evoked an image of a frightened creature cringing with its tail between its legs. That was how Kara felt, like she couldn't curl up small enough.

"I have good news, child," the Sleeper repeated. "We have won."

THIRTY-SEVEN

There's Nothing Left to Say

Aru Shah had lost.

It was plain and simple. The realization didn't even hurt. Maybe it was even better this way. She'd been dreading the battle. She'd been terrified of the choice she'd make . . . whether she would somehow do the wrong thing in an attempt to do what was right.

Even now, Lord Agni's words haunted her. . . .

All the weapons in the world cannot help you if you do not know what you'll do with them. What will you do, Aru Shah?

In the end, it was moot. The choice had been taken out of her hands. It was, she thought, the neatest solution to her problem.

You did it, Shah, she thought joylessly.

But then why couldn't she be the one sleeping forever instead of Aiden?

She blinked. The chaos of the dream world had been replaced with the sound of rain and birdsong. Aru shuddered as a raindrop slid down the back of her shirt.

Brynne, Mini, Rudy, and Aru stood in front of Lullwater Park, the entrance to the labyrinth. The Sun Jewel lantern dangled from Brynne's clenched hand, bright as hope. Around them joggers ran and dog walkers were pulled by their charges, oblivious to the four Potatoes peering through the iron gates.

"We got here right in time!" said Brynne, bringing a startled Mini into a hug. "You did it, Mini! I wanted to say that the moment you got your powers back, but then, y'know, demons and night mares and all that."

When Brynne set Mini down, the Daughter of Death was smiling, tears shining in her eyes. Aru was standing right next to her, but she felt as if they were worlds apart.

Mini looked taller and stronger, as if she had become more wholly herself. But it had nothing to do with the glowing Death Danda in her hand. Dee Dee looked like an accessory, a symbolic scepter, secondary to the power that was Mini through and through. It made Aru feel enormously proud....

And incredibly lonely.

Her sisters had surpassed her.

"This is amazing," said Brynne.

"Does this mean Aiden will come back now?" asked Rudy, excited.

"I think so!" said Brynne. "Nidra said that it depends on whether or not there's a world to save, remember? And now Mini has her weapon back!"

When Aru heard Aiden's name, her stomach gave an uncomfortable lurch. She touched her lips, remembering not only his kiss, but his words, too. *I lied, Aru* had hit her like a lightning strike. And then there was his wrong, misplaced, foolish belief in her.

You'll find a way out of this, I know it.

"But I didn't," she said quietly.

No one heard her. They were all too busy checking for

messages. Now that the Potatoes were back in the human world and within range of the normal Otherworld portals, their devices were syncing and gathering all the texts and emails they had received over the past few days. Aru couldn't even do that. Her phone had shattered somewhere outside Jambavan's cave.

A *ping!* came from Rudy's back pocket. He pulled out a thin geode.

"What is that?" asked Brynne.

"Emergency stone," said Rudy, sliding his finger down the front of the geode. Words flashed across it like a screen. His eyes widened. "Whoa. *Tons* of people are willing to show up for you guys. They're just waiting for you to shatter the boundaries to the labyrinth and let them in."

Brynne's chest puffed out a bit. "As they should."

Mini smiled. "Nikita and Sheela must have been hard at work in people's dreams."

Rudy nodded before swiping the screen one more time. "Nagas, too . . . Looks like I need to get back home. They think once you all shatter the boundary, other entrances will open. There's one in the sea that the underwater kingdoms are gathering around, which means . . . I gotta go. There's no way I'm getting in this way." He held up his palms. "No godly weapon."

"So, you'll meet us on the battlefield?" asked Mini.

Rudy winked. "You know I'll find you."

Faint color touched Mini's cheeks.

Beside her, Brynne let out a whoop. "Gunky and Funky texted me yesterday, but I only just got service," she said, holding up her phone. She glanced at Aru, grinning. "Your mom is the one who found the other access points to the labyrinth. She's been rallying everyone to gather there and wait."

"Well, that sucks," said Aru. "Who am I supposed to stay home and watch the war with?"

The glowing mood vanished. Aru watched them, a quiet fury vibrating through her bones. They hadn't even looked at her. Hadn't even *considered* that she couldn't access the Lullwater Park portal without her celestial weapon.

Understanding dawned on Mini first. Guilt flashed across her face. "Oh, Aru..." she started to say. "I'm so sorry—"

"For what?" asked Aru calmly. "Honestly, this is for the best. It's not like I can fight without Vajra anyway."

"You can come with me!" said Rudy. "We can go the naga route!"

"And after that?" asked Aru, sneering. "What am I going to do, stand on the sidelines and cheer? I don't even have pom-poms. Or are we picking some up on the way?"

"Aru..." said Brynne. "We can't fight without you."

"If I'm there, I'll just be in the way. You'll be worried about protecting me. I'll be a risk."

Brynne looked away. Mini frowned, biting her lip like she was trying to think of some way to make that statement less true. But there was nothing they could say, and their silence was all the answer Aru needed.

She adjusted her backpack. Her arms were still full of Aiden's bag, now a makeshift cradle for Baby Boo, who slumbered away. When she peered inside, the firebird looked even bigger than before. His tail feathers curled around him in a burning spiral.

"BB is too young to fight," Aru said. "I'll watch him."

She turned and made to walk off, when Mini grabbed her shoulder. "You can't go, Aru!"

Aru spun, her voice hot and sharp. "And I can't *fight*, either!"

"But—"

"This is all I have, Mini," said Aru, setting down Baby Boo and opening her own backpack.

There was hardly anything useful inside it. Nothing but some candy wrappers, the smashed remains of her phone, a key to the museum, the bangle from the poison maiden Aleesa, an extra change of clothes, Menaka's earring, Jambavan's bear claw, the anklet she'd snatched from Urmila, and a shard of porcelain tile that had once been in the Palace of Illusions. Not exactly the most advanced arsenal in the multiverse.

Brynne's phone began to *ping* loudly. Her face paled as she glanced toward the gate. "Reports are coming in that the Sleeper's army... That th-they..." she stammered, looking up from her phone, her eyes going straight to Aru's in what was both an apology and an explanation. "They have the nectar of immortality."

And there it was.

The others had to go. They had a world to save. There was nothing left for Aru to do.

"Go," she said.

Mini put a hand on Aru's arm. "We'll find a way to send word, or maybe get you armor, or—"

"JUST LEAVE ME ALONE!" shouted Aru.

Brynne flinched. Mini dropped her hand. Rudy stared at the ground.

Brynne set her jaw. "Fine."

Aru didn't stay to watch them enter the labyrinth.

She gathered the firebird in her arms and stepped into the rain, hoping it would wash off all the ugliness she felt. It was a long walk back home, and she wasn't sure how to make it without her mom's guidance, but for now, Aru couldn't care less. She just wanted to be away from everyone.

Aru trudged down the winding sidewalks, lost in her thoughts.... So lost, in fact, that it took a good minute for her to realize that there was a car moving slowly beside her. She froze, every STRANGER DANGER! instinct lighting up her brain.

It was a shiny silver sedan. The word UBER flashed across it—not on the windshield or any of the four windows, but in the air right above it. Like magic.

The passenger window rolled down and a smooth, melodious voice rang out:

"Hello! I'm here with U.B.E.R! The Underage Belligerent Emergency Response team for Otherworld youth? I was told to deliver you home safe and sound."

Aru groaned. She looked over her shoulder. The iron gates to Lullwater Park looked small and toylike now. Rudy, Mini, and Brynne were nowhere to be seen. One of them must have called a car to make sure she'd be okay.

"I'm fine with walking," said Aru.

"Oh, totally," said the stranger. "Nothing says safe and sane like war brewing with immortal beings."

Aru scowled. She tried to peer into the car, but she couldn't see the driver's face. All she caught was the suggestion of a warm, mischievous grin.

"Fine," she said.

"Good choice!" said the driver. "Trust me, you're in great company. *Everybody* loves a talkative U.B.E.R. driver! And there's not a single person in the world who wouldn't want to talk to me."

The car door swung open.

THIRTY-EIGHT

Can I Give a Negative Rating for This U.B.E.R. Service?

On the plus side, at least Aru was out of the rain. Her clothes felt damp and her hair was cold to the touch as she slid into the back of the car, shrugged off her backpack, and put on her seat belt. Almost immediately, the rain picked up, blurring the windows. Aru looked around. The inside of the car was neat as a pin and smelled sweet and kind of buttery. Soft flute music floated from the radio, and a single peacock feather hung from the rearview mirror.

"Want a mint?" asked the driver, reaching behind him to tap a bag of candy that was hanging from the back of his headrest.

"No."

"How's the temperature? Okay?"

"Fine."

The driver settled in. "So...some weather we're having, right?"

"Yeah."

"Always love to hang around inside and play music on days like this. Do you play any instruments?"

"No." She wasn't going to tell him about the tambourine.

"Really?" asked the driver. "Music is amazing. It forces you to stay in the present, to tune out the outside world. Myself, I quite favor the flute."

"Uh-huh," said Aru, uninterested.

"Me and Lizzo have something in common."

Aru didn't say anything. She thought the driver would take her silence as a hint, but he kept going. "Tough day, huh?"

"Yeah, you could say that."

"Well, not as bad as *my* day. I stubbed my toe first thing in the morning. Horrible."

"Mm-hm."

"That war in the Otherworld looks pretty awful. Getting lots of calls from people who aren't sure where to go or what to do," he said, sighing. "You know, people always think they don't know the answers, but if you ask me, they just haven't looked hard enough."

I didn't ask, thought Aru mutinously. But years of ingrained Southern politeness made her smile instead, even though her eyes screamed *NO SPEAKING!*

"You know, the *last* time there was a war this big, the gods got super involved."

Aru raised an eyebrow. She did know that. Even Lord Krishna—one of the most powerful avatars of the supreme deity Vishnu—had taken part, although he'd refused to wield a weapon. Instead, he'd served as Arjuna's charioteer, steering him through the battle.

Aru huffed. It wasn't fair. She had Arjuna's soul, but it wasn't like she was walking hand in hand with her best god pal and getting free advice like he did. With that kind of help, she probably would never have lost Vajra in the first place. And she wouldn't have had to deal with the Sleeper after their first encounter, because she wouldn't have hesitated to destroy him.

"The gods don't seem to care much this time," said Aru. "They've given up on the whole thing."

"Gods are mysterious beings."

Aru rolled her eyes. She knew that better than anyone at this point.

"Must've been really hard for Arjuna all those years ago," said the driver, humming as he turned on his light indicator to make a left turn. "All that doubt. I mean, that's where the Bhagavad Gita came from. It's a conversation between a demigod and the god driving his chariot. Ever read it?"

"No."

She knew what the Gita was. It was a deeply holy scripture. Sometimes her mom quoted lines from it, but it was complicated and unwieldy and half of it made no sense to her, so all Aru could do was nod sagely and pretend she understood. Most of the time that worked.

Maybe I should've paid more attention, thought Aru.

She peered inside Aiden's backpack. Baby Boo slept happily, his feathers glowing like banked embers. The crest of blue fire on his head waved up and down as he napped.

She wished she could talk to Boo.

Is this what you thought would happen? she asked him.

BB didn't respond.

I never even got to tell you how mad you made me, thought Aru. *I keep thinking about that. You made a mistake, but you did it because you loved us. My dad did the same thing. And my mom. What if I've made a mistake? What am I going to do? What's going to happen?*

"It's not really up to you, is it?" asked the driver.

Aru was startled out of her thoughts. "What?"

"Ah, that's just me putting my own spin on the sacred words. I mean, I can drive my car supersafely and wear my seat belt every day, but I can't stop other drivers from ignoring all the road rules, and I can't stop a meteor from hurtling out of space and striking me into oblivion."

"Uh...great?" said Aru.

"I *love* taking people places, but do I expect a massive paycheck?" said the driver. "Nah. It brings me peace of mind just to do what I feel is right. I find joy in the *doing* and not the *receiving*, you know? It's pretty great. Minus the Atlanta traffic, which, ugh, can get fairly annoying." The driver glanced in the rearview mirror. "Do you have a job? Babysitting or dog-sitting? Maybe some volunteer work?"

I'm a professional disappointer, thought Aru. *But I'm still working on my business cards.*

"Not anymore," she said.

"Why?"

Aru glared at him. "I quit."

"Oof. You're kinda young to give up."

"Yeah, well, it's complicated. I didn't..." Aru paused. "I didn't know what to do."

"Ah!" said the driver. "Well, that's always an easy solve."

"Excuse me?"

"Want to hear my life secret?"

Aru mumbled, "Not really," but the driver went on anyway.

"You just gotta show up...and let go."

Aru blinked. "What?"

"Good motto, right?" said the driver, laughing to himself.

"Just think about it. We all have a role in life. Maybe we're someone's sibling or spouse, a teacher or a parent, a ruler or a warrior. And with that comes a duty to show up for the situations life throws at you! After that, you do your best and let everything else go. The outcome? *Pfft.* Not your problem. People's opinions? Not the point! When you go home and look in the mirror, it's *your* face you've got to look at. No one else's."

Aru sat still. She had never thought about it like that. All this time, she'd been worried about what people expected from her, what they would think of the things she did or didn't do. But what about *her*? What about what *she* thought was right?

Granted, she didn't even know what that looked like, specifically . . . but maybe she'd figure it out if she just, well, showed up. Aru's heart raced. In the back of her head, something buzzed and sparked as an idea took shape. Thunder growled outside.

"Although being possessed would complicate that whole *look-in-the-mirror* thing. . . . I mean, would you even *see* your own face?" mused the driver. "Or would it be this creepy Sith Lord cosplayer—"

"Stop," said Aru.

"Rude!" said the driver.

"I meant the car!" said Aru. *Mostly . . .*

"*Here?*" asked the driver. "Kinda busy street. Folks may not like that."

Aru's heart was racing. "Turn around! Please. I changed my mind!"

What had she been thinking? What could she possibly have done at the museum? *Brood* indefinitely?

Aru couldn't stand the thought of *not knowing* what would

happen. If she could find a way to be at the battle, then she might still have some part to play in it.

The driver made another turn. It was impossible to tell how far they'd traveled. Outside, the rain slashed at the windows.

"No can do, kiddo," said the driver, tapping the screen affixed to his air-conditioning vents. "Gotta listen to the nav."

Aru sat up a little straighter. "I *really* need to go back."

"Why?"

"I . . . I left something behind!"

"I'm sure you can replace it."

"No!" said Aru, frantic now. "I *can't.*"

"It can't be that important," said the driver.

"Yes, it *is,*" said Aru, grinding her teeth.

The driver shrugged. "Sure about that? I thought you said you didn't know what to do?"

"Well, I don't, not exactly, but—"

"So, what's the point?" asked the driver. "What are you going to end up doing, then?"

This was the question that had haunted her for days. Maybe the zigzagging car was making all her thoughts collide properly. Or maybe it was that, in the moment where the worst had happened, she'd realized there was still a choice. A choice that was all her own.

Aru slammed her foot on the floor of the car. Thunder rattled outside. The hair lifted on the back of her neck, and when she spoke, her voice might as well have been shot through with lightning.

"I'm just going to do my best! That's all I got!"

The words seemed to hang in the air, sparkling.

"I don't know what to do," said Aru, breathing hard. She wasn't even sure if she was talking to herself, Baby Boo, the driver...or just the air. "I don't know if I'm going to make a mistake or if everyone's going to hate me. I don't know if it's going to work. And I don't even know if it will matter in the end...but I *have* to try."

The car jerked to a stop. The seat belt caught Aru, holding her back. Baby Boo let out an irate *Cheep!* Before Aru could ask what was happening, she heard the *click!* of the car door unlocking. It swung open.

In the rearview mirror, the driver grinned. Aru knew he had a face, but it was hard to really look at him, as if she could only see him in bits and pieces. Starry dark eyes? Skin the color of midnight? She couldn't be sure. It gave her a headache to try.

"I guess that's all any of us can really do, huh?" he asked.

The rain had stopped. The sky had cleared. Straight ahead, the gates of Lullwater Park gleamed. Aru glanced at the clock.

It was 11:07 a.m.

Hardly five minutes had passed inside the car. But how was that possible? Especially with all the twists and turns he'd made....

"Well, I guess that's the end of our drive, Aru Shah," said the driver. "Sorry we couldn't do this sooner, but, you know, I've got a lot of jobs to juggle." He winked in the mirror. "Anyway, you'll learn this on your own, but it's worth telling you. Life is a heck of a battlefield, but I gotta say, the scenery is totally worth it."

Aru didn't remember getting out of the car, but the next thing she knew, the door had slammed shut behind her. The driver revved the engine and sped off down the street. Mist still hung in the air and the sunlight had gotten all tangled up in it. When that happens, the world can play tricks on your eyes. Aru now knew that for a fact, because as the car disappeared down the road, she could've sworn it wasn't a car at all.

It was a chariot.

THIRTY-NINE

The Beginning of a Goat Song

Aru stared at the iron gates of Lullwater Park once again. The rain had cleared. The world smelled clean and fresh. When Aru looked up, she saw a thread of lightning snake across the sky and then hover there, as if waiting for a signal. She felt a growing static around her, a soft crackling of energy building in her very bones. Aiden's words floated back to her.

You'll find a way out of this, I know it.

She grinned. There was no way she was going to let him down.

Cheep?

"I know," said Aru, gazing down at Baby Boo in Aiden's backpack. "I can't walk into a battlefield with two backpacks. One, I'd look like a deranged tortoise—"

BB squawked, and Aru imagined her old pigeon mentor pecking at her and shouting: *NOT THE POINT!*

"And two, I'm going to need my hands free."

Baby Boo hooted, pleased with her words. Aru shrugged off her bag and laid it next to a lamppost, then slung BB's cradle across her back. Even through the pack, the warmth of his feathers reached her. It felt a bit like a hug.

Aru almost walked away, then she paused.

Nothing inside her backpack was useful, but some of those things had been given to her as gifts. She couldn't leave them like that. Aru opened her backpack and rummaged through the graveyard of candy wrappers until she found what she was looking for—Menaka's earring, Urmila's anklet, Jambavan's claw, and Aleesa's bangle. Last, her fingers closed around the small, star-shaped blue tile from the Palace of Illusions.

Years ago, the palace had given a piece to both her and Mini. *It can give you the part of me that matters most: protection.* When Aru squeezed it in her palm, she felt a little stronger.

Aru smiled a little as she stuffed the small treasures deep into her pockets. Then she flexed her hands.

Thunder clattered in the sky, and once more, rain began to pelt the sidewalks. She'd meant what she said in the U.B.E.R. She didn't know what she would do, but she was going to give it her best.

Right now, the Sleeper and his army had the nectar of immortality. Getting it back was the first step.

"Ready?" she asked Baby Boo.

From behind her came an enthusiastic *Cheep!*

With that, Aru closed her eyes and walked straight through the boundary. The enchantments on it pulled at her. And yet she felt veiled in crackling static and the smell of ozone that always followed a thunderstorm. If she wanted to, Aru knew that she could reach into her pocket and find a small Ping-Pong ball awaiting. . . .

But she wasn't ready yet.

She could feel her power like a string pulling tauter and more powerful with her restraint. And so Aru held off for the right moment...the right action.

Aru imagined a hundred things waiting for her in the labyrinth. Maybe Brynne and Sheela, Nikita and Mini were already locked in battle. Maybe Rudy was creating chaos with his sound stones. Maybe, just maybe, the goddess Nidra had released Aiden and his feet had just hit the ground, his scimitars waiting for her bolt of electricity to light them up....

She envisioned the sky split down the middle while the Otherworld's army and the Sleeper's troops charged one another in the most epic showdown the multiverse had ever seen. And there would be outcries of joy when she showed up, alight with all her demigod power.

What she did not imagine when she stepped into the labyrinth was...

"Ugh, it's just Aru."

Okay, one—rude. Two—the audacity?

Aru blinked. She, Brynne, and Mini were standing in darkness, their faces barely visible in the light cast by the Sun Jewel lantern. As her eyes adjusted, Aru caught a faint shimmer far above them, like the skin of a great membrane blocking the labyrinth from sight. Far away came the grunts and shuffling of soldiers.

"What—"

Brynne lifted a finger to her mouth, shushing her. Mini waved a hello with one hand. In the other hand, her Death Danda was raised like a scepter, casting a violet shield over them that was almost invisible except for the slight oily iridescence it left in the air.

Nikita and Sheela said everyone has gathered at the access point, said

Brynne through the mind link. *All they're waiting for is for us to break the barrier.*

Hi, Aru! came Sheela's voice.

Aru jumped a little. Usually you had to be somewhat close to another Pandava sister for them to hear you, but Sheela had spoken directly into her head.

I found a new power. I like it. See you soon!

Hi? And, I guess, bye? said Aru, but one half of the Pandava twins had already disappeared.

We knew you'd get here soon, said Mini, smiling.

Yup, added Brynne. *We figured it'd only be a matter of time before you realized how to get your powers back. And then you'd charge through the gates, lightning bolt blazing and all that. . . . By the way, where is Vajra?*

Waiting for my signal, said Aru, glancing up at the pitch darkness above them. She couldn't see it, but she knew her lightning bolt was there. *But how did you know I'd get it back? I was so . . . mad! And . . . and . . .*

At your lowest point? suggested Brynne.

Despairing? added Mini.

Aru swallowed hard. *Yeah.*

We figured, said Mini. *That's how I felt before Dee Dee came back.*

Same thing with Gogo, said Brynne.

I guess sometimes it takes being powerless to understand what it means to be powerful, said Mini thoughtfully.

Huh, said Aru. *I like that. Now what?*

Brynne held out her hand. *Now we find our way to the center and we blast this thing apart. We're going to move fast. You ready?*

Aru grinned and clasped her sister's hand and reached for Mini with the other. *Ready.*

Brynne hooked the Sun Jewel lantern to the end of her wind

mace. She raised it slowly, and the wind picked up, swirling around them, ruffling her hair and lifting her feet inches off the ground. Brynne breathed out a word before slicing her weapon through the air....

Fwoomp!

Aru felt like she was flying. The Sun Jewel lantern burned away the shadows as Brynne maneuvered them through twists and turns of volcanic rock. They cut through caves full of deep pools and narrow channels of rock that towered hundreds of feet above them. The wind stung her eyes, so Aru had to squint until, finally, they came to a stop before a great boulder. The gust died down as Aru's feet hit the ground. Mini kept up her shield and put a finger to her lips. Here, a circle of fire pits held back the darkness.

They were not alone.

Aru took a cautious step forward, peering around the side of the great boulder. The Sleeper was pacing just a few yards away. She couldn't see his face, only his broad back and the sherwani he wore, the hem of which curled into smoke and shadows. Beyond him was the sprawling mass of his army. Even from a distance she detected their restlessness. Frustration rolled off them in waves.

"I do not understand why we cannot take the nectar for ourselves as you promised! The troops are not pleased," hissed a pale naga—a lieutenant, maybe?—rising up on his orange-and-green-banded tail. "This is not what you promised us, Suyodhana."

The Sleeper did not turn his head. "I am your general, am I not?" he asked calmly. His hands were clasped behind his back as he surveyed the sky. "It is my judgment you trust.... It is *I* who have gotten us this far."

Overhead, thunder rattled, but the sky was still hidden behind the labyrinth's barrier.

"Have you noticed how quiet it is?" the Sleeper asked the naga lieutenant beside him.

The naga nodded. "And what of it? Surely that is good!"

"Why is that? Hmm? Is it because the gods have managed to trick us once more? Do they know something terrible will happen to us when we imbibe the nectar of immortality? If it is the grand treasure we were told it was, then *why has no one come to claim it?*" The naga hissed, his snake hood flaring out as the Sleeper turned sharply to face him. *"Do you understand?"*

Now that the Sleeper's head was turned her way, Aru flinched…and felt a familiar wave of emotion. It was hard to look at his features and see only the bad. She could still envision the person who had wanted to be her father. Aru pitied him, and she grieved what they had both lost….But it didn't change the fact that what he was doing wasn't right.

"Yes, sir," said the naga, coiling down on his tail. "But does that mean we are waiting for a battle?"

"Not exactly," said the Sleeper. "If we can accomplish this without bloodshed, that would be ideal. But I am not opposed to violence, if it is necessary."

"Then what *are* we waiting for?" asked the naga lieutenant, growing bold again.

"Test results," said the Sleeper, turning away again. "Kara has some power over truth, and she told me she had to perform some tests on the nectar to make sure it is safe for our consumption."

The naga paused for a moment. "And you believe her?"

The Sleeper froze. "Why wouldn't I?"

Aru was so absorbed in their exchange that she almost yelped when she heard Nikita's voice in her mind. *We will be there soon. Start thinning the barrier.*

Won't they notice? asked Brynne.

Not if I show them an illusion, said Mini.

We're on it, said Brynne, smiling.

The Sun Jewel lantern—concealed by Mini's ever-expanding shield—emitted a ray of light that pierced the darkness. Through it, Aru saw a patch of sky ... and a flash of lightning. Aru's gaze flew to the Sleeper, but he didn't seem to notice. The naga's question had frozen him on the spot.

"I said, *why* do you think I wouldn't be able to trust my own daughter?" he asked, his voice rising.

"Well, she ... She ... It is rumored that she has a fondness for the Pandavas," said the naga lieutenant.

The Sleeper snorted. "That is a feeling she no longer entertains. I am sure of it. Nevertheless, she should have her results soon. Bring her to me. Now."

Can you extend the protective shield, too? added Nikita.

Mini worked her jaw, then stretched her neck. *I can manage.*

She whispered something to Dee Dee under her breath, and the violet-tinged veil slowly expanded across the terrain behind them. Aru watched in awe as it stretched hundreds of feet. Mini's teeth were clenched and sweat had broken out across Brynne's forehead. Aru wanted to help, too, but her talents were significantly *louder.*

"Dad?" called a familiar voice.

It was Kara ... Aru's sister. She looked tired, with dark circles under her eyes. Her brown hair was greasy and pulled back in a messy ponytail. She wore ratty pajama pants and a hoodie two sizes too big with the words THESPIAN CAMP 1986 splashed across it along with a picture of the ancient Greek tragedy and comedy masks.

Aru recognized the hoodie immediately. It had belonged to her mom—*their* mom—and Aru had loved wearing it to bed. She'd let Kara borrow it one time, and she remembered her sister laughing at the logo.

"Goat song!" she'd said.

"What?"

"Goat song," repeated Kara, tapping the tragedy mask. "That's where the word *tragedy* comes from! *Tragos* or *goat*, and *oidos*, which means *song* in Greek. Scholars are pretty divided on how it got that name. People used to compete by performing songs and skits. I think the winner took home a goat."

"I would *riot* if someone gave me a goat as a prize," Aru had declared.

Kara had laughed.

Aru felt a lump in her throat as the memory washed over her. When did Kara get the hoodie? Had she gone back for it when the museum was empty?

"You owe us an answer, child," said the Sleeper now.

He snapped his fingers and the great golden kalash holding the nectar of immortality appeared in their midst, dragged in by a pair of shadows who gingerly set down the glowing liquid. Even from a distance, the air hummed with the presence of the amrita. A sweet perfume infused the air, and Aru felt a little light-headed. Here it was. The nectar that had united gods and demons, split oceans, summoned wonders, and destroyed lives. Such was the cost of attaining a sip of the eternal.

"What news of the amrita?" asked the Sleeper, gesturing to the pot. "Is it safe for us to consume or not?"

Kara fidgeted. Her eyes were fixed on the ground.

I know that look, said Mini through the mind link.

No, we don't, said Brynne stubbornly. *Clearly* we *don't know her* at all.

Part of Aru—the wounded part—wanted to agree with Brynne. Kara might be her sister, but she was still a traitor. The Sleeper was her father, after all, and look what he'd done to them.

But something in Kara's stance nudged a memory in Aru's skull.

Yes, Kara had betrayed them . . . but, unlike Aru, she was a terrible liar. And whenever she was about to lie, she looked just like she did now.

"I can't tell if it's real yet. I'm sorry," said Kara, her gaze sliding away from the nectar of immortality. "I think I'm tired. My powers haven't been working as well. And . . . and my stomach is hurting."

Aru rolled her eyes. *Your grand excuse is "My stomach is hurting"? Seriously? Always say "I have cramps." It makes men freak out! No one asks questions after that!*

Aru, she does not *need—or* deserve—*your advice right now,* retorted Brynne.

I don't know about that . . . said Mini through the mind link.

The Sleeper regarded Kara calmly. "There are those in the camp who seem to think you are delaying us on purpose, child. That perhaps your true allegiance lies with those who betrayed you. I told them such a thing would be foolish. I am right, aren't I?"

"Of course!" blurted out Kara.

"Then what is the delay?"

Kara stammered, "I—I don't know!"

"Does your allegiance lie with *me* or with *them*?" demanded the Sleeper, taking a step toward her.

"You, of course!" said Kara.

But her gaze went sideways, and her right foot hooked behind her left ankle, and Aru knew without a doubt Kara was lying.

Brynne and Mini must have realized it, too. Mini's violet shield flickered, as if her shock had temporarily arrested her power. The cloud that Brynne had started summoning stopped. All of Aru's concentration honed in on Kara, and it was as if the past had peeled off the present for this one moment, leaving behind a simple truth:

Kara needed help.

But what could Aru do?

Just then, Nikita's voice rang out in her head. *So. We're going to need one last piece of help.*

What kind? asked Aru.

A distraction, said Nikita. *We need everyone's eyes on one person.*

Aru grinned. She looked at Kara.

I can do that, said Aru.

Aru had imagined a thousand different ways to enter the battle-field. Shrouded in celestial light, perhaps. Or on the back of a war elephant. Preferably one that could trumpet in time with each step.

But alas, it was not to be.

There was no time for her to make a plan. The moment Aru set down Baby Boo, everything changed within seconds. Mini opened a space in the veil and Brynne gave Aru a helpful boost with a small gust to her back. Unfortunately, that "small gust" ended up being a tiny hurricane that sent Aru tumbling head over heels across the rock to land facedown in the dirt ten feet away from the Sleeper.

As Aru scrambled up, she uttered a word that she probably shouldn't have said in front of a parental figure.

That elegant landing really inspired confidence, said Nikita through the mind link.

Aru ignored her.

It was an easy thing to do because the next moment Aru found herself staring down the three glowing prongs of Kara's trident. Her sister glowered at her with flinty eyes. Aru looked past her at the Sleeper's shocked face.

"Yeah, see?" said Aru. "She's definitely *not* on our side."

FORTY

On Your Left

Aru smiled.

In her head, she heard Nikita through the mind link. *Keep their eyes on you, Aru. I need five minutes for the troops.*

Aru stared up into the Sleeper's slack-jawed expression. "Aren't you going to ask me how I did it?"

He seemed to recover himself. He snapped his fingers and the nectar of immortality vanished . . . but not quite. The air where it had been looked wrinkled, as if someone had merely pulled a curtain in front of it. Aru could still smell its immortal fragrance.

He may have hidden it for now, but she'd find it.

"Kara, where are your manners?" asked the Sleeper. "Say hello to your sister."

"Hi," she mumbled. Kara swallowed hard, hoisting the trident a little higher. The glower had gone out of her eyes, replaced with something searching. "It wasn't supposed to be like this."

"Well," said Aru, "it is."

"Have you come to join us?" asked the Sleeper, his gaze sweeping over the empty terrain. "Perhaps you've seen the error of your ways? Already there are those who call me a liberator, for I will free them from the ugliness of this world. I will release them from the silence it inflicts, from the shadows it wraps around those who deserve better.... I will remake Time, child. Tell me, have you finally seen reason?"

"Reason?" said Aru, grinning. "Nope. Never met her."

The Sleeper frowned. "I have searched the perimeter. You are alone. You have no army."

"Mm-hmm."

Was it Aru's imagination, or did Kara's trident drop by a fraction? Her eyebrows furrowed in question.

"You don't even have a weapon, child," said the Sleeper, with a rueful smile. "What can you possibly do?"

Aru groaned. Why was everyone so *obsessed* with asking her this question? Why couldn't they just shut their mouths and...

"Watch," said Aru.

She raised her hand. The illusion of darkness overhead parted cleanly, revealing an open sky. Thunder rattled the world. Lightning splintered the violet clouds and rain pelted the ground.

Now, she said silently.

There was a screeching roar, like metal against metal. Around them, the jagged battle terrain was briefly illuminated and then swathed in the darkness that follows when a light flares in front of your eyes. But this was better than light. This was *lightning,* and Aru Shah had just pulled it out of the sky.

"Hi, Vajra," she said. "I missed you."

Her lightning bolt had gone from tame to semi-feral. Whips of electricity slapped the ground, rattling the rocks. Ribbons of light wound up Aru's arm with a gentle squeeze and tickle, as if Vajra purred with happiness.

Within seconds, the Sleeper's army manifested in the labyrinth. Their numbers were legion. Aru could hear them panting and growling even as they were momentarily blinded by her power.

Kara gasped. Sunny, her trident, looked like a candle next to the flare of Aru's lightning bolt. The two sisters were locked in their positions, weapons poised, the air so tense that a mere breath would snap it.

Out of the corner of her eye, Aru watched the pale naga lieutenant slither forward. "Orders, sir?" Followed quickly by: "Is she allowed to do that?"

Welp, that did it, thought Aru.

"First of all," said Aru loudly, "*she* can hear you. And secondly . . . *Yes, she is.*"

Through her mind link, she could hear Mini and Brynne cheering. Aru let her hands fill with energy. Vajra—who had climbed to a towering fifteen feet in height—cast sparks over the battlefield.

"I'm giving you one last chance," said Aru.

But when she spoke, she wasn't talking to the Sleeper. Her eyes were fixed on Kara. Her sister—even if that wasn't what she wanted to be—looked torn. The light of her trident flickered. It seemed smaller and weakened.

Kara looked between Aru and the Sleeper before casting her eyes downward.

"You may have power, but you have no army," said the Sleeper through gritted teeth.

"Yet," said Aru.

"What?"

"We have no army *yet*," said Aru.

On the left, said Nikita through the mind link.

"But you'll meet them real soon," said Aru. "In fact, they're here *right now.*"

Aru turned her head. And then she frowned.

Helloooo? she said through the mind link. *I just said something super dramatic. Back me up!*

I said on the left! said Nikita.

I am looking left!

No, you're looking to the right!

"I meant on *your* left, Aru!" said Nikita loudly, in a voice that was no longer in Aru's head.

Right then and there, Mini's violet shield pulled back like an eye slowly opening. The vortex of Brynne's wind power had kept them silent, but now the massive Otherworld army roared to life. Aru's heart soared, and for the next few seconds before the world broke apart, she stared at all the people Sheela and Nikita had gathered. All the people who believed in *them.*

In one corner, the vanaras from the Kishkinda Kingdom waited, their monkey tails switching like whips as they bared their teeth and stamped the ground. Beside them, Queen Tara stood as tall as a skyscraper and ten times as impressive in her battle regalia. She wore an ancient bronze helmet and gold-plated body armor covered in spikes. One hand was extended over the hundreds of gathered vanaras; the other held a conch shell war horn just inches from her lips.

Queen Tara caught Aru's eye and nodded in acknowledgment. In the skies, dozens of Maruts beat on war drums made of thunderclouds. They jostled together, their electrified daggers casting sparks over the battlefield. Otherworld creatures with great wings beat the air, their bows and arrows already trained on the Sleeper's army. Hordes of nagas slithered out from pools of water in the ground. Rudy was among them, wearing plate armor made of carved sapphires. His hands were full of gems, and the stones whined, low and angry and rattling enough to raise goose bumps on anyone's skin.

"I think we're ready now," said Nikita, stepping out of a portal a dozen feet away.

Aru was glad to see her, but she frowned. Where was Sheela?

Sheela has her own plan, said Nikita through the mind link, as if she'd read Aru's thoughts.

Behind her, Hanuman emerged at his full height of three hundred feet. Aru couldn't see his face in the clouds, but she heard his snarl and it shook the ground. Urvashi flew out beside him, all beauty and menace, shedding an enchantment of drowsy allure as she moved. She blew a kiss at Aru before disappearing into the sky.

The only one missing was Aiden, Aru thought with a pang. But they would have to do this without him. *For* him.

The Sleeper watched all of this with dispassionate calm. The only movement he made was the sudden arch of his left eyebrow.

And then there was silence.

There's an etiquette to war, and somewhere deep in Aru rose those ancient instincts. With that silence came a gravity, a weight to the air, a shift in her pulse that said this might be a beginning or it might be an end. Either way, there would be no going back.

"So be it," said the Sleeper.

He raised his arm, let it fall, and the world around Aru Shah broke into chaos.

Don't Worry, She's Got Help

Aru's first thought was to get to the nectar of immortality, but the moment she lunged forward, she was
lassoed around the waist by a rope of shadow and
yanked backward. Aru skidded, her heels kicking up
dust and rocks. Just as quickly the lasso disappeared, and she fell
on her face. She splayed her fingers on the ground as she gathered
her wits and energy.

Overhead, a group of Maruts clashed with fiery snakelike
creatures. Flaming droplets slammed into the ground. Smoke
roiled in front of Aru, and she lost track of where she was on
the battlefield.

Aru gritted her teeth and stood, looking up as a dozen of the
Sleeper's troops flew toward her, closing the space with javelins in
their hands. The Sleeper and Kara stood in the chaos. Kara was
nearly obscured by his shadow. She looked like a lonely candle
in the dark.

Aru braced herself for attack when the soldiers started shrieking. Huge vines ripped out of the ground, rearing up like cobras
and coiling around their bodies.

"Don't worry, I gotcha," said Nikita, lightly dismounting from a twenty-foot wave of earth. She looked like a small but fearsome war goddess.

Aru blinked up at her. "Are you . . . Are you wearing a *ball gown?*"

Nikita tossed her braids over one shoulder and straightened the gold lamé sleeves of her long dress, which was embroidered all over in a pattern of mango blossoms.

"Duh," she said. "What else does one wear to a battle?"

No visual on the amrita! shouted Brynne through the mind link.

"We'll discuss this later," said Aru to Nikita. "Gotta go."

A knot of soldiers rushed at the twin. The power in Aru's veins felt dangerously easy to tap into. With a flick of her wrist, Vajra flattened into a massive discus. "Go on," said Aru calmly.

Her lightning bolt shot into the air, whirling in a large circle before slicing through a swath of enemies in a crackle of light. Aru didn't even bother looking as she jumped. Moments later, her feet thudded down on Vajra, who had flattened into a hover-board. Aru zoomed over the churning battlefield, hunting for any sign of the nectar of immortality, but it was impossible to see.

Instead, Aru honed in on the flashes of blue and purple light some hundred feet away, which could only be coming from Mini and Brynne. Mini shot into the air, her eyes glowing purple behind her glasses. Shadows snapped out from the top of her Death Danda, grabbing soldiers by their throats and flinging them across the battlefield. She hovered, twirling the scepter above her head, casting shields as she saw fit.

A protective sphere surrounded a group of vanaras as a horde of rakshasas appeared above them with sharp scythes gripped in their claws.

"I know everyone is super preoccupied and all," Rudy shouted over the din of battle, "but I think I should take this moment to remind you that I WAS PROMISED A BOW AND ARROW ON A PREVIOUS QUEST!"

He lobbed enchanted jewels left and right. Wherever his anti-music grenades landed, the gems emitted shrieks that forced soldiers to drop their weapons and curl up on the ground, holding their ears. Rudy huffed, adjusting the sling he'd brought to hold Baby Boo. BB continued to nap, oblivious to the fact that Rudy had picked him up. He glared around before looking beseechingly at Mini, who hovered above him with her arms raised. "I would look *amazing* with a bow and arrow!"

"Rudy, I'm sure it can *wait!*" said Mini, aiming her shadow magic at a knot of bird-winged asuras. "Hey, Aru! Evil serpents on your right!"

Aru hopped down from her hoverboard and twisted her lightning bolt into a sparking net. She cast it out and the serpents shrieked as electricity clambered over their scales. The smell of smoke and singed flesh hit the air and Aru wrinkled her nose.

"I want a bow and arrow—" Rudy started to say when dirt and rocks exploded around them.

Aru was thrown backward, her head painfully smacking into a boulder. "Mini!" she called.

A feeble shield flickered around Mini and Rudy. He lay on his side, staring up at Mini in plain awe.

"I'm okay," said Mini raggedly. "But I've lost the visual."

Smoke and darkness were trapped inside the shield with them. Aru could taste the enchantments woven into the air, cutting off all sound. The hairs on the back of her neck prickled. Tiny dots of light glimmered in the sky. Aru blinked. Were those stars coming out? But wasn't it too early for stars?

FIRE ARROWS! shouted Mini through the mind link. She fumbled with her shield, but the arrows were too fast.

Aru wove Vajra into a net, fear making her hands shake. What if the net exploded? Who would she hurt? The arrows whistled, gathering speed....

And then a curtain of fire encircled them.

Cheep! Cheep!

Baby Boo flew above, squawking angrily. No doubt the fire-bird had not been pleased to be woken up so unceremoniously. BB exhaled a long flame, and the volley of arrows was incinerated.

Cheep! the firebird added.

Which Aru interpreted as *TAKE THAT!*

Baby Boo flapped his wings and the smoke pulled back. The ground was scorched, giving them a clearing of a hundred-foot radius. The firebird flew gracefully to the ground, alighting a foot away from Rudy and his outstretched sling. The bird tilted his head inquisitively and burped.

"Good job!" said Rudy, gathering up Baby Boo once more. BB promptly returned to his nap. Rudy clasped his hands. "Now can I have a bow and arrow?"

"Okay, *fine!*" said Mini.

She performed a complicated gesture with her hands. A shadow ribbon knotted around one of the asuras in midair just as he was trying to fly away. The demon's bow and arrow fell, dropping straight into Rudy's hands.

"Yay!" said Rudy, hopping in delight. He frowned. "What do I do with it?"

"Any visuals on the amrita?" asked Aru, ignoring Rudy and whirling in time to avoid an onslaught of rocks from above.

"No," said Mini, her eyes still glowing as she surveyed the battlefield.

"What about Brynne?" asked Aru. "Where'd she go?"

Aru got her answer from the calamitous shrieking nearby. A jet of blue light snapped across the battlefield. Silence reigned for a moment before a hundred of the Sleeper's first line of soldiers rose in the air and were thrown backward by a great gust of wind.

The ground rumbled. With a huge roar, a ginormous blue bear charged forward, scattering the troops. A rash of soldiers surged toward her. Bear Brynne shook her head, tossing the soldiers left and right with swipes of her massive paws. Aru polished them off with a neat whip of her lightning bolt, and for the next few moments, their section of the battleground was clear.

And yet, thought Aru as she looked around, the fighting was far from over. The sprawl of enemy soldiers covered more than half the wasteland. The vanaras and Maruts, rakshasas and asuras on their side fought valiantly, but they hadn't closed ranks on the Sleeper's army. They were holding them in a sort of limbo.

Brynne shifted back to human form and cast her gaze upward. "Should we call them in?"

Aru knew who she meant. The Nairrata army. The golden militia they had won from Lord Kubera in his gladiatorial contest.

"We can summon them now that we have our celestial weapons back," said Brynne.

"But so can Kara," said Aru, scanning the area. "They wouldn't know which side to fight on."

"I guess you're right..." said Mini from above.

"Take the lantern! It should still guide you to the nectar," said Brynne, preparing to toss it to Aru. "Once we've got the amrita—"

"We'll finish this war," said Aru.

As she caught the glowing Sun Jewel lantern, Aru felt a prickle of unease. She was going to try her best, but a solution that felt *right* still hadn't made itself clear in her mind. If she got her hands on the amrita, the devas would expect her to declare the nectar of immortality for them on the spot. But somehow . . . somehow Aru felt as if she'd missed a step.

"You got this, Shah," said Brynne.

"Let's hope so," muttered Aru.

Brynne didn't seem to hear her doubts. In a flash of blue, she transformed into a massive crocodile. With a wicked grin, she charged straight into the melee.

I'll cover you, said Mini through the mind link as Aru hopped back onto her hoverboard.

Aru had only just begun to speed through the ranks of the soldiers when a thick column of shadows appeared in the middle of the battlefield. The inky cloud was so dark it looked like a hole had been blasted through the earth. The column expanded to the width of a house and grew in height until it touched the sky.

In Aru's hand, the Sun Jewel lantern glowed like a beacon, tugging her toward the darkness. Aru's pulse ratcheted higher. Of course, she thought. *This* was where the Sleeper had concealed the nectar of immortality.

That he'd done it so obviously could only mean he was growing panicked, but then why hadn't he just consumed it already? What was he waiting for?

Aru moved closer and closer. His army had surrounded the tower of shadows, but Aru moved unseen through their ranks, cloaked as she was by Mini's shield.

That's as far as I can extend my power, Aru, said Mini through the mind link.

Aru knew she couldn't fly into that darkness. She needed to dismount, to get her bearings....

At that moment, the soldiers beneath her screamed.

"Get it off!" yelled one. "*GET IT OFF ME!*"

Aru looked down. Bugs surged out of the ground. Spiders the size of shoe boxes clambered up and over the two dozen soldiers on the north side of the shadow tower. The arachnids scuttled up their legs, hung from their arms, and began tapping on their shields and visors. Aru felt a little nauseated as she watched the soldiers flee, screaming and shouting.

"They're poisonous!"

"Flesh-eating bugs!"

The moment the soldiers left the area, the spiders slipped back into the ground. Even so, Aru shivered a little as she hopped down from her hoverboard. Where had they come from?

Me! said Sheela, in her head. *I thought you'd need us to cause a distraction.*

Wait, said Aru, stunned. *This is* your *magic?*

Uh-huh! said Sheela in her sweet, high-pitched voice. *Looks like I can get into the heads of lots of things, and if I ask nicely, they'll even do what I say.*

That's ... that's not creepy at all.

Sheela went quiet.

Sheela? asked Aru.

I'm sorry, she said.

Huh? For what?

"ARU!" shouted a familiar voice. "WAIT!"

Aru turned around, and her heart dropped. Krithika Shah

was running toward her. Enchanted armor glinted on her shoulders, but her head was unprotected and her long black hair streamed wildly around her face.

"Mom," said Aru, softly at first, and then loud. "*MOM!* What are you doing here? It's not safe! Go!"

"I couldn't!" said Krithika, catching Aru in a fierce hug as sobs racked her body. "I couldn't stay back and not know if something had happened to you. Or to Kara. Or even to ... to him."

"This is what I've been training for, Mom. You shouldn't be here. You don't have any weapons."

Krithika pulled back, her eyes flicking hungrily over Aru's face. She stroked Aru's cheek, her hair. "I am so sorry," she said, before her eyes swept toward the tower. "You can't go in there."

"But"—Aru held up the lantern—"the nectar of immortality is in there...."

"And so is *he*," said Krithika. "There has to be another way."

Aru's head started spinning. She thought of Sheela's wispy words: *I'm sorry.*

For what? thought Aru, panic racing through her veins. Sorry *for what?*

"Oh gods," said Krithika, her eyes widening.

Aru followed her gaze to where the shadows had begun to peel away from the column, revealing something in its depths, something backlit by the glow of the nectar that was tucked far into its interior. A tower of rocks stretched nearly fifty feet into the air, its pieces sliding in and out of place, making it teeter dangerously.

It was going to fall.

On them.

Now Aru understood Sheela's apology. If Aru struck the

tower with her lightning bolt, the rocks would fly in all directions and still hurt them. Mini was too far away to cast a shield, and for all Krithika's armor, her head was unprotected. Aru could turn Vajra into a hoverboard for a quick escape...but it would not hold both of them. Aru could cast a net of electricity, but it wouldn't be able to contain that many rocks.

The shadows cinched around them. Outside the circle, the growls and chattering of the Sleeper's soldiers returned. There was nowhere for Aru and Krithika to run.

"Aru," said her mom, her eyes wide, brimming with tears. "It's okay. It's going to be okay. But you have to get out of here. You have to leave. *Now.*"

Aru went numb. She was about to watch her mother die. She knew it in her bones.

No.

No.

No.

Aru grabbed her mom's hand. Overhead, the rocks slid and started thundering into the ground. A wave of dirt rushed up, and Aru couldn't find enough air to pull into her lungs. Pebbles slashed her face and dirt sprayed into her eyes. Vajra flashed wildly, sparks of lightning breaking against the sudden dimness.

Aru felt a sudden pressure in her ribs and the sensation of flying backward only for Vajra to catch her, suspending her in a net of light.

"*Mom,*" croaked Aru, blinking rapidly.

But her mother was fine.

And she was not alone.

The Sleeper stood in front of her, breathing heavily, his hand thrust out. Whorls of darkness swirled around them.

"Suyodhana," said Krithika Shah, taking a tentative step toward him. There was a world of feeling on her face.

"Why?" asked the Sleeper, staring down at Krithika with haunted eyes. "Why is it that no matter what happens, I can't seem to stop caring? I couldn't let it—"

He gestured at the rocks, which had now been reduced to sand by his own powers. Not far away, Aru saw Nikita locked in combat with Kara near the nectar of immortality. A cage of thorns closed up around them, cutting off all visibility.

"It doesn't have to be like this, Suyodhana," said Krithika. "Maybe there is some truth, after all, in starting over... but not like this. Not with so much damage. Not with Time overturned and the world laid to waste."

"I cannot see any other way," said the Sleeper, his voice hollow. His eyes met Krithika's, and a fragile wonder snuck into Aru's thoughts. When he had lassoed Aru and thrown her backward, had it been because he'd wanted to keep her out of harm's way? Was the real reason he hadn't drunk the nectar of immortality because... because he couldn't bear to do it?

Was it possible that *he* might change? Was this, perhaps, the solution she'd been looking for? That all would somehow be restored, and her parents might even find some way back to joy?

"Then let us help you see," said Krithika, holding out her hand. Her wedding ring glimmered there, and Suyodhana looked up at her.

His hand lifted.

Something shot out of the air. Light flashed. The illumination threw her mother into stark relief, and as the object met its target, Aru screamed with all that was left in her soul.

FORTY-TWO

Bliss

Kara had always thought the phrase "ignorance is bliss" was weak. The full line was "Where ignorance is bliss, 'tis folly to be wise," and it came from a 1742 poem by Thomas Gray. Kara knew this because she loved to read. She loved to wander through imaginary worlds. She loved the fact that with a book in her hand, she could be a warmhearted princess and a quick-witted heroine and a complicated sorceress between breakfast and dinner. She loved how knowledge let her mind travel across thousands of miles and hundreds of years, all while she was curled snugly in her blanket.

Knowledge had always made Kara feel *fuller*.

Until now.

"You," she said, her voice coming out like a croak. "It was you the whole time...in the dreams."

Sheela stood five feet away from her, wearing a silver T-shirt dress, striped tights, and platform sneakers. Her braids were gathered into a bun on her head that was held together with a silver ribbon. She looked like she was dressed for a party, not a war.

"It's me," said Sheela.

Beside her, Nikita looked furious. "How much time do you need?"

Sheela shrugged, completely unfazed even with the rocks flying around them and the jets of power blazing from both sides of the battlefield.

"Maybe ten minutes?" she asked.

"I'll give you four," said Nikita darkly.

Nikita glowered and a vine lashed out from her hand to snap at Kara's neck. Just as quickly the vine retracted, now coiled around its stolen prize. Then Nikita rotated her right wrist, and more twisted gold and thorns enclosed Kara and Sheela. Huge vines clambered over them, blocking out the light and the sounds of the battle beyond.

"That's better," said Sheela with a happy sigh. She plopped onto the ground and looked up at Kara. "Thought you'd need a minute."

Kara trembled and Sunny flickered weakly in her grasp. Her trident, forged from a single drop of sunshine, had been acting differently over the past few days. Maybe it was drained from cracking open the protective sphere over the nectar of immortality. But deep down Kara knew that wasn't the reason. Her celestial weapon's malfunctioning came from a place in her own soul... a truth Kara couldn't bear to realize until this moment, when it had been shoved into her face.

Her reflexes had lagged.

Her brightness had dimmed.

Minutes ago, when Nikita's vine had taken the astra necklace, Kara had hardly felt its loss. And when Kara realized what had happened, there was no heady surge of revenge, only *relief*.

Without the burden of her betrayal around her neck, she could breathe freely again.

Sheela stared up at her. "You can say it."

"I can't," said Kara, sobs racking her chest.

Kara tried to blink away the mess of tears, but when she closed her eyes, she saw the life that had been stolen from her. Something came loose in her mind, and for the first time in years, Kara clearly saw the woman in the backyard with the purple jacaranda blossoms and the fragrant lime trees. Kara saw her wide face, her smiling mouth, the nose ring winking in her right nostril. She saw her gray-streaked hair and chocolate-brown eyes. Her name was Rohini.

But Kara had called her *Amma*.

Mom.

"I had a mom," said Kara softly.

The admission broke her. In a flash, Kara saw the chaos of getting ready in the morning, lunch packed away in a bright yellow backpack, a dad—a round, fell-asleep-with-a-book-on-his-face-goofy dad—embarrassing her by picking her up at school. What had it been called? Who was her favorite teacher?

Those memories—true and whole and *real*—lay out of reach. She could see them clearly, but they were kept at a distance by the Sleeper's magic.

The Sleeper.

She would never call him *Dad* again. Every memory of him staying by her side when she was sick, every trip they'd taken together, every time he'd brought her a book...poison seeped into each moment.

"He took me," said Kara. "Didn't he?"

Sheela kept her gaze downcast. "Yes."

"Do you know how he did it? How long ago it happened?"

"Yes."

"Show me," demanded Kara.

"It won't help," said Sheela, flinching a little. "It won't make a difference. You know that."

In that moment, Kara realized so much. Too much, perhaps. She felt the weight of Krithika Shah's guilt over giving her up and knew it was genuine. She recognized the expression of bittersweet happiness on her biological mother's face as she'd stood outside Kara's childhood home and seen that her firstborn had found love there.

Kara had been kidnapped by the Sleeper, and her memories—those vital pieces that had made her who she was—had been violated by someone who had dared to call himself a parent. And yet, even after what he'd done to her, she was grateful for one thing: he had helped her find something precious.

She had found sisters.

She had found another family. Weekends spent watching movies. Weekdays locked in training. Nights spent laughing.

And then she'd lost that, too.

"Are you okay?" asked Sheela. "It's going to go away now."

Above them, the cage of gilded roses and thorns cracked down the middle. The sounds of clashing weapons and shouts poured back into the space, rattling Kara's thoughts. In her hand, Sunny glowed with infernal heat. Then her weapon shot up, towering over her. Her skin felt hot. Her veins glowed.

For all that she loved words, neither sound nor sentence could hold what she felt in that moment.

"I'm sorry for what happened to you," said Sheela, rising to a stand. "I'm sorry, Kara."

Sheela held out her hand, but Kara did not take it. Instead, her eyes roved over the battlefield, finally landing on the Sleeper. Krithika Shah stood in front of him and they were speaking. Kara was not interested in what they were saying. Alarms blared through her senses. All she knew was that the Sleeper had destroyed enough lives, damaged enough people.

Kara's eyes snapped to the figure behind Krithika. It was Aru, caught in a net suspended in midair, one arm flung out. Vajra's electricity spangled over Aru's body as if trying to blanket her. To *protect* her. Or perhaps, thought Kara with a sudden lurch in her stomach, to prevent damage to her dead body.

Suddenly, the Sleeper's shoulders sagged. His hand lifted, Krithika closed her eyes, and...

Kara aimed her trident and let it loose.

She did not miss.

FORTY-THREE

Sorry Isn't Good Enough

Aru Shah went numb.

There was too much to feel, and so her mind rewired itself to feel nothing at all—not the electricity wrapping around her body as Vajra shielded her from harm, not even the tears that she knew must be sliding down her face. All she could do was scream. She screamed as she saw the prongs of light slice through the Sleeper's charcoal jacket. She screamed when his eyes bulged and he sank to his knees. Eventually she ran out of screams and the Sleeper ran out of life.

The last thing he did was reach for something at his neck. It was the necklace that held his memories, the same one she had thrown around him when they'd fought before the Tree of Wishes. His hand fell and the necklace of memories skittered across the ground, landing near Aru. She didn't reach for it. She was too busy looking at her father's face, trying to catch his eye. But it didn't make a difference.

Not once did Suyodhana remove his gaze from Krithika Shah.

* * *

Run.

The word shattered through Aru's skull, forcing her to hop out of the net. Dimly, she registered that Kara was stumbling, dazed, toward the Sleeper. Her trident, Sunny, glowed bloody as a sunset. Krithika was bent over the Sleeper's chest, her hands shaking above the place where his heart had once beat.

"Mom?" asked Aru bleakly.

Her mother didn't turn.

Kara's gaze met Aru's. "I thought he...He was about to—" she said before stopping.

Aru understood, but she had no grief left to give. The only thing she wanted was for all this to be over. She'd thought that the Sleeper's death would bring the war to a standstill....

And yet it continued.

Something flew overhead. A creature that was all teeth and wings. Aru flinched, reaching for her lightning bolt, only for the creature to go *splat!* against a sudden, shimmering violet shield. Mini appeared. She was levitating, her eyes sheening purple as she looked at the scene.

"I'm so sorry, Aru."

Now's our chance! shouted Brynne's voice in her head. *Aru! Please!*

No one seemed to care that the Sleeper's body lay on the ground, protected only by the violet sphere Mini had cast moments before. None of his soldiers mourned him. Instead, they turned against one another, eager to claim the nectar of immortality for themselves.

"The nectar!" shouted one of the nagas in the Sleeper's army. "Take it! It can be ours! For the nagas!"

"For the rakshasas!" shouted a bull-headed creature who barreled into the knot of serpents.

Time slowed for Aru. She watched as the great armies churned. They had been displaced by the Sleeper's swirling tower of shadows, but now that it had vanished, the nectar of immortality shone. It was alone. Exposed. Ripe for the taking.

From hundreds of feet away came the thundering din of tails rolling over rocks, claws scarring the earth, wings bumping against one another. The Otherworld army chased close on their heels. High in the air, winged *kinnari* drew their bows and let their arrows fly.

Aru watched as Rudy weaved in and out between the soldiers. He still had a bow and arrow in his hand, but he didn't seem to be using them properly. He bashed an enemy naga over the head with them, yelling, "Bowed and arrowed! WIN!"

Flying above him, Baby Boo shrieked in agreement before releasing a jet of fire, neatly incinerating a javelin lancing through the air.

What do we do, Aru? asked Brynne.

Call in the reinforcements, said Aru. *Summon the Nairrata army. We'll catch them on both sides, kinda like a donut ring.*

Aru wasn't sure where those words had come from. Somehow a part of her brain was still focused on war strategy, robotically following the steps they'd planned long ago. Beside her, the Sun Jewel lantern had fallen to the dirt, its brightness dimming now that its purpose had been served. Aru didn't want to touch it.

Cut a clear path for me, she said.

On it, said Brynne.

I've got your back, added Mini.

I'll work the earth, said Nikita. Her voice seemed to come from far away.

Sheela, Aru noticed, was silent. She stood between Krithika, still kneeling by Suyodhana's body, and Kara...who hadn't moved since she'd let loose her trident. At that moment, Aru zoned out. Her legs moved of their own accord, stalking past her grieving mother, stricken sister, and dead father. Something glinted in her hand. Aru looked down to see the Sleeper's necklace of memories clasped tightly in her palm.

She didn't remember picking it up. Now she shoved it in her pocket.

As she envisioned the battle ahead, so it came to be.

Gold rained down from the sky as the Nairrata army fell from the clouds. Their armor sounded like thunder as the soldiers slammed into a perfect circle around the nectar of immortality. All one hundred of the golden troops dropped into a crouch. A demon rushed at one, and...

THUD.

Another golden soldier flicked the demon's armored chest plate and the creature flew backward. As one, the Nairrata army closed ranks, transforming into a barrier with a single opening to the nectar of immortality a hundred feet away.

Brynne and Mini dashed forward. But while the Nairrata army was blocking anyone else from entering, the Pandavas still had to face demon troops who had previously wormed their way to the inner sanctum.

One of them materialized in front of Aru, a sword in his hand. "You ssshould be thanking usss," said the rakshasa. He had a forked tongue, red skin, and a shiny scalp the color of a picked scab. "You could be on our ssside. You could be our *new* leader, ssseeing assss the old one isss nothing more than meat growing cold. Sssuch a waste, don't you agree? In fact—"

Anger rippled through Aru. Before Mini could turn around and cast a shield, Aru slashed upward with her lightning bolt and the smell of seared flesh filled the air. The rakshasa vanished, his sword clattering on the ground. Smoke rolled off of Aru as she stalked through the corridor to the amrita on the other side.

They hadn't respected him, she thought. The Sleeper had died for them and their cause, and they didn't even care. It made her furious. What had it all been for?

Aru wondered whether that thought made her a traitor to the Otherworld, but it was too late to take it back. Fury guided her movements. Rage lifted her hand. The lightning bolt sparked, slashing across a knot of asuras to her left. Aru didn't stay to watch them fall. She registered it only as a loss of noise.

Her sisters cleared the path before her.

"You got this, Aru!" screamed Brynne.

Brynne transformed into a massive blue elephant. She trumpeted loudly and trampled a band of rakshasas who were tunneling up through the ground. Loose rocks rolled under Aru's feet as she ran, and though she could've sped forward faster on her lightning hoverboard, she chose to take her time. She needed to rid the space of all her demons, not just outrun them.

Mini threw a protective shield around them as Nikita caught up, climbing the air as if it were a staircase. Her ball gown flowed around her. She stretched out her fingers. At her command, roots tore out of the earth. The roots clambered over the Sleeper's army and shrill screams tore through the battlefield.

Aru took a deep breath. The world stank of things left out to rot. Above, light shimmered and shifted. Rainbows arced from the armor of the Nairrata soldiers. Mini's shield turned iridescent, like a beetle's wing, deflecting arrows and spears, javelins and swords.

Aru staggered forward. She'd been running for so long that it wasn't until the bright glow of the amrita was *right* in front of her that she finally stopped. The kalash was inches from her grasp. Weapons lay scattered all around it. Small flames sputtered on the ground and smoke choked the air.

Aru could hear her sisters battling in the background, making sure no one could touch her. But still, Aru felt so alone.

Now what? she thought.

Vajra sizzled, abruptly condensing to the size of a Ping-Pong ball. The sudden loss of light made Aru feel as if a spotlight had been turned off over her head. She breathed deeply.

The smell of the nectar was intoxicating. The liquid rippled in the great metal pot.

Grab it! Declare it a victory for the devas! For the Otherworld! shouted a corner of her mind.

Aru's eyes fluttered shut. She reached for the pot when a loud clanging echoed nearby, followed by a rakshasa's furious growl. Aru lurched back to see a scimitar barely a foot above her head... held by a hand she knew too well.

"Don't worry," said Aiden, beaming down at her. "I've got you, Shah."

Aru's jaw dropped. How had he...?

And did that mean...?

Aru cast back in her memory for Nidra's warning. *What is the point of returning him if there is no chance of a world worth returning to?*

A world worth returning to. That *had* to mean they were on the verge of success....

"I'll explain later," said Aiden, smiling widely.

Near them, the rakshasa who had so silently stalked Aru wasn't done. The demon had the head of an ibex, with cruelly pointed horns and flat black eyes. It roared, revealing ugly, flat teeth.

"Could you do the honors?" Aiden asked Aru, holding out his twin scimitars.

Aru touched Vajra to his weapons, and electricity happily spangled up the metal, casting light across Aiden's face.

"I'll take care of this guy, and any others," Aiden said. "You take care of the nectar."

Aiden leaped off into his battles, and despite her joy at seeing him returned, Aru felt a clawing sense of helplessness.

What am I going to do? What am I going to do? What am I going to do?
The time was now.

ARU, WHAT ARE YOU WAITING FOR? yelled Brynne through the mind link.

Aru didn't so much as reach for the nectar of immortality as *collapse* against it. The kalash was halfway sunk into the ground, the size of a witch's cauldron, and when Aru tried to lift it, she fell, her shoulder thudding painfully against the god-smelted metal.

I just need a moment, she thought, sitting on the ground. She kept the thought all to herself, blocking it from the mental communication channels between her and her sisters. *Just a second to myself. I need to catch my breath. I—*

I was wondering when you'd ask, said a voice.

The war around her disappeared.

FORTY-FOUR

We Interrupt the Doom and Gloom for Ice Cream. Yayyyy, Ice Cream!

When Aru opened her eyes, she found herself sitting at the end of a formal dining table in a wing chair inside a kitchen. Well, *many* kitchens—at least fifteen—that had been stitched together so that it was like one large amphitheater . . . of kitchens. There were granite, marble, and maple countertops. Light fixtures ranging from Edison bulbs to bright spheres and modern-looking pendants. Wooden chairs, backless chairs, barstools, and velvet settees. All the differently shaped windows looked out into blankness, and there were lots—perhaps an excess—of subway tiles crawling up the walls that disappeared ten feet up to become a blurry, bright expanse of space.

"Do you like the renovations?! I have been watching lots of HGTV! I am going to grow a breakfast nook!"

Aru smiled and knew immediately where she was. The Palace of Illusions.

"Hello, palace," she said.

"Hello, Aru," said the palace. Its voice rose up from the ground, warming the kitchen. The smell of just-baked cookies and fall candles wafted through the air, and Aru curled her feet beneath her.

"What am I doing here?" she asked, and then paused. "I'm not...dead...right?"

"I promised to provide you with rest and shelter when you were in need," said the palace. "And you are clearly in need."

"Oh."

"Want some ice cream?" asked the palace excitedly.

Before Aru could answer, dozens of bowls of ice cream popped up on the table—mint chocolate chip, chocolate swirled with fudge, delicate rose falooda, and lemon curd.

"Yes? Wait, no! No, this is not the time for ice cream!" said Aru. She almost regretted that when she saw a flavor called the Milk at the End of a Bowl of Cereal but with Fudge. "I was... I was in the middle of a war! I just grabbed—well, kinda fell on the nectar of immortality..."

Aru's stomach dropped in horror. What was going on with everyone she'd left behind? Were they okay? Who had ended up with the amrita? Did this mean the war was over—?

"Don't worry," said the palace. "It's only for a moment."

"What?" asked Aru, looking around. "What do you mean?"

"The time you are here will not even be half a blink," said the palace proudly. "Are you sure you don't want some ice cream?"

Aru wanted to say yes, but even the delicious temptation couldn't distract her. All she'd wanted was a moment to herself, and now that she had it, she found herself shaking. She thought she'd cry, but she must have run out of tears hours ago.

Her mind turned to everything that had happened—the light going out in her father's eyes, Kara's trident glowing sunset red.

Last, her mother's trembling hand hovering over the Sleeper's still heart. The heart that, up to the end, had never stopped belonging to them.

Aru sank farther into the armchair and winced. Something sharp poked into the top of her leg.

"Check your pockets," said the palace.

One by one, Aru brought out Aleesa's bangle, Jambavan's claw, Menaka's earring, and Urmila's anklet. In her other pocket she'd stashed—and forgotten in the rush to get to the nectar of immortality—her father's necklace.

Aru held them all in her lap, a heaviness settling just behind her ribs.

"You can stay for as long as you like," said the palace hopefully. "I can make us some board games! We can build pillow forts! We could stretch a moment into a whole year, if you'd like, Aru...."

She heard the hopefulness in the palace's voice.

"I wanted to bring the others, too, but the rules are very strict about *need* and such. Although the youngest Pandava has managed to visit me in my dreams, and that is very nice. A welcome break from my nightmares about white picket fences. I hate those."

Aru laughed a little. As usual, the palace sensed what she needed and before long a mug of steaming tea appeared on the table. She dropped the necklace, earring, anklet, claw, and bangle onto the table, where they clattered loudly. Then Aru gripped the mug of tea in both hands and inhaled deeply. Truthfully, Aru didn't care for tea—it was literally *leaves* in boiled water—but she *did* like the warmth of the cup, the steam clouding her face, and the ritual of waiting for something to cool.

Aru focused on the steam.

It would be nice, she thought, *to stay here awhile. To rest. To sit in silence.* But she couldn't leave the world waiting.

"I have something to do, don't I?" she asked, exhaling.

"Eventually, yes," admitted the palace.

Aru curled a little more into the seat, staring at the tokens on the table. As a Pandava, her duty was to end the war, and she had vowed to try her best to do that.... But now that the moment had come, it didn't seem like a win.

Why did everyone want to be immortal, anyway? What was the big draw? Eventually, you'd get bored!

And what if it was like one of those cautionary stories where someone wished for eternal life but got stuck with eternal adolescence and ended up shriveling in eternal embarrassment?

If she gave the nectar of immortality to the devas, the jar would be moved somewhere else. Within another labyrinth. And there'd be more seething anger in those who had been denied it. There would still be too much power in one place, and too much temptation in the world, because it wasn't as though the nectar itself could be destroyed....

Aru inhaled sharply.

"But what if ..." she said quietly, her hands clasped in her lap as she stared down at all the mementos she'd gathered over the past ten days. "What if there was some other way?"

Aru thought of the poison maiden's grief and longing for a different life; the bear king growing old and dreaming of his former conquests; the apsara recoiling at her legacy and desperate not to be hurt; the princess who had sacrificed all her dreams and could not even claim to live in someone's memory; and then, of course, Suyodhana. His deepest desire had been to live in a world where he could be with his family.

Maybe what most people wanted wasn't immortality and fame, but the reassurance that their existence had meant something. No matter how long... or how brief. Maybe being eternal meant becoming a story worth telling.

"I know that look!" said the palace excitedly. "That's a sneaky look! Arjuna always looked like that when he had a good idea. Do you have a good idea?"

Aru sighed. "Well, I don't have any better ones?"

The palace was silent for a moment. "I guess that's better than nothing!"

"I have to go back now," said Aru, setting down the mug and patting the arm of the chair. "Thank you, palace. You were wonderful."

The lights in the palace brightened happily. "Really? Maybe next time you can stay longer! Although I hope you never need a next time.... Now I feel very confused. Good-bye, Aru Shah. I am happy I could shelter you once again...."

Back on the battlefield, Aru's ears filled with shouts. Her shoulder ached from where it had bumped the metal kalash. When she stood, the necklace, earring, bangle, claw, and anklet spilled onto the ground.

Vajra twisted in her hands as ropes of electricity converged and fused into the shape of a pointed spear. Aru felt the glow of the amrita on her skin. She closed her eyes and inhaled. She recalled the ghostly brush of Urmila's ankle, the scrape of Menaka's fingernails as she'd dropped the earring into Aru's palm, the warmth of Jambavan's fur when he'd held out his claw, the green tinge of Aleesa's poisonous skin, and last...the mismatched colors of the Sleeper's eyes. One brown, one blue. She exhaled.

As the breath left her lungs, Aru Shah hurled her lightning bolt at the nectar of immortality.

FORTY-FIVE

Potatoes, Assemble!

At the first shot of lightning, a long crack appeared in the middle of the pot holding the nectar. Golden liquid seeped from the fissure. The sky darkened as if some cosmic switch had been flipped. A bracing wind swept through the sanctum being protected by the Nairrata soldiers, and moments later, the kalash zoomed high into the air.

"*WHAT ARE YOU DOING?*" demanded Brynne. She alighted on the ground beside Aru, her wind mace angled up at the pot. Brynne had moved it out of reach.

"I know how this looks—" started Aru.

"*Do you?*" demanded Brynne.

"Aru…" said Mini, materializing next to them with a trail of faint purple sparks. Above them, the iridescent protective shield she had cast flickered as if with uncertainty. Her gaze flew up to the leaking pot of amrita. "What have you done?"

Aru took a deep breath. "Our duty."

Brynne frowned. "What?"

"What do you mean?" asked Mini.

Before she could answer, Nikita and Sheila winked into existence. They had someone with them—Kara, only dimly aglow.

Aru kept going with her explanation. "Our duty was to *end* the war," she said, gesturing around them. "If we shatter that kalash...if we *share* the nectar to the point where everyone has a drop, then there'll be nothing left to fight over! I mean, yeah, there's always going to be fights, but *this* specific, never-ending war over who gets the nectar of immortality? Over who gets to be immortal? Over who gets to be, I don't know, *remembered*? Well, *this*"—she flailed a hand toward the pot—"is the answer."

Aru took a moment to catch her breath. "We end the war, not by winning immortality for one side, but by sharing it with everyone."

Aru searched her sisters' faces for a reaction. In a way, she'd always known this moment was coming. She had pictured it a thousand different ways, a thousand different times. It had been the backdrop of a thousand nightmares ever since the Sleeper had shown it to her years ago:

Aru, with her lightning bolt in her hand, staring at the five girls who had become family to her. Her on one side; them in a half circle on the other, wearing matching expressions of shock and disbelief. A cold wind blew around Brynne. Violet light sparked around Mini's silhouette. Vines coiled beneath Nikita, like an agitated snake unsure who to bite.

"Pretty sneaky, Aru," said Sheela. But she was smiling.

Aru's eyes went back to her other sisters, but she couldn't read what they were thinking. Did they hate her? Would they cast her out?

Mini drew back her hand, her gaze still fixed on Aru. In a single, smooth motion, she hurled her Death Danda as if it were a boomerang. It thudded with a metallic *thwack!* against the side of the kalash. More cracks appeared, glowing like rivulets of gold.

"My turn!" said Nikita, stringing a bow of rose canes before shooting an arrow. "Sheela? Wanna go?"

Sheela nodded and picked up a nearby rock. She aimed and let it fly. Moments later, a warm breeze surrounded them. Gently, the kalash floated back to the ground, landing within their circle. Within it, the nectar of immortality bubbled, as if agitated.

Across the burning liquid, Aru met Brynne's gaze. Her mouth was a grim line, but when she looked at Aru, she nodded. Brynne raised her wind mace high over her head before slamming it down on the pot. Rays of golden light burst all around them. But the container was still mostly intact.

Maybe one last shot would do it.

Aru turned to her left. Kara hadn't moved from her spot a dozen feet away. She was in the circle . . . and yet somehow out of it, too. Her trident gleamed dully.

Aru held out her hand.

Thunder rattled in the sky and rain began to fall. Aru couldn't feel it on her skin, but she saw it plinking and sliding on the exterior of Mini's shield. She had expected it. After all, she had summoned it.

Kara looked nervous as she walked forward and took Aru's outstretched hand. They didn't say a word to each other, but in those moments before the world changed, Aru considered how they were like two sides of a coin. A really, *really* magical coin, obviously. Maybe they'd both always known it, but at the wrong time. Maybe that's why the Sleeper had wanted to keep them apart. Kara had always been the warmth and sunshine to Aru's thunder and lightning.

The world they'd lived in was an eternal winter, a place frozen over by the bitterness of others. But winter disappears in the presence of two things: sunshine and rain. Together, Aru and Kara summoned spring....

Together, they brought *change*.

Aru and Kara threw their weapons. Mini dropped the shield and the kalash was obliterated. Without something to contain the liquid, without two palms waiting to scoop it up or a mouth ready to guzzle it, the amrita vaporized within seconds. Bright golden droplets hit the ground or dispersed into the clouds or blew away on the wind.

Nectar mixed with the rain and flowed in streams of immortality that gradually narrowed. Aru imagined it encasing the earth like a great shimmering net. Moments later, any signs of the amrita's existence vanished completely.

Aru searched around her feet, but she could no longer see the anklet, the earring, the bangle, the claw, or the necklace. She wondered if the nectar had taken those pieces of people's lives and whether, even now, an immortal alchemy was slowly translating them into legends ... *stories*. Snippets of the eternal that could live forever in people's imaginations. Somewhere, Aru heard a sigh of relief ... but she didn't know who had breathed the sound.

For the rest of her life, Aru would never be sure if it was her lightning bolt or Kara's trident that had shattered the last bit of the pot holding the nectar of immortality. But in a way, it didn't matter.

In the end, it was all light.

FORTY-SIX

Here, at the End of All Things

A stunned silence settled over the area.

When Aru looked up, the Nairrata soldiers had frozen in place, their heads craned to look over their shoulders as if they were amazed by what had happened. There were gaps between the troops now, and through the spaces Aru could see disbelief rippling through both the Sleeper's forces and the Otherworld army.

Then dozens of voices spoke up, seeming to come from every direction:

"It's gone...."

"I can feel it in the ground, in the air..." said another.

"What have they done?"

The handful of rakshasas still lingering nearby lowered their weapons and stared in wonder at the Pandavas. A few nagas' hoods flared, their forked tongues flickering angrily. Nervous sparks of electricity flew off Vajra, and the Pandava sisters slowly moved toward one another, tightening the circle.

Aiden and Rudy broke through the crowd to join them. Baby

Boo soared overhead, cawing happily. A huge grin broke over Aiden's face when he saw the bird, and Aru was smiling, too, when a massive shadow engulfed the battlefield.

A powerful gust of air, like a helicopter landing nearby, whipped their hair and made them cower.

"Dee Dee!" yelled Mini. She pointed her Death Danda at the sky and cast a shield that stretched over the Potatoes and Baby Boo as a wave of dirt threatened to swallow them whole. Outside the crackling screen, Aru watched as weapons were blown out of outstretched hands. Rakshasas and asuras went flying. But they were not alone. Otherworld creatures also tumbled through the air, losing the weapons that they'd only clutched harder when it became clear that *no one* would receive the nectar of immortality.

Panic fluttered through Aru. Where had her mom gone? Urvashi and Hanuman appeared above them. The celestial dancer had cast an enchantment around her in the air, and Hanuman had shot up in height, closing his eyes against the wind. The gust couldn't have lasted more than half a minute, but by the time it passed, the Potatoes and their mentors were the only ones still standing.

Almost.

Hanuman opened one hand to reveal Krithika Shah sitting on his palm.

"Mom!"

Far above them, Krithika gave a little wave, and although there were tears in her eyes, Aru knew her mother was proud of her.

"So . . . it is decided," said an unfamiliar voice. "I had wondered what would happen."

Garuda, king of the birds, landed on the ground. His huge bronze wings, Aru realized, had created that powerful gust. He appeared as he had when they'd first met him—a tanned, muscular man wearing long silk shorts and a solid-gold baseball cap. His face was covered in bright green feathers, his nose was a sharp golden beak, and his hands and feet ended in talons.

When the Potatoes were looking for the Tree of Wishes, he had almost attacked them. Rudy clearly remembered, because he quickly slithered behind Aiden and glared at Garuda—a self-declared snake-hater—from there.

"Will you not greet me, daughters of the gods?" asked Garuda, fixing them with a burning stare.

Immediately, Mini lifted the shield, and the Pandavas pressed their hands together and touched the ground before them.

Garuda nodded in acknowledgment. Then he lifted his gaze to Hanuman and Urvashi. "It is done," he said.

Hanuman cleared his throat. "And it cannot be undone?"

Aru flinched at that, wondering if her old teacher was angry. But when she looked at his face, she saw hope there. It confused her.

"It cannot be undone," confirmed Garuda.

Hanuman smiled widely. Beside him, Urvashi positively glowed, clasping her hands in joy. With a warm glance at the Pandavas, Hanuman gently set down Krithika Shah. She looked as if she wanted to run to Aru, but she froze when her eyes darted to Kara. Aru could feel Kara holding her breath just as she could feel her mother's tense gaze, and neither of them moved.

"Aru Shah," boomed Garuda, and every nerve in Aru's body leaped with panic.

I don't know her? Aru wanted to say, but it was too late for that now.

"Hi?" she said instead, and then immediately wished she'd thought of something else.

"I once asked you what you know of wars and winning.... It seems you have shown me the answer today," said Garuda. "For thousands of years I have been tasked with protecting the nectar of immortality, and now there is nothing left for me to protect."

Aru frowned, exchanging worried looks with her sisters.

"Are you here to punish us?" asked Brynne.

"Why would I do that?" asked Garuda.

"Because we . . . I mean, *I*"—corrected Aru, so the gods wouldn't blame her sisters—"destroyed the nectar of immortality?"

"Destroyed it?" asked Garuda, looking around him as if he were hunting for pieces of the demolished kalash. "On the contrary, you shared it freely with the world. You turned it into a story that flows from one mouth to the next."

"Your duty as Pandavas was to end the war," said Hanuman in his rich voice. "And you did just that."

"It was a most elegant solution," said Urvashi, smiling.

"But . . . But what about the devas?" asked Mini. "If the amrita was solely theirs, doesn't that mean they lost?"

"It depends on how you look at it," said Garuda. "From where I'm standing, I see no loss. I see only the gains of many. You brought about a victory for all, daughters of the gods."

Aru thought of the Otherworld people who had clutched their weapons tighter once they saw what the Pandavas had done. She thought of the Sleeper's body somewhere on the battlefield and the bright sunset-tinged blades of Kara's trident.

"It doesn't feel like one," said Aru softly.

"Perhaps that discomfort is the mark of a true hero," said Garuda, before correcting himself. "Or heroine, as the case may be."

Aru almost smiled, but then Garuda's gaze turned to Kara.

"As for you, Kara… You may be a heroine, but that does not erase your act of villainy," said Garuda, and his voice echoed around them. "Your life was taken from you, and you took a life in return. For your good deeds, you will be rewarded. You will return to your childhood home and family. All will be as it was.…"

Kara's eyes went wide, and she snuck a nervous glance at Brynne, Mini, Aru, Sheela, and Nikita. A frail smile twitched on her lips.

But Garuda wasn't done.

"But you must also be punished. As a consequence of your actions, you will be stripped of your memories of this time. You will have no recollection of the Sleeper or of having powers bestowed by Surya. You are hereby divested of your celestial weapon."

Kara gasped as her trident, Sunny, flew from her hands. Its light flickered, as if it were panicking, until it was caught in a ray of sun. Then it dissolved into particles of light.

"B-but…" she stammered, looking frantically between Aru and Garuda. "So I won't remember the Potatoes anymore? I won't remember that I had…"

Kara couldn't finish, but Aru knew what she would've said. *Sisters.*

Garuda's fierce expression softened. "It is a kindness, child, though you may not see it as such right now," he said. "This is the balance that must be struck. Sometimes life is full of loss, but at least you will not know of it."

"But I just found them," said Kara, staring at her feet, and Aru felt as though someone had taken a hammer to her heart.

"And perhaps you will find them again someday," said Garuda. "There may come a time when you prove yourself worthy of the power you once held." His eyes narrowed at something in the dirt. Aru followed his gaze to where the Sun Jewel lantern rose out of the ground and flew into the bird king's taloned hand. Garuda stared at it thoughtfully. "There will be other trials, other wonders and terrors. And perhaps their stories will collide with yours. But until then, it is time to say your good-byes."

Garuda withdrew to speak with Urvashi and Hanuman, leaving Kara to stare wordlessly at the rest of them. Rudy started to say something, but Aiden wisely led him away from the group. He paused only once, as if he might look over his shoulder at Kara. But in the end, he kept walking.

Brynne didn't meet Kara's gaze. Her expression was torn, caught between anger at Kara's first betrayal and maybe sadness, too. Mini looked pityingly at Kara, but she also didn't step forward. When Sheela made a move to console Kara, Nikita grabbed her twin's hand and gave a fierce shake of her head.

Kara stood apart from the Pandavas, and while there might come a day when that distance could be crossed, it was not now.

Kara released a shaky breath and then turned to Aru. "I really wish we could've been sisters."

"Me too," said Aru, struggling to speak past the lump in her throat. "Maybe another time?"

"Yeah," said Kara, with an uncertain smile. "Another time."

The last person to say good-bye to Kara was Krithika. Aru didn't want to hear their exchange. It felt too intrusive.

Could you give them a privacy bubble? Aru asked Mini through their mind link.

Mini nodded and gently cast a sphere around Krithika and Kara. Aru couldn't help peeking. Her mother and sister stood barely a foot apart as they talked, and eventually they embraced. Kara started sobbing, her thin shoulders shaking, her brown hair falling in front of her face. Aru kept watching as the sunlight grew fiercer, forming a puddle at Kara's feet. Mini pulled back her shield, and Kara glanced over her shoulder at the Pandavas. Then she closed her eyes, stepped forward... and disappeared into the light.

The numbness of before hadn't left Aru. She seemed to be experiencing things in slow motion, as if Time itself wasn't quite reaching her. She startled when she felt a pair of arms wrap around her. It was her mother, pulling her into a hug as the sky turned bright blue and a warm breeze wafted around them. Aru didn't know what to do next, but she didn't feel panicked anymore. She felt anchored. The past held pain and the present bore a raw and tender peace, which left only one thing for the future....

Hope.

And Aru Shah had plenty of it.

FORTY-SEVEN

It Was a Dark and Stormy Night

SIX MONTHS LATER

"We *need* to be prepared," said Mini, leaning over the dining table with a thunderous look in her eye. "*Everyone* is our enemy. *Nothing* is safe. And *everything* is a trap."

"Mini," said Aru. "It's a standardized test, not a war."

The Potatoes were in Brynne's penthouse for their weekly study session. Mini hated it. *I'm the only one who's taking this seriously!* she would usually lament.

Which, Aru had to admit, was true. Nikita and Sheela were too young for the various perils that accompanied high school, like standardized tests and cafeteria "surprises," so Sheela usually took this time to read while Nikita offered unsolicited fashion consultations to Brynne's abysmally dressed uncles.

"Now can we eat?" asked Brynne, slouching at the head of the table.

Hira raised her hand. "I'm hungry."

Sometimes, when Mini wasn't looking, Hira would stand behind her, shape-shift into Mini's form, and pantomime tugging out her own hair and swooning dramatically. It was very funny. Of course, Mini didn't think so.

"Come help me in the kitchen," said Brynne, smiling at Hira.

Brynne thought of studying the way others thought about eating brussels sprouts—it's really good for you and therefore completely unenjoyable. Aru had once made the mistake of pointing this out, only to receive a lecture on the Various Ways Brussel Sprouts Have Been Disrespected by the American Palate.

Cool.

"Guys, *focus!*" said Mini, smacking the sheaf of papers in front of her. "This could really determine the rest of our lives!"

"Eh," said Brynne, reappearing in the doorway with a spatula in her hand. "*Part* of our lives. We're always going to have Pandava duties. There *could* be trouble down the road. Not likely, but definitely still possible."

Mini harrumphed. "Well, I'm not going to exist on demon standby. I, and by that I mean *we*—"

Aru grumbled. The whole Mini-stepping-into-her-power thing had come with some bad consequences. Mainly that the rest of them kept getting dragged in the wake of her ambition.

"—are going to contribute to society! We're going to go to school! And we're going to worry about our GPAs! And get a mortgage!" said Mini, clapping her hands with a savage glee. "Doesn't that sound *fun?*"

"No," said Aru.

"What Aru said," Brynne called from the kitchen.

"Ooh, what's a mortgage?" piped up Rudy.

Rudy was sitting next to Mini at the table, a pair of headphones dangling from his neck and a sheet of music composing paper in front of him. Aru still wasn't sure why Rudy insisted on joining their study sessions. They already saw him on the weekends during Otherworld training, and his underwater palace had become the go-to choice for movie nights. Rudy's parents were even considering letting him try a year of "human school." With Aiden.

Rudy was excited.

Aiden was not.

"A mortgage is how people pay off their houses," said Mini.

Rudy frowned. "For fun?"

"No," said Mini gently. "Houses are expensive, Rudy."

Rudy blinked. He did not seem to understand this word.

"If you want a house, I can build you a palace!"

"No."

"It'll have gold *everywhere!*"

"No, Rudy, that's not what I meant," said Mini, sighing.

Over the past few months, Mini and Rudy's relationship hadn't really evolved. Aru and Brynne had, of course, asked Mini about it, and she had responded with a vague *I don't know yet.* Her uncertainty hadn't deterred Rudy, who, for the most part, addressed Mini as *my dark, benevolent queen.*

He's a bit of a dork, Mini often said, smiling.

Now Rudy continued, "Or maybe a bunch of palaces that spell out your name . . ."

Mini gave up, putting her head in her hands.

Behind Aru, she heard the sudden whir and *click!* of a familiar camera. She turned around and immediately felt the sensation of butterfly wings in her stomach. Normally, she would consider that disgusting. Butterflies were pretty and all, BUT WHY DID THEIR TONGUES CURL LIKE THAT? And how come they tasted with THEIR FEET? None of that was okay!

But what was infinitely more than okay was the person standing in the doorway. Aiden. He grinned at Aru and lowered Shadowfax. Baby Boo was perched on his shoulder.

Cheep! the firebird said.

Which they had recently decoded as *COOKIES. I WANT. GIVE?*

"Where've you been, Wifey?" Aru asked.

He rolled his eyes at the nickname before plopping into the seat beside her. Her chair was a little farther away than Aiden seemed to like, because he reached out and dragged it closer to his, which made Aru's face burn.

"I was visiting my nani," he said. "She says hello. She also gave me a letter." Aiden held it out to Aru. "C'mon, I know you're curious."

Aru took the envelope from him. It was cream-colored and addressed as follows:

TO THE PANDAVA SISTERS,
WHO OWE ME A DEBT

Aru frowned. "Mini? Brynne? I think you should come read this." She looked around the room. "Where are the twins?"

"Gunky and Funky took them to get ice cream," said Rudy.

"There's no way I'm coming out there to watch you guys make *eyes* at each other for five minutes straight!" shouted Brynne from the kitchen.

"We don't do that!" said Aru.

You do, said Mini through their mind link.

Aiden pretended to be very preoccupied with Shadowfax.

It seemed silly to call Aiden her boyfriend when he'd started off as Wifey, so Aru had stuck with the latter. Her mom had laughed her head off at the notion of Aru and Aiden "going out."

"Going out *where*?" Krithika asked with a cackle. "With whose money? You're too young to have a boyfriend."

Aru had glared and crossed her arms. "But not too young to be reincarnated? Or to fight a battle? Or literally *enter* this existence with someone who, *thousands of years ago,* was my actual *wife*?"

Krithika scowled.

"What?" said Aru, feigning innocence. "You said we should be more honest with each other. I'm telling nothing but the truth."

"It's a little too much truth for ten a.m.," her mother had responded.

They had settled on a truce—supervised interaction. As in, no door closed at any time, absolutely no being *"alone* alone," but most importantly...

"Just talk to me," her mother had said. "Don't hide things."

Aru had smiled. "I won't."

She and her mom were getting pretty good at that. Maybe a little *too* good, considering the conversations her mother had been trying to have with her lately.

Aru opened the envelope. As she read the letter, she started to laugh. Brynne stomped out of the kitchen and grabbed the note from her. Mini hopped out of her chair, abandoning her standardized test practice session to read over Brynne's shoulder.

> I have come to collect my debt.
> Did you think I would forget?
> The time is now, the debt is called!
> Ignore me and I will be appalled....
> —V

* * *

A few hours later, the Potatoes exited the nearest portal and entered a dark forest. It was instantly familiar to Aru, even though she'd only been there once, years ago. She waited by the trunk of an oak tree until she caught sight of a line of ants.

This way, they seemed to say.

They followed the ants deep into the trees, where the great poet Valmiki was waiting for them. He looked just like he had when Aru and Mini first met him and ended up granting him the right to tell their story. Valmiki glared as they came into sight. He adjusted the huge scarf around his neck and lowered his reading glasses.

"First things first," said Aru, lifting her hand. "I *cannot* speak to you in iambic pentameter. I'm in high school. And I'm in Otherworld training. So, I've got, like, three brain cells left, and it would take at least four for me to come up with rhymes."

Brynne snorted. "I think you're being generous about the three, Shah."

Mini mumbled about the anatomical absurdity of Aru's statement. "You're literally born with billions of brain cells, and they're all linked through millions of synapses—"

Valmiki sighed. "Fine, fine. Tell me your tale! I was always curious about whether good or evil would prevail.... Do be mindful of the plot! Otherwise the entire story shall be shot!"

Aru eased herself onto the ground and stretched her neck from side to side. "All right, I'll start," she said, in her most dramatic voice. "It was a dark and *stormy* night—"

Mini frowned. "Wasn't it four p.m. on a Monday?"

"And you were still in your Spider-Man pajamas?" added Brynne, laughing.

"I hope you don't have those anymore," said Nikita. "That's horrific."

"*I* want Spider-Man pajamas," said Sheela, pouting.

"Shhh! *Stahhhhp*," said Aru, fighting back a laugh. "It's my story. I'll tell it however I want."

GLOSSARY

PHEW. End of the series. How. When. What is existence. I have … so many emotions. I also never want to write a glossary again. (Narrator: Roshani Chokshi went on to write glossaries for the rest of her life.) No doubt you are all experts by now, but kindly indulge me one last time....

This glossary is by no means exhaustive or encapsulating of all the nuances of mythology. India is GINORMOUS, and these myths and legends vary from state to state. What you read here is merely a slice of what *I* understand from the stories *I* was told and the research *I* conducted. The wonderful thing about mythology is that its arms are wide enough to embrace many traditions from many regions. My hope is that this glossary gives you context for Aru's world, and perhaps nudges you to do some research of your own. ☺

Agni (UHG-nee) The Hindu god of fire.
Airavata (AYE-rah-vaht-uh) A white elephant! And no, not the terrible Christmas tradition where someone steals the present you were secretly excited about because they're actual Grinches.

Airavata is said to be the king of the elephants, and he spends his time joyously knitting clouds. He supposedly arose out of the churning of the Ocean of Milk.

Amaravati (uh-MAR-uh-vah-tee) So, I have suffered the great misfortune of never being invited to/having visited this legendary city, but I hear it's, like, *amazing*. It has to be, considering it's the place where Lord Indra lives. It's overflowing with gold palaces and has celestial gardens full of a thousand marvels. I wonder what the flowers would smell like there. I imagine they smell like birthday cake, because it's basically heaven.

Ammamma (UH-muh-mah) *Grandmother* in Telugu, one of the many languages spoken in India, most commonly in the southern area.

Amrita (AHM-ree-tuh) The immortal drink of the gods. According to the legends, Sage Durvasa once cursed the gods to lose their immortality. To get it back, they had to churn the celestial Ocean of Milk. But in order to accomplish this feat, they had to seek assistance from the asuras, another semidivine race of beings who were constantly at war with the devas. In return for their help, the asuras demanded that the devas share a taste of the amrita. Which, you know, *fair*. But to gods, the word *fair* is just another word. So they tricked the asuras. The supreme god Vishnu, also known as the preserver, took on the form of Mohini, a beautiful enchantress. The asuras and devas lined up in two rows. While Mohini poured the amrita, the asuras were so mesmerized by her beauty that they didn't realize that she was giving *all* the immortality nectar to the gods and not them. Rude! By the way, I have no idea what amrita tastes like. Probably birthday cake.

Apsara (AHP-sah-rah) Apsaras are beautiful heavenly dancers who entertain in the Court of the Heavens. They're often the wives of heavenly musicians. In Hindu myths, apsaras are usually sent on errands by Lord Indra to break the meditation of sages who are getting a little too powerful. It's pretty hard to keep meditating when a celestial nymph starts dancing in front of you. And if you scorn her affection (as Arjuna did in the *Mahabharata*), she might just curse you. Just sayin'.

Ashvin Twins (ASH-vin) The gods of sunrise and sunset, and healing. They are the sons of the sun god, Surya, and fathers of the Pandava twins, Nakula and Sahadeva. They're considered the doctors of the gods and are often depicted with the faces of horses.

Astra (AH-struh) Supernatural weapons that are usually summoned into battle by a specific chant and are often paired to a specific deity. These days, I'm pretty sure it just means any weapon.

Asura (AH-soo-rah) A sometimes good, sometimes bad race of semidivine beings. They're most popularly known from the story about the churning of the Ocean of Milk.

Bansari (buhn-SUH-ree) A flute, the instrument played by Lord Krishna.

Bhanumati (BAH-noo-MAH-tee) The wife of Duryodhana, the main antagonist of the epic poem the *Mahabharata*.

Brahma (BRUH-mah) The creator god in Hinduism, and part of the triumvirate represented by Lord Vishnu, the preserver, and Lord Shiva, the destroyer.

Carnatic (kahr-NAH-tick) A type of music with roots in southern India.

Danda (DAHN-duh) A giant punishing rod that is often considered the symbol of the Dharma Raja, the god of the dead.

Devas (DEH-vahz) The Sanskrit term for the race of gods.

Dharma Raja (DAR-mah RAH-jah) The Lord of Death and Justice, also called Yama, and the father of the oldest Pandava brother, Yudhistira. His mount is a water buffalo.

Diadem (DAI-uh-dem) A type of crown, specifically an ornamental headband worn by monarchs and others as a badge of royalty.

Gandharva (GUHN-der-vah) A celestial being, specifically a divine musician.

Hanuman (HUH-noo-mahn) One of the main figures in the Indian epic the *Ramayana*, who was known for his devotion to the god king Rama and Rama's wife, Sita. Hanuman is the son of Vayu, the god of the wind, and Anjana, an apsara. He had lots of mischievous exploits as a kid, including mistaking the sun for a mango and trying to eat it. There are still temples and shrines dedicated to Hanuman, and he's often worshipped by wrestlers because of his incredible strength. He's the half brother of Bhima, the second-oldest Pandava brother.

Himavant (HEE-mah-vahnt) The personification of the Himalayan mountains, also known as the Himavat Mountains. He is the father of the river goddess Ganga and of Parvati, one of the most powerful goddesses and the consort of Lord Shiva. Himavant's wife is Menavati, the daughter of Mount Meru. If I were descended from a literal mountain, I bet I would never have been picked last for dodgeball.

Indra (IN-druh) The king of heaven, and the god of thunder and lightning. He is the father of Arjuna, the third-oldest Pandava brother. His main weapon is Vajra, a lightning bolt. He has two vahanas: Airavata, the white elephant who spins clouds, and Uchchaihshravas, the seven-headed white horse. I've got a pretty good guess what his favorite color is....

Indraasana (IN-drah-ah-sah-nah) The throne of Indra.

Ixtab (eesh-TAHB) Indigenous Maya goddess of the underworld.

Jambavan (JAHM-bah-vuhn) The divine king of bears, created by the god Brahma to assist the avatar Rama in his struggle against the Lanka king Ravana. Jambavan wrestled Lord Krishna for twenty-eight days straight.... Can you imagine? Just thinking about that makes my feet hurt.

Kalash (kuh-LESH) A metal pot with a large base and a small mouth.

Kalpavriksha (kul-PUHV-rik-shaw) A divine wish-fulfilling tree. It is said to have roots of gold and silver, with boughs encased in costly jewels, and to reside in the paradise gardens of the god Indra. Sounds like a pretty useful thing to steal. Or protect. Just saying.

Karna (CAR-nuh) Karna is the son of Surya and Queen Kunti, mother of the Pandavas. He is the archenemy of Arjuna. When Kunti found out that she could use a divine boon and ask any of the gods to give her a child, she didn't believe it. So...she tested it out on Surya, which resulted in Karna's birth. But Kunti was unmarried and a teenager. Out of fear, she abandoned Karna in a basket by the river, where he was found and raised by a kind charioteer. Karna became one of the most gifted and noble of warriors. He was a loyal friend of Duryodhana, the archenemy of the Pandavas. Karna was a rather tragic figure to me growing up. He's someone who was rejected a lot because of his perceived low birth, and yet he tried his best to honor and love the people who loved him back. Was he perfect? Nope. But I think he tried to do more good in the world than evil. And perhaps that's what matters most.

King Vali (VAH-lee) Vali, the son of Indra, was king of the vanaras and husband to Tara. He was blessed with the ability to take half his opponent's strength in any fight. He was killed by the god king Rama. While fighting against his brother, Rama hid behind a tree and shot him from behind.

Kinnari (kin-AH-ree) A celestial musician, part human and part bird, said to be extremely beautiful.

Kishkinda (kish-KIN-duh) Home of the vanaras, the semi-monkey race.

Krishna (KRISH-nah) A major Hindu deity. He is worshipped as the eighth reincarnation of the god Vishnu and also as a supreme ruler in his own right. He is the god of compassion, tenderness, and love, and is popular for his charmingly mischievous personality.

Kubera (koo-BEAR-uh) The god of riches and ruler of the legendary golden city of Lanka. He's often depicted as a dwarf adorned with jewels.

Kumbhakarna (KOOM-bah-KUR-nah) A well-known rakshasa noble and the younger brother of Ravana from the Hindu epic the *Ramayana*. Kumbhakarna got tongue-tied at the wrong moment, which is why he's usually asleep.

Kunti (KOON-tee) One of the panchakanyas, or legendary women, and mother of the Pandavas. As a young woman, Kunti was given the boon to invoke any of the gods to bless her with a child. This resulted in the births of Karna, Yudhistira, Bhima, and Arjuna. Nakula and Sahadeva were the children of her co-queen, Madri, with whom she shared the blessing.

Lanka (LAHN-kuh) The legendary city of gold, sometimes ruled over by Kubera, sometimes ruled over by his demonic brother, Ravana. Lanka is a major setting in the epic poem the *Ramayana*.

Laxmana (LUCK-shmun) The younger brother of Rama and his aide in the Hindu epic the *Ramayana*. Sometimes he's considered a quarter of Lord Vishnu. Other times, he's considered the reincarnation of Shesha, the thousand-headed serpent and king of all nagas, devotee of Vishnu.

Mahabharata (MAH-hah-BAR-ah-tah) One of two Sanskrit epic poems of ancient India (the other being the *Ramayana*). It is an important source of information about the development of Hinduism between 400 BCE and 200 CE and tells the story of the struggle between two groups of cousins, the Kauravas and the Pandavas.

Maruts (MAH-roots) Minor storm deities often described as violent and aggressive and carrying lots of weapons. Legend says the Maruts once rode through the sky, splitting open clouds so that rain could fall on the earth.

Menaka (MEH-nuh-kah) Menaka was born while the devas and asuras were churning the Ocean of Milk and became one of the most beautiful apsaras in the world. She was sent to distract (insert winky face here) the sage Vishwamitra, which resulted in the birth of their daughter, Shakuntula.

Mohini (moe-HIH-nee) One of the avatars of Lord Vishnu, known as the goddess of enchantment. The gods and asuras banded together to churn the Ocean of Milk on the promise that the nectar of immortality would be shared among them. But the gods didn't want immortal demon counterparts, so

Mohini tricked the asuras by pouring the nectar into the goblets of the gods while smiling over her shoulder at the demons.

Naga (**nagas**, pl.) (NAH-guh) A naga (male) or nagini (female) is one of a group of serpentine beings who are magical and, depending on the region in India, considered divine. Among the most famous nagas is Vasuki, one of the king serpents who was used as a rope when the gods and asuras churned the Ocean of Milk to get the elixir of life. Another is Uloopi, a nagini princess who fell in love with Arjuna, married him, and used a magical gem to save his life.

Naga-Loka (NAH-guh-LOW-kuh) The abode of the naga people, or snake-people. It's said that Naga-Loka is a place strewn with precious jewels. Again, deeply disappointed to have received no invite.

Nairrata (NAI-rah-tuh) The vast army controlled by Kubera, Lord of Wealth and Treasure.

Nakula (nuh-KOO-luh) The most handsome Pandava brother, and a master of horses, swordsmanship, and healing. He is the twin of Sahadeva, and they are the children of the Ashvin twins.

Pandava brothers (Arjuna, Yudhistira, Bhima, Nakula, and Sahadeva) (PAN-dah-vah, ar-JOO-nah, yoo-diss-TEE-ruh, BEE-muh, nuh-KOO-luh, saw-hah-DAY-vuh) Demigod warrior princes, and the heroes of the epic *Mahabharata* poem. Arjuna, Yudhistira, and Bhima were born to Queen Kunti, the first wife of King Pandu. Nakula and Sahadeva were born to Queen Madri, the second wife of King Pandu.

Prasena (PRUH-say-nah) Satyajit's brother, who made the very poor choice of climbing into a tree while hunting and also wearing a stupendously fancy gem around his neck. The gleam of the jewel attracted a lion, which ate him.

Queen Tara (TAH-ruh) The apsara wife and queen of King Vali of the vanaras. Tara is said to have placed a curse on the god king Rama out of grief when he slew her husband.

Rakshasa (RUCK-shaw-sah) A rakshasa (male) or rakshasi (female) is a mythological being, like a demigod. Sometimes good and sometimes bad, they are powerful sorcerers, and can change shape to take on any form.

Rama (RAH-mah) The hero of the epic poem the *Ramayana*. He was the seventh incarnation of the god Vishnu.

Ramayana (RAH-mah-YAWN-uh) One of the two great Sanskrit epic poems (the other being the *Mahabharata*), it describes how the god king Rama, aided by his brother and the monkey-faced demigod Hanuman, rescued his wife, Sita, from the ten-headed demon king, Ravana.

Ravana (RAH-vah-nah) A character in the Hindu epic the *Ramayana*, where he is depicted as the ten-headed demon king who stole Rama's wife, Sita. Ravana is described as having once been a follower of Shiva. He was also a great scholar, a capable ruler, a master of the *veena* (a musical instrument), and someone who wished to overpower the gods. He's one of my favorite antagonists, to be honest, because it just goes to show that the line between heroism and villainy can be a bit murky.

Sahadeva (SAW-hah-DAY-vuh) The twin to Nakula, and the wisest of the Pandavas. He was known to be a great swordsman and also a brilliant astrologist, but he was cursed that if he should disclose events before they happened, his head would explode.

Salwar kameez (SAL-war kah-MEEZ) A traditional garment composed of a tunic and pants, often with a dupatta (scarf) to accent the piece.

Sanskrit (SAHN-skrit) An ancient language of India. Many Hindu scriptures and epic poems are written in Sanskrit.

Satyajit (SAHT-yuh-jeet) A nobleman who received the Syamantaka Gem as a gift from the sun god but selfishly refused to relinquish it to help his people.

Shiva (SHEE-vuh) One of the three main gods in the Hindu pantheon, often associated with destruction. He is also known as the Lord of Cosmic Dance. His consort is Parvati.

Sita (SEE-tuh) The reincarnation of Lakshmi, goddess of wealth and fortune, and consort of Lord Vishnu. Sita was the long-suffering wife of the god king Rama in the *Ramayana*. Her kidnapping by the demon king Ravana sparked an epic war.

Sitar (SEE-tar) A stringed instrument of the lute family.

Surya (SOOR-yuh) The god of the sun, and father of many divine children and the demigod Karna.

Syamantaka Gem or Sun Jewel (SYAH-man-tah-kah) A divine gem with magical abilities in Hindu mythology. This precious jewel could provide gold on a daily basis.

Tabla (TUH-blah) A pair of twin hand drums.

Takshaka (TAHK-shah-kah) A naga king and former friend of Indra who once lived in the Khandava Forest before Arjuna helped burn it down, killing most of Takshaka's family. He swore vengeance on all the Pandavas ever since. Wonder why . . .

Tumburu (TOOM-bah-roo) The most skilled among the gandharvas (celestial musicians) and sometimes described as the best of singers. He is obliged to perform in the courts of the gods Kubera and Indra as well as sing the praises of the god Vishnu. He leads the gandharvas in their singing, and, for reasons that I could not find but am extremely intrigued by, is often depicted with the head of a horse.

Urvashi (oor-VAH-shee) A famous apsara, considered the most beautiful of all the apsaras. Her name literally means *she who can control the hearts of others.*

Vanaras (VAH-nah-ruhs) A supernatural race of monkey-like people who lived in Kishkinda Kingdom. Most notably, they assisted the god king Rama in building a bridge across the sea that went from Kishkinda all the way to Lanka.

Vishakanyas/poison maidens (VISH-ah-kahn-yah) Young women trained to be elite courtesans and assassins.

Vishnu (VISH-noo) The second god in the Hindu triumvirate (also known as the Trimurti). These three gods are responsible for the creation, upkeep, and destruction of the world. The other two gods are Brahma and Shiva. Brahma is the creator of the universe, and Shiva is the destroyer. Vishnu is worshipped as the preserver. He has taken many forms on earth in various avatars, most notably as Krishna, Mohini, and Rama.

Yaksha (YAHK-shah) A yaksha (male) or yakshini (female) is a supernatural being from Hindu, Buddhist, and Jain mythology. Yakshas are attendees of Kubera, the Hindu god of wealth.

Yama (YAH-muh) See: **Dharma Raja.**

Xib'alb'a (shee-bahl-BAH) Xib'alb'a, roughly translated as "place of fright," is the name of the underworld in Maya mythology, ruled by the Maya death gods and their helpers.

Enjoy this sneak peek at Roshani Chokshi's
next middle grade novel,

The Spirit Glass

ONE

Corazon Lopez possessed a rare and secret power, the kind that could make a river shrivel into a puddle or trap a tornado in a jar. She could climb the stars like a staircase and pull down clouds for her pillows. The only problem was that this secret power was apparently just *so* humongous and *so* hard to handle that it remained a secret... even from Corazon.

But not for much longer.

Hopefully.

Corazon had the blood of a *babaylan*, a rare mortal who guarded the boundaries between the human world and the realm of spirits. Some babaylans whispered to the weather. Others brewed potions that could lure a soul back into a dying body. Some could even sift through dreams to find glimmers of the future. It all depended on each babaylan's particular gift.

On a Saturday evening, Corazon stood in the kitchen and threw back her shoulders. She closed her eyes and reached for her magic. It always felt stubborn and sulking, like she was trying to pull it from a nice, warm bed and it didn't want to move. She held her squirming, scruffy magic with all her strength before taking a deep breath and shouting:

"Heed my power and heed it well, lift into the air as I compel!"

Corazon opened one eye. The spoon on the counter had not budged.

"Get thee to the dining table!" said Corazon, throwing up her hands. "Please?"

The spoon wriggled weakly. Ever so slowly, it rose from the counter and hovered in the air.

"It's happening!" exclaimed a small, bell-like voice. "Your gift is waking up!"

Beside the somewhat-levitating spoon, Corazon's companion *anito* poked his head over the rim of a teacup. The anito looked like a small, glowing blue lizard with bulging eyes, violet polka dots, and a long tail.

All babaylans have companion anito. They are the spirits of mountains, rivers, streams, and trees. The more powerful the babaylan, the more powerful and impressive the companion anito.

Corazon loved her small anito, but she was fairly certain that the most impressive thing about Saso was his imagination.

"Your gift is to preside over all . . . spoons? No, *silverware!* Yes!" Saso cackled, his speckled tail whipping out over the teacup. "Henceforth, all dining utensils shall answer to *us!* You shall wear a crown of butter knives, Corazon! Together, we will wage a war on blenders and—"

The spoon—which had lifted barely an inch off the tile and perhaps felt overwhelmed at the prospect of warfare—clattered back to the counter. With a final twitch, the spoon went still, and

Corazon dropped her hands. Even that small exertion of magic had left her feeling dizzy.

"Well, definitely no gift for metal," said Corazon.

"Oh," said Saso, his tail flopping. "Well…blenders would have made for a weak adversary anyway." He blinked up at her. "But if you like, we can still make the crown of butter knives?"

"That's okay, Saso," said Corazon, quietly folding up her disappointment. "We just have to be patient."

"Excellent notion!" said Saso happily. "You be patient, and I will be obsessive!"

"How is that helpful?"

"I don't know, but it's certainly inevitable."

"True," Corazon said with a sigh.

All her life she had been told that she would be a great babaylan. She just had to *wait*. But she'd been waiting for years, and in two days she would be twelve! That's when most babaylan started their official training…and Corazon still had *no* sign that her magic was anywhere near waking up.

"At least it's Saturday," said Saso.

Corazon grinned. Sometimes she felt that her week was one long held breath as she counted down the days until Saturday dinner. It was the best night of the week. But it was also the worst night, because it always came to an end.

Corazon held out her hand, and Saso hopped from the teacup to her palm. She looked around at the tidy white kitchen, with its ropes of garlic bulbs and bundles of drying herbs hanging from the ceiling.

"I'm going to need three plates," Corazon told the kitchen. "Actually, four. Just in case."

Corazon checked her father's watch. The timepiece had a cracked midnight-blue face and two worn leather straps that were so big that the watch would've fallen off her wrist if the House hadn't fixed it. The time was seven minutes past seven in the evening. Which meant Corazon had exactly twenty-three minutes to finish setting the table.

"Corazon, may I pick the movie tonight?" asked Saso.

A month ago, Saso had picked the 1933 *King Kong* film and spent the rest of the week crashing into pottery, swinging from the lamp fixtures, and shouting *"I AM HUNGRY! AND I CRAVE ARCHITECTURE!!!"*

Her aunt Celestina—Tina, for short—had threatened to sell him to a pet store.

"Maybe next time," Corazon said to Saso, gathering the blue plates that had magically appeared on the counter. "It's almost my birthday, and that's usually story night, remember?"

"Oh, that will be most excellent!" said Saso, swishing his blue tail. "Will the tale have lots of blood?"

"Probably not," said Corazon as she reached for a pitcher of water.

"No cries of mortal anguish?"

"Nope."

"I hate it already."

Corazon rolled her eyes. Saso, which was short for Samson, had been her companion anito for years. As far as he knew, he'd been asleep for a long time before he awoke curled up in the bassinet of a newborn Corazon.

It had been the same way for Corazon's mother, Althea. Her companion anito was a shimmering blue python, nearly twenty feet long in his full form. He was named Caching—improbably shortened from the name Escolastica—and was the spirit of a massive *toog*, a rosewood tree. By day, Caching transformed himself into an elaborate bracelet while Althea worked as a nurse on the hospital's cardiology floor. By night, he took on his true shape and assisted Althea in her healing magic.

"I think my camouflage is changing again!" said Saso. He sighed happily as he examined his reflection on the side of a pan. "I really am an incredibly rare and exquisite baby crocodile."

Corazon had never heard of a crocodile that could camouflage. And with his bulging eyes, stubby snout, and spotted tail, Saso looked a lot more like a small blue gecko.

But Saso didn't need to know that.

"You do look more...bluish," said Corazon.

Saso preened. "Good, good. It's very important to stay camouflaged. Otherwise, people would be so intimidated by me! And, by extension, *you*! Only a babaylan of extraordinary skill would have a crocodile anito." Saso blinked up at her affectionately. "And you, Corazon, are definitely extraordinary."

Corazon was beginning to doubt that she'd *ever* be extraordinary.

Corazon's mother had a true gift for healing. By the time Althea was ten years old, she could brew and bottle a year's worth of beauty tonic. Whenever Corazon tried to brew anything, the potion turned into useless sludge. And if Corazon so much as *poked* a bottle, it would explode. Althea was considered powerful, but her sister, Tina, was something else entirely.

Corazon had once seen her aunt shush a thunderstorm. The storm had been so embarrassed that it slouched across the sky, dragging its rain clouds behind it like a tail. Tina could coax the poison out of a rattlesnake with a well-placed compliment. She could catch the sparkles of light on a pond and turn them into diamonds.

Tina was somewhere in her mid-thirties and looked like a warrior queen. Wherever she went, her long black hair streamed behind her as if blown by an invisible wind. Her companion anito, a huge and graceful eagle named Luzviminda—Minda, for short—always soared above her, snapping at the air. Together they made a terrifying pair—Minda's ferocious grace was the perfect complement to the beautiful, elegant Tina.

Next to them, Corazon felt rather silly.

Whenever Corazon walked into the garden behind the House, the plants shriveled up. Once, Corazon had been convinced that the flora was talking to her when she heard a rosebush crying. Then the bush asked for a belly rub. And some yarn.

This had seemed like a very strange request until Corazon realized that it was not the rosebush speaking, but a dead cat buried under its roots.

When Corazon dug it up, the cat—which was mostly bone with a tuft of orange fur on its tail—had *mrrreowed*, rubbed its skull against her leg, and proceeded to hunt a bug.

Since then, Lazarus had become something of a guard cat who lived in the garden.

You just have to wait, Corazon told herself once again. *Be patient.*

As was her habit, she touched her necklace chain and the delicate golden key that hung from it. It was her most precious possession in the world. A true soul key gifted to her by her mother.

Corazon began to set the table. She put flowers in a pitcher of water and added big serving spoons to the bowl of pancit and steamed milkfish that had magically appeared. As she worked, she smoothed her dress. It was a family heirloom and made of black silk with enchanted silver threads weaving clouds across the fabric. Corazon only took it out of her closet on special occasions, although sometimes the dress liked to slip off its hanger and hover near the windows just to be closer to the moonlight.

"How do I look, Saso?"

"Delectable!" said the anito, hopping down from the ceiling to land on her shoulder. "The most mouthwatering babaylan in all the land!"

Once, this dress had belonged to Althea. She had worn it right before her own twelfth birthday, when *her* mother, another powerful babaylan, had taught Althea magic. Corazon had always imagined that Althea would teach her how to be a babaylan. But life had other plans, and now Tina would be her teacher instead. Young, powerful Tina who looked like Althea but had none of her warmth.

"Should I call you *Tita*?" Corazon had asked Tina the day they first met. Althea had never mentioned a younger sister, but then again, she rarely answered questions about her family. When Corazon had asked her father about it, his answer was short and cagey: "It wasn't easy for your mom to leave home."

The only person Althea had ever spoken of was her mother. *Oh*, anak. *I wish you could've known her. Once, she was the stuff of legends.*

When Tina had arrived on the scene, all of Corazon's imaginings of a kindly and fun-loving aunt had vanished.

"She looks like she eats nieces for breakfast," Saso had muttered.

"Do *not* call me Tita," said Tina.

And so, Tina had remained Tina.

Saso suddenly squeaked from his perch on her shoulder. "Corazon, do you think the House will make us cake? It's two days until your birthday... and though I dearly love the tender snap of femurs and tibias, I quite like chocolate cake, too."

By then Corazon had moved to the kitchen and started slicing up the tiny green calamansi fruit to squeeze over their dinner. To her left, the refrigerator door swung open. The collection of small black-dot magnets on the front zoomed together to form a frowny face.

"Yes, but also, stop nagging it?" translated Corazon. "That's the fourth time you've asked... today."

"I am an apex predator," said Saso. "I have *needs*."

The magnets dispersed and then rearranged themselves into a question mark.

Corazon smiled. "Two minutes and then they'll be here."

The question mark turned into a heart shape.

In many ways, Tina's House was a lot like other houses. The outside was the color of a robin's egg. The House had a sunny living room with two squashy sofas, a small dining room with a long table piled high with boxes Tina kept meaning to sort through, three cozy bedrooms, a kitchen, and a backyard with a garden.

But there were rather large differences, too....

Sometimes the House got bored with being the color of a robin's egg and changed its coat of paint from blue to pink. Occasionally it even sprouted bay windows and balconies. The living room sofa regularly watched dramatic romance movies, and at least once a year the sprinklers would go off during a particularly depressing scene. Upstairs, the bedrooms grew night-lights like mushrooms, and the kitchen huffed and puffed, always cooking or rearranging the silverware.

Tina's House was *alive*.

But more than that...it loved Corazon.

It was the House that tucked her in each evening and made sure she always had a sweater when it got cold outside. The House kept her company while she was doing Tina's endless homework assignments, and it made all her meals. And even if Corazon didn't like it when the curtains flapped noisily the second she dozed off mid-studies, or how the cookie jar would be full of cookies one moment and carrot sticks the next, Corazon loved the House, too.

At precisely 7:23 p.m., Corazon began to walk down the front hallway. As she walked, the soul key hummed against her skin. *Soon, soon, soon*, it sang.

The dark brown door to Tina's workroom glowed in anticipation. Here, Tina's House branched into its different sections. To the right was the staircase winding up to the bedrooms. To the left was the door that led to Tina's vast workspace. It was an ancient door made of Philippine agarwood, with the carved head of a carabao staring at her from the center. The water buffalo blinked lazily.

Corazon hadn't seen Tina all day. But then again, Tina never came out for Saturday meals. Even so, Corazon still asked the door, "Is she joining us for dinner?"

The carabao regarded her with its flat, dark eyes and then opened its mouth. *"ABSOLUTELY NOOOOOOOOOT."*

Then it swung its horned head and melted into the wood, taking the doorknob with it.

"What a rude swamp cow!" said Saso. "When I grow up, I shall *feast* on you and—"

Just then, there was a loud knock at the front door.

Saso wagged his spotted tail. "They're here!"

"I know," said Corazon, her heart beating a little faster.

Unlike Tina, Corazon Lopez's parents never missed family dinner on Saturday nights. Not even being dead for three years could change that.